Praise for *Secret W*

"Karen Lee Boren's new n
novel set in the 60's, uncov
of a family sustained by music and torn apart by it as well. All this
is backgrounded by the horror of the distant war. The book fairly
sings, and Boren is a writer with a good ear and a big heart. We
need to have more books by Karen Lee Boren."—Thomas Cobb
author of *Crazy Heart*

"Engaging characters, evocative landscape, beautiful writing: these
are the highlights—and the delights—of Karen Lee Boren's novel
Secret Waltz. I immersed myself in the lives of Sonya, Leo, and
Emelia as they navigated the tricky terrain of an adult world they're
not quite ready to face. Family secrets abound, as do tragic
consequences. Set against the backdrop of the Midwest in the mid-
Sixties, the story is told in a community of voices. Each character
has a stake in the narrative; each brings a perspective that in the
end satisfies and resonates with the reader."—Tina Egnoski,
author of *Burn Down This World*

"The personal? It's absolutely political, as Karen Lee Boren makes
evident in her compelling new novel set in the days when an
unwanted pregnancy could mean an end to one's ambitions—or
worse. With its spot-on depiction of life in middle America in the
1960s and its compassionate rendering of the emotional lives of
teenagers, *Secret Waltz* is an urgent reminder that hard-won rights
can be reversed. This is an important book—and a terrific read,
with characters you'll be rooting for even as your heart is breaking
for them."—Jane Eklund, author of *The Story So Far*

"…Karen Lee Boren's characters, each with their own compelling
combination of naivete and bravery, crackle with realism. These
teenagers and their imperfect compromises stay with you long after
reading. *Secret Waltz* is a quiet triumph."—Robert Arellano, author
of Edgar Award-finalist *Havana Lunar*

SECRET WALTZ

by Karen Lee Boren

Flexible Press
Minneapolis, Minnesota 2022

Print ISBN: 978-1-7364033-6-5
eBook ISBN: 978-1-7364033-7-2

Flexible Press LLC
Editors William E Burleson
Vicki Adang, Mark My Words Editorial Services, LLC
Cover via Canva
A different version of the opening pages was published in the following: "Secret Waltz: A Novel." (Excerpt) Mikrocosmos, 61 (2015). 46–51. Print.
Epigraph from Wide Sargasso Sea: Rhys, Jean, and Charlotte Brontë. Wide Sargasso Sea.
New York: Norton, 1992. (18) Print.

I thought if I told no one it might not be true.
—Jean Rhys, *Wide Sargasso Sea*

Buckhorn, Wisconsin 1966

Part One

Sonya

SHE NEEDS A full moon and a midnight train. At three minutes before midnight, with the tail feathers of winter still fluttering, Sonya Morrow balances on a single rail of the train tracks behind Carlssens bean fields, listening for the Union Pacific's 12:02 Cheyenne-Milwaukee line. She's got to be on the track at the first vibrations of the train or the ghost mother won't come. And who else can she turn to? She doesn't know the kind of people who would know the kind of people who would help her. She doesn't know anyone who will help her. She's trapped like a March hare, she thinks, not sure the phrase is right. No, she realizes, it's not right. Mad as a March hare. Tonight, both are true.

Consulting both the lunar calendar and the spring 1966 rail schedule, she found tonight is her only chance this month if she's going to follow the story to the letter. Every month that passes, every week, every day, hour, minute, every second the life inside her grows, her future shrinks to a pinhole.

Not that long ago, her future had been as open as the bean fields that surround her. She's the first girl in her high school to win a scholarship for science. Most girls in her school don't go to college at all, and if they do, they study teaching, nursing, music, or art. A few talented girls have even won scholarships. Her best friend, Stella, is up for a drama scholarship at a small college up north. But Sonya's the first girl ever to win a scholarship for science, for biology, a *hard* science. And hers is not a partial scholarship to a small school, which is the most she'd ever allowed herself to hope for. She's got a full ride to the biggest university in the state where the new research facilities are said to rival those in the East and surpass those in Europe.

But pregnant girls don't get scholarships. They don't get to go to school at all, not even high school, much less college to become botanists. And a pregnant girl without someone willing to marry her, well, they call a girl like her all kinds of things: fast, loose, wild. It's on the tip of her tongue. *Slut.*

She clamps her mouth shut, refusing to utter the words used for a girl in her situation. Not tonight. Not here. Not when there's still the slimmest of chances she can make everything okay. And she can. She will.

Despite her resolve, she feels desperation thick at her throat. "I wanted to *be* someone," she croaks so quietly sleeping field mice don't hear. She dreamed of spending her life in a lab and traveling the world, finding cures for diseases, maybe discovering a new species of flower. She'll name it after herself, the way men have done for centuries. *Marrowilium*, an herb with healing properties. A draft of wind brings her back to herself. She checks her balance and swallows her tears.

Girls in trouble can't afford to cry. Girls in trouble can't afford to whine.

"I want," she says, but her voice comes out as shaky as her feet on the rail. She stiffens and clenches the rail with her bare toes. She forces firmness into her voice.

"I *want* to be a scientist," she says.

But then, she thinks, hadn't the very act of wanting been her undoing? Wanting may have killed her future as completely as the oncoming train may kill her.

She nibbles the skin at the edge of her thumbnail, a habit she's been trying to break so as not to show her nerves to her parents and teachers. Girls in trouble can't afford to reveal anything. She pulls the thumb from her mouth. Instead, she twirls the pin tacked inside the waistband of her skirt. She'd been so pleased when he gave her the pin, thinking it meant the start of something. Only later did she understand he'd meant it as a memento. Something to remember him by, something to moon over.

She glances at the empty, moon-washed land surrounding her. The fields are between winter and spring crops, and the exposed soil soaks in the darkness while patches of snow glisten in the moonlight. To the naked eye, the land looks dead. But buried below the soil's surface are organisms just waiting for the sun's heat to send them squirming to life. Normally this thought would excite her, but tonight, the landscape brings to mind the word *barren* and the close call she'd had when she'd nearly exposed her secret.

In English class, Georgie Baxter had misspelled the word in his composition on John Steinbeck, writing *baron* instead of *barren*. As if they were in seventh grade and not within spitting distance of their graduation, an exasperated Mrs. Gramercy made the whole class write ten sentences using each word correctly. Sonya sat as frozen as she had when she'd first realized she was gone. Finally, her hand wrote one sentence round, round, and around like a broken record: *A barren field holds promise. A barren field holds promise.*

She kept writing after the bell rang and the other students had left. When she stumbled her way to Mrs. Gramercy's desk and handed in her paper, the look Mrs. Gramercy gave her seemed hard and knowing, and for one terrifyingly hopeful moment, Sonya believed this gray-haired teacher could help her. Wasn't it possible that when Mrs. Gramercy was younger, she'd needed help herself, or maybe she had a sister or a best girlfriend who needed it?

Sonya liked Mrs. Gramercy. She respected her. Mrs. Gramercy was a smart woman. Not only that, the way she read Keats's poems to the class, with her fist on her heart, she'd certainly felt things, experienced things. She insisted students needed to find the passion in *Romeo and Juliet* in order to understand its tragedy. She warned passion leads to a bitter end. "But isn't it worth it?" she said, her faint Irish lilt adding veracity to the sentiment. "Isn't love worth it?"

Sonya *had* loved. The pistil, the anther, the petal of a flower were as moving to her as poetry was to Mrs. Gramercy. Last summer, she created a new variety of tomato grafted from her mother's favorite yellow and red varieties. The striped skin and flesh that resulted had been as sweet to her as the cheeks of any man would ever be. Or so she'd thought.

5

"It's okay," he'd said at the crucial moment, and she believed him, not only because of his loamy voice, but because he smelled like the earth too, smelled of clay and sweat and pine needles, things she trusted and loved.

Sonya dug her fingernail into the wood of Mrs. Gramercy's desk. Teachers are supposed to help, aren't they?

"Do you know—?" Sonya started, but her voice broke, and before she could finish, Mrs. Gramercy pressed her lips together, shaking her head and Sonya's paper.

"Such a disappointment," said her teacher.

Her teacher's disappointment pulled Sonya's shoulders forward to cover her shame.

"You're better than this, Sonya."

"Yes," she admitted. Maybe if she admitted it, Mrs. Gramercy would take pity on her and tell her what to do. "I know. I was stupid, but—."

Mrs. Gramercy shook her head again, slashed a red check on the paper, and handed it back. "Go on," she said. "I'll trust you know better."

Her hand trembled as she took the paper.

In the hallway, her whole body shook with disappointment. As her classmates shuffled around her, she stared at the red check mark, fighting back tears. She didn't used to be a girl who cried. She used to be smart and flip. Quick. Too quick, one teacher had written on her report card long ago. Now she was simply too fast.

She stood in the hallway and muttered the words she'd written a hundred times until they took on the rhythms of a train. *A barren field holds promise.* Instinctively, her hand sought her belly, but she pulled it down fast, afraid the gesture would give her away. If they won't help, they can't know.

A barren field holds promise. The rhythms of a train.

"Ghost Mother," she whispered, a sprig of hope shooting up. Doubt shot up behind it. It's just a story. She swiped at the mucus dripping from her nostrils and thought, no, it's more than a story; it's an old wives' tale. Old wives weren't fools. Hadn't her mother advised her to give them credence? "That science you love so much usually backs them up. Cows really do lie down when it's going to

6

rain. Earwax really does cure a cold sore. A slice of bread stuck halfway in your mouth really does stop you from crying when cutting onions. Try it." She handed Sonya a slice of Wonder, a knife, and an onion, and it was true. The bread absorbs the onion's fumes before they reach your nostrils.

"Your science only confirms what we old wives already know," quipped her mother, taking the knife from Sonya and expertly mincing the onion slices.

Old wives, the ones who survived birthing ten, twelve, fifteen children, the ones whose bodies couldn't bear to bear one more, those old wives would have found ways. The ghost mother was one of those ways.

So now, tonight, with her shoes in one hand, her ankle socks tucked deep into the toes, Sonya continues to step tightrope style on the train's rail. She wobbles, catches herself, steps, wobbles again. Gravity's working against the body that's becoming stranger to her every day. To steady herself, she breathes deeply. The smell of manure that she inhales turns her stomach. She used to love the smell. Not that she and her little brother, Dean, are farmer's children. Buckhorn is a suburb that straddles Milwaukee and rural land. But their mother was a farmer's child and plants a backyard plot each summer. Since she was tiny, Sonya's helped her mother tend it. One spring, her mother fell on black ice and bruised her coccyx, and Sonya took over the garden. She spent hours with the hot sun on her back and the cool soil squishing between her bare toes. She staked tomato plants, and their tendrils clung and pulled themselves toward the sun. As she dug into the dirt to retrieve the carrots straining toward the earth's center, she understood that nature hid itself from the human eye. You had to look close to see its secrets.

She used her father's boyhood microscope to look at a cross-section of those carrots, stunned at the intricate order they contained, an order she longed to understand. By summer's end, she'd produced bushels heaped with crock pickles, yellow squash, kohlrabi, and tomatoes. She'd sliced and observed each species, her exhilaration growing. She knew what she wanted to do with her life.

Soil + seed = fruit.

Perhaps it's no wonder that twelve inches of snow covered the earth when she managed to ignore the basics of her own germination.

"I'm not stupid!" she calls as the rail's steel numbs her arches. "Not every seed germinates. Not all soil is fertile all the time."

Her nasturtiums never sprouted. Year after year, her mother's irises never flower, and they won't until her mother replants them into a sunnier spot as Sonya has told her to do. But even then, there are no assurances. Her parents had nearly a decade of fallow years between her and Dean. So there must be some element of alchemy to it. A seed of luck.

Until now, she hasn't believed in luck, good or bad. She's believed in the carpel, the stamen, the petal and sepal. Nose always stuck in a flower, her mother says. She calls Sonya her smart girl in apologetic tones. But her mother had been happy for her, or pretended to be, when Sonya won her scholarship.

Holding the award letter, Sonya felt as if she'd stepped into her real self for the first time. She could almost, *almost,* see the person she was going to be.

How had she let herself be distracted? How had she let herself go? She shouldn't be gambling with her life. She should be collecting specimens of moonflowers, some to dissect and some to press and mount because the face of the moonflower is as lovely as any human face she's ever seen. Even his.

No, she won't think of him. She looks up at the full moon and nearly falls. She clenches her fists and reestablishes her balance.

Of course, it's too early in the season for moonflowers. She places her palm against her belly. He'd said, "It's okay," and she'd agreed because she'd consulted the calendar herself. How foolish to have allowed herself to believe, even for a moment, that because she understood the cycles—the lunar cycles and her own—she would be safe, that the timing was all right, and that he'd meant all he'd said.

"No!" she calls out.

She can't allow herself to think about that. Not now. Not yet. Maybe not ever.

8

"This train better be on time," she says to distract herself. The patch on her chin that's always cold-bitten first when she ice skates has begun to itch. The pads of her feet have gone numb. "It better be on time."

A rush of horror hits her. What if there's a derailment or accident or some other interference, a cow on the tracks up the line maybe, or dumb kids playing the kind of kid games she used to play? Fear tips her balance. She stumbles off the rail and falls hard onto the stones strewn around the ties. A jagged rock pierces her knee.

"Stupid, stupid," she calls, desperation and pain slicing through her at the same time.

Stupid for so many reasons. Look at me, she thinks. She feels bloody dirt smearing her knees. Gravel has cut into the heels of her hands. On all fours, she's a cow in a field. What in the world ever made her think she was a smart girl, that she deserved to be anyone, anything other than what she sees around her. Mothers and housewives. Maybe a teacher like Mrs. Gramercy, or a nurse, at best. At worst, a waitress or a stewardess with children at home to feed.

But Marie Curie had dared. And Sonya still has her scholarship. She tastes her future in the loamy night air. She has to try.

Abandoning her shoes and socks, she scrambles up and hops back onto the rail. Blood dribbles down her leg. She can't miss the train. She can't miss it. Can't.

A gust of wind unbalances her again, but determined not to fall a second time, she throws her arms wide. According to the tale, if she falls now, it won't work.

She's got to be on the track at the train's first vibration. Also, be barefoot. And stay until the heat and smoke choke you. Stay until you're coughing, until your eyes burn and hot tears streak your cheeks. Stay until the arms of death pull you close. Only when it's life or death, when it's you or nothing, then and only then can you jump. If you miscalculate or chicken out, if you jump when you first spot the train's headlight, the ghost mother will steal your soul instead of your baby. And as you jump, you have to scream at a throat-scraping volume to be heard over the engine, "Mother, mother of the night, carry my child into light!"

Of course many of the details are fictional trappings, there to entice you into doing something foolishly dangerous.

But stay on the track.

That's the key detail of the story, the part that stands to reason. Parsing the story from the science, she hypothesizes that the vibrations of the train will be mighty, teeth splitting, fetus jarring. Added to this are the trauma of waiting until the last moment, the effort of jumping, the violence of landing.

So she has to be brave. She has to be steel. Cold-eyed. She has to believe in the heat and the headlight and the vibrations of the train. She has to endure her teeth being knocked to sawdust until her very viscera loosen.

Sonya has heard this story since she was a girl. At sleepovers, the tale was always told at midnight, long after the girls were supposed to be asleep. One girl whispered the words while another girl softly kept the *shug-a-shug* rhythm of the train in the background. Sonya shinnied deep into her sleeping bag, which still smelled of the northern birch forests where her father took the family camping in the summers, and where Sonya spent silent afternoons learning the Latin names of every plant in her identification book. At the sleepovers, she listened, fascination and disdain crimping her face, her arrogance taking root.

Pulled into the narrative details of the story, she had scoffed, "Why would anyone risk going to the ghost mother?" If you weren't careful, if you forgot to say the words at exactly the right moment, the ghost mother stole your soul instead of the fetus. If your timing was off, the train would kill you. It was such a risk.

Risk vs. shame? Sonya had been certain she would choose shame. But she had been more certain she wouldn't put herself in this position in the first place. Better not to have to choose between two such lousy options. *Trapped as a March hare. Mad as a March hare.* How childish, she thinks now, not to have known women don't create dangerous solutions like this without cause.

The wind gusts again, but she's braced and ready. Her feet are so cold she can barely feel the track. Or so she thinks until the vibrations shiver her arches, her ankles, her calves. She grabs fistfuls of air. The train slithers around the curve, moving like a giant snake, its Cyclops eye unblinking.

Her whole body jitters. Her teeth knock, just as in the story.

Maybe it will work. Maybe it is real.

"Stay," she whispers, forcing her toes to clench the track. "The smoke. Wait for the smoke." She sniffs the electrified air. Her ankles strain. She begs her body not to jump.

"Please, please, not yet, please."

But her body is smarter than her mind. Just as the heat of the train slaps her cheeks, her legs make their own decision. Her thighs, knees, even the soles of her feet know better than her, all exploding at once, rocketing her onto the embankment so she lands hard on her side. Hip bruised, thigh scraped raw, shoulder jammed, she heaves deep sobs of pain and relief in harmony to the train's rushing wheels.

"Too soon!" Shame and fear and urine drench her body. She howls so loudly she can't tell if what shakes the night is the train's whistle, the ghost mother's fury, or her own wild desperation.

Leo

SITUATED AT THE western edge of Buckhorn, the train tracks are a mile from Lake Michigan, which is the town's eastern-most edge. Between the two, at the same moment the train's whistle sheers the dark silence, Leo Meitka sits upright on his bed, wide awake and wishing he were on that train, going absolutely anywhere instead of stuck in his bedroom off the kitchen in his parents' house, desperately trying to figure out what to do.

Tell or keep his mouth shut?

A kid a year ahead of him at school ran away to join the hipsters in San Francisco. After what Leo saw earlier this evening, maybe he should do that too. Pack his guitar and go. Hitch or jump a train. That way, he wouldn't have to do anything about what he saw tonight. Wouldn't that throw his father for a loop?

Never *Dad* or *Pa*, Leo thinks resentfully. "Call me *Father*, with respect." Respect and loyalty, his father's prized possessions.

Yes, Leo would like to see his father's face when he realizes Leo is gone. He'd like to see any other expression on his father's face—surprise, guilt, anger—anything other than what was there earlier.

Leo's working hard not to name what he saw, not just his father's expression, but the whole scene, which threatens to unfold in his mind like a time-lapse nature film. He bolts upright from his bed to forestall the unfolding and crosses the small room in two strides. He slides the album cover to *Out of Our Heads* from the stack on his rarely used student desk. With his gaze fixed on the tight close-up of Keith Richards's face (Kirstin says Leo's eyes are smoldering like Keith's, but blue not brown), Leo hums the guitar part to "The Last Time," reaching, reaching for that place in his head where sometimes music takes him, replacing the chaos in his overactive mind with sound and color and light.

"Blessing and a curse, that imagination of yours," his mother, Anne, says. Despite all that's gone before, tonight is the first time he's really thought of her as Anne, a woman in her own right. With a husband, Stash. The kind of man Leo is supposed to be some day.

When Leo plays his guitar, his brain goes from churning to sparking. Sometimes all he has to do is run his mind over a trail of remembered notes to get there. But tonight, he can't focus. So he drops the album onto the turntable, places the needle, and listens, untangling Keith's guitar part from Brian's. Each note of Keith's solo in the middle eight is a cold bead of water splashing Leo's cheeks and easing his mind.

Not long ago, Leo had almost lost his music. He'd become bored after years of lessons on piano and organ, and yes, the accordion because of his father, "the sensational accordion stylist and bandleader, Stash Meitka," as the tavern posters call him. For Leo's fifteenth birthday, his mother bought him his guitar, and the moment Leo's fingers touched the strings, it was like touching the wall after a perfect swimming race, breathless and exhilarating and right, just damn-it-all *right*. From that moment on, he's heard music everywhere again, in pencils scratching against notebooks at school, in his friends' footsteps as they tramp Lake Michigan's paths, in the train wheels' distant *cha-cha-cha*.

He reaches down for his guitar to play along with Keith when a thud sounds in the kitchen, and the needle skips. Leo freezes, pure sensation a mile beyond him now. He recognizes the sound as the refrigerator door slamming against the wall. His father is home. He must be foraging for the dinner he should have eaten earlier that evening to cushion the impact of the scotch and sodas he probably shot down his gullet all night long. The drinks are gifts from the dancers and drinkers at Bernice's Danceland, the tavern where his father's polka band played tonight and where Leo would have been if he hadn't had to turn tail and run

If only his father hadn't forgotten his set list, if only his mother hadn't sent Leo to Bernice's with it, Leo might not have caught his father—the specificity of the phrase *red-handed* turns Leo's own face crimson, but he can't think of another way to put it. Had Stash (Leo can't bear to think of him as his father here) seen Leo too? Leo knots his fists with hope. If Stash didn't see him, if they never speak of it, maybe Leo can pretend it never happened.

The refrigerator door slams again, startling Leo upright. He refreezes, his hand still extended toward his guitar as if he's been spun and flung and stuck in the pose in statue maker, a game he and his friends played when they were kids. After a moment, Leo silently twists his torso, grasping not his guitar but the volume button on the record player. Turning down the sound, he hopes his father hasn't noticed the music and will think he is sleeping. The record continues to spin though, emitting a gentle *shoosh*. Already unbalanced, Leo doesn't dare set the needle right. He continues to stand motionless in the middle of his room, tracking his father's movements around the kitchen.

His father opens a cupboard to find a plate or bowl, pulls out the silverware drawer for a fork or spoon. Both the extra jerkiness in the sounds and the too-long pauses between them signal that his father is tanked tonight. For once, Leo's glad. Maybe he can blame what he saw on the booze. But then again, most nights his father plays a tavern job, the drinks arrive steady as a metronome from the audience and dancers. *Thank you, we love you, we look forward to you all week.* His father eats up the praise, or rather drinks it up. Does that mean on those nights his father also—.

In the kitchen, something crashes hard on the linoleum, and Leo cringes.

His father growls a slurry "Shit."

Leo listens and waits. A second train whistles, shriller it seems, rising in pitch with Leo's dread that his mother's sleep tonight is shallow. Leo is no longer glad his father is tanked. If his mother wakes up and sees how drunk his father is, they'll argue. When his father's not too far gone, his mother sometimes manages to let it go. And when his father manages to go teetotal, his parents have long periods without a fight. During these times, they can get so

14

affectionate with each other it embarrasses Leo. But when his father is bull-in-a-china-shop tanked, it triggers something in his mother, and she pushes and pushes until his father snaps back. They go at it until his mother exhausts herself or until his father passes out. Those nights, Leo tries to ignore his parents' roaring voices. He pretends they are the television, the volume turned high on *Perry Mason* or *77 Sunset Strip*. Tonight, though, Leo will be busy pretending other things.

"Oh, man," Leo whispers before he can think to silence himself. He rubs his eyes with the heels of his hands, wishing to smudge out the images that threaten to fire smoky and hot. So much is not what he thought. It turns out his mother isn't merely the jealous type as his father has insisted, not a green-eyed monster snorting steam, or anyway not snorting without cause.

As if Leo's thoughts have summoned her, his mother's footfalls hammer down the stairs, and guilt floods him. He'd always secretly—maybe not so secretly, he worries—blamed his mother for his parents' fighting. Leo didn't believe his mother when she shouted at Stash that he was a cad, not really. Sure, women fawn over his father when he plays. But that's part of being a musician, isn't it? Look at the way girls scream and faint for Mick and Keith and every one of the Beatles, even Ringo.

Granted, his father's no rock-and-roll star. He's just a guy with a local band who works on the line at the steel-forging factory during the day and at night plays the taverns with other workers. But still, there's something about making music, no matter how small the stage, that moves people, especially girls. They reach out to you. They want to touch you. Isn't that what clapping is all about?

Leo had a small taste of such attention when he played with his father at a church festival. Older girls who wouldn't give him a second thought at school came up to him during the break between sets, smiling and gazing at him with what his friends Kirstin and Emelia later called *dreamboat eyes*.

Leo can't deny he liked this attention, so why wouldn't his father like it? Doesn't it mean your music is good? Doesn't it mean you've moved your audience? So what if those girls went back to treating Leo like a drip at school the next day? They'd liked him when he played, and he wanted more of it. Like his father does.

No, not like that. No.

Still frozen, sweat slides down Leo's ribcage, a rivulet of guilt at having blamed his mother, and another of shame. For what? For witnessing? For being his father's son? After all, Leo had liked the attention from those girls.

This time, the image flashes in Leo's mind before he can drive it back: his father's arm, elbow-deep beneath a girl's striped circle skirt.

Set sheets in hand, Leo had approached Bernice's from the alley so he could use the back entrance to the tavern, the one behind the stage where the band members parked their cars and stashed their cases and might be having a quiet smoke. Grease from Bernice's Friday night fish fry hung in the air, dabbed with the scents of garbage and old beer. The tavern's back door was shut, but the back door to his father's Plymouth was ajar. When the car shook, Leo rushed to it, thinking he'd catch a thief red-handed. His father would be proud of him and would congratulate him in front of the band. Maybe he'd let Leo sit in for a song or two before sending him home. Leo's not yet allowed to play the tavern shows, only weddings and church festivals. But how could his father disrespect his hero son?

As Leo's fingers touched the cold metal of the car door's handle, he looked through the window and saw two pink high-heeled shoes with pointed tips. He stopped cold, his hand on the car door, but he couldn't stop his mind from taking in the whole picture. A girl's ankles wrapped around Stash's waist. His hand up her skirt. Her blouse unbuttoned, and Stash's face lost in her breasts.

Thank God the girl's eyes were closed, so Leo's pretty sure she didn't see him. Leo recognized her from the mushroom-shaped mole above her knee. Nora, just a handful of years older than Leo. Not long ago he'd played at her wedding reception with Stash, two days before the groom left for the Army. Leo had seen the mushroom mole when the groom removed her lace garter. He'd thought the mole sexy then, but seeing it on the leg wrapped around Stash had sickened him.

At the sight of Stash's tongue snaking up Nora's neck, Leo's mouth gaped. Shocked and disgusted, he backed away without uttering a sound. He stuffed the set sheets in Bernice's overflowing garbage can and ran home. A frightened rabbit in the night.

He said nothing to his mother when he got home. He'd stayed shut in his room, trying to decide what to do. Should he tell his mother she'd been right all along? Should he apologize for silently blaming her and agreeing with Stash when he called her paranoid?

"You're worse than McCarthy," his father has said to Anne so often it's a phrase Leo's caught himself using. But never again.

As much as Leo wanted to apologize to his mother, he couldn't bring himself to squeal on Stash when he got home. His father has drummed into Leo that loyalty is the greatest virtue, even above respect. Both an Army veteran and a union man, his father believes in the union mottos: *in union there is strength*, and *one for all, all for one*. He was on the front of the picket lines when the factory workers went on strike. No one hated the scabs more. And loyalty doesn't stop at the picket lines either. Once Leo had tattled on a friend at school for taking an extra carton of milk at lunch without paying for it, and it was Leo who ended up punished and feeling guilty. His father had grounded Leo for a week, saying, "For all you know, that boy was hungry. Maybe never gets a meal beyond that lunch. You stick up for your own. No son of mine rats out his friends." When Leo argued that the boy wasn't really a friend, his father wouldn't listen. "He's in your class. He's on your teams sometimes, right? So like and not like doesn't matter. A guy who rats is the lowest of the low. No son of mine."

If it's that bad ratting out a kid you don't even like, how much worse would it be to rat out your own father?

But it's more than just loyalty keeping Leo from telling his mother what he saw. If he told, what would happen to his family? Would his mother leave his father? Do wives leave husbands? Of course, he's heard of divorce, but he's never met any kid whose parents were divorced. What if his mother kicked his father out? His father would hardly go quietly. He'd scream and yell, and the whole world would know. Leo's friends, his teachers, those older girls at school, everyone would know his father was a cad and his mother had been jilted. And Leo would be humiliated too. People would think he was like them. Of course they would. They already compare him to his father. *You have your father's eyes. Do you have his talent too? Are you a charmer like your pa?*

And where would his father go? Would he be gone for good? What would his mother do then? Leo couldn't imagine it, and he didn't want to either. Bad as things were now, they could get a hundred times worse.

So alone in his bedroom, Leo turned on the Zombies loud. His mother left him alone. She can be good that way, giving him space, not complaining when he plays rock music loud—unlike his father who hates that Leo listens to rock and roll at any volume.

If only she would leave his father alone tonight. But her steps down the back stairs pound the steady rhythm of Los Bravos' "Black is Black." She lands in the kitchen with a stomp, and the song slips away from Leo as if the needle has scratched to the center of the record.

Biting hard on his anger and guilt, he opens his bedroom door. He owes his mother something after all the years of secretly taking his father's side. At the very least, he won't leave her alone tonight. Maybe he can stop his mother before things get too bad, but he hesitates on the threshold between his bedroom and the kitchen, not sure what to do. His father is seated at the table, a lit cigarette burning between his fingers, another in the ashtray on the table. His mother stands across from him, the sink at her back.

"Please," Leo says. Neither of his parents seems to hear him.

"You're drunk," says Anne.

Her voice is rough, with sleep maybe, hopefully. He doesn't like to think she's been crying, but her eyes are rimmed red. Maybe she will be too tired to go for too long.

"Why do you have to drink so much?" she says, whinnying deep in her throat to clear it. "Why can't you just go play your music and come home? Drink a few drinks if you have to, okay, but why drink the whole damn bar dry?"

"People want to spend their money on me. They sweat for it all week. I've got to take what they offer. I say no, it's a slap in the face." He warps the word *slap* to *shlaapp*. His eyelids droop. Beneath his fuzzy gaze, gravy coats his black mustache.

Leo's stomach turns as he realizes his father has drunk the gravy straight from the pitcher. The stink of pork fat, whiskey, and cigarettes steam from him.

"Slap in the face to say no to a drink," Stash repeats, sucking deeply on the cigarette in his hand. When he tamps out the end, he seems confused at the lit one propped on the edge of the tray. He lifts this one too and takes another long drag. Blowing smoke words, he says, "I do more *good.*" He slams his palm on the tabletop. Surprised by the sound or the sting, he stares at his hand before continuing. "More good work in a single set than priests do all month."

Anne shakes her head. "You're better than priests now?"

"I tell you one thing." He lifts two fingers and snorts a laugh when he spots his mistake. Leo tries not to remember where he'd seen those fingers earlier tonight. "Life's just about bearable if you know around the corner lies a little music."

"Music, okay, fine. But why the rest of it?" she says. Round shouldered, round bodied, she has the strongest hands Leo's ever seen. They gallop over piano keys like a breakaway horse. She's a better musician than Leo or his father could hope to be. But at the moment those hands grasp the back of the kitchen chair across from where his father sits. Her flowered nightdress has short sleeves, and her biceps bulge with the same effort Leo's seen in them when she slides kielbasa meat down pork casings. Her dark hair, usually pulled into a neat knot at the top of her head, is loose now, a thick tangle that reinforces the sense of his mother as one of those horses in Westerns, running full speed, mane and tail whipping.

"Cheap," snorts his mother.

"Free," says Stash.

"I'm not talking about the drinks."

"Annie, my dear-dear, you're imagining things," he says.

19

"Cheap," she repeats, her nails digging into the chair's wood. "And younger every year."

"Your ma's crazy," Stash slurs, facing Leo but unable to focus on him. "Wild imagination on that dear-dear. The real McCarthy, your ma-ma. Ha ha ha ha!" Gravy splashes from his mustache as he laughs. "Real McCarthy, you hear?"

"Be quiet," Leo says to both of them. "Go to bed, why don't you?"

"Smell him. Like a cheap whorehouse," she spits. "And we all know big-man-bandleader Stanislav Meitka never says no to anything cheap. Or free."

His father growls something indecipherable.

"Why do you do it?" his mother says, each word clipped and hard.

As much as Leo wants to know the answer to this question too, he'd rather his parents give up their fight and go to their separate corners to sleep off their booze and anger. He's never seen his mother this angry.

"Leave it alone," Leo says to her.

But his mother keeps pushing. She looks anything but tired now. She could beat back an army. It's as if she relishes the excitement of the fight. Is this part of why Leo has always blamed her? Is it true? Is she enjoying this?

Her usually pale skin is radiant with blood. Bare feet set hard, shoulders thrown back, her angry breath pushes her nostrils wide and white. With hands at least as quick as his father's on the accordion's keyboard, she reaches behind her and grabs a bone-handled paring knife from the drying rack.

"No!" Leo cries.

He moves fast across the kitchen to his mother's wrist, which he grasps. Her gaze remains firmly on Stash, whose own blurry gaze looks curiously amused. His gravy-crusted lips spread into a small smile. Leo has an urge to release his mother's wrist and let her slice the smile off his father's face, but he stands to his full height in front of her. He's been taller than her for years, and he breaks her view of his father. He keeps his own gaze on the blade.

"Stop, okay?" Leo says softly but firmly. He risks a glance at her face, pleading with his eyes.

When she looks back at him though, the skin at her eyes is creased not just with anger but with hurt too, and the flood of guilt returns. He nearly drops her wrist. He manages to whisper, "For me."

She pauses, takes a breath, and nods. She lets him uncurl her fist from the knife's handle.

Careful of its blade, he tosses it into the sink. She lets him press her down into the chair she'd been grasping.

His father allows himself to be pushed into the pantry to sleep on the trouble cot set up for occasions when he's too far gone to make it up the stairs. Leo gives him a shove past the shelves holding jars of his mother's preserved beets, pickles, and green tomatoes. Stash's body is so loose he crumples onto the cot. Pinned to the wall over the cot hangs an American flag along with his victory medal.

"You're a good son," he mutters, gravy smearing the pillow.

Leo pulls off one of his shoes.

"Just 'tween us," his father whispers, "she's a beaut." He smiles conspiratorially at Leo, whose already-flushed cheeks inflame.

What does he mean? Is he talking about Anne or Nora? Does he know what Leo saw earlier tonight? Is he counting on Leo to keep his secret? One for all, all for one. Isn't his mother one of them? As if removing his father's other shoe would imply some sort of agreement, Leo leaves the shoe on, steps out, and shuts the door tight.

To his relief, the kitchen is empty. His mother has retreated to her own bed.

His hands shaking, Leo removes the paring knife from the sink and turns on the water. As if the blade were coated with blood, he rinses and rinses it until the cold water numbs his fingers. As his adrenaline ebbs, he wishes one of his friends, Kirstin, Emelia, or Will, were awake for him to talk to, but they have normal families—or more normal than his—and are probably sleeping like babies. Besides, if they were awake, he couldn't tell them about

21

tonight anyway. You don't rat out your family, even to your friends. Not just because of loyalty either. There's guilt by association.

He suddenly feels more tired than he's ever been in his life.

He drops the knife into the drying rack, pushes in the chair where his mother sat, and turns off the light so tomorrow morning it will be easier for all three of them to pretend tonight never happened. He releases the breath he hadn't realized he'd been holding. If they pretend nothing happened, so will he.

He switches off the light as he enters his bedroom and shuts the door behind him. In bed, he can hear his father's graveled snores and his mother's pacing steps on the floorboards above his room.

To shut them out, he fingers the guitar part to "Ferry Cross the Mersey" on his stomach and tries to concentrate on the notes, but the song is too gentle to pull him in. Only violent things can block out all that's happened tonight, like Lake Michigan's waves crashing against the breakwaters. Maybe tomorrow, today really since the train's first whistle signaled midnight, he'll talk his friends into jumping off the end of the jetty into the near-freezing water. Maybe the waves can slam all the thoughts right out of his head.

Pleased to have something else to think about, his enthusiasm grows. It's a crazy thing to do, jumping off the jetty, but his friends won't call him crazy. They understand loyalty too. They'll take him seriously, analyzing the pros and cons of the deed. Man, it would feel great. And it would be the earliest any of them have gone into the water, maybe the earliest anyone's ever gone in who's managed to come out alive. So what if the temperature is low and the riptide strong? They're all good swimmers. And they'd watch out for each other. All for one. Imagine how famous they'd be at school if they could do it. But who would see? Without an audience, is it even worth the effort?

He closes his eyes. Is anything real if there isn't someone else there to see it? If he hadn't seen his father tonight . . . famous people must feel a hundred times, a million times more real than regular people . . . how wonderful to be famous, not local-famous like his father but Keith Richards famous . . . John Lennon famous. He's already a good guitar player, nearly as good as his father is an accordionist . . . He could be the next Lennon . . . Lennon hardly knows his father, who's some kind of sailor. John didn't need his father . . . Leo doesn't need Stash . . . He's going to be so much better a musician than Stash . . . play real music . . . play color . . . green and red . . . blue as the waves . . . gold records . . fans . . . girls throwing underwear to him . . . mushroom . . . pink shoes with pointed tips . . .

As he falls into sleep, he hears the sound of his fans, their screams a sharp wind, their applause fat droplets splashing over his shoulders. Once asleep, he dreams he's stuck in the pantry, the walls closing in. He's got to push past his father to get out, but Stash won't move out of the way. "A beaut," says his father, grinning, his arms handless stumps.

In the morning, Leo glares grumpily at his father over his cereal. Stash looks back innocently, all traces of his drunkenness gone. His mustache is clean of gravy, and his chin has had a fresh shave. His eyes are bluer than Leo's, his black hair a neat swoop like the statue of Big Boy above the restaurants. Leo used to be so proud of him. Watching him play music, Leo felt so lucky to have a father who was special. He could work a crowd like few other bandleaders. Charismatic, people said. They still do, but now Leo wonders how much of it has been an act. Who is his father, really?

At the moment, his father turns his charisma on Leo, smiling wide. Had he used that smile on Nora to get her into the back seat of the Plymouth? When he was little, Leo used to respond to that smile and jump into his father's lap. Now that he's older, that smile would normally encourage Leo to ask about last night's show, but this morning, Leo won't give his father the satisfaction.

Leo sneers back.

"Used to call you Snagglepuss when you were losing teeth. My little boy, Snagglepuss Leo." He lights a cigarette, and the smoke curls into the air between them.

Leo harrumphs, wishing he didn't remember. He loved it when his father called him that. On Saturday afternoons, he used to take

23

Leo driving in the country to small lakes where they'd sit side by side on the banks and fish for trout. When they came home, he told Anne that his Snagglepuss had caught all of the fish in the bucket. She would *ooh* and *ah* and call Leo a real little fisherman, just like his father. If Leo started to protest, his father pressed his finger to his own lips and whispered, "Our secret," before breaking into a smile as wide as the one he wears now.

Leo's resolve falters. Should he give a little? He looks down at the floor, and his gaze catches on a smear of gravy. The ugliness of last night returns, and he stiffens, his sneer deepening.

"Now sourpuss suits you better. You want to come to practice with me today, Sourpuss?" says Stash. "Boys and I are working up some new tunes."

Yesterday at this time, Leo would have given anything for such an invitation.

"No," he says, "I have things to do. I have my own life, you know."

To his surprise, his father looks hurt. After a moment though, he shrugs and says, "You're too good for us, huh? Well, you're not too good to play the church smoker next week. I'll leave you the set list. You be ready."

"I won't know the new songs."

"I'll leave sheet music. You're not too high and mighty to read notes on a page?"

Leo says nothing.

"I thought you wanted to play with band," he says.

Still Leo says nothing.

"Like I say," he says. "You be ready for the smoker. Get your mother to help you learn the songs if you can't on your own. I want you there, young man. I want my son playing with his father's band."

He opens the newspaper, shutting Leo out, not waiting for him to agree or disagree to play the smoker because it isn't a question or a request. Big-man-bandleader Stash doesn't care about what he wants. Doesn't care about what Anne wants. What anyone wants but himself. My son. My team. All for one. And Stash is that one.

Facing the wall of his father's newspaper and headlines about seven Americans killed in a Viet Cong raid, Leo fumes. In some vague way, those boys getting killed is his father's fault. Until recently, the war was background static he hadn't tuned in yet. But this year at school, after announcements about dances and club meetings, Morty Hermann, the senior class president, started reading the names of alumni who have been killed in action: Wozniak, Olsen, Schroeder, Romanshek. It seems every block has a house with a flag in a window hung by families who have had someone killed in action, the same kind of flag his father has over his trouble cot in the pantry. In a few years, his father may be pushing Leo toward a uniform instead of the church smoker. How can he preach about loyalty to your country, then go out and cheat on Anne?

As Leo grinds his cornflakes with his teeth, she walks into the kitchen, carrying full grocery bags from the market down the street. She wears a coat the color of the blue sky. Her cheeks are ruddy from the effort of the walk. She's a beautiful woman; Leo can see that. With her eyes bright, her energy bright, and her dark hair pulled back into its neat knot, it's hard to imagine her as the same woman who pointed a knife at Stash.

A pang of guilt stabs Leo. Why hadn't he believed her before last night? Well, he decides, he'll take her side now.

"Morning," she says, kicking the door shut behind her.

At the sound, his father jumps up from the table to take the grocery bags from her. Being a good boy after last night, Leo scoffs, expecting her to cold-shoulder him as he has. We won't give an inch, either of us, he vows.

She hesitates only a moment, though, before allowing his father to take the packages from her arms. She lifts his coffee mug and sniffs.

"Not Irish," he says, lifting three fingers to shoulder level. "Scout's honor."

She smiles grudgingly and lifts her cheek. He kisses it with a friendly smack.

The kiss twists Leo's anger tighter. He can't understand them. Do they hate each other or love each other?

Probably his father has promised to go teetotal again. And his mother is foolish enough to believe he will keep his word.

Leo's sick of them both. He drops his cereal dish and spoon into the sink and pushes past them. He slams the back door behind him. He needs to be around people he can understand. He heads to Will's. They'll collect the girls. Go to the lake. He stomps the tempo of "Satisfaction" into the sidewalk, punching the drumbeat into the air.

Three new flags droop from the triple-decker houses called Polish flats. Three more guys are dead. Why are there never flags in the windows of the neat, new boxes being built on the empty lots he and his friends used to play in? It's a question his union-crazy father would ask, and he shrugs it off.

At Bradley Avenue, Buckhorn's main street, he turns left, past the new library and post office, Woolworth's, and the Smoke Store with the wooden Indian out front. As upset as he is, he can't pass by the Hobby Shop without stopping to study the album display, changed weekly. He spends whole afternoons in the listening rooms here. This week's display comingles Bob Dylan, the Stones, the Beatles, the Kingsmen, Buffalo Springfield, Jefferson Airplane, Donovan, the Shangri-Las, and the Byrds with Eddie Blazonczyk's "Happy Polka Music," "The Polka World of Kenny Bass," and Frankie Yankovic's unbearably stupid "Who Stole the Keeshka?" Even his father won't play that song.

Imagine passing by a store and seeing your own record. Some days he can see himself there. In the mirror, he practices poses for his album cover. But today, as the dusty scent of Armour Steel Forging hits him, the thought feels as fanciful as being a cowboy or astronaut, and he turns away. The dusty scent grows stronger as he nears Will's. He passes Jablonski's Pool and Lanes, and hollow sounds skip through the open windows, pins falling and pool balls knocking together. Jablonski's and most taverns are open to accommodate all three shifts of workers, but it's Armour Steel that rules this street, taking up an entire side for the next sixteen blocks. Its frosted windows make sure no one can see in or out. Just one step better than working in a mine, or so his father says.

Mostly taverns and liquor stores line the other side of the street: On the Lake, Fritz's, Wet Draught, Nite Awl, Home Plate, among others, and Will's father's tavern, Heartwood. Once there, Leo circles the building, heading toward the back stairs leading to the flat above the bar where Will and his family live. At eight in the morning, the tavern's open door reveals a cavern as dark as a cave, with humpback man-beasts leaning over the bar top. Leo sidesteps the door as if dodging an outstretched arm grabbing to pull him in.

Emelia

EMELIA DEMSKI WAKES anxious without knowing why. It's Saturday, she reminds herself, so she can be a little lazy. As her Aunt Lou would say, no pencils or books or dirty looks from teachers today, not that she or her friends earn many. They're all decent students and polite enough that they don't merit much attention from school authorities, except for Will, who's liked all around and good at baseball and basketball. Kirstin is a brain and a girl and sometimes eyed suspiciously by kids, but she's admired by teachers, this year by Mrs. Gramercy in English and Mr. Trippsman in biology. Leo's more like Emelia herself, hard to pin down. He's athletic, but at swimming and cross-country running, not the big- man-on-campus sports like Will, so people don't automatically associate Leo with athletics. He's musical too, but he doesn't play in the school band. Most of their classmates don't know how good he is, but he plays guitar for the three of them sometimes when they gather in Will's bedroom to hang out. As far as Emelia can tell, he's as good as any of the musicians on the albums they play.

She'll get up and meet them soon. There's an area of the beach they want to explore today. This year Lake Michigan has become their world. They've lived near it their whole lives, seen it every day, and been to the surrounding park's playground areas and skating pond plenty of times with adults and school groups. In summer Will plays baseball at the three fields, and sometimes they watch his father play softball on the Heartwood team at night. They've spent hot summer days at the crowded outdoor pool that is painted so blue it feels like you're jumping into the sky.

But this spring, they go alone to Lake Michigan's secret places that are charged with mystery and therefore brand-new. They stand at the edges of the cliffs high above the shore and dare each other to step into the sky for real. In the woods, they've found abandoned lean-tos, smoldering campfires, and fresh paths, rocky and dangerous, down to the stony banks, which give way to the sandy shore and frigid waves that on windy days burst like fireworks over the concrete piers. Someone must have used those piers once, but now they're broken and abandoned and the perfect places to test your balance.

At the moment though, she's too lazy to move, one of the many character flaws she tries to hide from her aunts, who are strict and exacting in their efforts to teach her to be not so much a decent student ("Just do your best," they say) as a decent girl. She stretches cat-like, enjoying the soreness in her thighs and calves from yesterday's swimming practice, one of the last before the final meet of the spring season. She can't decide whether or not to go out for the summer team. At her best, she came in third in the hundred freestyle and second in fifty backstroke. She circles her feet to loosen her ankles. Second and third place, not good, not bad. Nothing to be ashamed of, but nothing to be particularly proud of either. Just as well. Pride is another of those character traits of which her aunts disapprove.

Well, at least she helped the team win. Both she and her aunts can feel good about that. Her aunts approve of teamwork, and Emelia too likes being on a team. She often wishes she had a big family and not just her aunts.

Having enjoyed her laziness long enough, she sits and stands in one motion. Hanging from one of the bedposts is the floppy hat with the floral pattern she bought yesterday at Woolworths. She's been trying to find her look, something that seems authentically her, not a kid playing dress-up. She pops it on her head and tries a few poses in the mirror. She wonders if she looks like her mother, Elisa, about whom Emelia knows little. When she was a kid, she saw the *Parent Trap*, and she wished aloud for a mother like Maureen O'Hara, but her Aunt Lou looked hurt and told her she was lucky to have two aunts who love her so much. Of course this is true, but she secretly hung onto this wish for a real mother for years.

She tries another pose. Maybe with her flamingo pink lipstick? Not that her aunts let her wear lipstick. Vanity runs neck and neck with pride and laziness in the flaws race. But what her aunts don't see won't hurt them. She's bought two tubes, the flamingo pink and a true cherry, which Kirstin holds onto for her, so it isn't really like they're her own at all. She's good at finding technicalities and loopholes in her aunts' rules.

She thrusts a leg forward, bends with her hands on the outstretch knee, pursing her lips so she's kissing the air. Is she more Ann Margaret or Julie Christie? It's so hard to know who to be. She widens her eyes into a look of innocent surprise. Susan Oliver, maybe?

Like Leo, Emelia doesn't fit easily into one of the cookie-cutter shapes most other kids at school do. Sometimes she thinks of herself as one of the monkey-puzzle cakes her aunts make from leftover bread, bits of lots of things squashed together without any real form. She's okay at sports and most subjects at school, but she's not great at any of them. She can draw passably, but she's not talented. Art teachers have never fawned over her work as they do Kathy Dorkhsen's. Even her aunts hang up the pictures she gives them for Christmases and their birthdays for only a few days. Then they presumably drop the pictures into the trash because Emelia never sees them again.

This year the home ec teacher likes Emelia because she can already bake most anything. Emelia enjoys the attention but understands she's not some whiz at baking. It's just that she's helped her aunts in the bakery since she was little. One of her earliest memories is of making measuring cup towers and hand impressions in bowls of flour the way other kids did in sandboxes.

She pulls the hat off and returns it to the bedpost, sorry now that she spent $2.50 on it. It's not *her*, whoever that is. Lately she's had a dream in which she's standing on the edge of a lake cliff. With one leap, she'll become the person she's meant to be, but she can't see that person, just the rocky sheer of the cliff's edge. In the dream, she stands frozen, fearing the free fall but also afraid of transformation. What if she doesn't like what she becomes?

She wakes from these dreams with the feelings she had this morning, anxious and unsettled and certain that sometime soon she's going to have to choose whether to jump blindly and take what she gets, or turn back and remain forever the formless dough she's been for the whole of her fourteen, no, *fifteen* years.

"Gosh," she says, a smile breaking through the nervous pinch of her expression. It's her birthday.

"Emelia, time to get up," Aunt Lou calls from the kitchen. "You're verging on lazy."

"I'm up," she calls back, her voice muffled from the nightgown she's pulling over her head.

"Well, come on then, birthday girl."

"I'll be right there. I'm getting dressed."

Hurrying now, she pushes into a plaid blouse and fawn slacks, and drops to her knees to reach under her bed for her Keds. She can already smell sausages and waffles with jam from the previous summer's raspberries. Aunt Lou promised to save the last jar for her birthday breakfast.

Fifteen. It sounds so much more grown up than fourteen. Her birthday is the one day she's allowed to feel special without her aunts telling her she's being conceited, another trait decent girls have to keep in check. Just yesterday, Aunt Lou admitted fifteen is a significant birthday. She called it a before-and-after birthday, her face creasing into thought, perhaps about what kind of fuss to make over Emelia.

Certainly there will be the usual fuss. Aunt Lou will have left the bakery to Aunt Genny's care and come upstairs to cook Emelia's birthday breakfast. Tonight after supper there will be presents and a cake. Her aunts' wedding cakes are renowned as elegant sculptures. The local paper once called them baroque works of art, which Emelia had to look up in the dictionary, then decided it was a good description of the piped swirls, fleur-de-lis, and rosettes her aunts pipe so expertly onto layers of Victoria sponge.

Her birthday cakes are more fun than the wedding cakes but still elaborate. Among Emelia's birthday cake highlights have been the Raggedy Ann cake, the Casper the Ghost cake, the Slinky Dog, the telephone, and, Emelia's favorite, last year's phonograph complete with a semisweet chocolate-fudge "Love Me Do" record circling the top. The best part is that they're always a surprise. Each year she tries to catch her aunts in the act of baking, but they always manage to elude her. She loves that they can be so sneaky. She can't wait to see what this year's will be. She ties her sneakers fast and hurries to the kitchen.

As she enters, the sausages' scents of garlic and fennel make her mouth water. She's surprised to find both Aunt Genny and Aunt Lou leaning against the counter. Usually just Aunt Lou prepares her birthday breakfast. Although she would never say this aloud, she thinks of her Aunt Lou as the nice one. Her smiles come often, and she's quick to laugh and joke with Emelia. They share a love for movie magazines, like *Movieland* and *Screen Stories,* which Aunt Genny calls a waste of money. And they both love the beach, which Aunt Genny hates, claiming sand is just dirt wearing its Sunday best.

This morning both women are dressed in their baker's whites, but over her whites Aunt Lou wears an apron with ruffles and speckled with yellow rosebuds. She's told Emelia that the customers like to see a soft touch on a working woman, which is why she works the front of the store dealing with the customers, while Genny remains in the kitchen. In a rare joke, Genny once said the softest thing about her is her buns.

Aunt Genny has taken off the baker's hat, whose shape makes Emelia think of muffin that's overflowed its cup. Her short hair, which used to be brown but has become streaked with gray this year, is still matted down from the cap. Of course, she's been baking since 4 a.m. Her spiky bangs stick to her glossy forehead. Spiky actually isn't a bad way to describe her aunt. If Aunt Lou is the nice one, Aunt Genny is, not mean exactly, but, well, spiky. She's quick to take away Emelia's privileges as punishment and is less likely to let Emelia go places beyond their immediate neighborhood, even if it's a school-sponsored trip. Emelia has often wondered if this is because she's the oldest sister and was made to take on the responsibility of watching out for her younger sisters, Lou and Elisa. Maybe she feels guilty that she didn't keep Elisa from dying. This is pure speculation. Emelia has learned asking about her mother brings dark clouds to both her aunts' moods and very few answers.

While Aunt Genny calls herself no nonsense and says she refuses to suffer fools, Emelia has seen the soft spots she likes to downplay, like the dish of milk she leaves daily for the tabby cat who comes to the bakery's alley door. Also, she slips in a slice of cake when she makes Emelia's lunch, and she recently persuaded Aunt Lou to raise Emelia's allowance fifty cents without Emelia asking for it.

"A girl needs her own pin money, Lou," said Aunt Genny. "How else is she going to learn to spend wisely and save generously?"

So Emelia's pleased to see both her aunts there for her birthday breakfast. After all, as Aunt Lou said, fifteen is a special age.

But when she sees their nervous expressions, her earlier anxiety returns.

"Who's watching the bakery?" she asks, sipping orange juice from the small glass placed on the table, as it is every morning. For the first time though, a coffee cup has been placed at her table setting above her silverware. Aunt Lou fills it two-thirds with coffee and a third with heavy cream. Emelia hesitates, looking first at Aunt Lou, who struggles to stretch her lips into a smile, then at Aunt Genny, who rarely smiles and doesn't now. However, Aunt Genny gives a small nod, and Emelia sips the warm liquid, which tastes sour and grown up and serious.

"Happy birthday, sweetie," says Aunt Lou.

She's the taller of the two women, somewhat thinner too, although they are both solidly built with muscular arms and red hands from kneading dough and lifting heavy trays.

"Yes, happy birthday," Aunt Genny says with a brusqueness that makes the sentiment feel perfunctory.

"Sit down, hon," says Aunt Lou. "We have something to tell you."

33

"What happened?" Emelia asks. "Who's dead?" The words escape her lips instinctively, like a curse when she stubs her toe. She'd like to take them back because they feel like an actual curse. The knot of anxiety tightens in her stomach.

"Sit," says Aunt Genny, kneading a dish towel in her capable hands. Emelia recognizes this as her aunt's nervous habit. But the severity of Aunt Genny's voice reassures Emelia. Years ago, Emelia had known her grandmother had died because Aunt Genny had spoken to her with unusual gentleness.

Emelia sits, but her aunts don't say anything for a while. Finally she says, "What? What is it? Just tell me. I'm *fifteen* now. I'm not a kid."

Still they say nothing. The toaster pops, and they all jump.

"Well?" Emelia says.

"Honey, it's about your mother," says Aunt Lou.

"Yes, what?" Emelia says eagerly, maybe too eagerly. "What about her?"

Emelia barely remembers her mother. The scent of lilacs makes her think of her mother, but she doesn't know if this is a memory or not. She has little else of her save the photos on the fireplace mantle and the comments of the customers who come into the bakery and tell her aunts how much Emelia resembles their little sister. Her aunts only ever confirm this with a nod and move the conversation to other topics. They never speak of her mother unbidden. They avoid the topic of Elisa the way they avoid speaking of sex and death and other shameful things.

Perhaps today though they will give her some tidbit, something to cherish, like the ring Kirstin's mother gave her on her fifteenth birthday. The ring belonged to Kirstin's great-grandmother, or maybe her great-aunt, anyway someone long dead. What Emelia would really like, more than a ring, is some edifying tidbit, a gesture her mother made often or some phrase she liked to say. Maybe if Emelia knew more particular things about her mother, she would come closer to knowing who she's supposed to be.

When her aunt doesn't continue, Emelia decides she'd better urge her on before she changes her mind and clamps her memory tight again.

"Yes, what about her? What were you going to say?"

"She's, well, she's . . ." says Aunt Lou, "in a hospital."

Emelia laughs.

"That's funny?" says Aunt Genny curtly. "A person in the hospital?"

"Well, yes, I guess. Isn't it? Isn't this a joke? Some kind of birthday joke?" She looks around the kitchen. "Is there a cake back there? Did I catch you in the act of decorating it or something?"

Her aunts exchange looks.

"Just say it," Aunt Genny instructs her sister, but Aunt Lou only bites her bottom lip. "Oh, for sweet Savoy's sake, I'll do it." She tosses the dish towel onto the counter and says flatly, "She's not dead. Elisa. Our sister. Your mother. She's in a—." Her voice breaks for a moment. "An asylum."

"A *hospital*," Lou interjects.

They go on to tell Emelia things her mind cannot take in, about her mother's sadness and an operation by a doctor with an ice pick. They use the word *lobotomy* only once but use *diminished capacities* a few times.

Finally Aunt Genny says, "We all agreed, your grandparents and us too, that we would tell you when we thought you were old enough to understand. You're fifteen now. We thought it was time."

Although she has a thousand questions, Emelia asks first, "Can I go see her?"

"No," Aunt Genny says fast and firmly. Aunt Lou confirms this with a shake of her head. The quickness of the replies suggests they were ready for this question.

"She's far away. And she wouldn't know who you are," says Aunt Lou. "It could be upsetting for her. And you."

"And, well, it's just not the kind of place a young lady should go. Not a proper one. Not a place for a decent girl like you," Aunt Genny says. After a moment she adds, "We've done our best for her."

"She doesn't remember me?" asks Emelia. For the moment, confusion has won out over anger, but she feels rage simmering. "Why did you tell me she was dead?"

"For your own good," says Aunt Genny. "We didn't want you to have the stigma of abandonment, worse yet the stigma of such a mother." She stops. After a moment, clasping her hands before her chest, she adds as if she has forgotten a portion of a prepared speech, "You're a good girl. We know that."

"But you always told me she—"

"A mother in such a place," interrupts Aunt Lou. "A hospital. We love you too much to saddle you with that. Mind you, none of this is Elisa's fault either."

Genny snorts. Her expression squishes her features into disagreement. "As I was saying, easier for you to have a dead mother than an insane one. One who leaves you in the lurch."

"Genny, it wasn't her fault. Don't give the girl that impression," Aunt Lou insists, her gaze hard on her sister, then on Emelia. "That doctor promised it would help her. The procedure. The . . . ice pick. It sounds horrible, but it was commonplace. Everyone said he'd had such wonderful results with others. Your grandparents, they wanted—" She turns her palms up and shakes them as if frustrated to find her hands are empty. "But your mother, she did nothing wrong. Nothing."

"Oh, come on, Lou. Nothing?" Genny says. "El was no innocent. You know she was wild. Later, yes, okay, the operation didn't go well, it's true. But you can't blame Ma and Pa for that. It's the doctors who advised them who are to blame. And, Lou, you can't deny, she was fast. Wild. Sometimes she was downright cra—"

"*Not* crazy. She wasn't. I never believed that, even when the doctors said it."

"Rebellious then. A miscreant. Untamed. *Untamable*." She gestures a hand toward Emelia as proof, sees what she has done, and slaps the table with the dish towel. She whispers through clenched teeth, "Those were the words the doctors used. Official diagnoses. She probably would have run off on the child anyway. Like the father."

"Johnny Angel?" says Emelia. This is the most Genny has ever said about her father, a cur never to be spoken of in this house on orders of her dead grandparents.

"Whoever that was," says Genny, flinging her arms to the heavens.

Any shard of information Emelia has managed to chip off has had to come from Lou's softer resolve.

"Johnny Angel," Emelia says to Lou. "That's who my father is."

Lou looks down at her hands or her shoes or the floor. Genny's gaze has dropped too.

"Isn't it?"

"Your mother never said," Genny says finally, a sigh of exasperation in the words. "Not right out. Not for sure. He seemed a likely suspect. He'd left town. But it's a guess."

"Genny!" Aunt Lou says. This time her voice is a caution, her eyes a warning.

"The girl should know. We said it was time. It's no good to sugarcoat it. Better that she learns something from it." Genny turns to Emelia. "Let that be your lesson, Emmy. Bad things happen to bad girls. Mark my words."

"We know you're a good girl. Decent." Lou has stepped in front of her sister as if to protect Emelia from vitriol that may fly from her sister like batter from a whisk. "The things we're saying, they may sound harsh. Hard, even. Nothing to do with your mother has ever been easy. Still, she's our sister, and we have seen she's had the best care we could afford. And it's been a joy to raise you. Our own little girl."

She reaches out as if to touch Emelia, but Emelia pulls back, and Lou's outstretched hand falls limply to her side.

"Honey, despite everything, we love your mother. Our sister. And we love you."

"So it's not true she wanted to abandon me. That she was a miscreant?" She's not sure exactly what the word means, *miscreant*, but its ugly sounds suggest the depth of its badness. She wants desperately for Aunt Lou to agree. Her mother maybe was bad, okay. But not that bad, not bad enough to abandon her own baby. But Lou has turned from her. Her hands crush the cold toast into the sink.

"So, now that you're fifteen," Genny goes on, something folded into her voice that causes Emelia to stiffen. "You're a young lady. A young *woman*. It won't be long before, well, you know."

"Before what?" Emelia insists. She's had her period for years now, as her aunts well know. This can't be what they're afraid of.

"Genny, stop," says Lou. "That's enough for one day."

"You think I'm enjoying this?"

"I didn't say that, but it's the girl's birthday."

"She's the spitting image, Lou. Too pretty for her own good. We have a duty to her." She whispers as if Emelia won't hear, as if they are again behind doors discussing her, deciding which mold to put her in as they would a bowl of cake batter, but it's the sensation of her dream that returns to her, a rocky terror as she looks out over the cliff. Before she has the chance to jump, her aunts are pushing her to the edge. Emelia feels their hands at her back.

"It's not her fault she's her mother's daughter, but she is," Aunt Genny continues. "Ma and Pa waited too long to rein in that girl. She was loose, indecent. A *slut*. And you know it. You know it, Lou."

"Genevia Maria Demski, you hold your tongue this instant!" Lou says.

Too late though. Their words have launched Emelia into the air. She doesn't have to wonder who she is anymore. No need to try on hats and pose in mirrors. No choosing to jump or not. She's her mother's daughter. Wild. Crazy. Miscreant. *Slut*. They're in her blood.

"I want to see her," Emelia says. Despite her shakiness, she keeps her voice firm.

"No," says Aunt Genny, just as firmly.

"Why?"

"No," Aunt Genny repeats, "absolutely not. No, no, no."

"Aunt Lou? She's my mother. I have a right to see her."

"For now, darling girl, you have to trust that we are doing what's best for you," Lou says so absolutely that Emelia knows there is no point in arguing further. Aunt Lou takes a step forward and reaches out a hand as if to touch her, but Emelia flinches and pulls her arm back, crossing both at her chest.

"I know this is a lot to absorb. You take some time. Maybe we'll talk again, hmm?" Without waiting for an answer, Aunt Lou opens the oven door and uses a dish towel to remove a plate with a waffle. She tongs two sausages from a frying pan onto the plate along with a dollop of raspberry jam.

"Happy birthday," she says as she sets the plate before Emelia. She pipes a whipped cream *1* and *5* onto the waffle.

Apparently *some time* is no time at all because Lou goes on as if compelled to explain further.

"Sweetheart, what you have to understand is that none of this means anything for you. Really, it doesn't. Nothing's going to change. We just felt you should know. We're your family, and we'll always be here for you. Nothing has changed."

Silently, Emelia watches the numbers melt into the waffle's squares. Aunt Lou is wrong. Everything has already changed. Her aunts were the most honest people she knew. They use words like *integrity, loyalty, decency*. All the time, they have been lying to her. Like Dorothy in Oz suddenly seeing in Technicolor, Emelia will never see the same again. Not her aunts. Not her home. Not herself. Nothing's changed? She's not an orphan. She's the daughter of a crazy woman. The mother she thought was a ghost is really a monster.

"There's one more thing," says Aunt Genny. Her voice has softened, but she swallows hard as if to get down a last leathery bite of overcooked liver.

"Genny, let me do the rest," says Lou.

"I will not. This is too important, Lou. You know it is. This is no time for softness. This is our livelihood."

"What are you talking about?" Emelia asks. "The rest?" Surely Aunt Lou is right. This is plenty for one birthday.

"Honey," Genny says, giving Lou a nod to affirm she's softening the blow as much as she dares. "We tell people our sister is, you know, *passed*, because it's best for everyone, and we believe it's best you not tell anyone anything different either."

Emelia feels anger bubbling. "Why?" she says tightly.

"An association with someone like—" Aunt Genny lifts her palm and corrects herself before Aunt Lou does it for her. "Some *place*, like that *hospital* can be far reaching. People take any excuse. We count on that bakery downstairs for food and fiddle. But there are two other bakeries within walking distance, and we don't want our customers taking their business to those. You understand?"

Stupefied into silence, Emelia simply looks at her aunts. Has she understood them correctly? Having finally told her the truth, are they now telling her to lie? Are they really warning her to be a good girl and in the same breath telling her to lie? Lie to everyone, her teachers, her friends, every person she meets on the street as they've been doing almost as long as she's been alive?

"You can't be serious," she finally manages to choke out. "I can't tell my friends I have a mother?"

"Emelia," Aunt Genny goes on. "We're trusting that you're old enough to understand. Family business isn't anyone else's business. Not even your friends'. You're a Demski. First and foremost. We've always done for you. Clothed you. Fed you."

"Loved you," Lou puts in.

Neither adds, *so you owe us*, but Emelia understands this is implied.

"So we'll keep this just among us," says Aunt Lou. Her voice is gentler than her sister's, but it's not a question. It's not a request.

"You're serious," Emelia says.

"Yes," they respond in unison. The effect is even more unsettling. It's as if they have melted into each other like the cream 1 and 5 congealing on her plate. They've always been Aunt Genny and Aunt Lou, but now they're a singular force that she can't possibly resist.

"All right, I guess," Emelia responds quietly. What else can she say? Apparently, together they have the power to lock people away, to keep them from their children. "I won't tell anyone."

"So that's that then." Aunt Genny brushes her hands together as if dusting flour from them after kneading dough. She looks to her sister and nods. A job well done. Well, done anyway.

"Eat your breakfast, young lady," Genny says. "Your Aunt Lou made it special for you." She moves toward the door. "Then go enjoy your day. We'll have a special dinner tonight." She pauses at the top of the stairs. "You're a good girl." She clomps halfway down before calling up, "C'mon, Lou, it's time. The Bruskis' cake is due at noon."

Before Aunt Lou shuts the kitchen door behind her, she peeks back and whispers, "Happy birthday, darling. Fifteen is such a wonderful age. So many new things. Many, many happy returns."

Emelia blinks at the closed door, at the food on the table, which she leaves uneaten. Will she ever want to eat again? What does her mother eat in that place? Her mother. Elisa Demski. Her ghost mother risen from the dead. But not quite.

She feels as if she's in one of those fairy tales where your wish is granted but you didn't wish right. Eternal life but without youth. The mother she's wished for is alive but insane and unable to recognize her. The mother she'd imagined as perfect and Maureen O'Hara beautiful is wild and indecent. A slut.

By the time Emelia gets up from the table and goes to meet her friends, her coffee cup is empty, and her birthday breakfast has gone stone cold.

The sun has risen to its midmorning height, warming the air to chilly by the time she shows up at the street corner, which is the center point among all four of the friends' houses. They greet each other without greetings. Kirstin is busy retying her Keds. Will and Leo pinch lit cigarettes in their cupped hands. Likely, Will has stolen them from his father's tavern.

"You really think no one's going to notice that your fists are on fire?" Emelia says because it's the kind of thing she would have said before she had to hide her living monster of a mother from her friends. The words feel like a script, and she's reading the part of Jokey Emelia. She's not sure she can keep it up. It takes all her will not to blurt out the news of her mother having risen from the dead, sort of.

"She's right," Will says, dropping his stub to the sidewalk and stepping it out. He gives Leo a c'mon-you-too look, and Leo takes a last drag and steps his out too.

After that Emelia says little about anything, worried her secret will slip out. She notices Leo keeps quiet too, which isn't unusual. He's prone to broody silences. Usually she will try to coax him into a better mood, but she feels wooden and false and is afraid of her own words. Kirstin and Will fill the silence with bitter complaints about the advanced math test facing them on Monday. Neither Leo nor Emelia are taking advanced math. With no complaints to voice, they lead the foursome, navigating to the place on the beach they want to explore, what the older kids call Fox Tail Point.

While collecting shells and rocks along Fox Tail's shore, they challenge each other to stone-skipping contests, which Will, with his outfielder's arm, always wins. Kirstin sorts pebbles into piles by size and color, as if trying to order the messy beach. Emelia and Leo pick through the remnants of older kids' bonfire-and-beer parties. Leo cracks a brown Schlitz bottle against a rock and smiles, seemingly pleased with the sound the glass makes on impact. His stare fixes on the broken edges until he shakes his gaze free and tosses the bottle into brown weeds.

Emelia finds a slender shard of stone and presses its tip against the flesh above her eyebrow, wondering how hard they pressed that ice pick to get to her mother's brain. When Leo catches her at this, he only smiles again, the way he does whenever one of them takes a risk—playing chicken at the cliff's overhang, walking on a jetty coated with ice, or spinning their bodies up and around a bridge rail as if it were a parallel barre in gym class. His expression says he understands the pleasure and pain of this risk, so she presses the stone's edge harder to see what he will do. At the very moment she's certain the tip will pierce her skin and explode her brain, Leo takes the shard from her hand.

"Come on," he says. "It's not worth it."

"No?"

They exchange looks, and she almost tells him. *My mother is alive.* But even in her mind, the words sound crazy. Crazy. Like her mother. Her aunts are right; she can't tell one part of the secret without telling the other parts too. *My mother is alive and in the nuthouse. She's a slut who abandon me, and they punished her by braining her.*

And telling Leo means telling them all because she can't ask him to keep a secret from Will and Kirstin. What if after she tells them, they think she's crazy too? Like mother, like daughter. What if they don't want to be her friend anymore? Who wants to hang out with a crazy girl?

Before today it would never have occurred to her that her friends would discard her. The four of them have chosen each other. They're only children in a place of big families where six siblings is more usual than none. Until now, they've shared everything. But a curtain has dropped between her and them. No matter how sheer, no matter how thin the curtain may be, as long as she keeps this secret from them, she will be separate.

But to tell them, that's an even bigger risk.

"Leo, I—" she says

"No, you don't really want to," says Leo. He thinks she wants to hurt herself for real. Does she?

"Oh, no," she says, not sure this is true. Not sure what's true.

But before she can go on, he tosses the stone shard into the fire ring and says, "You don't want them singing some 'Teen Angel' song for you."

"Yeah," she laughs nervously, thankful for his misunderstanding, feeling she has stepped back from a cliff ledge, one different from her dream cliff but equally dangerous.

"Or 'Last Kiss,'" she says. "I hate that song."

"Yeah, sappy crap. Vroom, vroom," he fake roars.

He continues his motorcycle roar as they trot to catch up with Kirstin and Will, who have moved farther down the beach, and Emelia thinks, what do I need a mother for, or my aunts? I have these friends. Friends are better than family even if they don't know all your secrets. You get to choose them.

They spend all day together, scrambling up and down the cliffs, over the fields of cattails and winter-wheatened grasses that the snow hasn't managed to strangle. They tramp over barely established paths and forge new ones. They call each other's attention to the sounds of the spring peepers near the marsh, signaling the season's change. With mud clinging to their shoes, they debate Beatles vs. Rolling Stones, Ed Sullivan vs. Smothers Brothers, orbiting the moon vs. sailing the world. Emelia loses track of the conversations and doesn't remind her friends that it's her birthday. She's glad they don't remember. She can't afford their full attention on her. In fact, most of the afternoon, she keeps her lips pressed tightly together. Surely once she begins talking, forbidden words will tumble from her mouth. *Lobotomy. Asylum. Abandon. Alive. Mother.*

By late afternoon, they're back on shore, unsure what to do next. They walk single file to the end of the jetty.

"Let's rip off our clothes and jump in," says Leo.

They debate frostbite vs. school fame. Frostbite wins when Kirstin points out Leo could lose a finger.

"No more guitar playing," she says. "No album cover."

"Yeah, okay. No one to see us anyway," he says.

"Don't we count?" says Emelia.

She must have been quieter than she thought because they all turn to look at her.

"No," says Will firmly. "A participant cannot be a witness." He holds a finger up as if counting. "A good witness is impartial."

"Is that in some rule book?"

"*Dragnet*," Leo says, and Will nods.

Despite her mood and all that's happened today, Emelia smiles. Leo and Will love detective shows. She bets only she and Kirstin know this about them.

Backing off the jetty and scrambling back up the cliff's face, they all agree they're too old for games of buried treasure.

"But it would be neat to find some," says Will.

So they decide to give the pleasure of discovery to some future children by burying a time capsule.

Pulling themselves over the cliff's edge, they head to the marsh.

It's been a dry spring, so the pond is really just soft mud. They collect cattails, and after stripping them clean of their fur, they light the ends of the punks. Squatting on rocks around the pond, they pretend the lit reeds are cigarettes, blowing invisible breaths to the gray sky.

"What should we put in the capsule?" says Kirstin.

The discussion turns lively. Worldly things like magazines and newspapers? Or personal things? Will and Leo's scout badges, Kirstin's rabbit's foot, Emelia's Kennedy campaign pin, maybe one of their favorite record albums, although initially no one wants to sacrifice one from his or her own collection.

"'Love Me Do,'" Emelia offers finally. *Someone to love. Someone like you.* She'll never listen to her cake-top song again, she thinks defiantly.

Leo frowns. "Lennon and Harrison play boring guitar on that song. What about notes?"

"Musical?" says Kirstin.

"No, each of us writes something."

"What would we write?" asks Kirstin.

"Depends on what messages we want to send into the future," says Will.

"We should write secrets," says Emelia, pushing the ragged stem of a cattail between her lips and sucking in the taste of earth. It's perfect. She can tell about her mother and not tell at the same time. "Things we would never tell anyone else."

"Yeah," says Kirstin. "Then whoever digs it up in the future will know, but who cares then? We'll all be dead from the bomb. Or from Martian invasions. Oh, hey, wouldn't it be great if some Martian teenagers dig it up!"

"Maybe we'll survive the bomb. Some people will have to make it. Why not us? Then we can be the ones who come back and dig it up," says Will. "When we're old."

"At least thirty," Leo says. "We can't dig it up until then."

Emelia's cheered by their enthusiasm. Do they all have secrets they want to bury? And what will it matter if they dig it up when they're thirty and Emelia's secrets are exposed? Thirty is a million years away. Light years.

"When I'm famous," Leo says, "my fans will pay loads for what I bury. There'll probably be an article in *Billboard.*"

"I can't wait for you to be on the cover of *Flip*," Kirstin says. "When you're big and famous, you better still talk to us little people. Or are you going to leave us behind and hang out with all your famous friends?"

"Of course he'll still be our friend. He's ours first," Emelia says sharply. She doesn't like this talk of death or of one of them leaving the group. She needs them, her siblings, her non-Demski family.

As they continue to discuss what to include, Emelia stands and the other follow suit. She looks at the flat land that hides bulbs, seeds, and roots. Until they sprout, there's no telling what they will be.

"Do you think anyone else has buried a time capsule up here?" she says.

"Gosh," says Kirstin. "Or something else?"

"Like what?" says Will.

"Anything," says Leo. "Everything."

They all stand very still. Emelia's gaze traces the horizon line from the forest to the washed-out grasses of the marsh to the cliffs. The wind finds an exposed patch of skin on her neck, and she shivers. Every inch of earth at their feet is a landmine of secrets.

Sonya

SONYA WAITS IN line at Demski's bakery for the rolls and petite fours her mother has sent her to buy for her afternoon card party, *club*, as she calls it, with *the girls*. The scents of yeast, vanilla, and cinnamon are thick in the air. Sonya's sense of smell has become so heightened of late she bets she could dissect each ingredient in every baked item just by holding it to her nose. She has been closely monitoring her body since the night at the train tracks. For the first few days, every minor discomfort was a twinge of possibility. By now, she has given up hope; so today when her stomach turns, rather than hope, she worries she might throw up if she moves an inch. She feels a tap on her shoulder from the woman behind her, who gestures for her to move forward.

"Oh, go on ahead," Sonya says, now dizzy as well. She can't faint here, not among all these women who will surely guess her condition.

"Still making up your mind, dear?"

"It all looks so good," she manages, smiling wanly.

She grasps onto the display case, pretending to decide between the *kolaczki* and *babka* that are turning her stomach. Actually, she focuses on the girl behind the counter, seated on the steps that presumably lead up to the flat above where the family lives. Fourteen, maybe fifteen years old, the girl stares at her aunts with a disturbing intensity that reminds Sonya of the way her little brother, Dean, has begun looking at her, with those jellyfish eyes of his that suggest he knows all the secrets of the universe, or her secrets anyway.

Yesterday she'd walked with him to the cliffs above the water so he could look out at the early-rising half-moon hanging low in the powder blue sky.

"Let's practice the names of the flowers," she said.

He placed his little starfish hand on her stomach.

"There."

She'd stiffened under his touch.

"Do you know the man in the moon?"

"No," she said, relieved, "I don't."

"Do so."

She said nothing, not wanting to spark his stubborn streak. He might fixate on her belly all day, calling her parents' attention to it. With Dean pointing it out, her mother is sure to notice.

Dean had dropped his hand and stepped forward until his sneakers toed the edge of the cliff.

"No!" She grabbed his arm and tugged him back. "Not so close. Do you want to fall?"

He gave her a smile that said maybe he did. "I can fly. Like Hawkman."

She crouched down so her eyes were level with his. "Listen to me. Don't you ever come here alone," she said. "I mean it, Dean. People fall and die. And we'd better not tell Mom or Dad we were here. Don't tell them anything at all, okay? Not about the moon or the cliff. Or—anything else," she added, hoping this would cover whatever that hand on her belly had meant to him. She shook him once, harder than she'd meant to, but she needed him to understand. "You promise me?"

His eyes widened, and his lower lip began to quiver.

"Do you promise?" she said, her voice gentle now. She wiped a tear from his cheek, which was red with windburn. "Our secrets? Just us? Brother-and-sister secrets."

Nodding, he repeated, "Just us."

She smiled and pecked his cheek, laughing at the *ick* face he made.

"Now," she said, "the names of flowers."

"I don't like flowers. I want to look for frogs." He ran up the path, slapping last season's withered coneflowers as he leapt.

She felt guilty as she followed him. Keeping secrets is a lot to ask of a little boy. A lot to ask of herself.

At the bakery case, another wave of dizziness hits her. She bends at the waist, hoping to get her head near her knees. No longer so easy to do. She glances toward the girl on the stairs, who might notice her ungainliness, but her gaze remains fixed on her aunts. What could they have forbidden her, a new dress or a record? No, the girl's look is too hard for something so trivial. Whatever it is, probably the aunts are right to refuse her. Sonya silently tells the girl to listen to them.

She breathes as deeply as possible without calling attention to herself. The line moves slowly, and the women seem happy catching up on news. For this reason, her mother usually comes to the bakery herself.

"We need bread, and I need gossip," her mother sometimes jokes.

Sonya has learned a lot from her mother's gossip. For example, the younger Demski sister who works the counter is called Lou, a nickname for Louisa; the other one is Genny, for Genevia. "Used to be another sister," her mother whispered once to a new neighbor woman. "Elisa, Ellie, they called her, or El or Lis, something like that. She was at school with me, but a few years ahead. Beautiful girl. Too beautiful by half, turned out. Had boys falling at her feet until . . . Well, you know what happens to fast girls. She never would say who the father was. Had the child, then she just ran off. Or maybe the parents threw her out. Either way, no one heard hide nor hair of her for months. Ended badly for her." Her mother mouthed the word *dead*. "The family kept it quiet."

The neighbor woman looked shocked, then shook her head and said, "It's the children you feel for."

Sonya's mother added, "Just goes to show."

Her mother isn't usually mean, so the ring of satisfaction in her tone surprised Sonya.

"What does it show?" Sonya asked.

"Nature asserts itself," she said, nodding to the neighbor woman.

"It does," said the neighbor woman, adding, "Not that I'm judging."

"No, no." Her mother waved aside the notion. "Of course, they should have forced the girl to name the father and made the boy marry her. Although maybe the girl knew the boy was the wrong sort." Her mother wrinkled her nose as if she'd sniffed spoiled fish.

That spoiled fish look is why Sonya hasn't told her mother of her condition and why she's sworn Dean to secrecy. And while her mother's reaction would be bad, her father's would be so much worse, a disappointed fury Sonya tries not to imagine. After the initial upset, they would insist she give up her scholarship. They would expect him to marry her. Her father would try to force him.

Stinging with humiliation at his certain refusal, she reminds herself that she doesn't love him. She'd been impressed by him. Charmed. No one had ever given her that kind of attention. But she doesn't love him, she insists. Even if she did, even if he wanted her, which he's made clear he doesn't, she *can't* be married. To be a woman scientist will be hard enough. A married, pregnant woman scientist? Who ever heard of such a thing? Her scholarship would be gone in a snap as quick as the one Lou uses to move along the ladies in line.

Ironically, despite her scholarship, despite all she wants to do with her life, what her parents really want is for her to get married and have babies.

"You're going to college?" her mother had said when she got the award letter.

"It's an honor," Sonya said. "I'm the first girl to get it."

"When did you apply for a scholarship?" her father said.

"The school sends in the top five students' names," she said. "The teachers make recommendations."

"Oh, well," her mother said, clearly perplexed. "How wonderful. I think a girl from my class went to college. Left after a year to get married." This thought seemed to cheer her mother. "Right, there will be plenty of boys there. With so few girls, you'll have your pick," she said, as if college were simply this bakery case and not the chance to learn, to do something, to be something bigger than herself. The whole natural world is out there to explore, but her mother can't see past her kitchen door.

Her parents' dream for her is marriage and children, but pregnant without being married? They'd flip their wigs. They'd throw her out. Or lock her away. Locked out, locked up, or wedlocked. She imagines two white-velvet handcuffs tightening around her wrists.

Sonya's stomach clenches. She swallows a yelp. Have her efforts at the train tracks worked after all? The pain passes, her dizziness too, and she stands upright as Genny Demski barrels in from the kitchen with a large tray of turnovers over her head.

"Quit mooning on the stairs, Emelia," Genny snaps, her tone directive rather than unkind. "We're working here, and you have chores." She flicks her chin upward and turns her back to the girl. She slides the tray of pastries into the case, steam frosting the front glass.

Emelia's eyes narrow as if she were squeezing darts from them straight into her aunt's back, but by the time her aunt turns around, Emelia has banged up the stairs and slammed the door. Lou looks up at Genny and shakes her head.

"Go easy on her, Gen," she says.

Genny harrumphs and hurries back to the kitchen. Lou takes a deep breath before forcing a smile to her lips and calling, "Next!"

A woman brushes past Sonya, happy to skip, and says, "You got a pineapple upside-down, Lou?"

Lou's walnut-colored hair is pulled into a bun at the top of her head. Her neck is long. The skin on her hands is ragged, with no rings on any of her fingers. These women, Lou and Genny, haven't married, and they've done all right. They run their own business. Is this what they've chosen, or couldn't they find men to marry them?

They're pretty enough, or would have been when they were young. Now Lou's white pants and shirt hang loose, covered with an apron, so Sonya can't see what her body looks like, if her hips curve or drop straight to her knees, if she has small breasts as Sonya does. Or did.

Sonya's mother was right. Nature asserts itself. It's asserting itself on Sonya's very body. Even naked, Sonya can't look down see her own thighs anymore. Clothed, they're hidden beneath circle skirts she wears too often these days. She needs something better. And soon. She's got to give herself time to find a solution. Her mother isn't stupid. She just sees what she expects to see. Her bookish daughter getting a little fat. That's why Emelia ate so little breakfast this morning, citing a desire to slim down for graduation photos. Boy, hadn't her mother been pleased about that. But before long, nature will assert itself like a volcano, and her mother won't be able to deny her daughter's belly is erupting right in front of her eyes.

Another lady in line taps Sonya's shoulder to move her along. She'd better order or she'll attract suspicion.

Lou looks up expectantly, showing Sonya eyes the same blue as the delphiniums her mother planted last year. Sonya orders fours.

"Rolls will be out of the oven in two shakes," says Lou. "Can you wait?"

"Yes, of course."

Lou's smiles, and her face transforms into what Sonya considers beautiful, but she no longer really understands what that is, not since he told her she was beautiful.

Sitting alone in his car with him was thrilling. He'd parked in an alcove by the lake, in an area of the woods she'd never been to before. A patch of moon reflecting from the lake's surface was visible between the tree branches. Drinking wine with him made her feel grown up. "You're a stunner," he said. She beamed. He saw in her what others had missed. "Beautiful." A man like him, someone people admired, saw her, really *saw* her. His words were maple syrup dripping from his lips. She wanted to lick them off his mouth.

He'd fastened a little pin onto her blouse, a symbol he said only they would know was theirs. After kissing the pin lightly, he kept kissing, outside her blouse, then inside. And then they had done the other things as—she admits, she must admit it—she had hoped they would do. Why else would she have checked the calendar and done her useless calculations?

Afterward, he had smiled vacantly at her and again called her beautiful. No, not beautiful. He had said *beaut*.

"A real beaut." The word cut like a knife.

Afterward, when she was a beaut rather than beautiful, he didn't see her the same way. A week later, he didn't want to see her at all. She stood outside the car, speaking to him through the open window. She glanced at the passenger seat, half-expecting to find herself seated there as if in a movie. He hooked his elbow over the door and leaned toward her. She thought he was going to kiss her, and she moved closer.

"You understand," he whispered. "It's dangerous. You could ruin things for me."

"But—"

"You being so young and all."

He couldn't be serious. Not after what they'd done.

But he was serious, and she realized she'd been half-expecting it all along, which didn't make it burn any less.

"I have a lot at stake. You too. You don't want to lose your reputation, do you? All a girl's got, right? And you're too smart to get caught."

She'd been speechless. Why didn't she tell him off, call him names like the jilted women in movies? At the lake with him, she hadn't given a thought to their future, but she sure hadn't expected he'd cut her dead.

"Here you go, hon," says Lou, handing Sonya two white cardboard boxes. "Here's a cookie for your extra time."

Sonya takes the bag and the cookie and leaves the store. The street bustles with purposefulness. People post letters and do other business at the newly built Buckhorn City Hall and Post Office. Mostly men hustle in and out of O'Carroll's Hardware, while women enter and leave Schumacher's Dry Goods. Muted rock and roll emanates from Jablonski's Lanes, next door to the bakery. A few younger men dash in, probably late for their pool or bowling league games, which run twenty-four hours to accommodate the three shifts of workers at Armour.

Her nausea gone, she's famished. She chomps the flower's face from its stem. The icing melts over her tongue. Sweetness pinches her glands, and she enjoys the sensation, happy for this one moment. The cookie is like the snowman cookies Lou sometimes gives to Dean in winter, just cut into a different shape. The taste reminds her of Christmas mornings, hot chocolate, and ice-skating.

Across the street, a group of boys from her class emerges from the Dutchland Dairy with malts and baskets of onion rings. They sit at one of the picnic tables in the parking lot, eating and talking. She has gone to school with most of them since she was five years old. She knows which ones are in the slow classes and which ones are in the smart classes with her, who is good at sports or music. She knows who smokes and who doesn't, although none of them are smoking now, not where they could be caught by one of their mothers. To be caught by one mother is to be caught by them all.

Last year at this time, she could have called out to the boys across the street, and they would have greeted her, maybe gestured her over to talk. But she doesn't talk to anyone at school except Stella, her best friend since kindergarten. Imagine if she walked up to them and announced her condition. They'd call her disgusting, or worse, just as he said. She would have a disgusting reputation in two shakes. And that would be it. Her scholarship and college, they're just the start of what would be stripped from her. She'll have to drop out immediately. She wouldn't even get her high school diploma.

Quickly, she backs into an alley, out of sight. Today is trash day. Cans and lids are strewn about the alley. She drops the rest of the cookie into one. The dough has left a sour taste at the back of her tongue. He'd had a sour taste from the wine. She probably had too, but she'd barely drunk more than two sips. He'd drunk most of the bottle by the time he called her beautiful. She had laughed and brought the glass to her mouth often, letting him think she was enjoying her share.

A gust of wind flutters open her coat, and she pulls it closed fast so no one can see her body. As if she were still that girl of last year, the cold wind makes her wonder if the pond is still frozen.

Frozen enough to skate.

No one looks twice when you fall ice-skating. You can fall and fall. People think you're having the time of your life. Who would suspect? It would be safer than the railroad tracks and Ghost Mother.

That afternoon, her feet swaddled inside her Brunswick skates, she slides onto the glassy ice of the downtown indoor rink. She has decided not to take a chance on the pond. The Zamboni has just smoothed the surface. She pushes off and glides, pushes and glides. To her surprise, the extra weight she's carrying has a balancing effect. She's steadier on these thin blades than she's been in months. Her body relaxes into the movement, and she hitches to the right, skating backwards, drawing parallel S-curves in the fresh ice. The little patch of skin on her chin itches. She rubs blood back into it with her wrist and extends her arms into a circle above her head, a position her mother taught her as a child. A longing to be that child again so overtakes her, she forgets why she's here. She shifts her body a half-rotation. Facing forward, she pushes off. It's good to move. Her thighs turn rock hard. *This* body she knows. *This* body she trusts.

The ice is fast, and she runs across it, blades slicing the surface, cold slicing her cheeks, and she is that child again if only for the time it takes a speck of ice to melt on her skin. She dips into a spiral and soars until her momentum dies.

In no time, the ice becomes populated with other skaters, including a couple of nuns with linked arms, their black habits billowing behind them. Small children skitter and flail, despite the hands held overhead by mothers who lift and set them right again. Older kids race and show off spins and jumps.

Nearing the showoffs, Sonya spreads her arms, bends forward at the waist, and lifts her right foot from the ice, again dipping into a spiral. For a split second, she feels her own beauty again. She points her toe inside her boot as her mother taught her.

She's a seagull, a swan.

But she has to give up the beauty and the joy if she's going to save herself. She forces her torso forward. Her belly is no longer ballast but an unsteadying force, and she tumbles. Unbidden, her knee and left arm break her fall in a shock of pain. She has jarred herself good. But good enough? Right enough?

She gives herself a moment to catch her breath and checks that she hasn't broken her wrist. While hauling herself up, she lets her skate slip from beneath her, and she falls again. She glances around. As she'd hoped, no one is paying her much attention.

She skates and falls for the better part of an hour until she can no longer stand it. In the rink's bathroom stall, she pulls down her tights and finds bruises rising on both knees and on her buttocks. Her wrists and the heels of her hands ache.

Her thigh muscles tremble as she pulls down her underpants to find them clean and white and hopeless. Not hopeless. Couldn't the effect be delayed? She clings to this possibility as she rights her clothing. Until then, she'll have to bide her time.

Exiting the bathroom, she sits on the bleachers, watching the skaters stream. The patch on her chin itches. Her bruises and bones ache, but she doesn't want to go home yet. Here, no one knows her, and she can relax a little. For all they know, she might be a young wife.

She wishes Stella were with her. She'd thought to call her, but remembered Stella would want to keep her throat warm for tomorrow's singing at the church smoker. Besides, Stella knows Sonya skates too well to fall as often as she's just done. If only she could tell Stella.

The words have nearly fallen from her lips a hundred times, but she's sucked them back because the moment she utters the words, the secret is out. Stella wouldn't mean to tell, but her father is a police detective. Despite all her acting in school plays, Stella's never been able to hide a thing from her father.

Farther down the bench, toward the exit, a couple finishes lacing up their skates. When they stand, they look as if they've stepped off the pages of an Archie comic strip, the boy wide-shouldered and blond, the girl slim but with ample breasts and a perfect hair flip. They abandon their coats and boots, along with the girl's purse and the boy's letterman sweater, on the bench before they skirr off, their blades whispering over the ice. They're good, graceful. They clasp hands, skating easily as if they'd been a pair their whole lives. They don't seem to notice anyone else on the rink except to avoid running into them.

What must it be like to be them, easy, free, carelessly together?

Sonya's never been so swell and simple with a boy. She'd never had a boyfriend before him. There'd been a few dates to movies and dances with boys whose damp palms felt like wet leaves clinging to her shoulder or arm. She'd kissed those boys out of curiosity, not anything anyone would call ardor. Do these two have ardor? Passion? These two cool pats of butter? No, she can't imagine them melting in a pan, steaming into each other's ears, her breath hot, his fingers coaxing.

Even after all that's happened, she feels desire flush her cheeks at the memory of his coaxing fingers. She can't blame only him. He hadn't forced her.

But all the aftermath has been left for her. Anger chases desire to her cheeks, and she pulls off her hat, suddenly hot and breathless herself. If today's efforts don't work, she will have no choice but to go to him. So far, he has all but refused to speak with her alone, but she must force him to understand that she can't keep this secret much longer. He's got to help her figure something out, or she'll have no choice but to sing like the mourning dove they both admire.

The side-by-side couple completes a revolution of the rink and nears her. The boy has hooked his little finger into the waistband of the girl's skirt and runs it over her belly. The girl's mouth opens slightly, the tip of her tongue glancing her top lip. Not such cold butter after all.

"Don't do it," Sonya whispers to the girl, her breath clouds of frost. He will slide away from you on a silent blade. She leans forward, hoping to draw the girl's gaze. She has to warn her. But they float past without giving her a glance. Her own gaze lands on their belongings, left on the bench with the certainty all will be there when they return. The purse, the coats, her salt-stained loafers, his clean sneakers. The letterman sweater.

At least she can let them know how vulnerable they really are, she thinks, and buy herself some time too.

Getting to her feet and unbuttoning her coat to act as a shield, she sidles between the bench and the rink's wall. As she passes their pile of belongings, her hand shoots out. She grabs the boy's letterman sweater, hugs it close, and closes her wool coat. She's out the door of the rink before they finish circling the ice.

She jogs across the street and shuffles two blocks north to the main library, which is five times the size of their local branch. Its Neo-Renaissance style, marble floors, and vaulted ceilings remind her of a church, and in a way, it is her church. She has haunted the stacks here since she was old enough to take the bus alone. Instead of the stacks, though, she ducks into the bathroom and peels off her coat. She hangs it on the hook at the back of the door, along with the boy's baby blue letterman sweater. She touches the plush white A on the pocket, recognizing the symbol for St. Andrews Academy, an all-boys private school on the north shore. So the boy has money. He's a good catch. Does the girl have money too? If those scarred and stained shoes of hers were a clue, he's slumming.

Sonya checks the label inside the sweater's pocket. Large, just as she'd figured from the boy's shoulder width.

Before putting it on, she checks her underpants again. White as a cloud. She bites her lip with disappointment. At least there, blood pools like mercury over her tongue. She catalogues her inkblot bruises. For the most part, they don't hurt. Only her wrist and knee ache as she slips into the cardigan. The sleeves hang three inches beyond her fingertips, the bottom hem at midthigh. Buttoned at the front, it's roomy enough that she could carry Dean inside it and no one would be the wiser. Finally, she transfers the pin he gave her from its hidden place on the lapel of her coat to a prominent place on the sweater's lapel, a gift from her new private-school boyfriend.

Exiting the library's bathroom, she instinctively heads for the section with books on botany. The library's holdings are considerable. Farmland, open prairies, and forests nestle the city. Nearly all residents tip their hats to nature, if only with window boxes or a few tomato plants in pots on a balcony. She runs her finger over the shelves absently, moving from gardening to agriculture. This is where she belongs, reading, studying, drawing bisections of stem systems, cross-sectioning violets and cattails.

Actually, the drawings in her nature journal are merely competent, but her observations have always been precise. She prides herself on being able to spot the difference in each blade of grass in a field. She can't wait to learn more. She wants to know every wildflower, every herb, its Latin name, its genus, its history. It amazes her how many have been used to cure and heal. The bark of the willow tree produces aspirin; foxglove's digitoxin cures the heart. The secrets plants hold are endless.

"Oh." The sound is a shot in the cavernous quiet.

How had she not thought of this before? Too much digitoxin can kill. *Atropa belladonna, abrus precatorius, nerium oleander.* Plants heal in many ways. Heal and harm.

She'd relied on myth and chance when science was there for her all along, waiting for her to come to her senses.

She searches with purpose now, finally selecting three books: *The Secret Life of Flowers, Wildflowers of North America in Full Color,* and *Culpeper's Complete Herbal,* the last a thick book, promising to be "the cure of all disorders incident to mankind."

She carries them to the counter where a librarian about her mother's age considers the books. Sonya has taken out similar books her whole life. When she was eight and nine, she loved it when the librarian looked at a book she'd selected and said, "This is rather advanced, a grownup book. Are you sure you don't want something from the children's section? I'll help you find something if you'd like."

"No," she would insist, looking skyward with superiority. "I read those long ago."

This time, though, she prays the woman will simply press a date onto the cards and slide the books across the counter. The librarian does look up. Probably her nervousness has drawn the librarian's attention because Sonya can't seem to keep her hands still. She's tapping her bitten fingertips on the counter, she realizes too late, stopping herself only by clasping the tips of one hand into the fist of the other.

Seeing this, the librarian tilts her head to the side, assessing her.

Sweat breaks out on Sonya's forehead under the woman's gaze. Oh, God, the woman knows. She can tell. Sonya imagines the truth is dripping down her temples with her sweat. Still clutching one hand with the other, Sonya wipes at her forehead with her sweatered forearm.

"I've seen you in here before," the librarian says. "But not for a while. You used to come a lot. I always thought, now, there goes a girl who loves science."

"Yes," mutters Sonya. Please, please, she begs silently. "I'm in a hurry. Could you—?"

"You have a boyfriend," she says.

Sonya says nothing.

"The letter sweater," she says, as if Sonya has asked how the woman knows about the boyfriend. "I like the pin. Is that from him?"

Sonya's fingers search it out, twirling it, hiding its features as she'd like to hide her own. She nods silently. She understands she should preen, show off the sweater, the pin, and smile, gush, diminish herself—*I can't believe my luck; imagine him with me.* She does manage to step back. In doing so, she realizes the sweater has unbuttoned itself, or she has done it unawares. Her hands are not her own anymore. Her belly feels like the moon beneath her skirt, just as Dean had said, fully risen and glaring, daring the librarian to notice it.

Sonya snatches the sweater's lapels and crosses her arms.

"It's so hot in here," she sputters. "I feel faint. Can't you check me out so I can get some fresh air?"

The woman bites her bottom lip, revealing tiny rabbit teeth.

"I had a boyfriend too," she says, turning her attention to the books again. "Died in the war. Same as a lot of girls back then. We married boys, and after we sent them off to die, we had to find ways to go on."

Sonya screams in her head, why is she telling me this?

As Sonya squeezes her elbows to her chest, the woman sets aside two of the books Sonya selected. She thumbs through the third, *Culpeper's Complete Herbal.* Quickly finding the page she wants, she stuffs a card with the library's hours into the binding.

"Those other two books aren't for you. This one." She taps it with a neat, unpolished fingernail. "It's a favorite. Has everything. I've marked a page for you. Specific to your interests. I like to match a reader with her interests." She presses a stamp on the card and slides it into the slot on the front cover. "Useful herb, pennyroyal."

Sonya takes the book and forces herself to walk, not run as she'd like to do, out the door. She manages to squeak a thank you to the librarian as the door closes silently behind her on its hushed hinges.

Riding the bus back to her house, Sonya opens the book to the page the librarian has marked, understanding now why she had found it so quickly in the tome. The page has been dog-eared several times over, both at the top and bottom corners. The print is warped as if droplets of liquid have fallen on it and dried.

If you weren't looking for it, she thinks as she scans the page, you might miss the relevant application, buried as it is among toothache, gout, and dropsy. But in the fading light, the tiny pencil marking in the margin burns like a neon arrow. "Being boiled and drank, it provokes women's courses and expels." Science has not forsaken her after all; neither have old wives nor young maids, all of whom are pointing her in the same direction.

Sonya closes her eyes, a strange feeling welling in her. This book, and the librarian too, prove it. She's not alone. There have been centuries of women like her, millennia of them, and not just in books like Hester Prynne in *The Scarlet Letter*. The ironic significance of the *A* on the letterman sweater has not been lost on her. Real, living women and girls have felt themselves drowning, choking and desperate for something to cling to. She runs a finger over the pennyroyal entry again, as if reaching back in time to grasp those women's hands. Not ghosts. Real girls, petrified and pleading, their lips whispering these same words, *provokes* and *expels*. We can't all be bad, can we, she thinks defiantly. If no one else will help us, don't we have to help ourselves?

As the bus chugs southward, her defiance wavers. She reads the entry over and over, but her eye catches on the water stains. Tear stains? Tea stains? She fiddles with the dog-eared corners, then touches a stain.

Did the girl or woman who marred the page feel selfish? Did she worry it meant she was abnormal? What woman doesn't want to be a mother first and foremost, under any circumstances? What kind of woman wouldn't sacrifice anything, everything, to be a mother?

For the first time she admits to herself that she might want a child. Someday. But she feels strangled, actually unable to draw breath, when she thinks about the fetus inside her now. It feels foreign and unnatural in her body, an entity to which she has no connection. To her shame, she admits that the thought of it disgusts her. Even more choking than the thought of it inside her is the thought of actually giving birth to it. What would happen to her then?

Panic shoots through her body, and her vision blackens and narrows until all she sees is the stain on the book's page. What kind of life could she give this child? When she presses the pad of her finger to the stain, she finds her hand is trembling. Her lungs seem to have compressed. She really can't breathe, yet at the same time bile rises to her throat.

What a monster she must be. An abomination.

These feelings are the real reason she's told no one, even Stella, about her condition. No one in the world is more hated than a bad mother. Her own mother had said exactly this last year when she showed Sonya the article from *Ladies Home Journal* about Viola Liuzzo. Viola felt so strongly about civil rights, she left her five children in Michigan and traveled to Alabama to help register voters. When the KKK shot and killed Viola, more than half of the magazine's readers blamed her, saying she had no right to put civil rights before her children, that to a mother, the world outside her door was of no concern. Sonya's mother had agreed, but Sonya respected Viola. Viola understood there was more to the world than just her and her family, and she felt connected, more than connected; she felt obligated to those things beyond her family too.

"I think she was brave," Sonya said.

Her mother had snatched the magazine from Sonya's hand so forcefully that the back cover ripped off. "Since when is neglect brave?" her mother said, her tone as jeering as Sonya had ever heard it. "Nothing this world hates more than a bad mother. You remember that."

Sonya had remembered. She *does* remember. She remembers that for a moment her mother's face had become pinched and as ugly as her tone of voice, and Sonya had felt disappointed she saw the world this way.

Now Sonya draws an imaginary line on the page from one stain to another. Maybe these women were like Viola, outward looking and impassioned, but not horrible. Maybe they—*we*, she corrects herself—would have been better off if we were like marsupial frogs, seahorses, and water bugs. In these species, the males give birth, and the females go back into the world.

She fingers the button he gave her.

Should she give him a chance to be like the frogs? He hasn't wanted to have anything to do with her, but she could try again. She could wait on the pennyroyal to see what he says.

Another wave of panic hits her, and a small moan erupts from deep within her. What if she waits too long? For what? For nothing? He will barely look at her, will not speak with her or be alone with her. What if she waits and it doesn't work? Or, horribly, what if it works too well? Can pennyroyal kill? She grasps the book's cover and pushes her fears down. She can't worry about that now. She has to be steel.

She swallows hard and forces her shoulders back. When she looks up, she finds a woman her mother's age, with blue cat glasses and a matching twill coat, studying her. The woman's gaze shifts between Sonya's face and the book's open page. Sonya slaps the book closed and shoves it behind her back. The woman *harrumphs* huffily, tossing off a look that says Sonya's not fooling anyone.

Sonya slumps in her seat, feeling cornered under the woman's gaze. She pulls her new sweater around her, hunches her shoulders, and looks out the window, but she takes the woman's point too.

Her time is running out. If the librarian could guess her condition, if this woman has, her mother will soon as well.

How much longer can they pretend? More pointedly, how long can Sonya wait on the pennyroyal before it will be too late? Or too dangerous. She needs to make him see her.

She's promised to go with Stella to the smoker. Of course, he will be there too. He's anywhere there's music and women and alcohol, and so much the better if the excuse is church. She'll give him one last chance. She'll show him her condition, *their* condition. She'll have to be strong to make him see. She'll have to be steel.

Maybe he will know what to do. If not, this science is her last resort.

After signaling her stop, she wobbles up the aisle toward the exit, her body aching from her falls on the ice. Stepping out of the bus into the purple light of dusk, she walks against a cutting wind. Wrapped around her wrist, the laces of her skates cut off circulation to her hand. As she readjusts the skates, she drops the book, and it falls open to the dog-eared page. The word *pennyroyal* seems to scream into the streets. Alarmed, she scoops the book up fast, presses it against her belly, and wraps the letter sweater around it.

"Steel," she whispers and keeps going.

Leo

AT THE CHURCH smoker, Leo leans against a green cinderblock wall near the middle of a room the size of the church above it. The ceiling hangs low, and although he can stand upright with a foot to spare, he feels he has to hunch not to brush the water-stained tiles above. Smoke billows over the rows of tables where people drink yellow beer from plastic cups and huddle over plates heaped with roasted chicken, kielbasa, and baked beans, served by ladies at the back of the hall, cafeteria style.

Although the crowd is made up of many of the same people who attend his father's night tavern shows, they're different at an afternoon church event like this. They doll up for a night out. Women wear crimson lipstick, charcoal eye shadow, and form-hugging dresses. Men unbutton their collars. They sport knife-edged trousers and greasy sweat. Showing off their sex appeal, Leo supposes with an itch of distaste and curiosity, a combination he can't rub off after having seen his father in the car with Nora. Even the older folks, the *babcie* and old war vets, splash it up with bright colors and low necklines for the tavern shows.

At church events, they show off their respectability. The ladies' dresses are the muted colors of Easter eggs, pastel pink and powder blue, violet and daisy yellow, and they cover knees and cleavage. Some older ladies wear velvet hats with netting that creates crumpled nests in their hair. The men's ties are gray or navy, and even if loosened, they will stay tied until the last cigarette is crushed out. Which are the authentic people, the sexy ones or the respectable ones? Why can't people just be one thing and not changing all the time?

Since the night he found his father with Nora and his mother wielded that knife, Leo's mind has felt strangled as if he were actually wearing the tie balled up in the pocket of his sports jacket. His father has been teetotal and on his best behavior. Both his parents are lovey-dovey, leaving Leo on the rails, uncertain what to think.

And what to do. Tell his mother or stick by his father and say nothing?

If only he knew what was real.

His father's peck on his mother's cheek when he comes home after work seems like a performance, yet his hand brushing her back as she cooks resembles his touch on the keys of his accordion, knowing and tender. The way his mother's body gives in to his father's touch seems like the simple love in the polka lyrics. But is it real? Or was her fury real? Would she really have drawn blood with that knife? Maybe she only picked it up to cut through his father's boozy haze.

More confusing is that both his parents have been nicer to him since that night. His mother doesn't hassle him so much about his messy room and homework. His father asks him about swimming practice, and they all watched *Bonanza* together one night after dinner. Another evening before dinner, his father hovered in the doorway to Leo's room, listening to him play along with Dylan's "Ballad of Hollis Brown." When his mother called them to come eat, his father shrugged and said, "Not bad." High praise from Stash Meitka. Leo hadn't asked if *not bad* was Dylan's tune or Leo's playing. Either way, Leo liked having his father's attention for a while.

They all had a good time at dinner until they were clearing the table.

"Going to step out to the jam at Ola's," his father said.

His mother's hands were submerged in soapy water, but her back stiffened. She crashed silverware into the drying rack without rinsing it.

"You promised," she said softly.

"I know," he said. "But I've got to see Joey about the new arrangements. I'm still on that wagon." He lifted three fingers in a Boy Scout salute. "On my honor."

Leo waited to see. His father came home early. Leo poked his head out of his room to find him at the kitchen table, eating cherry pie with a fork and smelling of cigarettes but not whiskey. He slept upstairs, not on the trouble cot. The next day, his mother was more cheerful than ever, running out early to Demski's bakery for pecan morning cake.

Leo enjoyed every maple mouthful of that cake. Only later did he feel guilty, knowing that her good mood was based on her half-knowledge. And what does his father know? Does he know Leo saw him in that car with Nora?

So far, Leo has decided telling will only hurt his mother and make his father mad at him. Besides, maybe it was just that one time with Nora. Maybe his father will stay on the wagon. But his father hasn't played music since that night. Will his thirst be triggered today? If so, his mother is sure to see. She's at the back of the hall, serving the sausages.

His father waves him on stage to clear away the foam cross and rock left over from the Easter play.

"Where's your tie?" he growls before Leo even reaches the steps to the stage.

"I'll put it on later." Not only do they choke, they make his neck look weirdly skinny.

"You want to play today, you better strap it on this minute."

Leo climbs the stairs but says nothing. Who is his father to be barking orders after what he's done?

"You hear me?"

"Where am I supposed to put this thing?" Leo says, tapping the waist-high rock with his toe.

His father claps his hands and raises his finger as if a grand idea has just struck him. "I know. Maybe you should stand on it to play today, huh?" His father chortles, glancing around to see if anyone else has heard his joke. He adds in a louder voice, "My son, the no-tie rock musician!"

"What's the big whoop about a tie?" Leo mutters. In his tan slacks and sport coat, he's already looking like a square. At least at the tavern shows, the band members wear flashy red shirts and silk vests that sparkle in the footlights. His father wears a pin on his collar with a whole note on it that glints in the spot.

"Watch your tone, son of mine," his father says in the sneering way he talks when he's drinking. Has he already jumped down off that wagon?

"Heh, rock music," his father scoffs, nudging the air with his elbow and winking in Leo's direction but really at the few people looking his way. "You get it? He stands on a rock to play?"

He looks for confirmation of his hilarity at a group of teachers, many of them Leo's teachers. Oh, man, the ones who already think he's just a middling student: Mrs. Gramercy, his English teacher; Mr. Kildare, who teaches Kirstin and Will math; and Mr. Trippsman, Leo's natural sciences teacher. They stand in a loose group, talking to a few nuns and some kids Leo recognizes from school, including Kirstin. Please let her have not heard his father.

After laughing at something Mr. Trippsman said, Kirstin waves at Leo, then jerks her thumb toward the stairs to the gym, indicating she's going up to the area with the baked goods and craft booths.

Leo doesn't wave back, too stunned to move. Is that Nora with Kirstin and his teachers, in the St. Andrews letter sweater? No! Not here. She can't be here today, she just *can't* be. Not with his mother here too.

A moment later, he relaxes. This girl is taller than Nora and less shapely. Downright fat across the middle.

Shaken, though, his irritation at his father intensifies.

"Hey, rock star," his father jibes loud enough for the teachers and the first few tables to hear. "Shove your rock into the wings so we can set up. And put your goddamn tie on!"

Leo's irritation heats to anger. Why is his father riding him? He's making fun of him in front of everyone. Where's *his* loyalty? Leo kicks the rock, denting the foam.

"Gently, young man," a nun calls.

Grudgingly, Leo pushes the rock toward the wings. Passing his father, he sniffs. Soap and aftershave laced with a sour note of perspiration. So no drinks yet, but his hands tremble. Sweat has stained his underarms. How long has it been since his father has played music teetotal?

"That what you mean by rock, kiddo?" His father knocks on the foam as if testing its quality. "Hah, just what I've been saying. Nothing much to it."

Shut the hell up! Leo nearly says it. He should say it. He should shout that he's not wearing any goddamn tie, no matter what his cheating father says. He can almost taste the rebellion, a grain of salt on the tip of his tongue.

He holds back only because if he yells and his father yells too, his mother is sure to hear. What if she comes barreling on stage too, knife blazing? Leo will explode with humiliation if they go at it here.

Just as bad is if his father manages not to yell back. Leo's seen him fire *smart mouths* from the band in the middle of a show. And Leo wants to play.

He's worked since he was a boy to get good enough to be a full-fledged member of his father's band. The standards are high. His father's musicians need to be more than good; they have to be masterful. They need spirit too. "A certain flair," his father says, but not too much. No showboaters, save for Stash Meitka himself, leader, manager, and front man of the Meitka Band.

The thought of joining his father's band has kept Leo playing even when he's gotten bored. Leo has an ear, perfect pitch, and fast fingers, or so his mother says. She's the most formally trained musician of the family. He's got a good voice too, unlike his father who squawks like a wrung chicken. Even after Leo's voice change, he manages a three-octave range.

"No feel for the music though," Leo overheard his father say to his mother when he was younger.

Hurt by his father's words, Leo has worked to prove himself, to change his father's mind, enthusing about songs on the Saturday morning polka radio show and singing his father's favorite tunes while doing his chores. But his father was right. Leo's never felt about his father's music the way he does about his own.

A lot of polkas and waltzes are modified old-world folk songs with predictable lilting tunes. Some are still sung in Polish or Slovenian. Learning the words phonetically, the meaning dissolves for Leo. The songs with English lyrics are simple, about finding or losing sweethearts, or they're boozy, carousing celebrations, the famous happy polka songs for hopping and spinning and whooping along with the band.

Fun, sure, but shallow music. Rock music *means* something. Losing love really hurts. Authority's always getting down on someone. The war and the draft loom like bruised clouds on the lake's horizon. Serious and deep. Especially the moody stuff he's been listening to lately, the Moody Blues, the Yardbirds, the Animals, and that new band, Jefferson Airplane. This is *his* music. Listening releases his strangled mind. Playing along—the more complex the guitar part, the better—his mind is *blown*, a cool phrase he heard recently in Dylan's "115th Dream." His father doesn't have any idea how deep this music is, or how deeply it touches Leo. If he did, maybe he wouldn't make such easy fun of it.

Still, his father's band is Leo's only chance to play live, and even with polkas, there's nothing like playing live. It's the difference between swimming laps in practice and stepping onto the starting blocks for a race. Everyone shares a nervy tingle as you wait. Then the starting gun pops, or the drum counts you in, and *bang!* You all explode, riding the air together, feeding off each other until the air itself crackles like static. Then silence. Maybe his father guzzles more whiskey as the night goes on because there's nothing emptier than the patch of silence after the last note.

After playing live the first time, Leo can't get enough. He'd give anything to be on stage playing rock. But kids like him don't really become musicians. Not really. They grow up and work full-time jobs at Armour and play music on the side in church halls and in taverns. With his father. Or they play piano for the ballet company downtown, like his mother. No wonder his parents fight.

At least Nora's not here.

Leo clears the stage of the rock and cross. "What now?" he says to his father.

His father's desire to make fun of Leo seems to have passed. Sweat beads Stash's forehead, and he's breathing heavily. "Get the music stand. The girl, what's her name? Stella? She's going to need it," he says.

Leo has forgotten about her. One of the music teachers at Leo's high school asked if Stella could play the smoker with the band before the teacher decides who to put up for some award. It burns Leo a little that his father didn't hesitate to let Stella join the band for the day. He makes Leo audition in the living room, playing every song on the set list but only letting Leo on stage for one or two of them each gig.

"Hey, Rockhead," says his father. "We're on in thirty minutes. Get your finger out of your ass and get a move on."

Stella's eyebrows rise at his father's words. Leo's face burns with humiliation. He fears his bladder may release, and he may wet his tan pants. His own underarms are now soaked more thoroughly than his father's. He fists the tie in his pocket, wanting to shove it into his father's mouth.

He glares at his father, at the same time catching sight of his mother watching them from the serving area at the back of the room. Silently, Leo fumbles to assemble the music stand.

Stella steps past him, saying so gently that it deepens his humiliation, "Is that for me?"

He nods dumbly, taking in her scent of citrus and powder. He suddenly wants to touch her wild hair almost as much as he wants to hit his father.

His father snaps his fingers again to call Leo over to help the drummer unpack his equipment. "Get a move on, Leo," he says. "What's with you today? Useless as a sack of shit."

Anger flaring, Leo thinks, one word. That's all it would take to shut him up. Should he say it?

He walks over to his father, who kneels on the parquet to sort sheet music. Leo taps a fingertip on a drumhead, the resulting *thunk* getting his father's attention.

"You with us today or not, Leo?" his father says. "You put your tie on now, or you can walk off this stage. I'm through fooling around with you. Get your tie on, and get these drums set up."

Leo scrapes his fingernails over the drum's skin. His father's head twitches at the hollow scrape. Sweat has greased his mustache, reminding Leo of the gravy that had smeared it. How dare his father humiliate him. He should be thanking him, kissing his goddamn feet. If he doesn't know Leo saw him with Nora, well, maybe it's time he did.

Leo grabs onto the drum to steady himself. He gets so close his lips nearly touch his father's ear.

"Nora," he whispers.

His father pops up and looks around. Seeing that Nora isn't actually there, he spits, "Get off the stage, you little shit. Get off now." He brushes his wrist over his forehead before adding, "But don't you leave. I mean it, young man. I want to talk to you later."

Leo rushes down the stage stairs and across the room, grasping onto a concrete beam to steady himself. What has he just done?

He feels the whole room of people watching him. He feigns studying a framed photo of local soldiers who died in the two European wars. When he sees his father's squinting gaze on him, he steps to the side, putting the concrete beam between them again.

He waits to feel pride bloom at having finally stood up to his father. All he feels though is worry. Has he ruined everything? Oh man, he should have kept his big mouth shut.

Eventually it registers that the photograph before him is of six local soldiers, helmets on their heads, a rifle at each man's side, the caption reading, "Firing Squad." The riflemen look only a couple years older than him. One guy is named Schwartz. Leo goes to school with Alvin Schwartz. His father is too young to be this man. But maybe it's a grandparent or uncle. Alvin is part of the group of seniors who wear T-shirts that say stuff like, *Speak Out Against the War* and *We Won't Go*. Maybe Leo should get a shirt like that. He doesn't want to go kill people. He wants to play music. Imagine stepping on stage wearing even a peace symbol. Man, oh man, his father would freak. So would all these people, their respectable or sexed-up versions. He'd be stoned with kielbasa and beer.

He longs for a cigarette. Like his guitar, he was hooked the first time he picked one up. He spots an open pack of Player's Navy Cuts next to a leather flask, a bingo card, and a small stuffed dog that he recognizes as a prize for the game up in the gym where you knock down milk bottles.

He eases over to the table with the unattended cigarettes. Seated nearby is a lady with a blue-black beehive so tall it must brush the low ceiling when she stands up. She watches Leo through her pinpoint cat glasses. Suspicion pinches her face, and instinctively Leo smiles broadly, diverting her gaze from his shaking hands, holding it until he's jigged loose two cigarettes from the pack on the table and slipped them into the back pocket of his pants.

"You're Stash's boy," she says after a moment, a half-smile lifting a doughy cheek. "I'd know that Meitka grin anywhere."

Leo's smile melts to a frown. He's about to deny his parentage when she taps a red fingernail to her chin.

"Yeah, you look just like him. Go on then," she says, extending her own pack of Chesterfields. "Take a few. It's okay, go on. I won't tell. Our secret."

A poster from grade school about not taking candy from strangers flashes through his mind, but silently he slides two cigarettes from the pack. As he's backing toward the wall, she says, "Say 'thank you,' son. Your father always thanks a girl for a smoke or a drink or—"

Leo stumbles over a metal folding chair before she can finish, and his face heats under her trilling giggle. His smarting shin is a small price for not having to hear what comes after that last *or*. Nora is bad enough, but would his father really fool around with someone like her?

As if the wall were glue, he hangs there, crushing the Chesterfields in his fist and dropping them on the floor. Smoking them would feel like he approves of the woman, which he doesn't. *Cheap women.* His mother wasn't wrong about that.

Avoiding her gaze, Leo spies Kirstin's back at the teachers' table, probably sucking up to Kildare, although it's Mr. Trippsman who nods and laughs at something Kirstin says. She looks pleased as punch to be getting this reaction from him. But when

Trippsman reaches out to put his hand on her shoulder, she turns deftly. Leo finds himself glad to see Trippsman's hand brush air even though he's been angry with Kirstin for the past few days, ever since she said Leo looks like his father.

Like Beehive, lots of people say Leo has the same square jawline, the same black hair and blue eyes, the same damn smile. Leo's used to hearing it, yet after Nora, it felt like a slap coming from Kirstin.

All four of them had been laid out on the floor of Will's bedroom, listening to the Byrds and Barry McGuire. Leo had brought his guitar and softly played along with the records.

"It's not just your features," Kirstin said. "You move the same as your dad too." Her tone was analytical, as usual, and he felt like a frog she was dissecting, labeling his parts. "Maybe it's your long legs and arms. Aren't I right, Em? Aren't his arms and legs extra long? Doesn't he move like his dad?"

Emelia had also given him an assessing look. To his surprise, she said firmly, "Don't do that, Kirstin. Don't make him into his father. We don't have to be what our parents are just because we look like them."

"Hey, Stash's boy," Beehive calls.

She's been joined by a woman in a dress made of silky red fabric cut so low at the chest it reveals two inches of cleavage. Someone should tell this woman you don't wear a tavern dress to church, even a church smoker. At least she's not pretending to be something she's not.

On stage, his father hoists his accordion onto his shoulders to test the positioning of his music stand. He plays a quick run of the "Laughing Sailor" polka, which Leo hates. The melody is moronically simple. Happy, happy, twirl and drink some more beer. His father nods to Stella, who plays a quick lick of flute, which improves the tune a little.

She's pretty, even with her crazy hair. Leo recognizes her from school. She pals around with the drama set and a few of the guys Leo knows from the cross-country team. She's not Joan Baez pretty, but she's got thin arms like Joan. When she taps the keys of his father's backup accordion lying on the table, she works it piano style, with both hands, soundlessly without the bellows. Fast fingers, his mother would call them. Leo calls them graceful.

Leo's father breaks out his showman smile as he helps Stella size the microphone stand to her height. Leo winces when he touches her shoulder as Mr. Trippsman had Kirstin's earlier. Stella doesn't deflect, and Leo checks for his mother. She's busy tonging chicken onto plates and doesn't seem to notice.

The girl Leo mistook earlier for Nora joins Stella. He's seen her around school too. She's on the varsity swim team, or was last year. She has a smooth freestyle stroke and a sharp flip turn. Now, though, she's so lumpy in that letterman sweater, it's hard to believe she can do anything athletic. Was it just her dark hair that reminded him of Nora?

She hands Stella a bottle of ginger ale. His father gallantly offers the dark-haired girl a stool, his smile wider than his accordion at full extension. The girl scans the crowd before seating herself when his father lays his hand on her knee in such a familiar way it's as if he knows her.

On her knee?

Is his mother watching?

"Hi," says Kirstin, suddenly at his side. Leo barely hears her. "Hey, earth to Leo."

"Hey, yourself," he growls.

Distantly, from the gym upstairs, Leo hears someone cry out, "Bingo!"

"I can't believe this," he says. How the hell is he supposed to stop his father from crashing their family straight into a tree? If saying Nora's name hasn't stopped him, nothing will.

"I've had enough grief for one day." He stomps toward the back of the hall without slowing down for Kirstin to catch up.

"Emelia's still stuck up there," says Kirstin, jogging behind him. "Her aunts are making her man the baked goods table with them. I offered to help, but she said no reason we all have to suffer. Her aunt Lou said she'd let her off the chain in half an hour."

Leo doesn't respond. He reaches the back of the hall near the exit, but he can't bring himself to defy his father and leave. Again, he leans against the cream-colored brick wall. At least he can give

Kirstin the freeze. How dare she think he's like his father? She leans next to him but doesn't say anything, so he can't tell if she knows he's giving her the cold shoulder or not.

"Where's Will?" he says, although he sees him talking to Lisa Smolinski. Leo doesn't want to care about what his father does, but he can't help himself. He looks past Will to the stage. His father stands behind Stella, the dark-haired girl beside them, seated on her stool. At least his hand is no longer on her knee.

Instead, his father leans over Stella, shuffling through the sheet music on her stand. He's all but touching her. How can she let him get so close? Why doesn't she tell him to leave her alone? Leo's glad when Joey Katz, the sax player, joins them onstage and starts unpacking his gear.

"Shouldn't you be up there too? Aren't you playing with your dad today?" says Kirstin.

"Not if I can help it," he says, although now that Joey Katz is there, Leo wishes he hadn't tanked his chance to play. He likes Joey, who's younger than Stash by a decade and a century hipper. He doesn't have a day job. All he does is play music, shifting from band to band as a hired gun.

"Why don't you want to play with your dad anymore? I know it's not rock and roll, but people like the polkas. They like to dance to it. Everyone gets really happy."

"No-taste L-7s," he spits.

"L-7s?"

"Squares. See, you don't know everything."

"Okay, they're squares, but they love your dad," she says. "Sometimes I think my mother's in love with him. She's such a spaz."

"He's an asshole," Leo mutters. "Tell her that."

Suddenly his father's voice booms from the speakers, "Gentlemen, it's time to clear the tables from the dance floor."

"You better get up there," says Kirstin.

"Or what?"

Kirstin shrugs.

"Who are they?" she says, pointing to the girls on stage.

The dark-haired girl has climbed down from the stool. The letterman sweater hangs to her knees. But his father isn't paying her attention anymore. Beehive has approached the stage and offers his father a large plastic cup filled with beer.

Leo's body goes rigid. What should he do? Should he rush the stage and tackle his father to keep him from drinking it? Should he go to the kitchen and head off his mother?

"No, no," he whispers as softly as he'd whispered in Stash's ear earlier.

His father takes the beer from Beehive, but rather than drink it, he offers it to the dark-haired girl with the flourish of a high-class waiter or a knight. Stella giggles before turning back to sorting through her sheet music.

The tables moved to the side, people now stand on the dance floor, watching the show as if his father were Ed Sullivan and handing Dark-Hair a beer were a planned skit. The girl is supposed to look flustered and refuse. Instead, she stands up, squares her shoulders, and extends her hand as if daring his father to give her the beer.

His father loves it. He clowns it up now, placing the cup on his head like a Russian dancer, and waltzes around the girl without spilling a drop of beer.

In response, the girl unbuttons the top button of her letter sweater, then the second button, threatening to, but not yet exposing her body. Brazen hussy, his mother would call her. Please, please, let his mother not be looking. Leo checks and sees she's occupied by slathering melted butter over trays of buns.

The girl keeps the game going by twirling as she opens the sweater wider, pausing at Joey Katz, at the teachers grouped together in stunned silence, and finally at the two parish priests on the far side of the hall. Leo catches only a glimpse of her lumpy body beneath the sweater.

"Oh, my God, what's that girl doing?" Kirstin says. "What's she got under that sweater? Do you think she's naked?"

"Don't be stupid," Leo says. "She's probably wearing, I don't know, a potato sack maybe."

"A potato sack? Like in that episode of *I Love Lucy*?"

"That's what it looks like to me," he says. To his shame, he feels an erection. He kicks the wall with the heel of his sneaker. He crosses his right leg over his left, hoping Kirsten doesn't notice what's happening at his crotch. "Anyway, who cares?"

"She sure knows how to command the stage," Kirstin says. "Look, your dad's just staring at her. Everyone's staring at her."

As if woken from a dream, the girl suddenly shrinks like a water-deprived plant in one of those time-lapse films they show in science class. She slams the sweater closed and dashes from the stage.

"Hey," Stella calls after her, as if nothing strange has happened at all. "Get me a brownie, would you?"

But the girl has vanished behind the curtain, leaving his father on stage still holding his beer.

"Who *is* that girl?" Kirstin asks.

"Who cares?" Leo says. Then he whispers, willing his father, pleading with him, "Don't drink it."

"If you don't like your dad's music, you should start your own band," Kirstin says, shifting into the sightline between Leo and the stage. "You could play what you like. Play the dances at school and the beach parties. Graduation and birthday parties." She ticks events off on her fingers. "People would pay you. You could save up."

"Maybe I should," he says, grateful that he no longer has to look at his father. If he drank the beer, if he didn't, it's no longer Leo's problem. Not for this moment. "C'mon, let's get out of here. I'm not playing stupid polkas today. My father can go fuck himself."

"Okay. You get Will, and I'll see if Emelia can leave yet."

"No," he says. He's got to get out now, before he starts kicking over every beer in every beehive's hand. "If we wait, my father will nab me. Let's just go."

"You sure you don't want to get the others?"

He shoots Kirstin a smile, adding extra charm. He doesn't trust himself to be alone right now, but he can't wait for the others. His head is already starting to feel clenched. On impulse, he brushes Kirstin's cheek with his finger.

"Just us," he says, "You and me." He deepens his smile. Like father, like son.

The wind off Lake Michigan blasts more like January than April, but Leo's blood races so fast, he sweats through his suit jacket. He breaks into his cross-country stride. Kirstin's long legs manage to keep pace with him. Their shoulders brush as they cross the highway and enter the park. He leads them through the marsh's tall grasses, through the woods, toward the cliffs without consulting her. She follows his lead wordlessly.

He's glad she's here. He's afraid he'd jump in the freezing water and drown himself. That would show his father. And his mother too, for that matter. He's sick of both of them.

Still jogging, he smiles at Kirstin, not flashy now but genuinely. She talks a lot sometimes, but she's smart, and usually what she says is worth listening to. And she doesn't seem to like her parents much more than he likes his. Maybe that's why it bothered him so much when she said he was like his father. How would she like it if he said she was like her mother?

Kirstin calls her mother *a drinker* as if it's a fact like her height or hair color. It doesn't seem to bother Kirstin that her mother drinks. Does her mother do stupid things like his father does when she drinks? He would never ask her, would never make her choose family loyalty or friend loyalty. Of course, Emelia doesn't have any parents, so she doesn't really get how complicated it is between Leo and his father. And Will, jeez, he could never tell Will about how bad Stash is, not really. Will's father, Otto, earned a Purple Heart in the war. Will beamed with pride when he showed it to Leo, who'd been pretty impressed back when he didn't think there was anything wrong with war, when it never occurred to him he might really have to go to one. What's more, Otto Brauer has a business all his own. Okay, it's a dusty tavern for shadowy third-shift factory workers, but Will's father owns it outright. He doesn't punch a clock or have a boss he's got to answer to like Leo's father and most of the guys in his father's band. And Leo's sure Will's mother, Greta, a jolly woman who keeps their flat above the bar spotless and insists Will keep his bedroom strictly ordered, has never pulled a knife on Otto.

When they reach the cliff edge, Leo chooses a path down to the water. The ground is spongy from recent rain and the dregs of the last of the winter snow. Leo manages to stay on his feet, although mud smears his Florsheims. What does he care? Just let his father or mother try to give him grief for getting his good shoes dirty. Kirstin slides down half on her bottom. She lands hard, a little *oomph* escaping from her. She springs up with a nimbleness that reminds him of a story he read when he was younger about a playful colt.

"Your skirt's ruined," he says, noticing a tear.

"Yeah." She shrugs, brushing at clay smudges on the fabric, smearing them more. She adds matter-of-factly, "It's old. It's ugly. It was my cousin's. Most of what I wear was hers first. She has terrible taste. Or her mother does."

She's right. The worn brown-and-red check pattern is hideous. Lots of Kirstin's clothes are, or would be on anyone else, but somehow Kirstin manages to make them look cool.

"Yeah, it's really ugly," he says. This strikes him as hilarious, and he bends over laughing. It feels so good to laugh. It feels so good not to think about his father for a while. It's not really funny, but he lets the laughter overtake him. He falls to his knees onto the stones, unable to stop the spasms. He can't control them and starts to hiccup and choke, straining for breath. His head pounds painfully.

Kirstin crouches next to him and places her hand against his jerking back. Her touch instantly quiets him, and he gulps and gulps, brushing tears from his cheeks. Kirstin keeps her hand on him, and eventually he quiets. She balances against him, and he relaxes against her.

"Thanks," he says, gladder than ever she's with him. Any other girl would have run off or made fun of him. Well, not Emelia, but he's still glad it's Kirstin with him. If her mother's a drinker, she's the safest of his friends. Besides, he likes the way she smells of salt and caramel.

"How come you're so cool?" he says.

He feels her shrug, but she says nothing.

After a moment, he asks, "Is your mom really a drinker?"

"A lush," she says flatly. "That's what my dad calls her. When he says anything."

"How can you stand it?"

"I think about leaving. I'm going to get a scholarship at a college far away and study something that will make me a lot of money. Then who'll care about them? Did you hear? A girl at our school got a scholarship for science. So maybe I'll get one too. Or for math. I'm good at both."

Leo's impressed. She has plans. He's always known she was a brain, but she has dreams as big as his own dreams of playing in a real rock band. He sits up and looks at her in a new way. Her eyes are ice blue, her cheekbones sharp. He realizes she's not beautiful now, pretty maybe, but one day, soon, she will be beautiful. Beautiful and smart. Smart enough that he believes her when she says she'll get a scholarship. Why shouldn't she?

"I'm going to play music. For real. In a rock band, but real music. Music that matters," he says, blood rushing to his cheeks before the last word is out. It sounds ridiculous saying it aloud and not joking around. What does he know? What does he have to say that matters, that's real? He's just a silly kid who plays guitar in his father's polka band. And he probably won't get to do that anymore after ditching the smoker.

But Kirstin says, "Yeah, I know," her tone as matter-of-fact as when she calls her mother a drinker or when she's in class and proclaims an answer she knows with absolute certainty.

Her certainty makes his plan possible. His blush of embarrassment ebbs, replaced by a sensation that must be what people call joy. He's going to be a rock star. No, a musician, which is better, more serious. Kirstin believes it, so why shouldn't he?

She shifts from crouching to sitting on the stones next to him, and he decides he wants to know her thoughts on something else. The cliff blocks the wind, so it's not too cold, even with his sweaty shirt beneath his sport coat. He leans back on his hands and tips his head up so it feels like what he says next is to the powdery sky.

"Did you see my father with that girl back there?"

"Yeah, I saw them," she says.

Suddenly, doubt is back, and Leo doesn't know how to say the next thing. Working up his courage, he waits for a cloud to pass the sun. Before it does, Kirstin says, "I don't think it was anything."

"It looked like something," he says quietly.

"No," she says flatly. "Forget it. It wasn't anything."

"It wasn't?"

"Nope. Just for show. Some people like to show off."

"My father."

"Yeah, but that's what makes people want to watch him. He's a showoff. It's why he's good."

"Yeah," he says. She's so certain, so smart, he decides to believe her. He decides he was imagining things. Nora was a one-off. She must have been. "Yeah, okay. You're right. It wasn't anything."

He's so glad for her pronouncement he kisses her on the cheek. She kisses him back on the lips. Then they're kissing together, not just lips but tongues, warm and cold melting into each other, the wind and the sun, and it feels right, so he leans his body toward her, over her. He wants to press his whole body against hers, but she places her hands on his shoulders and pushes him back.

"No, Leo, I can't," she whispers, her voice husky and as breathless as his own. She shifts from sitting to crouching again in a single motion.

"It's okay," he says, although he wants more of that sensation. Why would she stop, why ever stop?

Hands hugging her chest, her weight rocking heels, then toes, heels, toes, she says, "My mother. You know what happened to her. How she is. I can't let that happen to me. I'm going to college. I'm going to make my own money so I don't have to stay with some man I don't even like. No way I'm getting stuck like her. I have to be smart."

She jumps up and runs to the edge of the water. She grabs a handful of pebbles and shoots them into the waves with such force Leo imagines she's fighting back her mother's fate with every stone. He's frustrated, but he understands her. She doesn't want to be her mother any more than he wants to be his father.

After his body calms, he follows her.

"So you're never going to have a boyfriend?" he says, picking through the stones for flat skipping ones so he doesn't have to look at her.

"Maybe in college. Maybe not until after. It's too big a risk. Life and death. Really. As much as the draft is for you." She throws another pebble before kneading him in the shin with the toe of her shoe. "It's not that I don't want to, Leo. I like it. With you. But all my mother does is talk about how having me ruined all her 'prospects.' She was smart too. Just not smart enough."

"Yeah," he says. "Okay."

"Really? You don't hate me? We're still friends?"

"Of course we're friends. Anything else is a stupid thought. You're too smart to be stupid, and I'm not as stupid as you think."

"I don't think you're stupid." She pushes him playfully. "Why, Leo Meitka," she feigns a Southern accent, "I think you're *dreamy*!"

"Shut up." He laughs.

"Dreamy, dreamy. Oh, dreamy Leo, play me a dreamy song on your dreamy guitar." She laughs, tossing a pebble at his chest.

He laughs too and grabs a handful of sand and pebbles and tosses them her way. Together they run on the shore, spinning stones into the waves. Leo's Florsheims get soaked. His mother will give him hell when he gets home, but he doesn't care. He's already going to catch hell from his father.

"How come you don't throw like a girl?" he calls to Kirstin after a particularly good toss.

"Physics," she shouts back, the wind a force away from the protection of the cliffs. "That's all it is."

An image of the dark-haired girl from the church flashes into his mind, and the surge of joy dies. Physics. Yes. Something about her body's balance was strange. Kirstin is wrong. That girl. Her show. It was something.

The feeling unsettles him again, so he focuses all his energy into his torso and arm, turning each toss of a stone into a release. Kirstin matches him toss for toss, and they shoot until their shoulders ache. Then they clamber up the cliff path fast and recklessly, slipping and grasping onto bushes and saplings to keep from tumbling down. By the time they reach the top, Kirstin's calf is scraped, and Leo has a gash in his palm near the thumb. Forgetting her own injury, Kirstin gasps when she sees the blood on his hand.

"Jeez, Leo," she says. "That's a deep cut. You should go home and wash that off."

"It's no big whoop."

"If you hit a nerve or it gets infected, you'll never be able to play guitar the same again."

He stares at the gash.

"Go!" she says.

He does as she directs him, his panic rising as the blood flows over his fingers.

Once home, he leaps up the three porch steps, slams open the front door, and runs to his bedroom. With muddy, bloodstained fingers, he plays a lick on his guitar, one with the most complex fingering he knows. He plays it flawlessly, every note clean, and he falls onto his bed, breathless with relief. He lays there for a long while. His cut has stopped bleeding. It barely hurts. When he finally gets up and runs cold water over it, he sees the wound isn't as deep as he thought, just bloody. But rubbing his finger over the bandage's rough gauze, it spooks him to think how easy it would be to lose everything, how quickly his future could shrink to a pinhole.

Emelia

IN THE CHURCH gym, Emelia begs to be set free from the aunts' baked goods stand while there are still plenty of cookies and cakes left on the table. Her aunts will have to finish selling off the goods and clean up, which should take a while. Then they'll go down to the dance, eat sausages and coleslaw, and drink a beer each. That should give her plenty of time. But she's got to get away first.

She whines as she hasn't for years.

"Please, please, please let me go hang out with Kirstin."

"Hang out?" says Genny. "What does that mean, *hang out*?"

"Nothing. Just spend time with her, be with her. She's got a new Petula Clark album she wants me to hear." Her aunts approve of Petula Clark, although not necessarily of going downtown where murders and worse happen. To her aunts, the world beyond the bakery and their neighborhood is to be feared and avoided. Does this have something to do with her mother? Elisa is the only one of the sisters who was born here. Is this why her mother was so different from her sisters, a wild miscreant? Or does her aunts' fear of the world have to do with where they came from in Poland, Lou as a baby, Genny a toddler? Or is it because of the Great War her grandfather fought in before they came to America? Or the next great war, which he was too old to fight in?

How can Emelia know? They're as tight-lipped about the past as they've been about her mother. Did they think talking about the past would open the door to her asking about her mother? Or is their silence because of where they came from in Poland? Or the first Great War, or . . . ?

She's a cat chasing its tail. Well, no longer. If she wants to know anything, she'll have to find out herself, and that's just what she plans to do.

"Please," she says again. "We won't get into trouble. I promise."

"Sounds like a waste of time. We've got a job to do here, Emelia," says Genny.

"Oh, let her go," says Lou, who has been especially kind to Emelia since her birthday breakfast.

Not surprisingly, there has been no further mention of her mother by either of her aunts. The one time Emelia brought up Elisa, asking what exactly is wrong with her mother now, years after the ice pick, Genny ignored her, saying to Lou, "Didn't I tell you? The girl is too young to be trusted." Genny huffed out of their kitchen and downstairs to the bakery kitchen, shaking the entire house as she descended.

"Please, Emelia," Lou said softly. "I'm the one who insisted you were mature enough to learn the truth about your mother. You know all you need to know. Don't make me wish we hadn't confided in you."

"Okay." Emelia nodded, but the rope knotting her stomach since her birthday tightened. Confided? Elisa is her mother, not a secret recipe. "Okay," she repeated, afraid any other response would confirm her lack of trustworthiness. The *okay* had a false ring though.

Alive, Elisa has turned out to be more of a specter than ever, a presence out in the world. Elisa holds the answer to who Emelia— her spitting image by all accounts—is now and will grow up to be. *The spitting image.* What a disgusting phrase.

She more than *wants* to see her mother. She needs to see her. She's got a natural right to see her.

Now Genny harrumphs but waves her hand in assent. "You want to go? Fine, fine," she says. "Go. But we aren't cooking dinner tonight. You'll have to make your own."

Emelia wastes no time. She ducks under the stand's counter.

"Thank you," she remembers to call over her shoulder, hurrying out of the gym. She hops down the stairs and into the church hall. The first notes of "Ponytail Polka" sound as she steps onto a folding chair to locate Kirstin. Leo isn't playing with his father's band. He'll catch hell if he ditched. What's up with him? He's been as moody as she is lately. Does he have some long-dead relative come to life too?

She can't see Kirstin, but she spots Will sitting with his father and mother, and she dashes over to him.

"Hey," she says, whispering in his ear. "If you see Kirstin, tell her to tell my aunts I was with her, but then I remembered I had homework to do and went home, okay?"

Will looks like he's about to ask why, but shrugs and says, "I think she left anyway. You're clear."

Emelia squeezes his shoulder and smiles, "Thanks, Will. Did Leo ditch?"

"Ditched," says Will.

"If you see his mom, just tell her he threw up and went home."

Will grins and nods. "I should have thought of that."

"You're a pal," she says.

She means it. His friendship, Kirstin's and Leo's too, means more to her than ever now. The four of them have always been more than a mere set. In some essential way, they act as counterbalances for each other because something is off in each of them. Kirstin is too smart, Leo too charming, Will too strident. And her? She's too Demski. Her aunts are right. People take any excuse.

Did Elisa know she was branding her daughter a bastard by making her a Demski instead of giving Emelia her father's name, even if it was a fake father, a Johnny Angel father? Only one boy has ever called Emelia a bastard to her face, Tony Elman, in third grade. He'd been angry that she beat him in the fifty-yard dash, so he spit it at her from his breathless red face. After school, Will and Leo and Kirstin cornered Tony and threatened to tan his hide if he ever said a word to Emelia again. The eldest in his family of five, Tony didn't have older siblings to help him out. Emelia remembers he cried and said he didn't actually know what the word meant. He'd heard his mother say it. She'd felt bad for Tony when a dark stain spread on his pants, but after looking the word up in the dictionary, she was especially thankful to her friends for looking out for her. A name like that could stick to a kid for good.

That Emelia has no father is bad, but it isn't so strange. Fathers seem to slip away oftener than mothers, running off, dying in wars, working night shifts and overtime that are nearly the same as being gone. But to have no mother too? And no siblings? Most kids she knows have at least three siblings; some have six or seven. To be only children, as the four of them are, marks them as different. To be an *orphaned* only child makes Emelia a Martian or freak show creature with other kids. With adults, it ensures she's coated with a glaze of sugary pity. Emelia's always felt that syrupy sweetness was supposed to cover up a belief held by grownups that she must be more than unlucky to have lost both parents. She must have done something terrible.

Her aunts have made it both better and worse for her; better because at least she has some family, worse because they're spinsters, a word whose very sound is spidery and suspicious. "Give this note to one of your spinster aunts," teachers used to say to her when she was small, their tongues *tsking* disapprovingly on the *p* and *t* of the adjective unless, of course, they were spinsters themselves. Genny and Lou are right about this much. If they didn't make the lightest cakes in town, if they didn't bake bread with the best chew, make pies with the flakiest crusts and fat with filling, they'd be passed over in favor of the other nearby bakeries run by proper families with decent men bakers heading them up.

For the most part though, Will, Kirstin, and Leo have kept her safe. Their solid friendship suggests to other people that she's okay, or okay enough to be left alone. And she looks out for her friends as much as they look out for her. All for one. So now Will won't ask why Emelia needs him to fib for her. He'll simply do it as she would for him.

She feels a fresh stab of guilt at having to keep the secret of her mother from her friends.

"You're a pal, Will," she repeats, squeezing his shoulder.

Lou and Genny should know her friends wouldn't tell anyone about Elisa if Emelia asked them not to. Of course they wouldn't. She's almost spilled the beans a few times, but in the end, her aunts' trust means more to Emelia than she likes to admit. As they remind her, she's a Demski first and always. And as much as Emelia doesn't want to believe this is true, there is also the chance that if her friends know she has a crazy mother, they will look at her differently. She'll be too tainted even for them.

"Yeah, a pal, that's me," Will says, adding quietly, "Go out through the tunnel so your aunts don't see you leave alone."

She gives his shoulder another squeeze before turning away. She takes the tunnel between the church and the grade school as he suggested, then the shortcut home, through the Rendells' back yard, up the alley, entering the bakery through the back door.

After the blush of late-afternoon sun outside, the sudden darkness in the kitchen startles her senses, and it takes a moment for her eyes to adjust. Even then, the calm is eerie. This place should bustle with giant mixers whirring, mammoth baking sheets sliding over countertops, flour puffing in the air while Genny and Lou weave and spin like the arms of some great sea creature. Now, with the mixers stilled and the countertops and floors scrubbed clean, it looks, not like a sleeping sea creature, but a dead one.

The front of the store is even darker than the kitchen, the shades having been drawn over the display windows. At least the high windows in the kitchen provide enough illumination that she doesn't have to turn on a light and risk one of the neighbors noticing someone was here during the smoker and mentioning the fact to her aunts later. As she weaves her way among the marble and butcher block countertops and the shelves filled with bulk sacks of flour, sugar, and other ingredients, she admits that since her birthday, a queer feeling has hovered over the whole house that no amount of hurly-burly, as Lou calls the bakery's busy time, has been able to dispel.

She and her aunts have become awkward with each other, so much so that Aunt Genny seemingly can't stand to be alone with her, and when forced to be, she's brusque and even more over-efficient than usual. Aunt Lou's become over-kind, baking foods Emelia liked as a little girl, increasing her allowance by a quarter, yet occasionally doing chores that have been Emelia's for years.

For Emelia's part, her aunts lying to her so easily and for so long has made her wary of every encounter she has with them now and every experience she's ever had. When she blew out the fifteen candles on her birthday cake, this one in the shape of a handbag, frosted poodle pink with a white ribbon-candy scarf tied around the handle, Lou snapped a photo of her as she always does of Emelia with her cakes. But instead of making a wish, Emelia glanced at the photos of the dead relatives atop the fireplace mantel—or in the case of her mother, presumed dead—and realized she never sees any of the pictures Lou takes of her.

Lou always has a camera, the leather strap slung around her neck. She takes it to Emelia's school events, the student art show where Emelia's painting of the lake won a prize, and her swim meets. Presumably Lou takes photos at these events. Of course, she does; Emelia's seen her focusing the camera, seen the flashes as she snaps. Yet Emelia never sees the developed photos. Only her current school picture shares mantel space with the dead relatives. Each year Lou pries the back off the unvarnished rosewood frame and replaces last year's stiffly posed photo with the most recent one. But what's happened to all those other pictures? Does Lou bother to have them developed? Is the film in the attic in a box? Or does Lou throw them away? And if so, why take them in the first place? For all Emelia knows, there's no film in the camera.

Likewise, every word out of her aunts' mouths takes on additional significance now. The other day, Genny handed Emelia an armful of clean laundry and told her to put her things away in her mother's dresser. Before, Emelia would have corrected Genny's mistake in her mind—her mother's *old* dresser. But Genny was right. The dresser is still her mother's, isn't it, now that she's alive again?

Nothing is really Emelia's anymore. It never was. Her bedroom is her mother's room. She sleeps in her mother's bed, puts books on her mother's shelves, does her homework at her mother's desk. Only the closet is her own territory. Inside it, her aunts allow her to hang the posters they say will damage the primrose wallpaper her mother picked out and that Emelia's grandfather pasted on every wall more than twenty years ago. Emelia used to like the idea of being surrounded by her mother's wallpaper and of using her mother's things. She'd felt close to her, or close to the mother she'd imagined was hers, someone tragic and stunningly beautiful like Catherine in *Wuthering Heights*, one of the books from her mother's shelves that Emelia has read, imagining her mother's fingers turning the very same pages. The image of her mother as a delicate waif, whose life was tamped out by a broken heart, was so vivid to Emelia, she assumed it was not just true, but a memory.

She used to bring her mother to mind through other memories too: the scent of lilacs, the nubby feel of seersucker beneath her fingertips, and a slash of cherry red lipstick on her own lips. But Emelia's no longer sure these are actual associations from actual memories. Maybe she's just conjured them from books or from the lies her aunts and grandparents told her when she was little and asked about her mother. Probably she's constructed some of these images from the photographs on the mantle, for there are plenty of pictures of her mother there—in a tiny ice-skating outfit, in a plaid school uniform, in a beaded dress and high heels, her smile wide, her eyes glinting. She really had been stunningly beautiful. Was she still?

Emelia has always known she'd never be as beautiful as her mother, spitting image or not, but she hadn't minded when her mother was dead. Emelia felt she was carrying on the only remaining traces of that beauty. She quite liked it when people who knew her mother came into the bakery and said, "You look so much like her." When people plotted Emelia's future from her mother's life, it was as if there was a map drawn for her. "Oh, I can see you'll be nearly as tall as your mother . . . You'll be almost as beautiful . . . nearly as lovely . . . almost as spirited."

Nearly. Almost.

Close enough had been okay before. But now existing in her living, breathing mother's shadow makes Emelia feel as she did in third grade when she swiped Jenny Grossman's piggy-topped pencil, which Emelia had admired and envied for weeks. Finally, she couldn't help herself, and as she passed Jenny's desk, she slipped the pencil into her own skirt pocket. At home, it had been so odd to see her hand wrapped around the pencil instead of Jenny's that she'd worried her writing would be Jenny's too, that whenever she held the stolen pencil, her thoughts weren't hers but Jenny's. Emelia had snuck the pencil back into Jenny's desk the next day.

What Emelia's doing now with her mother's life is so much worse than stealing a pencil. Her mother has always lingered in this house like the scent of butter. She was an apparition that might visit Emelia at any moment. But her mother isn't a ghost anymore. What if one day her flesh-and-blood mother escapes from the crazy house and comes back, furious with the girl who has stolen not just her things, but her life?

After all, it's Emelia's fault Elisa never made it out of this house until she went into the loony bin. No one has said this outright, but Emelia understands that once Elisa fell pregnant, her life was over. "She wasn't ready," Lou said. Emelia can see this is true. Elisa never had a house of her own, no job other than working at the bakery, and no husband or a family of her own. Just Emelia, who'd made Elisa go bonkers and had gotten her locked up in a place where some mad doctor had taken an ice pick to her brain.

Lying awake at night, surrounded by her mother's things, Emelia can't help but wonder, will this happen to her too, the crazy if not the ice pick?

Nearly as crazy. Almost as nuts. Wild. Miscreant. And the last, the one that haunts her the most. Slut.

And what of her father, whose name Emelia has been told is Johnny Angel, like the Johnny Angel in the song? Her elusive, winged father. He boarded a bus for an army base in Virginia and disappeared into the morning fog. His parents never heard from him again, or so Lou told her years ago when Emelia found her birth certificate and saw the father's name was left blank.

"Why didn't they write his name there?" she asked Lou. "Why not write *Johnny Angel*?"

"Your mother wanted you all to herself. She wanted you to be all Demski, all ours," her aunt said, stroking her hair.

Isn't it more likely he simply left Elisa high and dry when he found out she was pregnant? Did he know? Does he know I exist?

Does *he* exist? Maybe Johnny Angel is no more real than her memories of her mother. There's no Angel family in the neighborhood. Maybe he's fiction like her mother's death, a name picked from a song.

Emelia wants so badly to know. Where did her mother meet him? Did they dance together? Did they go down to the lake to watch the sunset? Maybe he was an older man, a married man. At the smoker, looking around at the men eating and laughing with their families, she realized her father could be almost any one of them, and a new—another—flesh-and-blood ghostly presence materialized before her. How awful that every man she sees, every man she meets above a certain age, *could* be him.

How can she possibly begin to know who she is going to be if she doesn't know where she came from? Only knowing the truth can be the gust of wind she needs to clear her mind of these ghosts, and only her ghost of a mother can tell her what's real.

Unable to take the quiet in the bakery kitchen any longer, as she passes the pans hanging from a cast-iron ring over the stove, she backhands them, the clatter startling and satisfying but not enough to chase back the feeling that she's about to step onto a cliff's edge.

Well, a plummet is better than teetering forever. At least once you fall, it's done and over.

Determined now, she shudders off the creeps, plunging past the machines and running hard up the steps to the family kitchen. She takes a key from a hook inside the doorway and gallops back down the stairs.

She unlocks the door to the bakery's office, opening it slowly as if someone might jump out at her. The office is a cramped afterthought beyond the kitchen's open work spaces and sales area, no bigger than the walk-in freezer, with a high single-hung window on one wall that lets in a yellow swath of sun. Despite Genny's rigid system of order in the kitchen, she's hopeless with the books, leaving Lou to keep the numbers. By all appearances, Lou keeps looser order here than on the bakery's shelves, which are as strictly organized as a library's shelves. The papers are stacked untidily on the rather grand oak desk that belonged to Emelia's grandfather. More papers wait in wire baskets or in the pigeonholes above the desk, and Emelia can picture Lou hunched before the desk like the mouse under the chair in the "Pussy Cat, Pussy Cat" nursery rhyme, small and skittish, shoving morsels of paper into her mouth so as not to have to file them.

Emelia feels rather small and skittish herself as she enters the room and considers where to begin looking. She's drawn to the large file cabinet against the back wall, on top of which is a black-and-white photo of the three Demski sisters posed in front of some bulky old Ford car. Emelia has always liked this photo and has sometimes imagined herself in the position of her mother.

In the picture, Genny stands stiffly with her hands clasped at her stomach. Lou, between the two, has one arm thrown over the shoulder of each of her sisters. Elisa's right foot rests on the running board, her skirt pulled up over her knee, exposing a thin but strong calf that could be Emelia's. She looks like a normal girl there, maybe two years older than Emelia is now. Does that mean Emelia has only two years before she goes crazy?

Nearly. Almost.

She takes her gaze from the photo and the file cabinet, deciding instead to start with the pigeonhole marked *To Be Filed*. She sorts through receipts for the dairy and dry goods suppliers. She tosses aside the business card for a plumber.

She finds what she's looking for beneath the water and electricity bills, both marked *paid* in Lou's flowing script. The receipt bears their bank's letterhead. Under the description of services, Emelia reads, *LONG-TERM CARE OF E. DEMSKI*.

A shiver passes over Emelia. *E. Demski*. That's her.

But it's not, she insists. She's not her mother.

Reading carefully, she sees her aunts have a standing order with the bank for quarterly payments to Red River Care Facility, which is located in Cortland, a city whose name Emelia vaguely registers from a grade school civics unit on state geography.

She copies the address onto a notepad and returns all of the papers to the pigeonhole. Cortland is too far to walk; she knows this much. It's not even a place the local buses go. So she'll have to find a ride. Maybe she can bike? Even then, she supposes it will be a long ride, farther from home than she's ever been before. But she's got to get there. She's got to tell her mother it isn't her fault. She didn't mean to steal Elisa's life. And she's got to get some answers.

The sun has dipped, dimming the office further. With her mother's address in hand, she looks out the small alley window at nothing but the navy sky. Determination has carried her to this moment, but now her nerve wavers. Are her aunts right? Does she know all she needs to know about her mother? No, she thinks, slapping the desktop in anger. At the very least, she's got go to that crazy house and ask Elisa a few questions. She's got to give her mother a chance.

Her determination back in place, she hugs herself against the settling cold and the feeling that a shadowy presence lurks in the near dark.

In the morning, Sunday morning, the bright sun swishes away the shadows like a broom to cobwebs. Lying in her mother's bed, surrounded by the faded primrose wallpaper her mother chose, Emelia finds her determination solidified. She sneaks a map from the "stuff" drawer in the kitchen and locates the route, going north up the shore to Cortland. It doesn't look that far when she traces the route with a pencil tip, just the distance from her wrist to her elbow.

Sunday or not, her aunts are already in the bakery, having risen at four in the morning as they always do. Although they are church members, they are not church-goers, believing God gives bakers special dispensation. "Someone has to bake that bread the Lord breaks," Genny says.

So they don't see Emelia make a ham salad sandwich. She wraps the sandwich and a few oatmeal cookies in wax paper and places them and a thermos of water in her school satchel. In her bedroom, she dresses neatly, a simple skirt and blouse, no dungarees. She wants to be presentable. She's meeting her mother. On second thought, she stuffs her good dress and a hairbrush into the satchel with the sandwich and water. She'll find somewhere to change clothes when she gets close to Cortland. There isn't room for her Mary Janes in her satchel, and she can't ride her bike with them, so her saddle shoes will have to do. She doesn't bother to leave a note for her aunts. They will assume she's with Kirstin, Will, and Leo for the day. A note saying as much will only make them suspicious.

She feels bold as she pedals out of the garage, down the alley, and up the street. Her aunts believe they can decide what she knows and what she doesn't. But Elisa is *her* mother. And she's not *their* daughter. Her mother will understand her the way her aunts don't. She and Elisa will have a special mother-daughter link that they'll keep to themselves. She has no intention of letting Genny and Lou know she's seen her mother, and she's sure her mother won't tell them. Her aunts assume they're the only ones who can keep a family secret. But as they've said themselves, Emelia's a Demski too.

She passes Harlen's Hardware, Schumacher's Dry Goods, Nordczyk's Grocers, and Constantino's Supper Club, where her aunts have not eaten one single time as far as she's aware.

Another few blocks and she's as far as she's ever ridden before. Bradley Avenue merges onto Lakeshore Drive, which turns into the highway that will lead her through Milwaukee and most of the way to her mother. It takes longer to put the city behind her than she'd thought.

Keeping the lake on her right side, on the left she passes newly sprouted soybean and corn fields, cranberry bogs, and apple orchards. She admires the huge red barns with silver silos bulleting to the sky. The sun is warm, and she wrinkles her nose against the smell of the cow pasture. When a cow glances up and drones a long moo at her, she moos right back and keeps riding.

Although a few pickup trucks and cars pass her, mostly she's alone on the road. The sound of her breath is loud in her ears. To cover it, she sings "Last Train to Clarksville," "California Dreamin'," and other songs that keep time with her pedaling. After a while, her thighs burn, but she keeps pedaling. The sun rises to its full height and begins to fall before she stops, her legs cramped to stones, her lungs sore. She leans her bike against a maple tree, near a sign that reads *Lawrence Pond*. She dodges behind a dogwood bush to pee. Maybe she should change into her dress here. She must be close to Cortland, but she'll check to see how close before changing. She wishes she'd brought a hand towel to wash away the film of sweat and grime from the ride.

She devours the sandwich and every last drop of the water in her thermos, planning to fill it up when she gets to her mother's place. *Her mother's place.* It doesn't sound so bad when she says it like that. She won't use the words *asylum* or *institution* when she tells her friends about her mother, which she'll do as soon as it's safe. Of course, she certainly won't ever mention the ice pick.

So far, the ice pick has made it easier to keep the promise to her aunts that she won't tell her friends that Elisa is alive. That ice pick gives her the creeps. Emelia swiped one from the drawer in the kitchen and took it to her bedroom. Looking in the mirror, she pressed the pick against her forehead. How had they done it? How had they gotten to her mother's brain? Wouldn't they have had to drill her skull or cut her scalp? Does she have scars? Have they made her mother hideous? Is that why she's locked away? How could her grandparents and her aunts have let anyone do that to her mother?

She shakes off the thought of the ice pick and disfiguring scars and chews oatmeal cookies as she locates the pond on the map. She starts at Cortland and moves her finger down the pencil line she drew this morning. At first she's puzzled. She can't find the pond. She glances up and sees a sign that confirms she's on the right highway. Maybe the pond is too small to be on the map. She runs her finger farther south, then farther.

The cookies go dry in her mouth when she finds the pond on the map and realizes she's gone no more than a fingernail's distance. She's nowhere near Cortland. It will take her days, weeks of riding nonstop to get there. Tears burn her eyes. Her mother is still so far away. As far as she's ever been.

Wishing she'd brought her watch, Emelia looks to the shadow cast by the maple tree. She and her friends have become pretty good at telling time from the sun, and she figures it's early afternoon. If she turns around now, she'll just make it home before dark.

She looks again at the map. How could she have misjudged the distance so badly? All her effort, and she's hardly closer to her mother than she was this morning.

Exhausted, she lies back in the grass. She can't face riding home just yet. She's glad she hadn't told her aunts of her plan. They would have laughed at her. Imagine thinking that they'd stash her mother a mere bike ride away. She can't stand the thought of going home without having seen her mother, but she's got to. She'll be lost in the dark if she carries on, and she still won't have reached Cortland. Not even close. She won't be anywhere but alone.

So she won't meet her mother today. Her disappointment is keen, but despite her desire, she thinks of the ice pick and the scars, and she's also a little relieved. Maybe her aunts are right. She isn't ready to meet her mother. If she can't even read a map, is she ready to face what her mother may really be? Isn't it more likely that Elisa is nothing like Emily Bronte's heartbreakingly beautiful Catherine and more like that other Bronte sister's creation, the wild-haired arsonist, Bertha Rochester, who gets locked up in the attic but still tries to murder Jane Eyre?

With the grass cushioning her body and the sun warming her face, she closes her eyes just for a moment, just to let her mind empty her thoughts. As the sun dots the darkness beneath her eyelids, it occurs to her that no one in the whole world knows where she is. She hardly knows. She could be in California. She could be floating in the middle of the lake. Her arms and legs feel like they're floating. She feels like she's pedaling over the lake, waves crashing at her ankles, the breakwater far behind her. She waves to her friends on the shore, who are shouting something she can't hear at first. "Riptide!" Leo's voice reaches her at the same time she feels the current's pull; then she's sinking and pumping the bicycle, but the pedals have disappeared and so has the lake and her friends, and she's struggling up a urine-soaked mound of cow manure, her feet disappearing into the muck.

She's awakened by the sound of a radio blaring "Wooly Bully." Disoriented and stiff, she sits up just in time to see a yellow pickup truck speeding north. She watches it crest a hill and disappear. If it had been going slower, maybe she could have hitched a ride. The thought cheers her. Okay, so she can't ride her bike to her mother today, but she can hitchhike to her another day, when she's ready. Leo says kids hitch all the time now. He says he's going to hitchhike to California or New York the minute he turns eighteen.

She checks the shadow from the maple tree. She's been asleep for at least an hour, maybe two. Her muscles ache as she gathers her things and climbs back onto her bicycle. Her aunts are going to kill her if she gets home after dark. She pedals fast. She'll be in big trouble if the streetlights come on before she gets home. Her aunts will start calling her friends' houses looking for her. She knocks the handlebar with the heel of her hand. She'd forgotten to tell Kirstin and the boys to cover for her.

The thought she had before she fell asleep returns. No one in the whole world knows where she is. She pedals faster, wishing again she'd brought her watch. And she wishes she hadn't drunk all of the water in her thermos. She's thirsty. Going north, it had felt like there were plenty of downhills to coast and rest her legs. Now it feels like she's going uphill the whole way.

With the sun dropping, the wind suddenly shifts, coming off the lake now. The cold air feels fat with a storm. "If it starts raining," she threatens the threatening sky. Then, feeling tears brimming, "Please don't rain."

She can't believe this was all for nothing. She feels stupid. She should have read the distance scale on the map. She should have planned better. She can hear Genny now: *She's too young to be trusted.*

But it's not her fault, she insists, trying out the stance she'll take with her aunts if she ends up having to admit where she'd gone, or where she tried to go anyway. It's all their fault. She wouldn't have had to lie to them and go through all of this trouble if they hadn't lied to her first. They've duped her for her whole life. How could they do it? Not just deceive her, but throw her mother away like that?

Anger fuels her pedaling. It feels so good to be angry, she wants more. Why didn't her mother fight harder to stay with her? Good mothers don't just abandon their children. Everyone knows abandoning your child is the worst thing a woman can do.

99

Struggling up a long hill, the lake on one side, the jaunty beginnings of a hayfield on the other, her anger drains. She uses her whole body weight to push down each pedal, which still isn't enough to keep the bike moving. Halfway up, she gets off and walks the steepest part of the hill.

Behind her, she hears the song "I Want Candy" before she hears the truck approaching. Glancing back, she finds it's the same canary yellow pickup she'd seen going in the other direction. She steers the bike toward the shoulder of the highway so the truck can pass her. But it doesn't pass her. It rolls alongside her and keeps pace with her. Inside, two boys, who look to be a few years older than her, wear crew cuts and white T-shirts streaked with dirt. Their faces and arms already have the deep tan of midsummer. Of course, they're farm boys. They're outside year round.

"It's a girl," says the boy in the passenger seat. He's got a square jaw and a beer in the hand that dangles out the open window.

"Of course it's a girl," says the driver, who Emelia sees also has a beer secured in his crotch. His hair is a dusty red, and his cheeks are splattered with freckles. "Don't be an idiot, Theo."

"Hi, girl. Like he says, I'm Theo. This is Danny," says the passenger. His eyes are the same green as the new leaves on the trees. "I've never seen you around here before. And we're always on this road."

She doesn't answer. She's not sure what to say or how to judge if these boys are okay like Will and Leo, or if they're dangerous like some of the shadier boys at school.

"I guess she's shy," says Danny.

"You shy?" asks Theo. "No need to be shy with us. We're harmless. Where're you going? Maybe we can give you a lift?"

"Thanks, but I've got my bike."

"We can toss it in the back there," says Danny, jerking his thumb toward the truck bed.

He stops the truck, and she stops walking. Now that she's still, she feels colder. The sky is definitely darker, and droplets of rain splatter her arms. She hadn't even thought to check the weather report before she left home this morning.

"I don't know," she begins, but Theo's already out of the truck and lifting her bicycle. He holds the door open and gestures for her to get in. She hesitates, not sure what other option she has now that they have her bicycle. The sprinkling has turned to rain, and a charcoal ceiling of clouds hovers over the hayfield. Still, she doesn't know these boys.

As thunder growls in the distance, Theo leans in and says, "We won't bite." His warm breath brushes her neck. He smells slightly of beer and loamy soil and fresh sweat.

She climbs up and slides across the bench seat. She settles herself with the gearshift between her legs. Danny smiles at her so sweetly that she smiles back. So what if she doesn't know them, she thinks as Theo climbs in after her and shuts the door, the loamy beer scent heady in the enclosed space. She won't know any of the people who give her rides when she hitchhikes to see her mother. Maybe if they're nice, she'll ask these boys to take her someday.

"Where you going, shy girl?" asks Danny.

"Home," she says. She unfolds the map and shows them.

"You rode your bike all that way? Why?" says Theo, immediately understanding the distance scale better than she did.

"I just wanted to see how far I could go," she lies, hoping they don't notice the pencil mark. Probably everyone but her knows the crazy house is in Cortland.

"Well, you got pretty far," he says.

"I forgot about getting home though." She realizes this isn't a lie. She hadn't thought at all about what she would do after she'd seen her mother.

"Yeah," Danny says, nodding, as if forgetting about returning home happens often to him. "We'll get you there."

"Here," says Theo, pulling a can of beer from a Styrofoam cooler. "You gotta be thirsty."

She's thirstier than she's ever been in her life, and she drinks deeply, her eyes tearing at the carbonation and the bitter taste. Still, it's good, a taste that feels natural and reminds her of the sourdough bread Genny makes. She drinks more.

"Do you always give people you don't know a ride?" she asks.

"We're building up cosmic credit," says Danny. "After we graduate in a few months, Theo and I are hitting the road, going to California before we get drafted."

"Yeah, but his dad won't let us take the truck, so we're hitching. Like you."

She wants to point out that she wasn't actually hitching, but it seems like bad manners to correct him.

"That's neat," she says, trying to sound casual. She's just now understood these boys are graduating. They're two or three years older than her. She wonders how old they think she is. She spots her saddle shoes and wishes she were wearing something more sophisticated, wedge-heeled slip-ons or fashion boots, not that her aunts will let her buy either of these. She wishes she'd at least put on her good dress at the pond. She tucks her feet behind the cooler, hoping the boys won't notice her little girl shoes.

Theo says, "We figure if we give folks rides now while we have the truck, maybe the universe will repay us later."

"My friend Leo wants to do that, hitchhike to California. He's a musician."

"Oh, yeah?" says Theo.

His tone suggests he's put out by the mention of Leo. Is it rude to mention another boy to the ones you're with, even if he's just a friend? Or is it that she's suggested their idea isn't as unique as they thought it was?

To change the subject, when "Mr. Tambourine Man" comes on the radio, she cries, "Oh, I love this song. Turn it up!"

Danny does, the loud music dispelling the awkwardness of having mentioned Leo. In fact, for Emelia the music is such a relief she sings along loudly, getting lost in the tune, clapping and shaking the fresh beer that has appeared in her hand as if playing the tambourine. Theo and Danny laugh when the beer sloshes onto her lap, and Theo brushes it off her thigh. His skin is warm and calloused. Emelia likes the dual sensation on her skin.

"She knows all the words," says Danny, smiling wide. Seemingly delighted with her now, they sing along to the parts they know too.

She hardly feels her sore legs anymore. And the anger at her mother and her aunts that's been clinging to her like fog drips away. She spills beer again, and the boys laugh harder. She loves these boys. They're beautiful. They're going to California. So's Leo. Why shouldn't she go too? And why just California? Maybe she'll go someplace even better, someplace no one's ever thought of before where everyone's happy and no one ever lies to anyone. So what if her mother abandoned her? When she turns eighteen, she'll abandon her mother right back.

After the song finishes, she swallows what beer she hasn't spilled.

"I want another one," she says, shaking the empty can.

"I like this girl," Theo says, winking at her.

He pops the top on another beer, and she drinks deeply. They keep singing to "Under the Boardwalk" and "Doo Wah Diddy Diddy." What fun it is to be with these boys who don't know her name and don't seem to care what it is. She's no Demski to them. She's not Elisa's daughter or her aunts' niece. She's not even Emelia. She could be anyone. She could tell these boys anything, and it wouldn't matter.

"My mother's crazy," she calls above the music.

"Aren't they all?" says Theo.

"Yes." She laughs, lifting her beer. "Every last one of them."

She's having so much fun she doesn't notice when Danny turns off the road down a path that leads to an inlet of the shore, wooded with birch trees whose buds have just recently burst into tiny leaves. He turns off the engine but keeps the radio blasting "Last Train to Clarksville." The rain thunders the hood of the truck as Theo leans toward her and kisses her. She kisses him back, letting him put his warm tongue between her teeth. She doesn't realize he's pressing her back against Danny until Danny grasps her shoulders and turns her toward him. He kisses her, his lips thinner than Theo's, but his tongue more insistent. Theo lifts one of her legs over the gearshift and runs his tongue up her thigh. She knows she should stop them. But she feels dreamy and sleepy, and it's delicious having these boys who don't know her name touching her.

"My mother is crazy," she manages to whisper when Danny releases her for a moment so he can unbutton her blouse.

"They all are," he says, his hand inside her bra. Theo's pulled aside her underpants, still kissing her.

When a siren whoops twice, Theo and Danny abruptly sit up, sit her up, and shove the beer cans beneath the seat. Beyond the thin trunks of the birch trees, she dizzily registers the black and white of a police cruiser. The officer whoops the siren again and says over a loudspeaker, "Break it up now, kids."

Theo puts his arm out the window and waves as Danny starts the engine and backs out of the inlet and onto the highway. With few words, she directs them the rest of the way back. The rain has stopped by the time they drop her in front of the Woolworth's as she asks them to do. She can't let her aunts or anyone else who might report back to them see her with these boys. They still haven't asked her name, and when Theo refuses to meet her gaze as he lifts her bike out of the truck bed, she knows they won't.

"See you 'round," he says, closing the truck's door.

"Okay," she says, wishing now he knew her name to at least say goodbye. Watching the truck retreat, she changes her mind. She's glad they don't know who she is. Later, when they talk with their friends, as they're sure to do, telling them about the easy girl they picked up on the road, a loose, wild girl who has a crazy mother and let them do anything they wanted with her, at least they won't be able to use her name.

Standing in front of the store's display window, she smooths her hair and skirt. The skirt is so crushed, she might as well not bother. She uses the hem to wipe the bicycle seat dry. Why didn't she tell the boys to stop? They weren't mean boys. They would have stopped if she'd told them to. She's pretty sure they would have stopped. But she hadn't wanted them to. She's barely kissed a boy before today, only once at a birthday party in a basement darkened for a Laurel and Hardy movie. With fifteen other kids around them, Arnie Kushman had pecked her lips. She hadn't especially liked it. His lips were scaly, and his bobbing head made her think of a chicken. But today she recalls Danny's tongue in her mouth and Theo pushing aside her underwear, and she flushes. She didn't want them to stop. What would have happened if they hadn't been interrupted?

She must be just like her mother.

Her flush deepens. Her mother had been wild. *Johnny Angel.* Is this why her aunts decided to finally tell her about Elisa? Did they recognize the daughter was turning out to be just like the mother? *E. Demski. Almost as loose. Nearly as wild.*

Emelia hadn't heeded her aunts' warning. She hadn't understood it. But she does now. Watch yourself, or you'll end up strapped down, brained with an ice pick, and locked away forever.

Sonya

PAIN IS COLOR.

The blood smeared over her thighs is the red of the coleus leaf. "Genus *solenostemon*, species *solenostemon scutellarioides*," Sonya hisses through grinding teeth.

Her clenched fists are the white of the paper birch. Her bare calves are splattered with charcoal dirt. Closing her eyes, yellow yolks and saffron rods sear her brain.

"Stupid," she grunts. "Stup——. Sm—aaart."

Grunts dissolve into huffs as the pain releases her.

Nauseous and shivering, she opens her eyes. She's thankful for the ashen clouds. Fewer people are likely to be out on a wet afternoon. Fewer still will be willing to brave the muddy paths down the cliffs to the shore.

Sodden weeds scratch her bare back. Pressed against the foot of the cliff, the overhang above her canopy, she's somewhat protected from the weather and completely hidden from view. Maple saplings and last year's cattails dribble water over her, but crashing waves and the splatter of the driving rain drown out the cries she can't manage to grit back.

At the next contraction, she sputters in a husky voice, "Mother, mother of the night, carry my child into light."

In this moment, it's all the same, spirit and science, myth and materiality, the sky and the water and the grainy sand coating her skin, her clenching belly, her heaving breaths.

"Mother, mother . . ."

She's never been so alone.

She thought nothing had worked. The train tracks didn't work. The ice-skating didn't work. He wouldn't speak to her, brushed her off when she waited in the church for him. So she'd had no other choice but to reveal herself at the smoker. Even there, he turned from her, refusing to look. After exposing herself on that stage, she waited again, outside the church, listening to the music, praying for it to end and for him to emerge. When he did, his arm was hooked over the shoulders of a woman in a hideously tight red dress, and she knew she was on her own.

So she steeped pennyroyal, but she was afraid of it too. She didn't know its other effects. Still, she drank it down and waited up all night. By morning, it hadn't worked. Nothing, nothing had worked. She tried again, two times, and three, growing more desperate each time, so she brewed the tea stronger. On the fourth effort, last night's effort, she brewed it black as dirt, six cups, and she drank all of them down, hot as sin.

This morning she wept her pillow sodden. It hadn't worked. None of it had. Myth, physics, chemistry. The old wives, the kind librarian, and him—most of all him—they'd all failed her. None as badly as she failed herself.

But she had been wrong. By the time the bell rang for homeroom, her belly was screaming. She tried to make it to lunch so she could slip away unnoticed. But in home ec class, it was all she could do not to double over. Mrs. Nardinski could see Sonya wasn't faking cramps the way some girls do to get out of classes, gym, or biology lab. Sonya's pain was real.

Abandoning her sewing pattern of a circle skirt, Sonya bit her cheek and gripped the pinking shears in her fist. From behind her sewing machine, Stella gave her a worried look, but Sonya rushed past her without returning her gaze, afraid the intensity of her pain would show in her eyes, and Stella would have to admit she knows what's going on and be forced to help her. The least Sonya could do is keep Stella out of it.

With a pass from Mrs. Nardinski dangling from her fingers, Sonya staggered down the hallway, past the nurse's office, and out the door. She took the alleyways, stopping to tuck herself between garage doors and garbage cans when each teeth-splitting pain hit.

Crouching and biting down on her sweatered arm until it passed, she tried to remember what the books had told her to expect. There'd been so little information for her that she'd relied on an old animal husbandry text in the school library with a section on birthing cows.

In the alley, with the reek of moldy bread and rancid meat in her nostrils, she decided that whatever was going to happen now, she had to move. She had one choice: where. She refused to let it be next to a garbage can or a hospital where they would record her shame to carry with her for life or mark her in death. At worst, if she didn't die, they might arrest her if they deciphered the bruises from skating or figured out what she'd swallowed.

She chose the lake. Let nature do what it would do. Now, she squeezes clay and stones in her fists. She sucks on a pebble, the taste of sand and lake water grainy on her tongue. Her whole body writhes. Her entire being is a ball of pain. At the worst, she spits the pebble into the air and yells, "Mama!"

The world goes black.

When she awakens, she looks at the boy, who is as tiny as a kitten and glows the pearlescent blue of the lake. She picks him up and holds his body to her chest. She's so cold, she can't tell if he's cold too. But he looks cold. She rubs his spindly arms and legs, his sunken belly, and the tiniest buttocks she's ever seen. His blue limbs don't move. A film covers his mouth.

Tears fall over the dark wisps of his hair. Her brain spins. She vomits into the weeds. Liquid feces smears her thighs. *Mother, mother of the night. Carry my child . . .*

Her mind spins. Ghost Mother has stolen her son.

And she's the one who summoned her.

The world goes black again.

This time when she awakens, she removes from the pocket of the letterman sweater the pinking shears she'd held onto as she rushed out of the classroom.

She cuts the cord, surprised at its thickness. She buries the placenta in the sand to give her time to get away before an animal comes to eat it. She crawls herself and her boy to the edge of the shore and into water so cold that she feels woozy again. Still on her knees, sand and pebbles digging into her skin, her teeth chatter as she rinses off what blood and fluids the rain has not managed to wash away.

He's no bigger than her brandywine tomatoes, but clean now, he's more ethereal than ever.

"Baby, baby," she coos to him. She holds him up to the gray sky. He's the color of a storm. "Do something, baby." Shiver or cry. Her brother, Dean, used to shake his fists angrily at the world as he screamed himself beet red. "Do anything." Anything at all to prove Ghost Mother hasn't swooped in at the last moment.

His limbs hang limp and motionless.

It was what she wanted, but not what she wanted at all. Not this. Not like this.

Above, a turkey vulture glides, squawking over the sound of the waves. She curls her body over her boy.

"No," she says to the bird. "You can't have him."

She carries him back to the high, dead weeds at the foot of the cliff where she does her best to dry him with the letter sweater, running her numb fingertip over his gray pearl toes and his tiny shell ears. The ears, the jawline, maybe that little reedy nose are *his*. But the purple lips, full on top, fuller on the bottom, turning his expression into a pout, those are *hers*.

If he would only move.

"Just open your eyes," she whispers as she runs a sleeve around his moon face. A little moondrop fallen from the dark sky. If he would only look at her, claim her as his own, she knows, as she knows seasons follow seasons, she would claim him right back, claim him with a roar. Her parents be damned. Her classmates be damned. Science and *him*—especially *him*—be damned.

She holds the boy to her breast as she'd seen her mother do with Dean when he was an infant. She sings softly, "Baby Love," and "Turn, Turn, Turn," and "Puff the Magic Dragon," weeping onto her moondrop when Jackie Paper kills Puff by growing up. The world is so cruel.

She dozes again. This time when she wakes, the rain has stopped, although the air is foggy and every surface drips. Moon Boy has turned from blue to gray.

If she returns him to nature, maybe he will come back to her someday. She'll be ready for him then.

She carries him to the calm side of the breakwater, unwraps him from the letterman sweater, dropping it onto the sand. She wades knee deep and sets Moon Boy into the water. She gives him a push. But the waves, forceful even on the calm side of the breaker, push him back toward land. She walks farther out and tries again, but the waves push him back. She carries him to the side of the breakwater with the riptide. She swims out as far as she dares and releases him with a shove. First, the current spins him, but he's so small that the current can't get a grip on him, and the waves again push him back toward shore.

Feeling dizzy, she realizes if she doesn't get out of the water soon, she's going to faint again.

"Hypothermia," she says vaguely.

Holding him to her, she wades back to shore, her own lips feeling as blue as Moon Boy's. She wraps him in the letterman sweater. Cradling him in one arm, she scrambles up the cliff path, her wet sneakers slipping often. She plods to the marshy pond where she takes Dean to play, although she'll never bring her brother here again.

This is Moon Boy's place now.

The earth around the pond is squishy from the rain. She lays the bundled infant down and uses the pinking shears to cut through roots and gouge the soil. She deems the first spot too wet and looks for another where the earth is drier. She scoops the dirt with her hands. Grit splits the tender skin beneath her nails, but she keeps scraping, excavating up to her wrists, to her elbows. Finally she lays the woolen bundle of Moon Boy in the ground. She sits back on her heels and opens the sweater. She snaps the wet stems of crocus and wild daffodils and places them in his miniature fists. She's never seen hands so small, so perfect. Her moon boy is perfect. Too perfect for this world. Hadn't she always known that? He wasn't ready for this world.

Using the pinking shears, she cuts the tips of her hair, sprinkling the bits over his chest and face. He will need something of her to remind him who she is when he comes back to claim her, when she's older and ready for him.

But the hair doesn't seem enough. It's dead matter. She unbuttons the top of her dress. Clamping her lips between her teeth, she pinches the skin over her ribs between two fingers. Using the pinking shears, she cuts a small swatch of her skin. The pain stuns her. She's already lost blood, and for a moment blackness obscures her vision.

When the world rematerializes, she dabs at the wound with the hem of her skirt, which is sopping and muddy and only manages to smear her stomach with bloody dirt. Ignoring the mess, she places the small diamond of translucent skin against Moon Boy's breast. Then she closes the sweater. She turns over the lapel and removes the pin he gave her.

She pauses with the pin in her hand. Why had he given her the pin if he didn't want her? He should have helped her. Someone should have helped her before it got this far. The moment she knew she was gone, she should have been able to go to someone. It wasn't right. Not now. Not yet. She wasn't ready.

"When I'm ready," she says softly, "you come back to me."

But that jawline, those ears. Shouldn't the boy also have something of his father's? No matter what she thinks of *him*, Moon Boy should have something of his father's. She retacks the pin to the sweater. She touches the bundle one last time before again using her hands to shovel dirt on top of it.

"Soil is life giving," she says, patting down the earth until only a small mound remains. She pats the soil, caresses it with her fingertips. She rips a wild tulip from the pond's edge, bulb and all, and pushes it into the dirt at the foot of the mound. "Soil plus seed equals fruit."

Except for the tulip, she doesn't mark the spot. She doesn't need to. She'll always know where her moon boy is. Soon, she vows, she'll return and plant spear thistle to protect him.

"One day, I promise I'll be ready for you, Moon Boy," she whispers. "Like your grandmother's irises, I'll plant you in the right place, and you'll flower. You'll come back to me."

Exhausted now, she cups her hand over the wound on her rib. The bleeding has lessened. The raw tissue gapes and throbs. She rebuttons her dress and hauls her body to her feet. She aches all over. She'd like to sleep for a week. With any luck, her mother will be out shopping with Dean. Not that she believes in luck, she reminds herself. Except bad luck. She hopes Stella hasn't called round to check on her. Maybe, just maybe she'll make it home and into the bathroom without being spotted.

It takes so much of her concentration to move one foot, then the other, that she doesn't look around her, so she doesn't notice the sky clearing, or rabbits venturing from their holes to nibble dewy grass, or four sets of eyes watching her from the reeds as she lurches away from the pond.

Part Two

Leo

"WHAT'S WRONG WITH that girl?" says Will as Sonya stumbles away.

"I don't know, but did you see what she buried?" asks Emelia.

Leo jiggles the hatbox Kirstin brought for their time capsule. He didn't see what the girl buried, and he doesn't know what's wrong with her, but he recognizes her from the church smoker. She's the girl who was nothing. Or something.

Would his father dance around with her now, with her dress dirty, her skin ghostly, and her dark hair stringy and slapping her face as she pawed the ground like some coyote burying its prey? She bounds off through the dead grasses toward the road.

When he first saw her, Leo almost called for her to stop. Before he could yell, Kirstin threw her arm out and crossed her lips with a finger to quiet the group. She pointed to the girl. They all stopped walking, but Leo froze as he had when he'd first seen her at the smoker and had mistaken her for Nora. Had Kirstin recognized the girl from the smoker too? Would she say anything to the others?

No, she's a good egg. She can keep her mouth shut. She hasn't told anyone about kissing at the beach, at least not as far as he knows. He'd been so mixed up that day that kissing Kirstin had been more release than anything.

She's like his sister, she and Emelia both. People have sometimes mistaken Emelia for his sister, but never Kirstin with her snow-blond hair and his dark hair. He's glad it was her idea to stop messing around. The next day she looked at his bandaged hand. He wiggled his fingers to show her he was fine, and she punched him lightly on the shoulder, as any sister would. The punch said they were friends again and the kiss was a blip.

"Let's go see what she buried," Kirstin calls over her shoulder, already on her way toward the mound that the dark-haired girl has just left.

Despite himself, Leo can't help noticing the curve of Kirstin's leg as she high-steps over the tall grasses. She's lovelier than any deer. She's wearing another ugly skirt; the pattern on this one is a mass of squirmy tadpole shapes. Her mustard yellow tights cling to her thighs, which are strong from swimming and tramping.

Like father, like son?

Ashamed, he focuses on stopping her from investigating what the girl buried. He's got a bad feeling. The wild way she looked, something bad lies beneath the ground.

"Leave it alone," he calls.

"Maybe that girl made her own time capsule," says Will, following Kirstin. He holds the shovel he brought for burying their capsule above his head. Emelia follows too, twisting the trash bag Will took from his father's bar to protect the hatbox from disintegration.

"Isn't it bad luck or something to dig up a capsule before you're supposed to?" tries Leo. "Don't you have to wait at least ten years?"

Kirstin and Will ignore his protest, but Emelia gives him a quizzical look. She's been strange lately too, sometimes goofing it up like some cartoon character, all loud and bossy, other times giving him a run for his money on sullenness. It drives him crazy that the only record she wants to listen to these days is *Pet Sounds*. At first Leo couldn't understand how the Beach Boys managed their cool harmonies and tight instrumentation. It both fascinated and annoyed him when he read in a magazine it was done with multi-track tapes. He'd give anything for a chance to make music like that, layered and full. A wall of sound, the magazine called it. Music's never sounded like that before in the history of music. What annoys him is that even the Beach Boys' saddest songs make it seem like happiness is just around the corner. As amazing as "God Only Knows" is with all that multi-tracking, it's really no better than a polka. The dark throb of the Kinks and the Animals, they match Leo's moods better. He'll even take Buffalo Springfield over the Beach Boys. At least they say something. They have cool harmonies too. Sometimes unstringing them can block out his thoughts for a little while.

"C'mon, leave it," he says. He doesn't want anything to do with that girl. He's decided what to believe about his father. Nora was a blip, like Kirstin was a blip. His parents' cease-fire is holding. That's all he cares about.

The moment he woke the morning after the smoker, Leo's apprehension weighed on him like wet clothes. He hadn't heard his parents come home. Had he slept through his parents' argument? His jaw ached as if he'd been clenching his teeth all night, and his cut hand throbbed.

Pulling on his blue jeans, Leo half-hoped his father had told his mother about Nora. The anticipation was grinding his teeth to sawdust. As he put on his T-shirt, he made a deal with himself: If his father had fallen off the wagon last night, if he'd drunk even one drop, Leo would tell his mother about Nora. If not, Leo would keep his trap shut.

He opened his bedroom door and entered the kitchen warily.

His mother was alone, standing at the stove frying eggs and sausages. As far as Leo could tell, no anger tightened her shoulders. She wore the navy wool dress she often wore to church. The accompanying hat and gloves lay on the counter along with the today's church bulletin. He glanced at the clock. It was already 11 a.m. She rarely let him stay in bed so long.

The buttery smell from the eggs made his mouth water.

"Sit," she said without turning around.

He sat at the table and drank the entire glass of orange juice at his place.

She set down a plate with sausages and eggs. "Eat," she said, "sleepy boy."

"Where is he?" Leo ventured.

"Up early this morning," she said. "He'll be gone all day."

"So he—?"

"Bright-eyed and bushy-tailed. Good as gold these days." She ruffled Leo's hair and smiled down at him. "So ease up, okay? You have to appreciate how hard he's trying. And with his new project, he's got a focus. Your father's never so happy as when he's working on a project."

Relieved that his father hadn't hopped off the wagon, that he wouldn't have to tell his mother about Nora, and that he wouldn't have to see Stash for a while, Leo shoveled an egg yolk into his mouth whole. It popped sweet and creamy. It was the best egg he'd ever tasted. He chewed three sausages before asking, "What project?"

"You'll see. He said he'd tell you when he's ready. I won't ruin his surprise." As if it just occurred to her, she asked, "Hey, what happened to you yesterday? Your father was upset you left. Will said you were sick and went home." She placed her wrist against his forehead. "You feel all right this morning? You're not hot."

"I'm okay."

"Probably all that smoke yesterday. I felt a little ill too."

"I'm fine now," he said, wanting it to be true.

His mother was more than fine, happy. Obviously his father hadn't said anything to her about Nora. Well, a deal's a deal. So far his father has remained good as gold. Leo would keep his mouth shut. Besides, why should he have to be the one to ruin his mother's happiness? And if his father never said word to him about Nora either, Leo would take that deal too. They'd all go on as if nothing happened. For his mother's sake.

He finished his breakfast, grabbed his jacket.

"Wait," she said. "What happened to your hand?"

"It's nothing," he said. At least this much he could be truthful about.

"Are you sure? You want me to look at it? You want to tell me how it happened?" She laid her hand on his shoulder, gently holding him there.

"No," he said.

"Really, son, anything you want to tell me? You can tell me anything."

Could he? He wished this were true.

"I know lately . . . Your father—"

He cut her off. "I'm fine, Ma. There's nothing wrong at all. I like you happy though," he said. "So be happy." Without realizing it, he flashed her his smile, his father's smile. He thought she would see right through it.

"You're a good son," she said, smiling back at him.

A glint of surliness rose in him. She's as blind as a bat. Or she's choosing not to see what's right before her. He shrugged her hand off and got up from the table. He put his plate in the sink and said, "I'm going to Will's."

Right now, Leo wishes they were in Will's bedroom listening to music instead of here in the cold wet about to unearth Dark-Hair's secret.

"Let's go to Will's," he says. "I've been working on a new song I want to play for you."

"It's okay, you don't have to look," Emelia says. "I get it. Sometimes it's better to not know." Her tone is kind, almost gentle.

What's with her? Does she think he's a coward? Or has Kirstin told her about their kissing and she pities him for finding out Kirstin doesn't want him that way?

"I want to see as much as you," he lies. He pushes ahead of her, following Will.

They stand over the mound in a circle that reminds Leo of playing ring around the rosy when they were little. *Ashes, ashes, we all fall down.*

"Okay, who's digging?" says Kirstin.

Will looks to Leo, but Leo doesn't move. The girl's handprints are visible in the damp soil surrounding a wilting pink tulip. He glances at his hand and stretches his fingers. The girl's reach is tiny compared to his, which easily manages a five-fret stretch. His father wouldn't really have done something with this small-handed girl, would he? Just because she looks like Nora doesn't mean anything. He was just goofing around with her on stage, hamming it up the way he always does in front of people.

Leo looks to the break in the grasses where the girl ran. She's gone. It was nothing on that stage. He turns back to the mound. Kirstin agreed it was nothing.

"Come on. Someone dig. We won't hurt anything. We'll just look," Kirstin says.

"Fine. Give me the stupid thing," Leo says, snatching the shovel from Will.

Maybe whatever is in the earth will prove this girl has nothing to do with his father besides stupid antics. Heck, his father didn't even drink that beer. He's been good as gold, just as his mother said.

"You don't have to do this, Leo," Emelia says quietly.

"I'm not afraid," he spits back, tossing her the hatbox.

"I didn't say you were," she says. "I just think sometimes it's better not to know things."

"You don't have any idea what you're talking about," he says. "It's always better to know what's what." If things turn out okay, you can relax. He remembers the way the girl stumbled away from the mound. If you know the worst, maybe you can do something to save your family.

"It's probably something stupid anyway," he says, piercing the muddy earth with the tip of the shovel.

"Yeah," says Emelia with a nervous laugh. "Maybe it's a voodoo doll."

"Or money," says Kirstin, rubbing her palms together. Will gives her a cross look, and she adds, "Not that we'd steal it. But if she buried it here, she must know the risk. I mean, it's a public park. Not that we'd steal it. But wouldn't it be neat to find a sack of money?"

The digging takes little effort. In only a few shovelfuls, Leo reveals a bundle of white yarn.

"Stop!" says Kirstin. "Let's use our hands now so we don't ruin whatever it is. That's what they do at archeological sites."

They all kneel around the hole and scoop earth.

"It's a sweater," Emelia says. "Why bury a sweater?"

Leo notes the red letter *A* and recognizes it as the cardigan the girl wore at the smoker.

"Boring," says Kirstin.

"Just a stupid sweater." Leo's so relieved he giggles. "Some stupid guy's stupid letter sweater."

"I bet whatever boy owns this sweater broke up with her," says Emelia. "Left her high and dry. I bet when she buried this, she put a curse on him."

"Ugh, even more boring. I hate when girls get all soppy over some boy," Kirstin says. Her glance shifts quickly to Leo and just as quickly away. "I'm never going to do that. I'm focusing on school, not boys. Let's go find a good place for the time capsule now. This spot's ruined. That girl might come back and take our stuff."

"Wait, I think there's something in it," says Will. He grips the neck of the shovel, sliding the tip beneath the sweater. "Yep, there's something inside." As he lifts the bundle, the sweater falls open.

"Shit," he spits, dropping the shovel. Will's swearing intensifies the shock of the gray creature that looks like it's been dropped from a spaceship. Will usually never swears, but he repeats now, "Shit."

"Shit is right," says Emelia,

"It's a Martian!" says Kirstin.

"It must be fake," Emelia says, leaning over and tapping its rubbery arm. "Is it a doll?"

"Don't touch it!" yells Will.

"It's a *baby*," says Emelia. "Sort of."

"You're right. It looks fake. It's fake, right?" says Kirstin. She leans over it, placing her hand near the mouth and nose. She gets closer and sniffs. She sits back on her heels. "Nope, it's real. Really, really dead too." After a moment she adds, "Poor thing."

Leo hasn't moved. He hasn't taken a breath. He's waiting for his brain to catch up with his pounding heart. The way the girl stood on that stage, daring the men to look at her, daring his father to look. Is this what she wanted them to see?

"She killed it," Emelia says. "That girl killed her baby."

"Maybe not," says Will, his voice tremulous. "Look how small it is. And . . . weird. Maybe it, you know, came out this way. That happened to my mom. It came out too early." They all look at him, and he adds, "A really long time ago."

"Even still, that girl just abandoned him," says Emelia.

"Wow, it's such an odd color," says Kirstin. She leans over the baby again and brushes its cheek. Leo catches her glance at its tiny penis and then away. "The color of the water."

"He's holding flowers," she says. But before anyone can comment, she exclaims, "Wait, what's this?" Perched on her index finger is a colorless swatch of something Leo can't identify. She sniffs it, and for a moment Leo thinks she may actually taste it. Instead, she says, "I think it's skin." It takes a moment to register. When it does, she calls, "Ugh!" and flicks the swatch into the pond and shivers her whole body. "Ugh!"

Leo feels bile rising at the back of his throat. He turns away from the others and vomits into the weeds.

"Are you okay?" says Kirstin as he wipes his mouth. From the look on her face, his vomiting seems to have repulsed her as much as this creature shedding its skin.

"I'm fine," he insists.

"You don't look it," she says.

"I said I'm fine."

But he's not fine. He's shivering. He's never been so cold in his life. He wants to ask Kirstin if she still thinks there wasn't anything between his father and the girl. He wants to run home to ask his father what the fuck is going on.

If it were just Kirstin here with him, he'd tell her everything, and she would help him figure it out. Man, if only they hadn't come to the lake today. They should all be in Will's bedroom listening to the Kinks, or even the Beach Boys, not burying some stupid time capsule. He wants so badly to go back in time, before today, before the church smoker, before he saw his father in that stupid, stupid car with stupid, stupid fucking Nora. Emelia was so damn right. He should never have dug into the earth. He should never have looked. Why did Will have to pull back that sweater and expose the ugliest thing he's ever seen in his life? Even uglier than Nora.

The foul creature is hideous enough, but Leo sees what the others don't, or if they do, they don't understand its meaning.

Attached to the sweater is a circular whole note tie pin. A fat circle on a red background. The same kind his father wears on the collar of his band shirt. He bought a whole bunch of them to give to the members of his band.

"Why would she come here?" Kirstin asks. "Why wouldn't she go to a hospital?"

"Because she's crazy," says Emelia. Leo can't believe it when Emelia drops the hatbox and picks the—thing—up. She cradles it like it's a real baby. "Only crazy mothers abandon their kids."

"I don't think you should do that," says Will. "My mom says you aren't supposed to touch dead birds because of the germs."

"He's not a bird," says Emelia.

"This is worse," says Leo. "Emelia, cover it back up." He can't bear to look at it. He can't bear to think what it has to do with his father.

"What should we do with it?" says Kirstin.

"Cover it up!" insists Leo. "Put it back in the ground."

"Okay, okay," she says.

She spreads the sweater out in the hole so Emelia can place the remains on top of it. Kirstin covers the body but leaves the face showing.

"We should tell someone," says Will. "Our parents or a policeman."

"No way." Leo's voice is firm, even to his own ears. That girl is awful and ugly. She might even be crazy as Emelia said. But she was smart to keep this thing a secret. His mother would kill this girl if she knew.

"Leo's right," Emelia says, her voice as firm as Leo's. "He's ours now. We found him."

"Yeah, but—" says Will.

"We're not dumping him on someone else," Emelia says.

"We're going to rebury him. It's the right thing to do, the *honorable* thing," says Leo. He knows Will may skate the edge of a few rules, but he believes in honor. He always wants to do the right thing. Leo must convince him the right thing is to keep their discovery a secret.

"I don't know," says Will.

"Leo's right. We should rebury him," Kirstin ventures. "Then some archeologist can dig him up later."

Yeah, after he and his parents are long dead. Leo forces himself to smile at Kirstin's good idea.

In the smile she gives him in return, he can't tell if she understands what she's done for him or not. He can't tell if she's recognized the girl or the sweater, but he can tell she's on his side. Whether she knows it or not, she's saving his family.

"Emelia and Kirstin are right," he says. Will always crumbles when faced with a united front. "He's ours now. We've got to give him a proper burial."

"We can put him in the hatbox," says Kirstin. "Like a tiny coffin."

"I suppose," Emelia says. "It will protect him. A little."

"Yeah," Kirstin says in her lecturing voice. "A respectable burial always includes a container. Of course, a sarcophagus would be best, but that's carved out of stone, and I don't see how we could do that. Still, the cardboard on my mom's hatbox is thick; that and the trash bag should preserve him. He'll be like a local Tutankhamen. I read about it for that project we had to do in civics in eighth grade when the tour came through a few years ago." She's warming to her subject. "To properly mummify him, we'd have to remove all moisture from him. Unfortunately, we don't have the right equipment for that." She pauses before adding affectionately, "He's really special. Our own baby king."

"He's not a king," Leo says sharply. His father is the farthest you can get from royalty. "And he's not a mummy."

"No, he's not. Not because he's not a king though. Anyone's a mummy if you mummify them. It's a process, not a ranking," says Kirstin. "But yeah, he won't be a proper mummy without the full process."

"I still think we should tell someone," says Will. "If we don't tell and someone knows we found him and didn't tell anyone, we'll be in trouble too."

"No!" Leo and Emelia say at the same time. To tell or to bury? It's no choice at all.

"C'mon, Will," says Emelia. "He deserves people who care about him. We'll do it together, and it will be something special that's just ours, like Kirstin said. We'll have this secret that binds us together for life."

"Like soldiers," Leo adds.

"Or a family," says Emelia.

"Maybe . . ." Will says.

"Okay, so we're all agreed?" says Kirstin as she lifts the top from the hatbox.

"Agreed," Emelia says, giving Will a pointed look. "Right, Will?"

When Will doesn't respond, Leo goes to him and puts his hand on his shoulder the way his father does when he tries to get Leo to do something by using his man-to-man approach.

"We all have to agree," Leo says. "All for one, you know?"

"Like a family," says Emelia.

"Like a band of brothers," Leo says, looking at Will. He looks to Kirstin, adding, "And sisters."

"I know, we'll swear an oath," says Kirstin. "Do a spit circle."

"Good idea, but only if Will agrees," says Leo, giving Will's shoulder a squeeze. "How about it, Will?"

Will hesitates. Finally he says so softly that Leo has to lean in to hear him, "I guess he's already dead."

"Right," says Leo nearly as softly. "It won't do him any good to have a bunch of grownups poking at him. He's not some Martian, not some science experiment. When you think of it, we're saving him. Other people would only see him as some freak."

"We're protecting him," adds Emelia.

"Yeah, I suppose," says Will. After a moment, he shrugs and nods. "Okay."

"Should we put in our time capsule stuff?" asks Kirstin. "In Egypt they put things in the tomb that the dead will need in the afterlife, things of value that they can give the ferryman taking them over the river Styx."

They all open their school satchels and pull out their time capsule items. They had agreed not to show each other what they'd chosen for the capsule until they were ready to bury it. Although they look with interest at each other's offerings, it no longer feels like a game. Their belongings no longer feel like treasures but offerings.

"Is this stuff any good?" Will says, looking at his Braves booster club card and Kirstin's *Seventeen* magazine with headlines for the articles inside: "How Much Freedom Is Too Much Freedom?" and "Facts about Your Bosom." Emelia lays her 45 record of "Love Me Do" in the empty box.

"I wish I had something better for him," she says.

"It's a good song," assures Kirstin.

Leo drops in a Gibson guitar pick but decides against the *Mad Magazine,* whose cover shows a soldier aiming a rifle at a dopey-looking gorilla. The ape has his finger stuck in the gun's barrel.

"Weirdo," says Kirstin.

"I didn't think we'd be . . . you know," Leo says defensively. "I thought it was going to be just a regular time capsule."

"Yeah," she says.

"Okay, what about our secrets?" says Kirstin.

"I think we should give them to him," says Emelia. "They're a part of us."

She'd been insistent they all seal their secrets inside white envelopes with no names on them. Leo thought about writing about Nora, but even to write her name felt like a risk. Instead, he wrote, *I want to be a rock musician.* His desire looked silly written out like that, a foolish dream, and he'd quickly folded the note and sealed the envelope. Now, as he drops it in the box, he feels more foolish than ever for having believed what he wanted to be true. Better to believe what you fear. Believe the worst. At least then you'll be prepared.

The others drop their envelopes into the box. Then Emelia places the sweatered bundle on top.

"Should I cover his face or not?" she whispers.

They look at each other uncertainly.

"I'll cover it," Leo says. He feels bile rising again as he touches the gritty sweater, but this time he pushes down the urge to vomit. He's got to keep his nerve. "Before we put the top on, I think we should close our eyes and someone should say a prayer."

They all look to Will, the only one whose parents make him go to church every Sunday. He grimaces but says, "Okay, but just the Our Father, and everyone has to join in."

"Close your eyes, or it doesn't count," says Leo.

He makes sure his voice is loud enough for the others to hear. When he's sure their eyes are closed, he removes the tie pin from the sweater and slips it into his back pocket. At least if someone else finds the box, there will be no connection to Stash.

When they've finished with the prayer, Kirstin puts the cover on.

"It's so sad," Kirstin says. "Make the hole deeper. Too deep for an animal to smell. It's the least we can do for him."

Leo nods. This time he welcomes the effort of digging. He'd like to dig to the center of the earth and drop the box in, but he stops after going down another two feet and widening the hole. They place the box in the plastic bag, cinch the end, and tie it off. Leo wedges the container against the muddy sides of the hole. Water is already seeping in, and it splashes his shirt. He doesn't bother to wipe it off. He's going to burn this shirt anyway.

"Everybody has to take a handful of dirt and drop it in," says Kirstin.

"Do they do that in Egypt?" Will asks.

"Well, they do it here. We did it for my grandmother," she says.

Afterwards, Leo lifts the shovel to finish burying the box, but Emelia says, "Wait! We have to give him a name."

The last thing Leo wants is for it to become more real by naming it. He's about to protest when Kirstin says, "I know, let's call him Water Boy because he's blue-gray like the lake today."

Water Boy. It's not a real name. Not the kind of name a brother would have.

"That's okay, I guess," he says.

After Will and Emelia agree to the name too, Leo scoops the wet dirt and drops it on the box. It splatters over the slick plastic of the trash bag. When the hole is filled in, they all step on the grave to flatten the soil.

"Should we mark it with something?" says Will. "Like a headstone?"

"No," says Leo. He doesn't want anything to remind him of what's hiding beneath the crust of a world that feels more unreal than ever. He wants to believe what's under there has no connection to him or to his father, and he wants no evidence, no reminder that it does. A month from now the grass and weeds will be so thick all traces will be gone.

But Emelia has already placed a pink stone the size of his fist at the top of the area and a larger gray one at the bottom. She looks at Leo and says firmly, "He deserves something. We can't just ditch him here. These will do for now. Maybe we can come back later and put something better up."

With her jaw set as it is and with her eyes narrowed, her face has turned hard. He can see there's no changing her mind. If he insists, she may well hurl the gray stone at his head, retrieve it, and place it just where she wants it anyway.

They're just rocks, he assures himself. Out here, who will take any notice of them?

"Now we spit-swear," says Kirstin.

At first, it feels like a childish thing to do, given what they've just buried. But anything so they keep this secret. They stand in a circle and spit into both of their palms. Emelia thrusts her left hand into the circle first. Leo and Kirstin follow. When Will hesitates, a dart of panic shoots through Leo, and he acknowledges that swearing secrets isn't childish at all. Not if the secret is deadly serious.

He bites his lip to keep from yelling at Will, who sometimes digs his feet in when pushed and may yet decide to say no just to be contrary. Give him time, Leo thinks. Eventually Will places his hand over Kirstin's. By this time, Leo's bitten his lip so hard that blood trickles over his tongue. The taste brings a new wave of nausea, but the pain feels good, solid and familiar.

They continue piling their hands in the center of the circle until the last hand lands on top. Usually they all shout, "Swear!" as loudly as they can and reach for the sky. But today they hold each other's hands longer than usual.

"This is a real pact," Leo says into the pause. "This one matters. Everyone understands that, right?"

127

"Of course we do. We keep this secret to ourselves. Everyone ready?" Emelia says. Without waiting for a response, she starts, "One, two, three."

Their shouts are quieter than usual but firm enough that Leo's assured it counts. They will all keep his father's secret, even if they don't know that's what they're doing.

After reaching for the sky with the others, Leo slides his hand into his back pocket. He presses the pointed metal at the tip of the pin, which isn't sharp enough to pierce the calluses he's developed from playing guitar. He rubs the smooth side, using his fingertip to read the raised whole note. Once he asked his father if he could wear this pin to school. His father had said no, not until he was a real member of the band. "Only the full-timers get one. Something for you to work toward," Stash said. "You have to earn it."

What had the girl done to earn it?

The answer to that question makes him feel sick again. When the others are walking away, he turns back and hurls a thick globule of spit at the pink stone and curses the grave of his half-brother, who, after all, might have turned out to be the son his father really wanted.

Emelia

EMELIA SKIPS LUNCH to go to the school's library.

"I'm still deciding about whether to go out for the school paper or the yearbook next year," she says to the gull-faced woman behind the desk. "I want to look at some of the recent yearbooks to help me decide."

It's a dull lie and therefore easy for Emelia to deliver offhandedly. Then again, she's become so practiced at lying by now that the complicated ones are pretty much a snap to tell too. She's figured out the trick to pulling one off is to believe the lie is really the new truth, and sometimes it really *is* the new truth. For example, her mother's new truth is that she's not dead. Emelia's new truth is that she wishes Elisa were.

No, that's not the whole truth and nothing but the truth, as they say on *Dragnet*. As neatly contained as her mother was when she was dead, alive she's a world of possibility. She's the key to Emelia's past. She's the harbinger of Emelia's future. She's confusion made flesh.

Today, though, Emelia's not here about her mother, or maybe she is. Maybe she's here on her mother's behalf.

She's on the trail of the girl at the lake.

In Emelia's mind, the two have become linked. The girl burying her secrets in the earth and vanishing, it was as if Emelia's mother suddenly materialized to abandon her all over again. The difference, though, is this time Emelia was there to watch her do it. Holding Water Boy was like holding herself. And having been taught by her aunts to never, *never* pity yourself, Emelia felt she had free license to pity Water Boy. She allowed herself to weep all night for him. Moaning into her pillow so her aunts wouldn't hear, she wept for the moment Elisa was taken from her, and she wept for the grief she feels at her mother's return. Of course, Elisa didn't get away with it. For what she did, she was sent away, locked up, and brained. This is what bothers Emelia most. It's not fair this girl gets to go scot-free while Emelia's mother was punished so harshly.

The bored librarian accepts Emelia's fib without much interest. "Down that aisle." She points with a grizzled finger. "You'll find a shelf with yearbooks from the past twenty-two years."

Emelia locates the shelf and removes last year's edition. Unless the girl has only recently moved here, she'll be in these pages. Since the day at the lake, Emelia's seen the girl in the hallways, going slowly from class to class, her face expressionless, her books propped on her hip like any other student. No one would guess just by looking at her that she's got a secret even bigger than Emelia's. Except maybe from the eyes. The girl has hollow eyes.

At first, this hollowness made Emelia feel sorry for her, but she's forced those feelings away. She's got to make things as hard on this girl as they've been on Elisa. As hard as they'd be on her, she admits, if more had happened with Theo and Danny. As hard as they'll be if Emelia turns out like her mother.

She opens last year's yearbook, admitting it's a relief to aim her hard feelings at this girl instead of her mother or her aunts. But her relief is tinged with this new understanding that having a baby and being a mother aren't the same things. The way mothers are shown in the magazines Aunt Lou sometimes gets, *Good Housekeeping* and *Family Circle,* or in movies and on television, it makes you think giving birth magically stops you from being who you were before and transforms you into this other thing: a Mother. On television, even monster mothers like Morticia Adams and Lily Munster are good mothers. And in home ec, Mrs. Nardinski promises outright, "You'll see, when you become a mother, you'll be the happiest woman in the world."

But it isn't true. Elisa and this girl show that the magical transformation doesn't always happen. What then?

Then you get locked up. Then you get an ice pick in the brain. In this girl's case, you get, what, nothing? How is that fair? Emelia won't betray the girl's secret. The revelation of one secret might start a chain reaction, and the others could come tumbling out; but someone needs to spell out to Water Boy's mother just how bad it could be for her, that she should count herself lucky.

Paging through the yearbook from last year, Emelia decides she can ignore the senior pictures, unless the girl is stupid enough to have flunked last year and had to repeat. She turns to the juniors and runs her fingers over the faces, first spotting the frizz-haired girl she's seen with her in the halls. Beneath this frizz-haired girl's photo is the name Stella Bronski. She participated in drama club, girls chorus, operetta, music festival, and all of the school plays and revues put on last year, including *Hamlet*, which Emelia admits is pretty impressive.

Emelia finds the girl from the lake in the middle of the class.

Sonya Morrow.

She's a junior in this photo, so a senior now, although the term will be over in a matter of weeks, and she'll be out in the world. As with the other students' black-and-white photos, Sonya Morrow's shows her from the torso up. She wears a shirt with a Peter Pan collar and a smile that reveals a small dimple in her round cheek. Her hair was shorter last year, brushed back from her face with a flip at the end. The way she wears her hair now—straight down past her shoulders with a deep center part—makes her look older, and not just a year older. *Haggard*, thinks Emelia, pulling a word from one of her seventh-grade vocabulary lists.

Besides her hair, her face is leaner now. Surprisingly, she's chestier too. Is that because of Water Boy? There's also a more indefinable difference between the picture and the girl. Emelia can't express it except to say, here she's a girl; the Sonya Morrow walking the hallways is a woman. So some transformation has taken place.

Emelia's mind flashes to Theo and Danny. How old had she looked to them? She glances down at her chest and legs. She's grown taller in the last year and gone up a cup size too. The saddle shoes are a sure giveaway, but in other shoes, her Aunt Lou's navy suede heels maybe, would she look like a little girl playing dress-up, or has her body changed in this same enigmatic way? Maybe it only happen after you've gone all the way with a boy? No, her aunts look like women, but as far as Emelia knows, neither one has ever had a date to Constantino's Supper Club or the movies or anywhere.

She didn't try to fool those boys into thinking she was older, she insists. But she bites her lip when she remembers how she hid her saddle shoes from them.

If the police hadn't interrupted them, how far would she have gone? Danny's tongue in her mouth and Theo's lips moving up her thigh. Would she have let them? No, she insists, stopping her thoughts. She's not Elisa. She's no way like Sonya Morrow. She swallows an uneasy feeling that reminds her of her dreams of falling down the cliff.

She turns her attention back to the yearbook. Sonya looks like any other girl. Under the photo is listed Sonya's participation in the science club, the math club, and the varsity swim team. Strange that she and Stella Bronski are friends. They have nothing in common. Obviously, given the math and science clubs, Sonya Morrow is not a stupid girl. And she must be a good swimmer to have made varsity as a junior. Emelia and the others had gone out for junior varsity swimming last fall. She and Sonya Morrow are almost teammates.

Emelia's affronted by the girl's normalcy and her successes. How dare Sonya be good at swimming? How dare she ever swim again? How dare she ever smile or study or eat ice creams with that frizzed-out Stella Bronski, as Emelia's seen her do in the cafeteria? How dare she conduct experiments in Trippsman's lab and read Shakespeare in Mrs. Gramercy's class? How dare she carry on as if she hadn't thrown away her baby?

Sonya Marrow needs be shown what a narrow escape she had. But how? Emelia considers taking up Will's suggestion of telling someone outside their foursome, a teacher maybe, or the girl's mother. No, as much as she wants Sonya to acknowledge that she's gotten away with something, Emelia can't betray the girl to the people who might lock her away. Those people, the authorities, they're on the other side of some line that was drawn the moment Emelia found out about her mother being alive.

Emelia closes the yearbook and slides it back onto the shelf. She spends the rest of the day considering what to do. She's so preoccupied that she startles when, in geography class, Darlene Schlotzke slides a note onto her desk that reads, *Pass it on to Jenny*.

She passes it forward without reading it. Strange the way people honor the privacy of notes passed in class. A silent understanding circulates with the note that to break the chain of delivery is to break a deal with all the other students in the class. Turning the note over to a teacher is the ultimate betrayal, but just reading someone else's note, you can expect your own to be blasted from the school loudspeaker during morning announcements. It pleases Emelia, the fairness of this agreement, and in this pleasure she finds her solution.

By the time class is over, the idea is fixed.

Anonymous. Not physically harmful. A secret kept among them. Just enough to let Sonya know she hasn't gotten away scot-free.

The trick will be to get Leo, Kirstin, and Will to agree to her plan. Well, she'll make sure to have everything in place before she brings it to them.

After her last class of the day, Emelia rushes out of the room, down a flight of stairs, and into the science lab. There she is, Sonya, coming out of the lab with Stella Bronski.

"Hello, Emelia." Mr. Trippsman is suddenly at her side. "You look very serious. Do you need something from me? You want to talk about your last test grade?"

Emelia had done poorly. It's been hard to concentrate since her birthday, and science has never been her strongest subject. But if she doesn't escape her teacher and get a move on, she's going to lose Sonya.

"I just wanted to let you know I'll do better on the next one. Thanks, Mr. Trippsman. I've got to go," she calls, jogging down the hallway in the direction Sonya and Stella have gone.

She locates the two of them in the seniors locker area. Standing across the hall and five lockers down, she pretends to study announcements on a bulletin board as the two girls switch books and tablets and put on jackets, chatting the whole time, although admittedly Stella does most of the talking. Sonya's gaze pretty much sticks to her chunky Mary Janes, whose bright red color and big round buckle Emelia can't help admiring. She glances at her saddle shoes, and her anger at Sonya flares. How dare she wear such cool shoes? Why is she allowed to think about clothing at all as if she's some regular girl?

Sonya and Stella part ways down the hallway. Stella goes through the auditorium door that leads to the theater. Emelia follows Sonya through the school's front doors. Keeping a half-block between them, Emelia trails Sonya, hoping to find out where she lives so they can deliver their notes to her there without risking them falling into the wrong hands at school.

Instead of going home though, Sonya walks to the grade school five blocks away. On the playground, kids are jumping rope and playing tag and four square in small groups. Emelia hangs back, pretending to watch a game of hopscotch. In the lower field, boys play a pickup game of baseball, some outfielders with gloves and some without. Sonya grasps the chain-link fence and calls to a towheaded boy, who looks to be about six years old, playing alone on the swings. He stands on the canvas seat, occupied with a finger in his nose.

"Dean!" Sonya calls.

The boy briefly looks Sonya's way but then ignores her except to remove his finger. He bends his knees to start the swing swaying.

"C'mon, Dean, we have to go," Sonya says.

Her tone is sharp, but the boy still doesn't obey her. He bends his knees more deeply, swinging himself so high he's almost parallel to the ground. Emelia and Sonya watch the boy for a while. As if gearing up for the fight the boy will put up, Sonya grasps the fence harder.

Finally she calls, "Okay, fine, Deanie-Beanie. But Dad's coming home early today. He'll be mad if we aren't already there, but I'll tell him you didn't come when I called because you had to swing more."

Emelia shakes her head and sucks her tongue. Surely this is lie. Something to get the boy to obey. She bets lies slip off Sonya's tongue like shortening across a hot pan.

The ruse works though. At the height of the swing's arc, the boy leaps off the seat, his small body suspended in air before landing hard in the dirt and rolling into a ball. He pops up from the ground, stretches his finger and thumb into a gun, and pretend shoots Sonya, his mouth erupting with *pshew pshew* sounds for bullets. He shoots her the whole time he trots to her side. Without a word, Sonya lays her hand on her brother's head and ruffles his hair.

As they pass her, Emelia hears Sonya say, "C'mon, curious boy."

"Curious," he repeats, then asks gravely, "You won't really tell Dad, will you?"

"No, I won't tell. We don't tattle on each other, do we?" She places her hand on his shoulder. "You're such a curious boy, though, I should call you cryptic."

"Cryptic!" he squeals, jumping up to touch a maple branch overhanging the sidewalk.

Emelia finds herself smiling as they move up the block and out of earshot. Sonya loves her brother. She isn't a complete monster.

She again follows them, taking care not to let the boy notice her. As they turn the corner, the girl's heel slips out of one of her cool red shoes, and she stumbles a bit, sliding her foot back into the shoe.

Emelia's anger flares again. Serves her right. Does Sonya think that dressing well and being nice to her brother make up for what she did to Water Boy? Aren't her aunts nice to her most of the time? Does that make up for them lying to her for her whole life?

Sonya rights herself. Dean grasps her hand as if to keep her from falling again. Watching the boy gives Emelia another idea, a better idea than giving the notes to Sonya at school or at home. Dean is the perfect reminder of what Sonya threw away.

At the next corner, Emelia watches the small and tall figures continue up the block. She turns toward the bakery, satisfied she has a clear course of action. Tonight she'll tell the others of her plan.

After dinner, she meets the others in Will's bedroom. The room has two twin beds, so Will can have a friend stay over, which Leo often does, or did. Emelia's not sure if he still sleeps over much. Emelia isn't sure why, but unlike girls, after a certain age, boys become too old for sleepovers unless they take place in the woods in tents. So the boys haven't mentioned sleepovers lately, but that doesn't mean they haven't happened. This year they've all become, if not more secretive like her, certainly more private, even before Water Boy.

Ever since finding Water Boy though, fields of silence have opened up among them. Leo most of all has become terse, grunting more than talking, making cutting remarks when he does talk, and generally acting as skittish as a stray cat about almost every subject, but especially about Water Boy. The only thing that makes Leo more peevish than Water Boy is the mention of his father.

As far as Emelia can tell, Kirstin and Will remain mildly interested in Water Boy. As if he were one of the baby dolls Kirstin played with until she was far too old, in Emelia's opinion, Kirstin makes up stories about Water Boy, which, despite herself, Emelia enjoys hearing. She even throws in a few details of her own to make them better. The one Emelia likes best is where Sonya is a mermaid who believes Water Boy will have gills like her and be able to breathe underwater. So she swims to the middle of the lake to give birth to him. When he turns out to be human, she has only one minute to get him back to shore before his lungs fill with water. She swims desperately, but the evil seaweed sprite grabs her ankle, trying to keep the boy for himself. By the time she frees herself, it's too late. Water Boy dies just beyond the breakwater. Although Sonya wants him to remain in the water with her, she understands he needs to be buried in the ground because he was of the earth, and maybe, just maybe, he will grow into a beautiful tree and look out over the water where Sonya still swims.

It's a pretty story and one Emelia can't help liking it. But it has nothing to do with the real Sonya, who has legs, not fins, and no evil seaweed sprite as an excuse for abandoning Water Boy.

Will rarely adds to the stories, but he listens, keeping a keen eye out for discrepancies in the details, interjecting when Kirstin gets too loose with facts. For example, when she tried to suggest something about the boy being born under the full moon at high tide, Will gave them an excruciatingly detailed description of a tide versus a seiche, which Emelia understood to mean Lake Michigan is a giant sloshing bowl of water. She reminds herself to get Will to help her study for Trippsman's next test.

Only Leo seems as bothered by Sonya and Water Boy as she is but in a different way. Whenever Kirstin starts one of her stories, Leo's shoulders tense, and he drills his thighs with his fingertips, a practice he claims strengthens his hands for guitar. But Emelia can tell the action is more like slitting the top of a piecrust to let steam escape so the filling won't explode.

So she will have to be careful about how she presents her plan to him. Leo is their group's unofficial leader. He wouldn't admit it, but they usually end up doing whatever Leo wants, even if they've spent hours debating the options. If she can convince him, she's pretty sure the other two will join in.

Emelia peels off her saddle shoes and flops onto the spare bed. The bedspread releases a woody smell she used to associate only with Will and Leo, but which now also reminds her of Theo and Danny. She covers her cheeks with her palms, hoping no one has noticed her flushing at the thought of them. Only at night in bed does she allow herself to relive those moments in the truck. Then her whole body flushes. Under the blanket of darkness and her mother's bedspread, her hand slides down her belly, and she lets herself explore what might have happened and how good it would have felt.

But now, Leo's occupied with putting a stack of albums on Will's record player. Kirstin and Will rework a conjugation they both got wrong on their Latin exam. By the time they've found their common mistake, the Zombies are playing, and Leo has dropped to the floor and leans against Will's bed reading the liner notes on the album cover.

"Haven't you read that album cover about four thousand times already?" she says, jostling Leo's leg with her socked foot.

"Your feet stink," he says. "I thought girls' feet weren't supposed to smell."

"Who told you that?" says Kirstin. "Girls sweat just like boys."

"No, they don't," Will says. "My mom told me only pigs sweat. Men perspire, and women glow."

"That's ridiculous," says Kirstin.

"Yeah," says Emelia. "You should see Aunt Genny in the kitchen in summer. She gets soaked. Then she leans over and sweats right into the dough. Saves money on salt, she says."

"Really?" says Kirstin. "That's disgusting."

"No, not really," snaps Leo without taking his gaze from the album cover. "She's exaggerating, Kirstin. Don't be such a square drip."

Obviously hurt by Leo's comment, Kirstin looks at her Latin book, but her gaze keeps sliding to Leo. Oh, Emelia thinks and almost says, but she catches herself before speaking aloud. Kirstin likes Leo, she realizes. Has Leo noticed? He doesn't seem to notice much outside of music these days.

He picks up the guitar he always brings over these days when they hang out. He fingerpicks the notes of "Woman," rocking his head in time to the beat, seemingly oblivious to Kirstin, oblivious to them all. As he gets deeper into the song, his playing takes on such intensity, Kirstin and Will look up from their textbooks and watch him. His fingering is fast but precise. He must be practicing a lot because his playing used to be muddy and he'd fluff notes sometimes. He doesn't get a note wrong, and when the song's over, they exchange looks and then clap enthusiastically. Emelia pats him on the shoulder. He smiles in a sheepish way that suggests he's both embarrassed and pleased. She realizes it's the first time she's seen him smile since that day at the lake.

"For the record, I don't think a drip can be square," Will says after their clapping dies out. "Although it's an interesting concept. Maybe if it's frozen, like a tiny ice cube."

Now or never, before Kirstin and Will go back to studying. She sits up abruptly and takes the guitar from Leo's hands.

"Hey," he says, reaching for it.

"I found out her name," she says, holding the guitar beyond his reach. She sets it on the opposite side of the bed so he won't be tempted to retreat back into playing until they've agreed to go along with her plan.

"Whose name?" says Kirstin.

"Dark-Hair. The girl from the lake. Water Boy's, um, I guess mother."

The last word trips her up. After seeing Sonya with her little brother, it feels strange to call her a mother. She's older, sure, but not like Aunt Genny or Aunt Lou. They're a different kind of grown woman. They run a business and pay bills and boss Emelia around with an authority that runs through them like blood. How can Sonya be a woman, a mother even, but not be a grownup?

"So what's her name?" says Kirstin.

She hesitates. Should she go through with it? She could still let Sonya off the hook.

"Who cares?" says Leo. He snatches up the Zombies album cover. He frowns at the liner notes, so she can tell he isn't really reading. "What's the point of going on and on about it? I'm sick of all these phony stories. You guys talk about that stupid girl like she's some fairy-tale princess. Well, she's not. So just shut up already."

"Leo," Kirstin says, "what's wrong with you?"

"Listen to me," insists Emelia, annoyed now because Leo is right. Turning Sonya into some fairy-tale princess the way Kirstin has done isn't right. But neither is forgetting about what they saw and letting her get away with abandoning Water Boy.

"Her name's Sonya Morrow. She's a senior," Emelia pushes on. "She's in the science club, or she was last year."

"Really, science club?" says Kirstin, alarmed. "I was going to join that next year."

"How do you know her name?" says Will.

"I looked her up in last year's yearbook."

"Why?" says Leo, scowling at her. "Why did you have to look her up?"

"I keep seeing her in the halls at school. Don't you? Doesn't it bother you?"

"I thought I saw her too," says Will. "But I wasn't sure. She looks so different than that day at the lake."

"Yeah," says Emelia, "you're right. She walks around like she's just some regular student. Like nothing ever happened at all. It makes me sick. Doesn't it make you sick? Don't you think she needs to know that she hasn't gotten away scot-free? Someone saw what she did. Someone knows. No matter where she goes, what she does, we'll always know."

The others look at her without speaking, the notes of "What More Can I Do?" not managing to fill their silence.

"Listen, I'm not saying we should tell on her or anything," she goes on. "But we have to do something."

"No, we don't," says Leo. "It's none of our business. She's just some girl. She has no connection to us whatsoever. None."

"How can you say that? *We* saw her," she says. "*We* touched Water Boy. *We* buried him."

"Exactly," Leo says. "He's buried. Gone."

Kirstin stands up from the desk and sprawls over the bottom of the bed. She touches Emelia on the knee.

"Leo's right," she says gently. "Water Boy is gone."

"You would agree with him," Emelia mumbles.

"What would we do anyway? If we were going to tell someone, we should have done it right away," says Will. "Exactly as I said at the time, if you'll remember. Now it's too late. Now *we'd* get in trouble for not telling someone right away."

"Who says we have to tell anyone?" Emelia says. "We can do it ourselves."

"Do what?" says Leo.

"I have a plan," says Emelia. "It will be easy."

As she explains, she eases herself onto the carpet between the beds. She makes her voice quieter until she's nearly whispering so

140

they have to move closer to her. Without realizing it, they've joined her in a tight huddle between the two beds. The Zombies album finishes. *Animal Tracks* drops, but Emelia barely notices, concentrated as she is on their reactions, which shift from intrigued to alarmed to intrigued again.

"I don't know," Kirstin says softly when Emelia finishes.

"She's right," says Will. "It's a good plan, but maybe Leo's right. We should just forget about it. It's almost summer vacation. We won't even have to see her at school then."

To her surprise, Leo says, "No, Emelia has a good plan, and she's right. That girl has got to know there are consequences."

When his lips twist into a wry, not-quite smile, she sees something's edged in, but she's not sure what. Does it matter as long as he agrees with her?

"Maybe we really can still make everything all right," Leo says, nodding.

She could kiss him. It doesn't matter why. Where Leo goes, the others will follow.

"Okay," says Kirstin, hesitation drawing the word out. "But we all have to agree."

They look at Will, who shrugs and says, "As long as no adults find out. I don't want to get in trouble. I can't do anything to mess up my chances at college. West Point won't let in a troublemaker."

They all look at him surprised.

"My dad's been talking about it for a while. He says that it's better to be an officer than a grunt. Yesterday I told him I'd think about going."

So they all really do have secrets, thinks Emelia.

"Well, if we *all* keep our mouths shut, no one has to find out," says Leo.

"So we agree?"

Emelia wants to kiss each of their nodding heads. When Leo says, "Spit?" she's the first to wet her hand.

Sonya

WORDS HIT SONYA like molten grains of sand. *Van der Waals bonding. Bond polarity.* Each syllable burns a little. The whole world feels like a desert. Her tongue is sandpaper. Her feet sink when she walks. She's sinking now just sitting in chemistry class.

"Let me blow your mind," says Mr. Trippsman, "with ionic bonding."

It's his first year teaching at the school. He's one of a recent wave of young teachers who have replaced a wave of retiring teachers: Miss Norris teaches art; Mr. O'Lynn teaches French and Latin; Mr. Anderson teaches history and government, and his support for the kids wearing antiwar T-shirts has upset a lot of parents. Many parents also disapprove of the casualness the new teachers have brought to the classroom—the men teachers don't wear ties, the lady teachers wear skirts that hit above the knees. But more kids have gotten scholarships to college as Sonya has, so the rules have loosened. The young teachers are popular with the students too. Behind his back, some of the girls call Trippsman dreamy. To his face, the science boys call him Trippy. He laughs good-naturedly at the nickname. At the beginning of the year, Sonya liked that he didn't just pay attention to the boys in the class. He called her smart. He used to think the world of her. He put her at the top of the list for her scholarship.

"A full ride," he said when she showed him the letter from the university in February, an early offer, so she wouldn't consider going elsewhere. "Good girl!"

What does he think when he sees her now? What do they all think?

It feels like everybody knows. Her expanding body before. And now her deflation.

Chemistry used to be so liquid and clean. Now everything is muddy. Sandy, muddy sludge. Her grades are plummeting. If she can't focus, she'll be lucky to graduate. Goodbye, scholarship. Goodbye, future. After all she's done.

She dips her head, hoping to make herself invisible. If he calls on her, she may atom bomb dive under her desk. She studies her fingers. The swelling has disappeared. They look like her hands again.

After the lake, after Moon Boy, it's as if a spell cast upon her has been broken. Her whole body has transformed back into one that looks like hers again. But it's not. Her body will never be hers. The oversized letterman sweater is gone and buried, along with the rich across-town boy, who she claims has broken up with her.

Wilting with sympathy for her jilted daughter, her mother has let Sonya cry without question. She's taken Sonya shopping for new clothes to cheer her up, saying, "We'll make you so pretty, boys will be falling at your feet." Sonya managed to hold in the guffaw she felt bubbling inside of her at that thought, afraid it would erupt into hysterical laughter. Pretty? Her? Impossible. She's soiled as dirt.

"Besides," her mother had continued, "none of those old clothes fit you anymore. You must have had some kind of growth spurt. You're not taller, but you've thinned out so. You're getting a real nice figure, hon. Boys love a nice figure. Don't you worry. There'll be others."

"A spurt," Sonya said. "Yes, a spurt." She touched the gauze taped over the wound on her ribs.

Sonya took the new clothes on offer because refusing them would take more explanation than accepting them. She managed keep her mother out of the changing room as she tried on styles she would never have chosen for herself before. Before, Sonya liked skirts and blouses in soft pinks and blues, polka dots and gentle patterns. Now she wears dresses with straight lines and thick slashes of hard color—charcoal, basalt, siren red. The blocks of color cut her body at sharp angles, scribbling out that other person, drawing a new one in her place. Or so she'd hoped.

But the new clothes aren't working. Foolish to have thought they would draw a line before Moon Boy and after, allowing her to move on.

Afterward, she stayed home for three days, claiming stomach flu, which was easy enough because the pennyroyal kept her throwing up the whole next day. She's hardly been able to eat since then. Sick as she was, she can't bear to think where she'd be now if that librarian hadn't helped her. She feels something almost like relief. Relief soiled by grief. If only it hadn't gotten so far. Maybe if she'd had someone to help her earlier or if she'd figured out what to do sooner, she wouldn't still feel swaddled in steel wool.

When she returned to school, Mrs. Nardinski had looked kindly but knowingly and whispered, "Are your lady troubles better, hon?" Her gym teacher, Miss Potts, hadn't given her any guff when she handed over the note from her mother, excusing her from class. But the teacher gave Sonya's belly a long look. Unable to withstand the scrutiny, Sonya had hidden her stomach with her hand. Nodding, Miss Potts pointed to the bleachers and said, "You'll be back to yourself soon."

That nod was knowing, too knowing, and Sonya hunched on the bleachers chewing her fingernails raw. Who knows? Who doesn't? Every look seemed an accusation. Then actual accusations arrived.

Keeping her eyes down so Trippsman won't notice, she reaches into her purse and fingers the slips of paper. Like her soul, she doesn't need to see them to know their ugliness. The first note had disturbed her: *Baby, baby, quiet and sweet. Close your lips, feel your heartbeat.*

The next one had frightened her: *You can't bury your sins.*

Yesterday's rocked her so she's barely functioning: *Infanticide: the act of killing an infant.*

When a finger taps her shoulder, she startles, retracting her hand as if the notes have grown thorns. She nearly does bomb-dive under the desk. She grasps her desktop and manages to stay in her seat, but she can't inhale, can't exhale. If she does, the whole world may disintegrate. She concentrates her gaze on the periodic table tacked to the wall. We're all just elements. The human body is mostly water. Moon Boy is in the earth. Dust to dust. Elements to elements.

After a moment, she tries a breath, then another. When the finger taps her shoulder again, she quarter-turns to find a folded piece of paper hidden behind Julie Stremski's palm, and she gasps. "No!"

She shakes her head, forcing herself to stifle the scream pressing at her throat.

Julie shakes the note insistently.

"Take it," she whispers.

Julie's hot breath against Sonya's neck smells of dill pickle.

Sonya stares at the white paper, her fingers welded to her desk. Julie sighs heavily, her dilly breath brushing Sonya's ear before she drops the note. The white paper lands quiet as a petal on Sonya's skirt. She cringes. It's an atom bomb ready to burn her into a shadow.

"Well, go on," dilly Julie whispers. "Open it, Eve."

Sonya flinches. *Eve* has become her new nickname at school. No one said why, so she had to ask Stella. At first Stella shrugged and said, "They're stupid drips. Don't listen to them."

"Eve from the bible?" Sonya had guessed. The most infamous of all the fallen women. All her classmates must know.

Eventually Sonya coaxed out of Stella that some girls, Julie's set, are calling her Eve after the movie *Three Faces of Eve*, which had played at the Royale a few weeks ago as part of a Joanne Woodward film festival. Eve White. Eve Dark. So these girls can see the change, the new ugliness. Why shouldn't they? Sonya sees it every time she looks at her hands. What they did. They can't be her hands. Her body, it looks like hers, but what it did. It won't ever be the same.

Sonya still hasn't touched the note on her lap. Wriggling with impatience, Julie spit-whispers in her ear, "Open it!"

Woozy, as if shaken from a dead sleep by Julie's voice, Sonya picks up the note. Unfolding it, she finds spiders sprawled on the page. No, that's just black ink. Stella's handwriting: *Meet me on the bleachers after school.*

Sonya huffs her relief. She should have known this wasn't one of the ugly notes. All of those have been on colored paper and given to her by Dean, who, thank God, can't read yet. Poor kid, slow for his age. He still writes some of his letters backwards. When she asked her little brother who gave him the first note, all he could tell her was, "A girl with sand hair. She said give it to you. She was pretty." Then it was, "A boy with squiggle hair." Yesterday, when all he could tell her about who handed him the worst note yet was, "A boy with dirt hair," she nearly shook him senseless.

"Was it a girl or a woman who gave you the first note?" she prodded Dean, her fingers pressing into his narrow shoulders. "A boy or a man who gave you this one?"

Was it *him*? Why would he send her these notes? Was the girl part of Julie's set? If so, who was the boy? It doesn't make sense. None of it makes any sense.

Dean had started crying, and Sonya had come to her senses. She released his shoulders and rubbed his arms. "Okay, okay, Deanie-Beanie, it's okay," she said, kneeling down to embrace him. "But if someone hands you another note, ask the person's name, okay?"

He nodded and wiped his nose on her shirt.

Now she refolds Stella's note, quarter-turns the other direction, and nods yes to Stella, indicating she'll meet her at the bleachers. Stella is her true friend. Stella will tell her everything will be okay. If Sonya can just hold on, maybe what she told Dean, and what Stella will tell her at the bleachers, can be true. Maybe it will be okay. If only she can find herself again. She stares hard at the periodic table. Element to element.

She's got to graduate. She's got to keep the scholarship. She owes it to Moon Boy.

She hears Trippsman say, "Okay, covalent bonding? Anyone?"

She straightens her new body in her desk. This one she knows. She pushes her hand into the air. Element to element. She will prove to him she's still smart.

"Atoms share electrons," she says, reflexively reaching for her lapel pin, which is no longer there. "Oxygen, for example, forms two bonds."

"Usually, not always," he corrects, his voice cutting rather than encouraging.

He no longer thinks the world of her.

At the bell, students leap from their desks faster than if the bomb siren had actually sounded. They scramble out the door. She lingers as she used to do often. He half-sits at his desk, shuffling papers to avoid looking at her. She's lost his favor.

When the last student is in the hallway, he finally addresses her. "You're failing. You're going to lose your scholarship. You *should* lose your scholarship. I should have known better than to put a girl forward for it. It's the only one offered for next year. There were *three* boys nearly as good as you. But no, I had to see if the fish could ride a bicycle." He slaps his desktop, and she jumps. "I wanted to believe you could do it, that a girl could handle it. We could have been the first. But I was wrong, wasn't I?"

"I know I'm behind," she says.

"You used to be so keen," he says, genuinely puzzled.

She waits for him tell her he knows why she's failing.

You can't bury your sins. The most recent note's message.

"Such a disappointment," he says regretfully. "And I went and put my efforts behind you. I took an interest. It's my own fault, really. I should never have let you get this far when it's clear, you aren't scholarship material. College is a lot of work. And a girl will have to work twice as hard to prove herself." He sighs. "I should have seen you weren't up to it. Maybe you aren't college material at all."

After all she has done to be college material, she can't lose this chance. She owes it to Moon Boy. She owes it to her old self.

"I can make it up. There's still time," she says firmly. "I can do it."

"Can you?" he says. "Because I went out on a limb for you."

"You used to think I was smart. That I was —"

"You're different now. Bill Clempson, he's best now. You know it's true, and I'm not doing you any favors letting you believe you're better than you really are."

She clenches her books to her chest to keep from throwing them across the room or at him. The door is open and anyone could see. Dark Eve. She won't give them the satisfaction of witnessing her humiliation.

"I'm smarter than Bill Clempson," she struggles to say. "You know I am."

"You used to be. I should have known though. Girls, once they mature, they lose their focus. I suppose that's why they've never given the award to a girl." He looks at her wistfully, as if he wishes this weren't true. "I should tell them to give it to Bill." He rubs his hands over his face. "Ah . . . maybe."

"That's not fair," she says softly. "I've given . . . I've given *up*—"

Before she can protest further, Mr. Gold, the vice principal, appears in the doorway. "Some freshmen are in the lab rolling mercury over the tables like billiard balls. Please attend to them, John, before they poison themselves and us."

"Right away," he says, nodding. At the door, without looking at her, he says, "One can't be soft-hearted when it comes to science."

"What does that mean?" she calls after him. When he doesn't answer, she says to the empty room, "It's not fair."

Alone with the formula for ionic bonding on the board, the names she used to recite as a litany come to her: *Marie Curie, Marie Joliot-Curie, Gerti Cori, Maria Goeppert-Mayer, Dorothy Crowfoot Hodgkins*. They hadn't lost their focus. They'd won prizes.

For them, for Moon Boy, for her old self, she has to find her focus.

If only she didn't feel as if she were trudging through sludge.

She hauls the body she now has to the bleachers to meet Stella. The afternoon is warm and sunny. Heat rises from the freshly cut grass on the football field, sending the green scent of spring into the air. Dry clay puffs around her ankles as she crosses the track that circles the field. She dodges the lithe bodies that swish through the white lines of the painted lanes. Climbing the bleacher steps, her new body's legs seem to work fine. But the new body's arms ache from carrying the schoolbooks she's hardly been reading lately.

She needs to get to work, but what's the point of studying if her scholarship gets pulled? What was the point of any of it? Bill Clempson? She'd been his lab partner in natural sciences freshman year. He'd shredded their gladiola flower during dissection. She'd re-dissected the flower outside of class. When he saw, Bill thanked her and called her a pal, and when it came time for grading, he grinned at Mr. Lawson and accepted praise for her work. He shared in the A she earned them without a second thought, and she hadn't said a word. Why hadn't she spoken up? It's not fair. It's not right.

Stella sprawls over a bleacher seat halfway up the stands, her skirt hiked up to her thighs, her knee socks rolled down to her ankles, her skin the fish white of winter. Even at rest, her calf and thigh muscles are sharply defined from the dance classes and early-morning runs she takes to improve her breath for singing. Eyes closed, she's pointed her face to the sky to catch the sun. Her halo of curls shivers like wings as she sings a Petula Clark song about going downtown where you'll be fine and happy again.

"Okay, let's go then," Sonya says.

Stella opens her eyes and lifts herself onto her elbow. "About time. I've been waiting for ages. What'd ol' Trippy-man want?"

Sonya shrugs. "Oh, you know, I need to do better." She can't tell Stella about the scholarship maybe going to Bill Clempson. If she does, Stella will want to know why Sonya's slacked off. Sonya feels her secrets welling—Moon Boy, the notes, now her scholarship. She looks to the blinding sun and blinks them back.

"He's so creepy," Stella says. "I always think he's staring at my chest and seeing test tubes. Did you hear he's leaving next year? He got some big fellowship to go to doctor school in California."

"California?" Maybe she should go to California, surf all day, slide into the water, and transmutate into a dolphin, into White Eve.

"Anyway, I'm hardly passing either. But who cares about that class anyway, right?" Stella wriggles back into her sun-catching position. "I'm going to be a singer, not a doctor." She sits back up quickly. "Not that you don't care. You could, Sonya, be a doctor, I mean. There are women doctors, aren't there? Well, maybe you'll be the first one. If anyone can do it, you can. Especially now that—" She lets the words drop like stones.

"Now that . . . what?" Sonya pushes.

Now that you won't have to take care of a baby.

She wants Stella to finally say it. She wants somebody to say it outright and clear the vapor and make reality solid. Even the ugly notes haven't said it outright.

"You *know*," Stella says, looking at her hard, her glance grazing the torso of Sonya's new body.

Say it, say it, Sonya pleads.

"Now that . . . oh, nothing," Stella says. "Nothing to worry about at all now." She tilts her head to the sky and sings the Animals' song about getting out. All the songs say there are better places. If only this were true.

The world feels so inconsequential. Moon Boy is gone. Her scholarship is slipping away. She feels the two mingle in her mind. She can't catch her breath. "Oxygen," she whispers, feeling the air on her lips but not hearing the sound. She grasps the bleachers' steel railing to steady herself.

Marie Curie. Element to element.

She owes it to them all.

She forces life into her new body and sings along with Stella. "Hey, you want to do something this weekend? Go to the movies? Go downtown? Or we could really get out of here, take the train to Chicago."

"I have the *play* this weekend." Stella looks at Sonya indignantly. "Jeez, don't you ever think about anyone but you? I've been rehearsing for a month." After a moment she says, "Sorry. I'm nervous about the solo. It's a really hard song. Just me on stage.

All eyes on me." She sticks the tip of her thumb between her lips and works her teeth on the nail. When she realizes what she's doing, she pulls her hand down and tucks it beneath her thigh. "You'll come, won't you? Please, please, please."

"Of course," Sonya says, ashamed. She had forgotten about the play. She can't lose Stella too. Stella's all she has left. Sonya feels like such a bad friend, such a bad person. Dark Eve. She forces her new body to laugh lightly. "I'll be there. Front row. You're going to be great, La. You know you have the best voice in the whole school. In the whole world."

Stella looks at her gratefully and says, "Thanks. I was a pill before. You're a real friend. You know, you can tell me anything." She arches her eyebrows for emphasis. *"Anything."*

"Thanks," says Sonya, "I'm going to walk home now, okay? I have homework."

Leaving Stella to her dress rehearsal, Sonya walks past Dean's school, a red-brick building with huge cracks down the facade. A few little kids flip on the monkey bars and swing on the swings, but there's no sign of Dean, who is grounded again and has to go right home after school. He said the people giving him the notes had found him on the playground. If only she could see their faces, she might remember seeing them at the lake. She remembers the oddest details about that day.

She remembers the feel of dry grass like straw against her bare back, fresh blood the color of the coleus leaf smearing her thighs. The little creature that came out of her glowed the color of the lake on a stormy day. He never got pink like a real baby. He stayed the color of a sky about to rain.

Scissoring the umbilical cord felt like splicing sapling branches.

The lake water was so cold, it nearly knocked her out as it washed them both clean and numbed her pain.

Moon Boy had *his* jawline, *his* ears and hair, and toes like blue pearls.

Moon Boy had her lips.

She remembers the rush of the wind and the smashing waves. There were no human sounds, not from her own mouth, not from Moon Boy's. This she knows: The note with the word *infanticide* is wrong. She didn't kill him, her little moondrop fallen from the sky. He never moved. He never opened his eyes.

On that day, she sat in the high, dead weeds at the foot of the cliffs, shivering, waiting for Moon Boy to move, to make a sound, to do something. She held him to her breast the way she'd seen her mother do with Dean when he was a baby. She sang to Moon Boy.

All for nothing.

She took him to the place where she took Dean to play. There the earth was soft, warmed enough by the sun to be marshy.

The note writers couldn't have stumbled upon that tulip and known. A tulip is no giveaway. So how do they know?

They must have seen her.

Grasping the chain-link fence surrounding the playground of Dean's school, she closes her eyes and concentrates. She presses the gauze at her rib, her eyes rolling up at the pain. She didn't know she would recover much faster from pushing Moon Boy out of her body than from the wound she scissored into her side. It's become infected. As she cares for the cut, dabbing on mercurochrome and changing its bandage, she thinks of pressing her flesh against the flesh of her Moon Boy.

She had looked around to see if anyone was watching her cut herself and plant Moon Boy in the ground. Hadn't she? She must have looked, but she hadn't seen a soul.

She hauls her new body home from the playground, dodging her mother, who is in the utility room folding laundry. Not today, she thinks. Not now. She can't bear to see her mother's earnest, inquiring face. She rushes past the door.

In her bedroom, she drops her books onto her desk. She sits on the bed and unsnaps her purse. She grasps the notes, tosses aside her purse, and without rereading the words, opens the door to her closet. She pushes aside the old-body clothes and the new-body clothes, some of which still have tags dangling from them. She kicks away the shoes neatly lined up in pairs and sits down in the dust on the oak floor, shimmying toward the back corner of the closet. Whether her father or some long-ago builder never bothered to cover the space with drywall, she doesn't know, but ever since she was Dean's age, she's used the two-by-one-foot space to store the shoebox that holds her treasures: her Girl Scout badges, a four-leaf clover she found in the park, the tag from their old dog Rumpus, who'd slipped the collar and run away. More recently she included the cork from the bottle of wine they shared. After that day, she put in a button from Moon Boy's shroud sweater. The picture of *him* though, that she's stashed elsewhere. She used to look at it when she needed to see his eyes. She hasn't looked at it in a long time. Should she put it in this box? Was he a treasure? Something to remember or something to forget?

She reaches into the opening and pulls out the box. She lifts the lid and pushes the three notes to the bottom. As much as she'd like to throw them away, they are clues—to what, she doesn't yet understand. She returns the cover to the box fast, as if the notes are bees trying to escape a jar. She places the box back in its hiding spot and props her rain boots in front of the opening. With no further business, she should get out of the closet.

She should find her mother and pretend to be Stella, act, act, acting her heart out, starring in the part of Just-Fine Sonya. But she stays in the closet, moving only enough to pull her legs in and close the door. The dark surrounds her, and she breathes more easily. Dark Eve. She hears her mother call for her, knock, then come into her room. Sonya listens to the opening and closing of her dresser drawers. Probably her mother is putting away her laundered clothes. As her mother's footsteps retreat down the stairs, Sonya pushes the shoes into a pile and settles herself on the closet floor. She can't remember the last time she felt so safe. The new body relaxes.

***

153

She falls asleep, waking only when she hears her father yelling at Dean. Although she can't hear why, she distinguishes the word *sissy*. Poor kid. She kicks open the closet door and crawls out. Cramped and achy, she stands, gazes in the mirror, and finds strange sleep lines striping her face. Yet her face looks more like her own than before. She feels refreshed too. Maybe all she needed to return to her old self was a good sleep.

She removes her dress, which is dusty from the closet floor. After choosing an old-body blouse and skirt from the closet, she tosses the skirt onto her sunflower bedspread and then slips into the shirt. She buttons it, noting the swelling has gone down in her breasts, which had never leaked milk. Dry Eve. She hadn't been ready for Moon Boy. Her body has made this much clear to her. She smooths down the shirt's collar. She runs her hands over the front of her torso, pausing a moment at the gauze square taped over her ribs. The pain is dulled. The wound finally seems to be healing.

She hadn't thought it possible, but her old body really is returning to her. Confident now that she will be able to button and zip the old skirt easily, she picks it up from her bed. The cotton is cool and crisp in her hands. She brings it to her nose and smells the brand of spray starch her mother uses. She recalls that as a little girl she sat beneath the ironing board at her mother's feet, steam rising from her father's shirts while her mother slid the iron over them like a magic wrinkle-removing wizard.

She unzips the skirt. With one leg in the skirt and one leg out, she stops cold. She drops the skirt to floor. She steps on it. Now it will have to be re-ironed before she can wear it. She doesn't care. All she sees is the folded piece of paper punctuating the center of her bed.

Dean must have left the note for her when she was asleep in the closet. Her hands tremble as she snatches up the paper and clutches it to her chest. She glances around the room as if someone could be hiding beneath her desk or her dresser. Holding her breath, she opens it and reads.

Baby killer. We know what you did. Make it right.

Slowly, the note still in her hand, she opens the door to the closet. She steps back in, sinks to the floor, and closes the door behind her.

Leo

"LEO, COME QUICK," his mother calls from the front porch.

In his room, Leo reluctantly stills his fingers, which have been tracing the sitar part on "Paint It Black." He'd been trying to see if he could replicate the sitar's twang on his guitar by bending the strings. He's also been trying to slide into the sound, alternately using one of his father's old sockets and the top of a Black Bear soda bottle, which Will helped him cut with a wine bottle opener he borrowed from his father's tavern. But Leo's sliding comes out sounding more like a wailing cat than music. He turns the sound down on the record player and listens to his mother's tone, braced for alarm or anger. He feels as if he's always bracing for something bad these days.

"He's here. It's time!"

Leo rolls his eyes. He'd forgotten to brace himself for excitement.

Over breakfast, his mother told him his father would be revealing his big project today. The news sparked no curiosity in Leo. He didn't say a word. Instead, he pictured his father's last projects, a Martian called Water Boy buried in a hatbox, a girl in a letter sweater, and Leo's throat shut like a vise. Since Water Boy, he struggles to push out a grunt at his father. When his mother asks him what's wrong, he barely manages a grizzled, "Nothing."

What can he possibly say? There are no words for what's wrong—what *could be* wrong, he reminds himself as he tries to puzzle out what's true and what's not. After all, he's not sure, not absolutely, not of anything. The tiepin with the whole note on it isn't dead-on proof that his father is the father of Water Boy. Without knowing for sure, Leo won't drop the atom bomb that's etched with Water Boy's name on his family. Nothing would be left of them but shadows. What if it turns out he's wrong?

For a week after finding Water Boy, Leo simmered and churned, watching his father closely for some clue that would lead him to the truth. His father has remained on the wagon, busy in his attic den with his secret project. He's home for dinner most nights, and if he goes out, he's straight back from rehearsals or maybe the taverns or . . . Leo doesn't like to think where else his father might go. Wherever he goes, he comes home sober as a judge. In the morning, his mood is bright, kissing and goofing with Leo's mother like they're goopy kids. Good as gold, as she says.

But this behavior isn't necessarily proof of anything. His father was good as gold after Nora, who neither of them have mentioned since the smoker, holding firm to their unspoken deal: His father didn't hassle Leo for leaving the smoker without permission, and Leo doesn't mention Nora again. If not for that whole-note pin, Leo might have allowed himself to put his father's encounter with Nora behind them. Not forgiven, not forgotten. Knowing things a boy shouldn't know about his father. But having made his stand, having given his father fair warning, Leo might have allowed himself to trust that his father has changed as his mother seems believe, as if all is hunky-dory in the Meitka family, her husband never came home drunk, she never picked up a knife against him.

And if not for that stupid pin, Leo might have allowed himself to consider Water Boy and Sonya as nothing to do with his family. He might have let the whole damn thing go.

But that pin. He can't throw it away until he knows the truth. He carries it in the front pocket of his jeans, where it pricks him at odd times, during classes or smoking with Will behind the school's field house, when he least expects it. To leave the pin at home feels too dangerous though, a ticking time bomb his mother might find and question him about. He's not sure he can straight-face lie to her if she confronts him outright, accusing him of having stolen the pin from his father. It's galling that his mother might suspect him of stealing, that he might have to lie to her, when his father might be . . . could be . . . or maybe not . . . Each prick of that pin to his thigh is a fresh pang of uncertainty.

The uncertainty bubbling inside Leo is the reason he agreed with Emelia about sending the notes to Sonya. Just maybe, the notes would shake something loose and provide him with a clue to the truth. Not that he was sure what he'd do then, but at least he would know. And maybe he wouldn't have to do anything, he'd thought. Maybe the notes would force Sonya to lead them to someone else and get his father off the hook.

The first three notes hadn't worked out that way. Sonya didn't give away a thing, just mooned around the halls at school with Stella, who is the only nice thing to come out of any of this. Leo finds himself thinking about Stella when he plays guitar, imaging her being impressed with his skill, loving the same riffs he loves, and together they work out the fingering. He's decided Stella is pretty in a way that's different from Kirstin. Stella's graceful. She walks like willow boughs blowing in a breeze. He wishes she weren't associated with this mess. He'd like to ask her about her favorite bands. He'd like to talk to her about anything.

Only after the four of them handed off this last note to Sonya's bratty little brother did Leo realize what a risk he'd taken with its message. *Make it right.* What a mistake. They'd written a call to action, and the moment the kid ran off with the note pinched in his dirty fist, Leo wanted to snatch it back. What, exactly, had he thought the girl would do to make it right? What else could she do besides confront the father? His father? True, it may lead to someone else. But it may also turn out to be the very bomb Leo feared dropping on his family.

"Come on, Leo," calls his mother. "Trust me. You won't want to miss this!"

He lays his guitar on the bed and grudgingly joins his mother on the porch.

"Look," she says. "Just look at it!"

He tracks his mother's pointing finger to a beat-up old bus speckled with rust. The bus lumbers down the street more like charging elephant than something meant to transport humans.

"Wow," Leo says, his awe finally loosening his vocal cords. "No way that's—"

"Your father!"

When his father punches the horn twice, the bus emits an appropriately elephantine roar. He thrusts his arm and head through the side window, patting the outside of the bus as if it were an animal's rump.

"Got her for a song!"

He nearly clips the mailbox as he turns the beast into their driveway.

His mother claps her hands, her feet scurrying down the porch stairs. She Polish hops around the lawn, her cotton dress flapping at her knees.

Caught up in the excitement, Leo jumps down the porch's three steps and chases the bus up the driveway.

"Where did you get it?" he says, uttering the first full sentence he's spoken to his father in days.

"Police auction," Stash says, flapping open the bus doors and clambering out. "Ha-ha, no wonder it was such a steal."

"It's cool," Leo says. "But why would you buy something like this? I mean, what's it for?"

His father can't contain himself long enough to answer.

"Isn't she a beaut!" he says. He leaps over to Anne, and together they bounce around the lawn, hop-hop stepping, hop-hop twirling, squealing and laughing with delight.

Despite himself, Leo catches their happiness and giggles at their display of joy. They hop until they're breathless.

"Stop, stop," his mother says finally. "You'll give us both heart attacks."

His father stops dancing but throws his arms wide and howls to the sky in his typical off-key voice, "We're going to the Silo . . . We're going to the Silo-o-o. . . ."

"Hush." His mother laughs. "You want to kill all the birds?"

"The Silo?"

"Tell him," says Anne.

"My boy, my son, my progeny, it's a recording studio!" says his father.

"A real one?"

"My son, the skeptic," says his mother. "Of course, it's real."

"We're cutting a record," says his father, rubbing his palms together with relish. "And at the end of the summer, the Meitka Band is touring, going all the way to the festival in Cleveland. Show those Vadnal brothers some real music."

"You mean it? Cutting a real record? At a real studio?"

"A lot of the bands from around here record up at the Silo," says his mother. "Not just polka bands either. All kinds of music."

"Your mother's right," Stash says. "Country musicians and some of those Ukrainian folk groups and mariachi bands too because Mitch, the Silo's owner, his wife is Mexican. Even some blues musicians come up from Chicago. Some pretty famous ones too."

"Like Muddy Waters? John Lee Hooker?" Leo says.

"I'm not sure about Muddy and John, but some hotshots," says his father, as if he knows the blues musicians.

"Who? What hotshots?"

"I don't name names, sonny. Some of those fellas are breaking their contracts by recording with Mitch. But you know, they're top musicians who want to record something their fat-belly studios won't let them record."

"Why wouldn't a big studio let a hotshot record whatever he wants? Isn't that why he's a hotshot?"

"Those big-time studios are only in it for themselves. All they care about is money. Sometimes a musician has something really special he wants to keep for himself, record his way. Maybe not a money-maker but a heart project or something the studio bums don't understand. So the hotshots go to a small place like the Silo where you pay all the costs up front. Hotshot or not, Mitch gives you your studio time for free, and in exchange you've got to order a certain number of records from him. You split royalties if distributors come knocking for more. We're doing a 45, so I'm paying for five hundred records up front."

"Wow! How much do they cost?" asks Leo.

"I don't name names. I don't name numbers. But I also have to pay the boys in the band their AFM scale, not Mitch. But Mitch will engineer the record, press it, and sleeve it before we drive away."

His mother adds, "Stories go around about the hotshot musicians sneaking out of Chicago under the cover of dark after playing a job. They drive up to Luste City, record at the Silo in a couple of hours. Have breakfast while Mitch finishes mixing and pressing. The hotshots drive away with their records literally hot off the presses. They can do whatever they want with them then, sell them to friends or other musicians, slip them to their DJ pals, sell them to the tavern or club owners or to their fans when they play."

Leo's fascinated but still skeptical. How do his parents know all of this? "So you can just go there and play your music and come back with a record?"

"Exactly," says Stash. "As I said, if you have the money for the upfront costs, Mitch will engineer the record and press copies right there. He makes the sleeves and labels and everything before you drive away."

"Drive away from where?" asks Leo. "Where is this place? Luste City? The Silo?"

"In the middle of a cornfield. It's a real silo. You play inside it," says his mother. She laughs when Leo's eyes widen. "It's true! Look, Stash, our son thinks we're lying."

"Just imagine the acoustics in a silo," says his father.

"Bet your sweet bippy!" says his mother. "You and the boys will sound terrific."

"What about me?" Leo says. "I mean, do I—?"

"Of course, you're coming too," says his father, patting Leo's shoulder. "It will be educational seeing a real record get made."

"But do I get to play on the record?" Leo asks.

"Well, we'll see, we'll see," says Stash. "Right now, help me wrangle this beast into the garage."

It takes all three of them working together to park the bus in the garage. It's the most fun they've had together in ages. When his father hits the gas pedal instead of the brake pedal and smashes up an old card table, no one gets angry. They crack up laughing when they realize the bus is too long to close the garage door, and Leo thinks, why can't it always be like this, fun and easy? He's misses his parents, he realizes, wishing their present joy could cancel out the ugliness of the past.

As he wheels his bicycle from the garage to the back yard so they can get in and out of the bus more easily, Leo thinks that more than anything in the world he wants to play on his father's record. Imagine, a real record. And a tour too. So what if it's polka and not rock? He'd play hillbilly music if he could be on a real record and go on a tour. He wants it so badly, he'll practice his fingers numb until they go to the Silo. He'll do more than learn Stash's new songs. He'll give them his own flourish, show off the techniques he's learned from the rock music his father dismisses. He'll show his father just how good he really is, show him what music can be, and earn a place in the band. It's time to forget about Water Boy. Forget about Sonya and Nora too, he decides. Music is what matters, not just to Leo, but to his family. The Meitkas are musicians, and music may be the only thing able to cancel out their past.

A week later his mother jokes, "Our first family vacation." She packs the last of the sandwiches she's made into a Styrofoam cooler.

His father hasn't had a chance to get the refrigerator in the bus running, but Leo loves the bus anyway. The previous owners excavated the guts, pulling out some of the bench seats and converting the space to a caravan-style living area with shelves, a stove, and a small kitchen table with a red vinyl top. Outside, they covered the school bus yellow with red and white paint, detailing it in black. The overpaint has begun to chip off, but it's still the coolest vehicle he's ever seen. When his father first took Leo for a ride, the beast roared and spit, jerked and bucked, moving less like a multicolored elephant as it looks from the outside and more like a taunted bull. Leo held on for dear life, laughing and swaying and swearing that he wasn't going anywhere ever again in this death trap.

His father's friend Frankie, a mechanic from the factory, has been tinkering with the engine all week. Last night Frankie proclaimed the bus's engine ready, and today they're going to the Silo to cut a record. Leo can hardly believe it's really happening.

Since before sunrise, Leo and his father have been stuffing the bus with all the musical gear in the house, everything but the piano, and that would be going too if his father could find a way to strap it to the bus's roof.

"A vacation?" Leo chuckles, handing his mother the cooler's lid. "Isn't a vacation supposed to be waterskiing behind a boat up north or a trek down the Grand Canyon on donkeys?" The family of one kid in Leo's class actually drove all the way to California to see the Hollywood sign. Another kid's family drove the opposite direction to see the White House. "Why is it we never go on a real vacation?"

"You know why. Your father plays every weekend in summer. You don't mean to tell me you'd trade going to the Silo for going to see a giant hole in the ground?" says his mother, sliding the cooler beneath one of the remaining bench seats.

"No way." Leo grins. "I want to go to the Silo."

"Silo or bust!"

"How long is the drive?"

She shrugs. "Two hours or so, northwest. Depends how fast this thing goes once we're on the road."

Leo can't wait to get there. His mother is right. The Silo is going to be so much better than some giant hole in the ground. Okay, maybe the Silo isn't Abbey Road or Sun Studios, but they were just small studios once too. Sure, the Meitka Band will never be the Beatles or Elvis, but neither were they before they cut their first records. And with Leo's new stylings, well, who knows?

Leo's secret hope, the one he barely allows himself to think about, is that the studio owner, Mitch, will be so impressed with Leo, he'll ask to him record solo. He'll see Leo's so good, he won't even make him pay the upfront costs. Leo's got a song ready, just in case.

Admittedly his father hasn't absolutely, one hundred percent for sure said that Leo gets to play on the record, but Leo's certain his father won't leave him out once they get there. Probably his father hasn't said Leo can play so Leo will keep practicing, so he'll be ready.

"We'll see, we'll see," his father has hedged all week when Leo has asked about playing, getting more and more impatient with Leo as the week wore on. "Don't nag. We'll see how it goes when we get there."

The last few days, Leo hasn't pushed him. His father's excitement has turned to the same kind of edginess Leo noticed at the smoker. Leo plans to convince his father by playing great during the session's warm-up.

The session. Leo loves the way that sounds. Warming up for the session.

And his father's ploy to keep Leo practicing hard has worked because Leo's spent the week holed up in his room, guitar in hand. Each morning before school, he performs the vocal exercises his mother has taught him. He knows forward and back, upwards and downwards all five of the songs his father plans to choose from for the record. Leo's as ready as the bus and determined that today he'll show his father he's a musician in his own right. Not only does Leo deserve to play on the record, he deserves a spot in the band, and he deserves to go on the tour.

Man, if only they were playing real music. Rock music. Then Leo could show his father the song he's written, and maybe it could go on the B-side. It's the one he plans to play if Mitch asks him to record solo. A bluesy-rock number, whose entire instrumentation Leo can hear in his head. *I've got a fistful of secrets I've hidden from the world. But come a little closer, sweet. Let me open my hand and whisper you my soul.* It's the kind of song Mick might sing, or Denny Laine.

Leo starts toward the bus stairs for the last load of extension cords when his mother grasps his forearm and stops him.

"Help me up," she says.

"Oh, sorry, here."

He puts his arm down for her to lean on. He's surprised how much support she needs to shift from sitting on the bus's grimy floor to the slightly less grimy seat. It wasn't long ago she was

164

bouncing around the yard. Once seated, she doesn't let go of his forearm, and he notes again how strong her grip is.

"Listen, Leo. I want to say something to you before the boys get here. This record, it's something your father has dreamed of for a long time. He's worked hard for it. Saved his money. Gone without sometimes to make it happen. He's bringing in extra musicians, so he's got to pay them too. Today's big for him. So, son of mine, you be happy for him. Play music when he asks you to—"

"Did he tell you he's going to let me play?" Leo says eagerly. "I'm ready. You've heard me practicing."

"Your father hasn't said a thing either way. But *if* he asks you to play, you play." She puts a hand up to stop him from interrupting. "*If* he tells you to sing, you sing."

"Oh, man, I might get to sing? Really? That would be great! I've been doing the vocal exercises every day."

"I didn't say that. Your father didn't say that. But if he does say sing, you sing. If he says play, you play. Otherwise—and I mean this, Leo—otherwise, you keep that smart mouth you sometimes open shut today, *capiche*?"

Piqued, Leo licks his lips, which tingle with the urge to open his smart mouth and protest that there's no one better in this world at keeping his mouth shut. The things that could spill out if he ever really opened his smart mouth could fill ten buses. But he only nods. Because he wants to play music today. He wants to place a vinyl pancake on a record player, drop the needle, and hear his guitar stylings, maybe even his voice. Oh, man, what an absolute knockout it would be to hear himself sing on the radio.

But even if there was no recording session, Leo would keep his smart mouth shut because after the close call with the last note, he and his friends have sworn yet another oath. They've all agreed to keep their own brand of radio silence. Even Emelia has agreed to say nothing about what they've seen or done. Sonya, Water Boy, the notes, not a word. Not ever.

His mother releases his arm and lays her palm against his cheek. Her fingers tremble, but her gaze is fierce. For a moment, he thinks she might slap him. But instead she caresses his cheek with the back of her index finger.

"Let the man be happy," she says. "We're both happy for once. You must see that."

"I know," Leo says.

Despite his father's increasing edginess, his mother has managed to keep him calm. Yesterday Leo caught them kissing at the stove as his mother stirred oxtail soup. When they saw him, they smiled at him vacantly, as if he were a stranger. Then his mother used tongs to fish a knuckle of bone from the pot. She held it over the pot and said to Leo, "Your father made sure I could cook oxtail soup before he married me. Of course I could. It was my favorite too."

"Liquid gold," his father said, leaning down to catch a drop of broth on his tongue.

Now his father peeks his head into the bus. He hands Leo three rolled-up extension cords.

"It's going to be a long day," he says, gazing through the windshield at the tawny light of early morning.

"We're all packed," Leo says.

"You sure? You got everything on the list? I'm going to double-check," he says before Leo can confirm that he's already double-checked.

An hour later, the band members climb aboard the bus with cups of coffee, the scent of stale booze escaping with the steam. All of them played at Ritczi's Tavern last night, and they greet each other sleepily but with grins that suggest their excitement will rise as their hangovers ease.

"You're driving?" Leo says when his mother perches herself in the driver's seat. She wears a flowered sunhat and has an unlit cigarette dangling from her lips.

"Of course, she's driving," says Stash. "Your mother was driving tractors on your grandparents' farm as soon as her legs were long enough to reach the clutch."

"And don't forget," Anne says. "When I wasn't much older than you, I drove the bus for my church chorus. We competed in three states. We won plenty of times too. Best chorus in the region. So no matter what your father thinks, you got your vocal range from me. Now go get your jacket from the laundry line in the back yard in case it gets cold tonight after the sun goes down."

Leo groans.

"March," she says, pointing to the yard.

To Leo's surprise, he finds Emelia seated on the back door's concrete stoop, her body hunched over her thighs, her arms hugging her knees. She's laid her cheek on her knees, and her hair falls to one side in a thick drape. For a startling moment, that hair makes Leo think Sonya has materialized, and he stumbles as he jogs to the clothesline. When she lifts her head, she's pure Emelia, her brows dark branches above her eyes, her lips a twig below. She wears denim dungarees, the bib's straps clasped loosely around her waist rather than over her shoulders. She's turned up the cuffs, revealing the thin skin of her ankles. The wooden handle of a hairbrush sticks out of one back pocket, the end of a pen out of the other.

"What are you doing here so early?" he says.

"You're leaving. Where are you going?"

"My father . . . that music thing I told you about."

Superstition suddenly taking hold of him, he can't bring himself to say he's cutting a record today. He doesn't want to jinx it. It's already too absurd. He won't believe he's playing on a record until he's in the studio.

"I can't wait to play it for you," he says.

"Oh, yeah," she says. "That's really cool. How long will you be gone?" Without looking, she reaches for the hairbrush and fingers the end of the wooden handle.

"Just today. Emelia, what's wrong?"

"Can I come along?" she says.

"Why would you want to do that?" If Emelia comes, Sonya and Water Boy and all the rest of it will climb on that bus too, tainting the whole experience. "There's not really room on the bus. And my mother said it's mostly going to be a lot of waiting around. It's probably going to be really boring most of the time."

"So don't go. Stay with me. We'll do something fun. I know, we could get all the neighborhood kids together and play kickball. Remember when we used to do that, have those big games that lasted whole days? One out seemed like life or death. Remember?"

"Emelia. We haven't played kickball in years."

"Or, I don't know, we could go somewhere."

"Go where? Emelia, what wrong? Has something happened?"

"We could mess around downtown. Or get a bus to Chicago. We could go to California. You said everyone's going there. I bet it's beautiful. I bet the ocean is so much better than the lake." Her expression shows real interest. "Yeah. C'mon, Leo, let's go. What's keeping us here? We could hitchhike. It'll be okay with two people."

The bus's horn honks loud staccato pops.

"Today? Now?" he says.

"Why not now? Now's perfect. It would solve everything."

"What do you mean, everything?"

"It's all so mixed up."

"Yeah," he admits. "I know. But leaving? I can't, Emelia. Not yet. Not today."

She nods and picks at a loose piece of rubber on the side of her sneaker. When she yanks it off, she rips the canvas, revealing her little toe. Leo taps the pink patch beneath the cloth, but the callus on his index finger is so thick the sensation is dulled, so he barely feels her flesh.

"I don't want to be alone today," she says quietly.

"I have to go, Emelia," he says. "I really do, but what about Will and Kirstin?"

"They're on the college tour. They won't be back until this evening."

His mother lays on the bus's horn.

"Sounds like an elephant farting," she says, smiling a little.

His mother pop, pop, pops the horn, then lets go another long one, and they laugh together.

"Oh, go, Leo. Enjoy your ride on Dumbo," she says, getting up. "Make a good record. I want to hear it when you get back."

"Will you be all right?"

"Where the hell is that kid?" his father yells. Christ, thinks Leo, his voice could carry two miles with a good wind. "Get your ass out here now, Leopold!"

"Go on, Leopold," she says. She gives his shoulder a push with the heel of her hand.

"I'll call you as soon as I get back. Oh, wait, we're going to be back late. So tomorrow. I'll call you tomorrow."

"Sure," she says.

He tugs his jacket from the laundry line and waves as he jogs to the bus. By the time his mother closes the doors behind him, Emelia has left his back yard. The bus clatters away from the curb. He holds tight to a chrome railing and watches her shuffle up the street. Her shoulders slump so deeply she looks as if she's carrying pails of water in her fists. She and the bus reach the corner at the same time. She pauses, cocks her head as if trying to decide something. Then she seems to shake off the weight.

Leo keeps watching Emelia while the bus lumbers up a hill. At the crest, he sees her turn away from the bakery and stride toward the lake. Just before she disappears from sight, she removes the hairbrush from her pocket, but where the bristles should be, the sun glints from a metal shaft of, what, a screwdriver maybe, or a knife? No, it's an ice pick like the one he used to break up the ice block for the coolers.

"She all right?" his mother says.

"Fine," Leo says, not at all certain this is true. Maybe he should have let her come along. Suddenly, his mother turns the bus left, and he's thrown right, his shoulder hitting the chrome railing hard.

"Emelia's doing better than me," he mumbles, rubbing his bruised arm.

"Quit your grumbling and sit down," his mother says. "Take a sandwich with you."

Any response he might have given her is drowned out by the sudden blast of polka music from a transistor radio. He lifts the lid on the cooler and takes a liverwurst sandwich.

He eats as he minces his way through the legs of the men lounging across the bench seats, their feet propped on instrument cases, hands palming cigarette smoke into their mouths. The scents of Vitalis and coffee mingle with the thickening smoke. Mostly they're the regular members of his father's band, with a few hired guns thrown in, presumably for musical finesse. Leo notes that at least two hired guns play guitar, although one is mostly a banjo player.

He slumps onto the last seat in the bus, his own guitar case jostling beneath him.

Sprawled out asleep on the seat in front of him is Joey Katz, the youngest hired gun. He plays regularly with the Meitka Band, but he isn't an official member. The other musicians call him Kid, although his real name is Janek Karczewski. Joey irritates his father, who takes Joey's name change as a personal insult, sneering at the *Joey Katz* stenciled in big red script on his instrument cases. To his face, the older musicians call him runt of the litter, giving him guff about playing the field with women and playing the blues clubs in Chicago when he doesn't have a polka job. Before Nora, Leo used to laugh along when they said things like, "Kid puts that sax of his in any old case."

Behind his back, his father calls Joey flashy and phony, but he can't deny Joey's talent and skill. To Leo's mind, Joey's the best musician on the bus. He's got perfect pitch and can play any instrument within reach, not just sax. Leo's heard him plunk ragtime tunes on piano and drum as well as Ringo with the same loose quality. He's got style too. Leo covets the sunglasses with pine-colored lenses Joey has perched on his mountainous *schnoz*, his green sharkskin blazer, and the black wingtips shined to a gloss that reflects the egg yolk sun streaming through the bus's windows. He wears his wheat-colored hair slicked over his jackrabbit ears. He's not so much handsome, not movie star handsome, but what both Kirstin and Emelia agree Mick Jagger is—ugly-sexy.

Unlike the other musicians on the bus, Stash included, he holds no day job as a machinist or a plumber or a manager of a grocery store. He plays music.

At the moment though, he lies perfectly still with his arms crossed over his chest and his fingertips tucked under his armpits. Only his thumbs show, the tips perfectly filed ovals, which Leo would swear are painted with a layer of clear polish.

Leo props his elbow against the window's frame. Passing the endless green carpet of soybean and corn fields, his excitement ebbs, and his thoughts return to Emelia. She's been strange ever since they found Water Boy, but this morning, turning up in his back yard, talking of running away? Something must have happened, but what? Probably a fight with her aunts. Lately, she doesn't have a good word to say about them. It's weird the way she cares so much about Water Boy. Although now that he thinks of it, it isn't Water Boy that she's fixated on. It's Sonya. He understands why he's concerned with Sonya, but why is she?

Of course, it was her idea to send the notes to Sonya. And she's the one who pushed them to keep sending the notes when they didn't seem to be having much effect. The uneasy feeling that they've gone too far returns. That fourth note, it's still a time bomb. Why had they told Sonya to do something?

Because Emelia insisted.

When nothing much happened after they sent the first two notes, Will and Kirstin seemed relieved. They turned their attention to other things, reminding Leo and Emelia that it's the end of the school term, so they have tests and papers to write. They're going to college, Kirstin said, striking a sore spot with Emelia, who claims she only has baking cupcakes alongside her aunts to look forward to after high school. Is that why she pushed them to carry out their plan to deliver four notes?

It was her plan from the start: one note for each of them to deliver. One for all and all for one. Kirstin insisted the last message be clear. "The others were just weird," she said, looking hard at Leo, who had suggested the cryptic lyrics on the first note. The four of them sat on a busted-out picnic table on the beach. "If we're going to do this, let's at least do it right."

Baby killer.

"That will get her attention. You know, shock her," Kirstin said.

171

We know what you did.

"It's always worse when someone knows you did something wrong," Emelia said. "Even if you didn't get caught." Leo shot her a hard look. Was she implying something about Stash? Did she know things she wasn't saying?

Make it right!

Who suggested it? Leo can't remember. Kirstin wanted to add "or else," but Will said it sounded babyish. Kirstin insisted on the exclamation point though, and they all agreed it was a reasonable compromise, Leo doing so with a reluctant nod.

They all had to agree on everything. That was the deal. Equal risk for everyone.

It had been Will's turn to write, and he pressed the pen so hard it embossed the second and maybe the third sheets of paper beneath the top one on the tablet, but Leo could tell that like Kirstin, Will's effort was more about doing the job right than out of strong feeling. To Will's mind, this note finished things. Four notes. Each of them written on a different colored piece of paper: green, yellow, pink, and blue. Now, with note four, it would be a job done. Each of them had penned one note, and each had delivered one to the little brother.

For the fourth time, they stood together outside the grade school's chain-link fence, watching the strange boy with the white hair and pale eyes, who seemed a little slow. Emelia said she learned the kid's name was Dean by following Sonya and the boy home one day. He doesn't seem to have any friends. He stood alone on a swing, gazing at the kids playing together: marbles, hopscotch, or playing catch with a baseball. The boy cocked his head as if trying to figure out how or why the other kids played together. At five, maybe six, years old, he's unable to recite the alphabet. Emelia tested him on it before handing him the first note to check if he would read it before giving it to Sonya. When Emelia pushed him to get past the letter "j," he balled his hands into fists and held his breath until his face rose scarlet. But Emelia held out the oatmeal cookie she had brought from the bakery, and the boy released his breath, sniffing the treat's scent like a dog. He ate the cookie greedily, then calmly told her he liked peanut butter better.

Will delivered the second note with a sense of authority that impressed Leo. The boy responded with fearful eyes, taking the cookie and the note without complaint.

When it was Leo's turn to deliver the third note, it was a bright day, and the boy's hair was so white, his skin so pale, it seemed that when the sun hit him, Leo could see his skeleton through his skin. As he approached the boy, Leo smiled the smile that usually melts teachers and girls, even boys sometime. His father's smile. This kid didn't seem to understand that when someone smiles at you, you smile back.

Leo held out the note to him and said, "Give this to your sister." With a web-like hand, the boy reached for the peanut butter cookie rather than the note, but Leo pulled the treat back, thrusting out the note instead. The kid hesitated but eventually clapped his fingers onto the paper. As he did so, Leo noticed greenish dirt under the boy's nails, and his stomach lurched. Instinctively he pulled the cookie away, and the boy's other hand swished the air. The boy waggled on the swing before regaining his balance.

The gaze he fixed on Leo suggested he wished him dead on the spot. Genuinely disturbed, Leo tossed the cookie at the kid, figuring it was a fifty-fifty shot whether Sonya would get that third note. The kid probably blew his snotty nose in it and threw it away. Or burned it. He looked like the kind of kid who plays with matches. But later, at school, Leo saw Sonya pull out the pink sheet of paper, look at it, and shove it back in her purse.

The last note was Kirstin's to deliver. She bounded over to Dean like a happy bunny. When she got within reach, the kid thrust a foot out to kick her, wobbling the swing. She dodged him easily enough, saying something Leo couldn't hear. At first the boy shook his head, presumably refusing to take the piece of paper. She held out the peanut butter cookie Emelia had brought from the bakery, but still he wouldn't take it. Dean said something to her, and Kirstin looked back at them as if uncertain. Finally, she fished a nickel out of her coin purse, and Dean's greedy hand shot out.

Kirstin trotted back to the group and said breathlessly, "He almost kicked me, the little stinker! And he made me pay him a nickel. He even had the gall to ask my name."

173

"What'd you say?" said Will, alarmed. To learn one of their names was to learn them all. "You didn't tell him did you?"

"I started to tell him not to be so nosy, but then I thought fast and said my name was Jiminy Cricket, which is sort of true. We're kind of like her conscience, right?"

"Smart answer," said Emelia.

"Yeah, really smart," Will agreed.

As they walked away from the playground, Leo glanced back at the swing one last time. The boy's gaze was stuck on the four of them. Leo was suddenly reminded of his uncle Fritz, who sometimes stayed in the attic den. A near twin to his father, Fritz had a disturbing way of making Leo feel he saw more of him than other people did, and that he was storing up what he saw for future use. Then it struck Leo that if Water Boy had lived, this boy, Dean, would have been the child's uncle. Would that have made this boy related to Leo too? Leo puzzled over the genealogy. Would it have made Dean family? The possibility made Leo shudder.

"And then I told him," Kirstin went on as they pulled open the door to Dutchland Dairy and slid into a booth at the back of the diner, "if he gives the note to his sister, he'll get a big surprise, which is a fib, but who knows? Maybe he will get a surprise."

"So we're done now, right?" said Will, passing out plastic menus none of them really needed to look at.

"Now we watch," said Emelia. "We see what she does. Then we decide what to do next."

"What if she still doesn't do anything?" said Kirstin.

"Who cares?" whined Will, slapping his menu on the tabletop. "I'm sick of this. I have a history paper to write and math test to study for. I don't like this anymore. Doing this feels . . . I don't know . . . creepy. That little kid is spooky. And I feel weird about these notes. They're spooky too."

"She'll do something," said Emelia, ignoring Will. "Let's just hope it's the right thing."

"What is the right thing again?" asked Kirstin. "I've sort of lost track."

"Yeah," Leo said, only then realizing the mistake they'd made in that last note. *Make it right.*

"Who cares?" repeated Will. "It's not really any of our business anymore. She's not our responsibility."

"How can you say that?" Emelia started. "She—"

Kirstin cut her off. "Not again, you two. Listen, I'm four-square with Will this time. We've done what we can. We did what we did for the good of Water Boy. Now it's up to her."

Emelia looked about to argue, but this time Leo cut her off.

"Whatever happens, we all have to agree," said Leo quietly, his throat tight with fear. *Make it happen.* "Let's just wait and see."

Will and Kirstin nodded readily, but Emelia pouted and refused to eat any of the French fries or onion rings they ordered to share. She kept her arms crossed over her chest as they walked home. Leaving Kirstin and Will at the corner, Leo walked Emelia back to the bakery. She looked as miserable as he felt.

"It's not right," Emelia said. They had reached the bakery's door. Nearly dinnertime, the Closed sign was up, but the scents of yeast and powdered sugar lingered in the air. "None of it."

"I know," he admitted. "I'm beginning to wonder if there is such a thing as right."

"Of course there is," she said angrily, narrowing her eyes and focusing on a point in the distance. "I'm sick of people pretending they don't know the difference between right and wrong. Everyone knows. Some people just decide they don't like it, or they get caught up, or I don't know. But if no one knows the difference, how are we supposed to know how to act?"

"Emelia, what is it you want Sonya to do?" Leo ventured. "Make it right?"

"Don't you know?" she said, exasperation tightening her face. "Isn't it obvious?"

He bit his lip and pushed his hands deep into his jacket pockets. Finding his father's whole-note pin there, he ran his finger over the nubs of the symbol.

"Sure, of course it is," he said quickly.

She shook her head. "None of you understand anything," she said. She stepped past him and pushed through the bakery door, the little bell tinkling as she slammed it shut behind her.

***

Once again, the bus makes a sharp turn, throwing Leo against its side. Coffee sloshes over the lips of cups, and the men grumble, brushing liquid from their laps and shirtfronts.

"Sorry, boys. Which way now?" his mother calls, her alto voice piercing the balloon of polka music that bounces from three separate transistor radios, turned up loud and tuned to the Saturday morning polka show, which blares a new song by Hank Thunander and the Vadnal brothers. The high notes of accordions ricochet from the bus's metal walls, a contrast to the men's faces, which, despite the coffee, still droop with exhaustion.

"Next week that will be us," his father announces to the bus at large, gesturing to the radio and winning approving, if tired, head nods all round.

"Left on Route 52, Annie," calls Dinky, the band's gray-mustached drummer. A stout man, his bulk barely fits on the bench seat. According to Anne, he's been to Luste City and Silo Records before to record, so he knows the way. "Then a right turn at the feed processing plant."

Leo looks out at a vast orchard of apple trees, their blossoms bursting in what's now full morning light. His gaze falls on the dead one in the nearest grove. Its gnarled presence alters the scene, but Leo can't decide if it makes the other trees more or less splendid in comparison. They pass a pasture with a few horses grazing peacefully on its rolling hills. One horse canters and bucks, racing at the fence rails, mane and dust scrubbing the dry morning air. Leo thinks again of Emelia. Is a confession what she wants from Sonya? Or is it something else she's looking for? Leo can't imagine what. He thought he knew his friend well, but he's beginning to doubt if you can ever really know another person. He believed he knew his parents too.

As the bus continues to lurch over the increasingly patchy highway, Leo's stomach churns, liverwurst bile burning the back of his throat. He's dizzy, and his whole body feels clammy. How the hell can Joey Katz sleep through the jostling and the noise of those radios and the men's shouted conversations? Whiskey and a skunky odor like burning cattails emanate from Joey. Desperate, Leo forces open a rickety window. He lets in a gasp of apple blossoms, chased by the smell of recently turned soil, which reminds Leo of digging up Water Boy. Quickly grabbing a discarded piece of wax paper from the sandwich his mother insisted he eat, he retches into it.

He drops the paper out the window, hoping no one noticed. But Joey's sunglasses lift slowly. After shooting a glance at Stash, who's now occupied with sheet music, Joey slides a hand-rolled cigarette from the breast pocket of his suit jacket and presses it into Leo's palm. Leo can think of nothing worse than tobacco right now.

"Hide that. Smoke it later where your papa won't catch you," he whispers. "It'll settle your stomach. Make you play better too."

Leo slides the cigarette into his back pocket just as his father glances up. Leo holds his father's gaze for a moment. Then he turns on his father the very smile handed down to him. To Leo's surprise, the smile works. His father grins back before returning to his music.

An hour later, his mother turns the bus down a swath of dirt road cut through acres of feathery barley. Leo wants to die. Greener than the young grasses and trembling with motion sickness, he barely notices the silver bullet of a silo in the distance or the ramshackle barn and three-story house alongside it. As they approach the silo, a wall of a man in overalls stands wide-legged, waving his mother to park next to a combine. The moment the bus jolts to a stop, Leo pushes open the rear door, jumps out, and runs to the edge of the barley field where he drops to his knees and vomits again.

When he manages to raise himself onto wobbly legs, he sees most of the musicians have exited the bus and stand with the bibbed man, chuckling at Leo. Someone says, "What's the matter, son? Ain't got your road legs yet?" Another says, "Gut like that sure as hell won't make it on the road."

"You all right there, son?" calls the man in the overalls.

Before Leo can answer, his father calls, "He's fine, Mitch. Get over here, Leo. Fellas, for those who don't already know him, this is Mitch Meyers, sole owner, engineer, and producer of Silo Recording. This place is as homegrown as the seed store in town. Mitch started it in the basement. Moved it to the silo when one of the field hands stumbled in drunk one night and started singing 'Home on the Range.'"

"His voice was that good?" says Zach, a button-box man.

"Nah, he was a howling chicken," says Mitch, grinning. "But the acoustics made him good as a rooster."

The men laugh and murmur greetings. Still green, Leo can barely raise his hand, and he bends over, resting his elbows on his knees to keep from falling down.

"Leo!" his father says. "Get over here and help get this gear off the bus."

As he shuffles to the bus, Joey says quietly, "Two tokes of what I gave you, you'll be fine."

"I don't know," says Leo, the thought of smoking turning him green again. "A cigarette right now is going to make it worse."

"Trust me, little man. This ain't no Lucky Strike," he whispers. "And listen, hold the smoke in your lungs for a while before you exhale."

Leo lifts his eyebrows as Joey pats him on the shoulder.

"Trust me," Joey says again. "I'll cover for you."

Seeing that his father has moved inside to set up the instruments the boys are unpacking and that his mother is busy cleaning out the bus, Leo lopes behind the silo and lights the cigarette Joey gave him. Already lightheaded from vomiting, Leo inhales carefully, but still the smoke burns his throat like no other cigarette he's ever had. It tastes different too, more like the bonfires they light on the beach, or the cattail punks they fake smoke, but not quite. Hot and harsh and musty.

Looking out at the soft barley-tipped fields waving against the breeze, Leo imagines he's sucking in the earth. Just like Water Boy. His brother. He inhales again, holding the smoke in his lungs longer as Joey told him to do, and he feels the world around him hum and loosen. Did Water Boy ever get to feel air in his lungs or only sand? Or nothing? How good it would be sometimes to feel nothing at all.

So this is marijuana, he thinks, having only read about it in magazines and books. He likes it. It's done the trick with his nausea as Joey promised, replacing the green feeling with a floating feeling quite different from dizziness. In fact, his whole body relaxes into the morning air, now crisp and refreshing. He inhales and decides he likes the apple-blossom smell lacing the wind from the orchards beyond the field. He smokes half the joint, stubs it out carefully, and returns the rest to his pocket. He knows he should get inside and help set up, otherwise his father will be angry. But at the moment, Leo doesn't care what his father thinks. He doesn't care about anything, and he stays right where he is, seated in the dirt, resting against a rain barrel, sniffing sweet manure. It's so nice not to care. Why has he always cared so much what his father thinks of him? Crazy, when it feels so good to just be.

Stray notes skip out of the silo. Leo plucks one out of the air and sings softly in a falsetto that strains his newly raw vocal cords. "Ask me, baby, I'll make it right. You been home, I been out all night." A piebald cat sidles up to him, rubbing against his leg and mewing harmony, which makes Leo giggle.

He reminds himself it matters what his father thinks because he's the one who decides if Leo gets to play on the record and tour with the band this summer, so he hauls himself up and follows the notes to the silo's entrance.

Instinctively, when Leo steps inside the silo, he looks up. The spiraling walls and domed ceiling make him feel like he's in the eye of a tornado. Truly dizzy now, he stumbles over a music stand, rolling his ankle before tumbling to the ground. He finds the searing pain in his leg hilarious. Waves of laughter splash over him, and he collapses into them. Around him, the pips and screeches of instruments being tuned make him giggle more until he's all but choking.

"Oh, man, be cool, little man," says Joey, who's suddenly at Leo's side, pulling him to his feet. "Aw, look at you. You're all messed up. Ain't you a beaut. Here, hold onto this." He pushes

Leo's guitar into his arms. Leo finds it's already tuned, and he stares at the instrument as if it might tell him who's been handling it today.

"Come on, kid, cool it!" Joey whispers. "Go on, play with me." He lifts his sax to his mouth and blows a few notes Leo's way.

Leo's fingers move before he thinks to tell them to, playing the bass line to "House of the Rising Sun," then slipping into the guitar part so naturally it feels like he's entered warm water. The two play together, passing music back and forth, easy and sweet. This is what real musicians do, thinks Leo. They ride the sound, surfing it. For the first time, he gets what Brian Wilson was doing on "God Only Knows." Man, he'd love to play that song here in the silo or, better yet, play "Revolver." Oh, man, he wishes he had a sitar right now.

"For Christ's sake, Leo." His father's voice cuts through Leo's music and thoughts. "Get your finger out of your goddamn ass and get over here. We've got real work to do."

Leo stops playing and stares at his father. Normally, such a rebuke would turn Leo's cheeks hot with humiliation and fury. But Joey chuckles, which makes Leo giggle too and mutter, "Heil, Stash." Joey chuckles again as Leo hurries to his father's side.

When Leo gets close enough for Stash to whisper in his ear, he finds his father's breath as sour as the sweat rising from Stash's body, not with booze but with nerves. When his father speaks, his voice is a mixture of threatening and pleading.

"Don't ruin this for me, Leo," he says softly.

Mitch steps out of the control room that Leo hadn't yet registered.

"Wow, look at that," Leo says.

A cubed room juts from the round side of the silo, a large window cut into the center-facing wall of the room. Behind the window, Leo sees the mixing console laid out like the deck of a spaceship. Leo looks around the rest of the silo, noting the wooden platform that covers what was probably a dirt floor when the silo held barley. Wires, spots, and cords are hooked to boards secured to the metal walls, providing lighting and electricity.

"I think this is the neatest place I've ever been," says Leo, but his father has already crossed the silo and is setting up a mike in front of one of the accordionists.

"All right, boys, let's go," calls Mitch. "Warm-up session. Let's see how you sound. Stash, when you're ready, take a listen in here. See if you like what you hear."

Leo sees now why his father was so exacting in the week leading up to this session. He's only got a few hours to get his record perfect.

Leo comes down from his high long before the actual recording begins. Although they're recording only two songs, one each for the A and the B sides of the 45, his father has the band warm up all five songs that may make the cut and numerous versions of each one. Meanwhile, Mitch tests microphone placements, dodging in and out of the small room.

The silo becomes clouded with cigarette smoke, and his father orders those not playing to step outside to smoke, which they do, lounging on broken-down couches and chairs, eating sandwiches from the cooler. Leo's mother spends the whole day outside, seated on a washed-out rocker with a missing spindle. Mitch's aged hound dog, Rocky, sleeps at her feet. Leo steps outside only occasionally, preferring to watch every minute of the process, aching to join in the collaboration but recalling his mother's words, "If he asks you to play, play."

A few times, his father does ask Leo to play, but all he wants from him is basic rhythms. If only he could show what he's been experimenting with all week. Once, Leo risks it, bending a few notes of the lilting tune they're warming up for the B side, but his father immediately chops the air with his hand, halting Leo. He catches Leo's eye and shakes his head.

"If you'd just listen," Leo tries.

"For Christ's sake, Leo," his father snaps. "This is no time for fooling around. We're not playing your goddamn rock music."

His own temper flares. This isn't turning out at all as he'd imagined it. His father isn't looking at him as a real musician. He doesn't care if Leo has ideas to contribute. He doesn't want to collaborate. He's as selfish as ever. It's Nora all over again, with his

181

father thinking only about himself. Frustrated, Leo grasps the guitar's neck while he's still miked, and his fingers audibly bend the strings out of tune.

"Get out!" Stash yells so loud all the musicians stop and stare at Leo. "Take that instrument outside and retune it! Then give it to Harlow. He'll play it right."

"Never mind, kid. I'm tuned. All set to go, Stash," Harlow says, smiling uncomfortably and lifting his own guitar. "Whenever you're ready."

Embarrassed but still wanting to stay, Leo pauses, but his father spits, "Get out, Leo. Now!"

Outside, Leo ambles over to his mother and sits down in the dirt next to Rocky, his guitar on his lap. Sulkily he pets the dog's silky ears.

His mother stops her rocking and says, "Give that to me." He realizes she can hear everything going on in the silo from here, and his sulk deepens. Why didn't she come inside and stick up for him? He hands the guitar to her. She cocks her head, thumbs strings, and adjusts a few pegs.

"Here," she says, passing the tuned instrument back to him.

He scowls and plucks "Apache" with vehemence.

"Stop that. You'll throw it out of tune again," Anne says. More gently she adds, "Don't let your father get to you."

"Why won't he let me play?" he says.

"What do you mean? You were playing just now."

"I mean really play. You should hear what I've been working on."

"They're his songs, Leo," she says. "He hears them a certain way."

Leo snuffles the dog's fleshy fur with his cheek and says nothing.

"Let him have his day," she says. "He's worked a long time for it. You keep playing, keep working, you'll have yours."

"Yeah, right. When?"

"Write a song of your own," she says. "Write something you love."

He looks up sharply. Can she tell his song is on the tip of his fingers, that he's longing to play it here, do exactly what his father is doing, re-create the sound in his head in the actual world?

"Go on. Play it for me."

His fingers hover over the strings, aching to play the way he aches when he thinks about Stella. But he can't make his fingers move into his song. He feels frozen and trapped, and all he hears is his father telling him to get his finger out of his ass. He looks at his hands as if he's never seen them before.

After a while, his mother says quietly, her voice sad, "I see. I've always had the stage fright too."

"If he didn't pick at me all the time," he grumbles, wanting his inability to be someone else's fault.

"Your father is who he is. He's not going to change. If you expect him to, you'll always be disappointed."

"You tell him to change all the time. You almost stabbed him because you wanted him to change."

"Yeah," Anne chuckles, "I haven't changed much either. I've always been jealous of those women who flock to him. Little birds pecking, pecking at his feet. Pathetic."

"Why does he let them?"

She grimaces and pushes the chair so hard that Rocky raises his head and gives her an examining look before dropping his chin back to his paws.

"I suppose he needs those women to assure him he's more than some old Polish factory worker."

"Is he?"

"Hey, show some respect. He's in there cutting a record. And he's my husband. Your father."

"Okay, so why do those women bother you so much?"

"Enough to grab a knife?" She smiles. "You get older, you'll learn, understanding isn't the same as approving. Not even the same as accepting. One day maybe it will go too far, and who knows what then."

"Maybe he's already gone too far," he mutters. As soon the words are out of his mouth, he wishes he could suck them back in. The hard look Anne gives him makes him sink into himself.

183

"Has he?" She stops rocking. "What do you mean?"

He plucks the notes of his song on his guitar, but she doesn't seem to hear them. He studies her pink toes inside her white sandals, refusing to look at her.

"Leo, answer me. What do you mean, he's gone too far?"

At that moment, Dinky appears in the silo's doorway. "Your father says come back in if you want."

"Leo," his mother says. "Tell me what you mean."

Silently he stands up. His mother catches his hand as she had earlier in the bus. He can't meet her eye and looks toward the silo's door. Does she know how hard her thumb is digging into his forearm? If he told her, not about Water Boy and Sonya but about Nora, which he knows for sure, would she shut down the session? Would she break every instrument in the studio? With his free hand, he grazes the pin in his pocket. He really could ruin this day for his father right now if he wanted to. The record would never get made. He would certainly never get to play on it.

"Leo?" she says, her thumb digging deeper, her nail breaking the skin.

"Nothing," he says. "I don't mean anything."

He tugs his arm free. As he walks back into the silo with his guitar, his arm burns, not from his mother's grip, but from the knowledge that he's as selfish as his father has ever been. It isn't his family he's just chosen with his silence. He wants the record to happen, and he wants to be on it, even if he's got to play his father's way.

Back inside, his father directs him to play something Leo could have strummed after six weeks of lessons, but his hands are leaden, and he messes up again and again. On the third take, his father sighs, and Mitch moves the microphone away from Leo, so as to pick up less guitar. Even more frustrated than before, Leo wants to spit at his father, *I know what you are. I know what you've done.* Instead, he says he needs to pee.

Ignoring his father's annoyed sigh, he shuffles out back and smokes the rest of the joint. This time he's ready for the floating feeling, and for a moment after the first breath, he fears it won't come. But a moment longer, and release douses him. He looks at his hands, and for the first time since he played with Joey, they feel familiar.

Back in the silo, he says to his father, "One more time." His voice is so definitive, his father nods. Leo steps closer to the microphone, closes his eyes, and finally the music in his father's head enters Leo's hands. When he opens his eyes, he catches his father smiling.

It's after midnight by the time Mitch brings out two cardboard boxes of freshly pressed records. The band has already broken down their equipment and reloaded the bus, and the musicians lounge near the bonfire one of them built, drinking beer and polishing off his mother's sandwiches. She quietly rocks in her chair, her hand draped over the side, caressing Rocky's fur.

The night air is crisp and fresh compared to the inside of the silo, which now reeks of sweat and moldy grain. Leo has followed Mitch through the whole process, and he's come away with one clear thought. He wants this for himself. Not this polka music. Not those two cardboard boxes of records Mitch has handed off to his father, who has tucked them snugly beneath one of the bus's seats. Leo wants *his* music, his way. He won't work in a factory all week, playing a few weekend nights, saving up years to cut one record. He's going to do it like Joey Katz. He's going to make music his life.

The men linger outside the bus, having one last smoke before boarding, while his father and Mitch discuss some final details. Leo stays in the shadows, seated on the beast's bumper. Joey Katz joins him. He lights up a joint, inhales, and offers it to Leo. Leo takes it, but he only takes a small toke.

"You played okay today," Joey says.

He shrugs. "I could have played better."

"Not so. You could have played easier. But your old man, he wanted what he wanted. No better. No worse," Joey says. "What you failed to understand, kiddo, is that we were session musicians in there. Nothing wrong with that. You wanted to play your way.

Nothing wrong with that either. But then it's time to start your own band."

"That's what I've been thinking. It's what my mother said too. Write my own songs."

"Anne Meitka's a wise woman. Stash hardly deserves her."

"I know."

"But I'm not one to talk. I never deserve the good ones either."

The overhead lamps attached to the silo are so bright that at first Leo can't single out the headlights from a Lincoln Continental snaking up the driveway. As they move closer, Leo stands up, squinting in the dark.

"Who's that?" Leo asks.

"C'mon, I'll introduce you," says Joey, jogging over to the car that has pulled up under the spotlights.

"Okay, boys, make sure you got all your gear," Stash says. "Mitch has plenty more work to do tonight."

As the musicians pick themselves up to take a last look in the silo, the darkest-skinned man Leo has ever seen, not that he's seen many, not in real life, emerges from the Lincoln. The man wears a white shirt and a sport coat that strains at the shoulders, suggesting he would be chubby if not for his height, which is a full head taller than Stash. Leo hangs back, but Joey jogs to the man's side. To Leo's surprise, his father walks over and shakes hands with the man too, greeting him as if he knows him. The man greets his father with familiarity right back.

To Leo's greater surprise, before Joey can call him over, his father raises a hand and waves Leo over.

He trots to his father's side.

"This is my son." Perhaps it's exhaustion or the dregs of Joey's cigarettes, but Leo thinks he detects a vein of pride in his father's voice. "Leo, this is Errol Brooker. Plays guitar, like you. Well, not like you. He's the best blues guitarist you'll ever meet."

"That's kind of you, Stash. What's your name, son?"

"Leo," he says, noticing how easily Errol accepts his father's assessment of his own skill. Will he ever be so good that when someone says he's the best, he believes it?

"Nah, your daddy told me a long time ago they call you Snagglepuss. Let's see them teeth."

"No, they don't call me that anymore," Leo says quickly, chewing his lip. "Not for years."

"Nothing wrong with a stage name, son. Folks call me Slide."

"Is that because you play slide?" Leo asks shyly.

"I do."

"Wow. I'd love to hear you play. I've been trying myself, but it gets all muddy."

"Muddy can be good. Can be bad, but can be good sometimes."

"C'mon, men," interrupts Mitch. "It's late already."

"All right, boys, let's set up," says Slide. "We won't need much warm-up. We been playing all night at Theresa's." Slide turns to Leo. "You want to hang around a while, Snaggle?"

"Can we stay?" Leo asks his father. "Just for a little while?"

"No," his father says. He ushers Leo toward the bus.

His mother leans against the bus's bumper, and when they approach, she says, "Let him watch for a while, Stash."

"I'm tired, Anne. So are these boys." He gestures to the other musicians, but many of them have already made their way over to the silo's open door where Slide and three other musicians are tuning up."

"You've had the whole day your way," she says. "Let him watch for fifteen minutes." He seems about to argue more, but she says flatly, "I've got the keys. Let him watch."

Leo leans against the silo's door, but with a tilt of his head, Slide gestures him in. "Sit right there, son."

Leo feels like Slide is playing just for him, although he doesn't look Leo's way once. He plays with his eyes closed.

"Trust your ears, not your eyes . . ." He narrates as if he's telling a story. "Works easier if you tune open E . . . you see here, raise that A string up to B . . . you whack that G up to G sharp . . . Keep that slide straight up like you've just seen a pretty girl prance by . . ." He laughs gently. "Then you mute the strings with your right hand, isolate the one you want . . . Vibrato stays below the note, see there, below . . . most human sound you can make slidin', listen here . . ."

He stops talking and plays. Leo tries to follow Slide's technique, but he gets lost in the feel of the music, which reaches inside him and seems to strike every emotion he has, evoking not the images but the sensations of the horse running in the field, and Kirstin spinning stones into the water, and Water Boy's tiny ears, and Sonya's wet hair slapping her face, and Stella's beautiful fingers, and the hard line of the horizon over the lake, and the scent of the apple blossoms. When Slide stops playing, the silence that follows is so charged, Leo's whole body hums.

After a moment, Slide opens his eyes and says, "Snaggle, that's all for tonight. I got to get recording before the rooster crows and ruins my sound."

"Thanks," says Leo, wishing he knew how to tell Slide how much it means to him to watch him play. He blurts, "I'm going to buy your record." His face burns with embarrassment as soon as the words are out.

Slide laughs. "Well, I hope you do, son. You and a million others. Nice to meet you, Snaggle. You keep sliding. Be patient. Takes time to get. And if you find yourself in Chicago, you come to Theresa's, maybe I'll be there. We'll slide a little more."

Back at the bus, Anne starts the engine. "What about him?" She gestures toward Joey, who's still inside the silo.

"Kid's staying. He's going to play a while. Besides, he's buying that old heap of Mitch's. He'll make his own way back," says his father. Before walking to his seat, he places his palm against Anne's cheek, bends over, and kisses her full on the lips

"My girl," he says quietly. Then louder to the whole bus, he says, "My girl!"

She doesn't laugh or smile. She says, "Let's go. It's late."

The beast shimmies as she guides it up the drive. Leo turns in his seat and strains to see inside the silo, but it's too dark to discern much. When they turn onto the highway, Leo sprawls out on the seat as Joey had done earlier, imagining what it would be like to play music with those men. Slide's a real musician. That music, it was more than something to make you forget your life, as his father claims his music does. Slide's music contains life, its beauty and sorrow, its ugliness and joy.

Leo closes his eyes and lets the junky road beneath the tires rattle his body. He recalls the pride he thought he heard in his father's voice when he introduced him to Slide. Had it really been there? Slide knew Leo's nickname from years ago. So Stash must have talked about him before. Imagine, Stash knowing someone like Slide. Sometimes he wonders if he knows his father at all. He should thank his mother for making his father let him stay and watch Slide. Right now though, he's too exhausted to think anymore about his parents. As the bus gallops into the night, Leo lets the dark wash over him. He imagines he's on his way to Chicago and Slide and Stella are waiting for him at Theresa's.

Emelia

THE MORNING LEO leaves for the Silo, Emelia glances behind her in time to catch a glimpse of his father's weirdo bus cresting the hill and disappearing. Will and Kirstin are gone too, college touring until tonight. In the empty street with the ice pick heavy in her hand, she feels utterly alone. All three of her friends are going to see new things today while she's stuck here. The day ribbons endlessly ahead of her, choking with familiar places she'd like to avoid: the bakery, the lake, the elementary school playground where they delivered those notes to Sonya's little brother. Not so long ago, she would have enjoyed a day kicking around doing nothing much, happy to browse the record shop and try on lipstick at Woolworth's, tramp the lake path to the beach. But now, the thought of the whole day alone unnerves her, and she draws the tip of the ice pick down her bare thigh for the solid sensation it raises.

At the corner, she turns left to avoid the playground and walks up a block of brick houses with big yards, neat lawns, and flower boxes spilling over with pink and yellow blooms. She's never lived in a house with a yard. She used to be jealous of kids who had all that space to play in. The bakery was her play area when she was little. It had been fun, hadn't it, warm and busy, butter squishing between her fingers, flour mountains disintegrating in her play mixing bowl? Had it mattered that Elisa wasn't there?

She shakes her head, disgusted with herself.

This is why she hates being alone these days. All her mind does is spin and spin with questions she has no idea how to answer. She walks faster, circling the neighborhood like a stray cat, avoiding the haunted places. Without her friends, walking is the only thing keeping her—the word comes before she can push it back—*sane*.

She stops. Without realizing it, she has placed herself on Sonya's street. She pivots and retraces her steps, afraid the little brother will spot her, point her out, and Sonya will rush out the front door and chase her. The feeling of pursuit is so strong, she starts running. Two streets up, she finally slows and stops. She braces her hands on her knees and gulps air. She glances back a few times. When she sees no one is chasing her, she muscles up some defiance. Show some gumption, Demski, she chides herself. It's Sonya who's done wrong, not her. All she did was send a few notes. But as soon as she catches her breath, the itchy feeling of being pursued returns, and she gets her feet moving again.

What a disappointment those notes have been, feeding her agitation rather than dispelling it. She insisted the notes were about justice, and maybe they were a little. When she looked at Water Boy, she saw herself, and in Sonya, she saw Elisa. Emelia couldn't lay a finger on Elisa, but Sonya was within reach. Emelia wanted to punish her. And she wanted her friends to help her so she wouldn't be in it all by herself.

But what Emelia had really wanted, even more than punishing Sonya, was to draw a line between her and Sonya, between her and Elisa too, proving Emelia was different from them. In TV shows and movies, when the gavel comes down and the jury decrees someone guilty, it's clear who the criminal is, but Sonya has gone on being a regular girl, doing regular things that are disturbingly similar to the things Emelia does herself, school and swimming and chatting with her friend.

Emelia pauses at a corner, waiting for a car to pass. Inside the car, a boy with a ducktail drives with one hand on the steering wheel and the other stretched over the shoulders of girl with blue-framed sunglasses. The boy smiles at Emelia before pulling away, reminding her of Theo, then of Danny, and her whole body seems to blush. She turns away from her neighborhood. She's got to get out of here.

She doesn't have a plan like last time, not really. She knows she can't get to her mother by walking, but she follows the path she'd taken on her bicycle anyway, and as the morning wears on, yards get bigger, gardens turn to fields, fields to pastures. Among all this space, she can breathe a little better, think a little clearer, or rather, think less, so she keeps walking, listening to the rhythm of her footfalls.

Her feet and back ache by the time she's on the long, straight stretch, which had gone by so much faster on her bicycle. When she was riding, she hadn't noticed how quiet it is out here. And when a car approaches, the desire to shatter the quiet and to get farther away prod her to put out her thumb, just as a test, just to see what it feels like. The car zips past her as if she isn't there. So do the next two. The fourth car is a wood-paneled station wagon with suitcases strapped to the roof. Children's arms and heads spill out. As they pass, the kids yell to her and throw peace signs, but they don't stop. She waves and lifts a two-fingered peace sign in return.

After a long while, she hears "Summer in the City" booming and sees a snow white sports car approaching. She raises her thumb, hoping the car stops, and hoping it doesn't. This time the thrill of not knowing hits her as strong as any Theo-and-Danny surge. Anything could happen. She should be frightened, and she is a bit, but her fear only makes it more exciting.

When the driver hits the brakes, she gasps and almost can't believe it. She hesitates only a second before running to the car and leaning into the open window on the passenger side.

"Hi," she says in a deliberately friendly manner. "Thanks for stopping."

The driver turns down the music and says, "Get in."

She pauses as wisps of caution and excitement brush her like the wind. Anything could happen, she thinks again. He's older than Theo and Danny. His neck has thickened in the way grown-up men's do, but he isn't a fatherly kind of grownup like Leo's and Will's dads. He's in that class of untethered men, the ones who ride alone in Westerns or become double agents in spy movies. Less James Dean sulk, more Warren Beatty aloofness.

After a moment, he says sharply, "I don't have time to waste. Get in if you're getting in."

She chews her lip. She could step back, wave him on. But then she'd be stuck again, sore and lonely and afraid every sensation or thought she has is the eggshell of insanity breaking over her. She doesn't want to think about any of it. She doesn't want to feel anything for a while but this excitement.

"Well?" he says.

She opens the door and slides onto the car's bench seat.

He pulls away with her foot still hanging in midair. The seat's leather is the red of a ripe apple. The same red leather encases the dash and the door, which she has to catch with two hands, leaning back to keep it from swinging wide as he pulls away.

He drives fast, the steering wheel tight in his fists, swiveling the white ring expertly. He leads them through, then beyond Milwaukee and onto the rural stretches she recognizes from her bike ride. Driving even faster now, he hugs the road's curves, tracing the bank of a small lake that has appeared from nowhere, as they seem to do everywhere beyond the city.

"All alone out there," he states finally. His gaze on the road, he scrapes grubby fingernails over his beard, scaling the skin beneath. His green undershirt with no sleeves shows off long arm muscles, the skin walnut brown, except the shoulder tops, which are burnt the color of the burgundy wine her aunts drink with Sunday dinner. Sunglasses with smoky panes cover his eyes, so she can't see their color even when he glances her way.

"Someone ditch you?" he asks.

"Why would you think that?" She has to shout to pierce the air swirling through the open windows.

"Look at you," he says. He says more, but all she catches is, ". . . hobo."

She glances down at her half-secured bib overalls and torn sneakers. She admits she looks a little like a hobo. She rakes her fingers through her hair, but strands jitterbug on the breeze, and she gives up trying to neaten it. Beneath her arms, half-moons of sweat have pooled in the pink cotton of her sleeveless blouse. She wants to lift her arms to dry them, but too embarrassed to do so, she wipes grit from her neck and squints against the sun's glare. Outside the car, islands of cattails jut from the small lake's surface.

Its banks must be shallow. Twenty feet in though, the islands disappear. A sheer drop. She wonders how far down, how deep whatever is rotting on the lake's bed has had to sink.

"I'd rethink that relationship with the friend who ditched you," he says.

"No one ditched me."

"Leave no man behind," he says, then snorts, "shit."

"Aren't you going to ask where I'm going?"

"If you wanted me to know, you would have already said."

He steers away from the water and into a forest thick with ash, sugar maple, and black walnut trees whose boughs form a canopy, leaves filtering the sun. She blinks in the sudden shadow. Can he see with those sunglasses on? He doesn't remove them, but the road is straight, if narrow, and he seems to know it well enough to steer through it blind. Still, she hopes no cars come from the opposite direction.

She feels him accelerate and watches the needle on the speedometer pass sixty and seventy. She slips her hand behind her back, into the deep pocket of her overalls where she fingers the wooden handle of the ice pick.

"It's a Falcon," he says as if she's asked him the name of something.

She looks to the sky but doesn't see any birds.

"No, the car," he says as the speedometer's needle pushes eighty.

After a while, he slows and pulls into a small clearing next to a green pup tent and a ring of stones marking a campfire. Whatever lake they passed earlier must not be round because here it is again, just beyond the tent, a kettle-shaped expanse of ginger water that laps its muddy banks. She calculates that in the short time since he picked her up, the car has traveled an hour's walking distance, at least that far. How far back was the last farmhouse? She can't tell. They were moving too fast. She curls her palm around the ice pick's handle and runs her index finger down the metal shaft.

"Get out," he says when the car stops. He pushes open the driver's side door.

She doesn't move.

"Where are we?"

"Nowhere. I'm staying here for a while. Go on, get out. I don't have time for games."

When she still doesn't move, he yells, "Get out, and get the fuck over here. Now!"

Her glance flits to the woods, searching for the entrance to a trail, which she spots about a hundred yards away. She's fast. She has the ice pick. She swings the door open and steps out.

"Come 'round, over here," he says, not yelling now but using a tone that suggests he doesn't tolerate those who don't obey him. He's still seated in the car.

She hesitates, her hand on the car's back fender.

He looks at her expectantly, annoyance pinching his features. After a moment, his expression softens. He takes off his sunglasses and seems to see her for the first time. His eyes are brown but bloodshot.

"Jesus, you're a kid," he sighs. He drops his chin to his chest, then lifts it and blows a hard breath into the branches above them. "What's your name?"

"Emelia."

"Okay, Emelia, I'm Ben. Now we know each other. So listen, I'm going to show you something, but don't be scared. First time's a shock."

He slings a single cowboy boot onto the ground, crunching dry leaves. He grasps the car's open door and the frame above and lifts himself onto his left leg. Even hunched, he's tall, taller than Leo, who'd shot up to 6'2" last summer. Using the hand on the Falcon's frame to support his weight, he clasps his right thigh with the other hand. His right leg emerges behind him. Below the knee, the cuff of his jeans flaps empty.

"Oh," she says, staring at the space where the other cowboy boot should be.

"You ever hear that saying," he says, his voice breathy with the effort of standing up, "you'd give your best friend your right leg? Well, an asshole named Ricky drove off with mine in his back seat. Some fucking friend."

She squeezes the fender and doesn't respond.

"Long story. You mind?" He loosens two fingers from the Falcon's frame and flicks them, motioning her toward him. "Come on, get the hell over here, little girl, and help a soldier piss." When she still doesn't move, he adds, "Please. Or you're going to see a grown man wet his britches."

She goes to him, her fear overshadowed by something else. Curiosity. Not just for the leg either. He's like no one she's ever met. Once there, he guides her to his right side. Draping his arm over her shoulders, he says, "Tuck in here."

She does, but her shoulder comes only to his ribcage.

"You're not tall enough," he says.

"You're too tall," she says.

He smiles for the first time.

"Oh, I see. Okay, well, how about you bend over, little girl?" When she raises her eyebrows, he adds, "Brace your hands on your knees. Leapfrog style. You're a kid, you play leapfrog, right?"

"Not for years," she says. "But I remember how."

She bends and locks her arms. His weight pushes the heels of her hands into her knees, so she widens her stance, managing to support him as he hops. She shuffles forward a few steps so he can hop again. In this way, they make it to the line of trees, where he leans on a paper birch and unbuttons his trousers. She waits for him to tell her to turn around, but he has either forgotten her in his urgency or he doesn't care if she watches. She curls her arm around a birch trunk as a line of urine riffles some fat ferns.

"Aaaah," he sighs. "Better than sex. . . . Don't let anyone tell you there aren't other sensations just as pleasurable as fucking."

She flinches at the curse word, which has more muscle than when she or her friends use it. When he says it, it's clear he's done the act it names.

He finishes urinating, buttons his fly, and says, "Can you get me to the tent? My spare leg's in there."

"Really, you have an extra?"

"It's crap. Army issue. The leg Ricky's hot-rodding around the state with is a honey. Smooth a ride as that Falcon." He flicks his fingers again. "C'mon, private, assume the position."

"It's a nice car," she says, bracing herself.

196

"She's a sweet ride," he agrees.

They make it to the tent, and he drops hard onto his buttocks. He unbuttons a flap, rolls back the canvas, and scoots himself into the tent's opening where he leans in and roots around before sitting back up. He emerges with a calf and foot that remind her of the legs of dolls she played with when she was a little girl.

She wants to ask him what happened, but she hears her aunts instructing her, don't ask questions, don't stare at cripples. Yet she'd like to know. She guesses he'd been a soldier. On television, she's seen the bloody bodies of soldiers in Vietnam. After dinner, her aunts read aloud newspaper articles about local boys killed there, even if they don't recognize the names. Out of respect, they say. The word *shrapnel* is featured a lot in the articles. It's an ugly word, far more hideous than *fucking* but just as foreign in her mouth. As he bunches up the cuff of his trouser leg, he doesn't seem to mind her looking, so she does, watching him expose the cupped end of his leg, a scar smiling wryly over the nub. Strangely, the stump suggests the leg that used to be there far more than the baby doll calf and slipper-like foot he's strapped on.

"Fascinating shit, huh?"

"Where is it?" she asks, her aunts be damned.

"What?"

"Your foot, your leg. Where are they right now?"

He glances at her, then at the water as if his limb might be one of the bloated things disintegrating on its bed. He turns his attention back to his plastic leg, which he secures with the same expertise he showed when handling the Falcon's steering wheel. She notes the flesh tone of the plastic is three shades lighter than the skin on his arms.

"I'll give you this, little girl, no one's ever asked after it before. But I dream about it. Spend my nights running around in forests and marshes and cities, looking for my damn leg. I must say, it's nice to run, even if it's in my dreams and my leg's rotting as I go."

"So you don't know where the real one is?"

"Probably still in a half-burned rice paddy, decomposing into manure." He shrugs, then laughs. "Harvest must have had a hell of an aftertaste."

Until now, she hasn't met anyone who's been in this war. She wants to ask him if he felt any difference between him and the men on the other side. Had there been a clear line? In war, at least, there must be good and bad, them and us. Afraid that asking this would be bad manners, she asks instead, "How do you drive without your foot?"

"Use my left. Didn't you see?" he says, rooting around in the tent again. This time he emerges with a cane. Through its varnish, the shaft retains the features it held as a tree limb. "Tried ten cars before I found the perfect fit though. My folks bought it for me. They own all this land. Biggest farm in the county."

"The lake too?"

He nods. "Great for trout. I was supposed to come back from my war, go to the agri college, and work the farm with my pa. But now, well, plenty of men have farmed with one leg. Farming with one arm's actually harder. But I lost the taste for it. Hey, you want to swim? I need to float."

Without waiting for her answer, he expertly flips to his left knee. Using the cane, he pushes himself to his feet and limps toward the lake. At the water's edge, he unstraps his leg and pulls off his undershirt and pants. She's startled when she sees he doesn't wear underpants and equally startled that she hadn't noticed this when he peed. At the sight of his sex, her cheeks burn with embarrassment, but she wants to see and doesn't turn away. He seems not to notice her looking as he slides his naked body into the water.

"Aahhh," he sighs as he'd done earlier when peeing. He flap-swims himself into deep water, eventually diving under and swimming the crawl with just his arms. He has a strong stroke, long and even. After a while, he turns onto his back and floats.

"Like outer space. Zero fucking gravity," he says, spitting water into the sky. "What do you think? Should I be an astronaut? Be the first man to hop on the moon?"

She can't tell if he really wants her to answer, but she says nothing, and after a while, he shifts from floating to treading water.

"Come on in. The water's fine." When she makes no move, he adds, "Can't you swim?"

"Sure, I can," she says. For only a moment does she consider that the water may even the advantage she has over him on land. If she needs to, can she outswim him? If she can make it to land, she can run up the bank to the trail or out to the road. He'll have to strap on his leg to follow her. But she finds she's not afraid of him. She feels something else, curiosity certainly, and a little thrill.

"So if you can swim, get your damn self out here," he says. As if her reason for hesitating has just occurred to him, he adds, "It's okay, you can keep your panties and bra on."

"All right," she calls.

She steps out of her shorts and pulls off her shirt. Stripped down to her underwear and bra, she steps to the edge of the water. The cool tongue of the lapping water licks her tired feet. How long had she been walking before he picked her up? She wades in up to her ankles, the cold and mud soothing her soles.

His gaze on her, she finds herself heating up. She thinks of the way he said the word *fucking*. With one leg, she kicks water into a high fan.

She can walk away right now. He could never catch her. He's a safe risk.

She unhooks her bra and lets it drop, quickly crossing her arms over her chest.

"No," he calls. "You keep the rest on, kid."

She steps forward until the water is up to her calves, her toes squishing into silky mud, arms still crossed over her breasts. He showed himself to her, she thinks, not only his sex, but his leg, the broken part of himself too. He let her ask questions. He's been places and seen things. Who better than him to look at her and tell her who she is?

She turns and surveys the tree line for watching eyes—the friend, Ricky, or someone from the farm. Seeing no one, she slides down her underpants and tosses them toward shore.

"Aw, man, what are you doing, girl?"

She pauses long enough for him to look, to see the whole of her, before diving cleanly into the water. She surges into a few strokes of butterfly, hearing him whoop on her third and fourth strokes.

"Look at that, the girl *can* swim!"

Energized, she swims a circle around him, finally sucking a big breath, pulling and kicking breastrokes beneath the surface, popping up an arm's length away from him. Silently they tread water together until he seems to have decided something and says, "Race you."

They swim freestyle to a raft anchored about fifty yards out. She lets him heft himself up before raising her own body up. She lies next to him, the sun warming her, waiting for him to touch her. But he lies still, his hands crossed over his belly.

The sun has mostly dried her skin by the time she finally speaks.

"Do you want to kiss me?" she says.

"What?" he says absently. His mind has been in the clouds or the rice paddies. He's forgotten about her.

"Don't you want to touch me?"

"You have a nice body," he says after a while. He reaches over and clasps her hand in his. "Don't ever be ashamed of it. But you're a little young for me, honey."

She goes hot with embarrassment, feeling more naked than she had when she first pulled off her clothes. His hand is strong and warm, and she longs to touch him more. She wants him to touch her. But he doesn't want her. He thinks she's too young. Should she tell him who her mother is, that she's the spitting image?

She turns onto her side and places her hand on his chest. His body startles at the contact.

"I'm not as young as I look," she says, trailing her fingers down his stomach.

He lifts himself onto his elbows and looks at her for a long moment.

"I see I've given you the wrong idea," he says, his voice even. He lies down again. "I'm sorry. You may not be as young as you look, but you're younger than you think."

She pulls her hand away as if burned and searches for something to cover herself with. Finding only words, she says fast, "I caught a girl burying her just-born baby down by Lake Michigan. It wasn't quite a baby, not yet. But it would have been."

"Oh, yeah?" he says.

"Don't you think that's the worst thing in the whole world a person can do?"

"Depends."

She feels him shrug.

"No, it doesn't," she says. "She buried her own baby. She's horrible. Maybe she killed it. We couldn't tell. It looked weird, you know, unfinished."

"We?"

"My friends and I. We—" She's about to tell him how they dug up Water Boy. How they reburied him and sent the notes telling Sonya to make it right, but the details and reasons are muddled in her head. How come what they did sounds as bad, worse maybe, than what Sonya did?

"No, listen, I'm not explaining it right," she says, sitting up. "You didn't see Water Boy—that's what we named it. Him."

"Like a pet, huh? I feel sorry for that poor girl," Ben says, muddling things further. "Stuck like that. Nowhere to run. No better than the draft."

"What do you mean?"

"I mean boys growing up now have that swamp monster called Vietnam and the draft dogging them. You girls got your own bodies doing the same," he says closing his eyes. He points at her belly. "Ticking time bomb, no way to defuse."

"You don't get it," she says, lying back down.

"Maybe not," he sighs.

As they lie together in silence, she decides to find a way to make him understand. She doesn't know why, but she needs to hear him say she's right.

"Water Boy, that could have been me."

He doesn't respond.

"My mom left me. She never even said who my father was, not even on my birth certificate. So Water Boy, he could have been me."

"In battle," he says, "*could have* is as big a killer as land mines. Could have stepped left instead of right. Could have been the one to put my head up and gotten it blown off instead of the guy next to me. Could have deferred and said fuck you to Uncle Sam, gone

201

to college, or fucked away up north the way the smart ones are doing now. The only way to really make it through a war is to focus on the situation at hand. Make the best choice at the moment you have to make a decision. Then live with it. Consequences are going to come, no matter what choice you make."

"I suppose," Emelia says.

He goes on. "You take the situation with that girl. Sonya you said her name is?"

"Yes."

"Well, the situation *could have* been a whole lot better if she'd had a good place to go to take care of things. Ideally before she got herself gone. They got pills now, you know. You should know that. Figure out a way to get yourself some. But after too. What was she supposed to do? Trapped like a March hare."

"What if everyone did that?"

"*What if* is just another way of saying *could have*. Anyway, we wouldn't be here to ask the question. Of course, you'll never know if having the kid was her choice or not because she didn't have one, not really. Hell, you don't even know if she had a choice at the moment of conception."

Emelia's taken aback. She hadn't thought of this. Water Boy's father. *Johnny Angel.* No angel at all? Is that why her mother named her Demski?

"*Could have* been he was married or cruel or had a strict family. *What if* she just didn't love him?"

"But it was wrong, what Sonya did. It must be."

"Maybe, but given your current state of undress, are you one to say? *What if* I weren't the gentlemanly man I happen to be?"

"It's not the same," Emelia insists, but her insistence sounds feeble even to herself.

"You sure?"

"You don't understand," she says.

"You're right," Ben says. "I guess that's my point. I don't know the whole story. I do know it's pretty hard to understand someone else's hell. To really understand it."

She stares at the empty blue sky, grudgingly acknowledging that she doesn't really know the whole story either. Not her mother's, which is her aunts' faults. Not Sonya's, which is her own. She never tried to find out Sonya's story. The shame of having sent those notes suddenly burns hotter than the sun on her bare stomach. Ben's right about another thing too. As much as she wants to pretend she's not like them, she let herself be kissed by Theo and Danny, and she took her clothes off for Ben and asked him to kiss her.

"You okay?" he says

"Are your parents mad that you don't want to farm?" she asks. She doesn't want to think about Sonya or Elisa or how much choice she has in who she will be. She wants to hear Ben talk. "You know, are they mad that you don't want to go into the family business?"

"Mad? Wouldn't that be a nice change? Don't you know it's not polite to get mad at a cripple? Mostly my folks are a shit pile of guilt." As if just remembering her age, he adds, "Pardoning my French. As I said, I could have deferred. Got accepted to college. Had a scholarship even. When the draft hit though, my folks started using words like *duty* and *freedom*. My pa started talking about his Army time being a character-shaping experience."

"Did you want to fight?"

"I think I knew they'd look at me differently forever if I didn't. It was my decision, but they feel like they convinced me to go. So now they feel responsible. Fact is, though, I've been milking them too long . . . I suppose one of these days, my sweet-lady Falcon and I will just hit the road. Let them get on with things. Let me be someone else somewhere else."

"Me too. That's what I want to do. I want to go to California."

"Kids do seem to be going to California these days. Me, I'd like to see the Rockies. Think a person can ski on one leg?"

"I don't know." She tries to imagine him in snow, but the sun burning her breasts and belly and thighs makes it impossible. "Were you scared?"

He takes so long to respond, she wonders if he understands she means *over there*, then wonders if he's fallen asleep.

"Anyone who tells you he's not scared most of the time is either lying or batshit crazy. In war or out."

203

They lie quietly for a moment.

"What scared me most over there were the nights," he says. "Humid. Man, a hundred times thicker than an August night here. And black as fury. And you knew there were people out there, but you couldn't see them. Not even your buddies. Sometimes a guy just had enough of wet darkness and started shooting at the dead black."

"Living ghosts," she says.

"Yeah, sort of. Daytimes, you'd see guys get blown up or shot down. Guy next to me was bull's-eyed, a hole right between his eyes. Perfect kill." He touches a spot between his eyebrows. "Shit, the expression on his face . . . not surprised, not angry, just . . . nothing. But you know what? That motherfucker survived. Blind though.

"Rather be a gimp than a blind man. Can't drive blind." He picks up her hand and places it on his right thigh. "That feels nice," he says.

She lets her hand lay lightly on his half leg, then heavier, until it feels like their flesh has melted together.

After a while, he props himself onto his elbows again. He raises his face to the sky and screech-sings, "Man, I love that pad-dy water!" He sits full up, lightly backslaps her upper thigh with his finger, and says, "Little girl, I need a smoke."

The wind has picked up, and they swim back against it, the water chilling her now; so she swims fast, easily beating him to the shore.

They dress with their backs to each other. She can't find her underpants and pulls her shorts on without them. Her shirt stinks of her old sweat and clings to her wet back.

"Going to be a storm," he says absently. "Think I'll sleep up at the house tonight."

She wonders if talking to her has leached something out of him.

"Give me a hand up," he says when he's strapped on his leg, "and I'll drive you home."

She says okay to the ride, which is no longer thrilling to her. She's just tired. For now, she wants to go home to her mother's primrose wallpaper and comfortable bed.

He grasps her arm and his cane with equal force. Despite them, he trips on an exposed tree root, dropping the cane. He gropes for her as he falls, wrenching her arm and bringing her down with him. She lands hard, scraping and bruising her thigh on the same tree root that tripped him.

"Goddamn it!" he shouts. "Motherfucking goddamn piece-of-shit leg!"

"It's okay," she says, pulling the fringe of her shorts down her thigh so he won't see the scrape on her leg and feel worse.

"Motherfucking Ricky!"

She doesn't know what to say in the face of his anger. She admires it though. It's hard as a steel rod, she thinks, wishing for a little steel of her own.

After a time, she helps him jostle himself back up.

"See, no harm done," she says.

But he's silent and moody as he drives her back to town, just as Theo and Danny had been. Are all men like this, she wonders, moody after they expose themselves to you?

Her arm aches, and her thigh burns, but she says nothing. The breeze is cold now. Its rush fills the silence between them, so she keeps the window rolled down. The sky has clouded up, and he doesn't need his sunglasses, but again, she can't see his eyes. He keeps them trained on the road. She sticks her arm out the window and hand-surfs the breeze, imaging she's on a real wave in a real ocean. When she brings her hand back in, her palm is moist. He's right. It's going to rain.

She directs him to the same spot the truck had let her off. He steers the Falcon to the curb just as fat drops of water burst against the windshield.

"I'll walk from here," she says, getting out.

"Showoff," he says, finally smiling at her.

She smiles back and slams the door. She's only taken a step when he calls her back.

"Hey!"

She crouches so she can see him through the open passenger window.

"Don't take no wooden legs, little girl," he says, forced jokiness in his voice.

"Okay," she says, disappointed this is all he has to give her. "I hope you get your Falcon leg back." She turns away, but he calls to her a second time. She leans her palms on frame of the open window but looks at him through the windshield.

This time when he speaks, his tone is sincere.

"Hey, look at me."

"What?" she says, shifting to the open window so she can meet his gaze.

"You swim a beautiful butterfly."

"Thanks." Now it's her turn to hold his gaze. "By the way, did you know your leg smiles?"

He looks at her questioningly.

"The scar. Biggest grin I ever saw. Didn't you know?"

He laughs and shakes his head. "No, I didn't know that." He sticks his hand out the window. "It's been my true pleasure, Emelia."

When she shakes his hand, she sees another scar, one she hadn't noticed before, a ruby thread, trailing up his inner forearm. When they unclasp hands, a twenty-dollar bill nestles in her palm.

"For California," he says. "Or somewhere. Go see something." He drives off, shooting a wave out the window.

"I will," she promises. "I'll see you out there, okay?"

He thrusts his thumb out the window as he U-turns and peels off.

Sonya

THE FOURTH AND final note has shaken Sonya from her lethargy.

Last week, crushed into her bedroom's closet, she focused on these words from the note: *Make it right.* After the initial shock of the others—*Baby killer, We know*—she'd ignored them. They're the music on the record that's been going round, round, and around in her head for weeks now. Nothing new. But the note sender's other point hooked her.

Make it right.

Moon Boy cannot be sacrificed for nothing.

Make it right.

Do something to make his loss meaningful.

After a long time spent on the closet floor, going from wretchedly frozen to rigidly determined, she slid open the door and dressed. Without taking much notice, she chose an old pair of pedal pushers and a new blouse. She sat down at her desk and opened her chemistry textbook. If she can ace the final, she can still pass the class, she thought. She'll do extra credit to improve her grade. Trippy will have to let her. She'll make him. And she'll talk to her other teachers too, go to the principal if she has to. She'll force them all to let her make it right.

She's spent the week buckling down, going to class and studying and doing little else. Most of her teachers have said they'll allow her to make up her work. Only Trippy has been resistant, and he's the one who matters. He holds the fate of her scholarship in his hands. She's determined to prove to him that the university hasn't made a mistake, and not just for herself now. *Girls, once they mature, they lose focus*, he said. For him, this was no longer a theory to be proven or disproven. Her actions turned this theory to a postulate, and in doing so, she'd stolen a chance from every other worthy girl to come after her. If he tells them to pull the scholarship from the first girl who's ever received it, who knows if they'll ever take the chance on a girl again?

Sonya spends her Saturday holed up in her bedroom reviewing her organic chemistry notes. It seems crazy to her now that these principles, the laws and theorems that prove the order of the natural world, had ever looked muddy to her. *Nature, synthesis, fermentation. Organic compounds have lower boiling points. Organic compounds are combustible. Every cell in the human body is an organic compound.* The order is there. You only have to seek it out.

This fresh clarity of mind and her renewed determination have returned something to her, a sense of herself. But she doesn't make the mistake of believing her old self has returned. That girl died on the shore of the lake and was buried with Moon Boy. *Moon Boy is an organic compound.* But she's not Dark Eve either. And she's not a smart girl. She never had been. That's where she'd been wrong. But she's wiser now than she was, wise enough to understand just how much she didn't know before Moon Boy.

And she's ready to be finished with high school. College will be a whole new world. New people who have never seen Dark Eve. There, she'll be Focused Eve, Inquiring Eve, Enthralled Eve. In those college classrooms and labs, the world itself will crack open like a milkweed pod revealing its silky seeds. She'll see beneath surfaces. She'll understand everything. She'll discover new things. Help people. *Make it right.* She's already learned so much since this morning. Even relearning material she'd known before but had forgotten has been thrilling. Her brain simmers with new knowledge and the joy of being stretched. Imagine how it will buzz after four years of college.

What a relief that science hasn't betrayed her after all. It was waiting patiently to bring her back into the fold.

After the second post arrives, Dean runs headlong into her bedroom. He crashes against her bed and scrabbles up, scattering her freshly written notes. She's been studying since early morning, and she scoops up the notes and sets them on her bedside table. She can afford a break. She knows the material. She'd been so far ahead of the class before, she hadn't really been behind.

Dean jumps pogo-stick style on her mattress, waving a white envelope above his head. He punctuates each syllable he utters with a leap, "You. Got. A. Let. Ter."

"Where's Mom?" she says, pretending to catch his bare feet as they spring into the air.

"Shop. Ping."

"Okay, then, give me the letter."

To prolong the game, he holds the letter high above his head, bouncing and kicking and giggling at her feigned near misses of his feet.

"Spe. Shul. Di. Liv. A. Ree."

"Gimme, gimme." She laughs, finally pulling his feet from under him so he lands on his behind, waves of giggles crashing when she tickles him. "Hand over the letter, buster boy."

"Stop!" He laughs, wriggling and wiggling and dropping the envelope into her lap. "Here!"

He springs down from her bed, flings his arms wide, and motors out of her room, growling the sound of an airplane engine at top volume.

The envelope bears both the special delivery payment stamp, dated yesterday, and the crest of the state university. Special delivery. Is that good or bad? Nervously, she pulls her hair from her damp neck and ties it into a knot at the back of her head before turning her attention to the envelope. She recognizes the name on the return address as the chair of the biology and natural sciences department. She opens the envelope, unfolds the letter, and reads.

> Dear Miss Morrow,
>
> I regret to inform you a mistake was made in the
> original awarding of the Louis Peret Naturalist
> Scholarship. The panel inadvertently read your

name as "Sonny," not "Sonya," and awarded you the LPNS in error. However, only young men are considered for this exceptional scholarship to ensure it best promotes and furthers Louis Peret's naturalistic goals through the study of botany. While this may be disappointing to you, I'm sure you'll agree that the University must consider who is truly most dedicated, most deserving, and will best serve the interests of the field of botany.

We are sorry that this error was brought to our attention so late.

We wish you the best of luck elsewhere in your future endeavors.

Dr. Edward Burton

Her mouth goes dry as her future disintegrates and scatters like pollen. Just as she'd tightened her grasp on it. She drops the letter on her bed, her disbelief surpassed only by her anger. Has Trippsman done this, contacting this Dr. Burton to point out the oversight, or had the panel discovered it for themselves when looking at the rest of her application? Either way, it's not right. After all she's done, no one is more deserving, no one is more dedicated than she is. No one has sacrificed as much.

She feels herself crumbling. Dark Eve hovers, threatening to return. But white-hot anger beats her back. Sonya's newly regained clarity of mind sharpens to microscopic. Every atom of her person trembles with anger, every atom in the world shivers with instability. Her bed, her desk, her books. Nothing is solid. It never was. What an illusion the world is. A stinging, buzzing hive of illusion.

"All *his* fault," she spits.

She has never thought this before. Not really. She always believed she was to blame. She should have been smarter. Everyone knows it's up to girls to keep themselves unalloyed. Bad girls get bad reputations, but stupid girls get them too. She'd been vain, thinking she was so smart, so special, it could never happen to her. Even when he turned his back on her, she hadn't believed he should suffer as she has, as Moon Boy has. No one should suffer so.

But now, to have struggled her way back to the surface, to finally be able to breathe again, only to be pushed back down. No, it isn't right. Not one iota.

She picks up the paper and tries to read it again, but the letters shimmer on the page. Why should she lose everything? She's already paid a high price, a queen's ransom, for her foolishness and naiveté. She gave up Moon Boy. Now she's lost the wide world too. Because she is *Sonya* and not *Sonny* or because of him? Because of her sex or because of sex? It hardly matters.

She refolds the letter and returns it to its envelope. She won't put this in any memory box. She's going to deal with it. She lifts the edge of her mattress and places the envelope on top of the picture she'd forgotten was there. *His* picture. It's been so long since she pulled it out to caress—did she really run her fingers over a photograph, she thinks disgustedly—to gaze at it as she touched herself in the dark.

She drops her mattress with a thump. She has nothing more to lose. But she will do as her other letter-writers have advised. *Make it right.* She opens her binder and writes on a clean piece of loose-leaf paper: *Meet me. Urgent.* She specifies the spot at the top of the cliffs where they had met before and gone down to the secluded area of the beach. They'd collected stones together. She let him teach her what she already knew, to select flat ones, to spin them to make them skip.

"It's physics," he said.

Be there Sunday at the break of dawn, she writes. She used to go out often at this time of day to watch the sun rise and to collect samples. She never sees a soul at that time, so they should be safe. Except for when she'd seen him there, and they'd walked and talked. No, he'd done all the talking, she realizes. A man used to being listened to, his voice the undercurrent to the rolling waves. But she's been silent long enough. It's time he acknowledges all she's sacrificed.

Before folding the paper, she adds one final line: *It's time to make it right.*

To ensure he sees it, she swipes an unopened bottle of brandy from her mother's secret liquor stash and tapes the note to the bottom of the bottle. "Never refuse a drink," he's told her. "It's ungracious." Good girls are never ungracious. She sipped every sip he gave her. Or pretended to, not realizing it was all pretend.

She waits for her mother to return so as not to leave Dean alone, but he still begs her to take him along.

"Not this time, Deanie-Beanie." She waggles his cheek. The brandy and note are hidden in her specimen-collecting bag. She'll sneak them into the spot in his garage where he keeps his equipment. He'll be sure to see it there. She calls to her mother, "I'm going to see Stella. I'll be back soon."

"Have a good time, hon." Her mother waves her out the door, all smiles that her daughter is no longer mooning around.

The delivery goes off without a hitch. Afterwards, the sudden lightness of her specimen bag gives her a feeling of being unmoored. Just when she'd rooted herself to the world again, she's been cut loose. But she jogs to the lake, the wind wet and fresh on her cheeks, her muscles taut and strong. She feared Dark Eve would return. Instead, the lightness is now freeing. Yes, she's unmoored. College is gone, but only for now. Her parents can't afford to send her, and if they could, she doubts they'd think it was worth the money. But with some money of her own, she could go anywhere. Do anything. See the great redwood forests, the Everglades. She's never seen a mountain or an ocean. She'll go learn the world for herself and bring it back to Moon Boy. And when the time is right, Moon Boy will return to her, and she'll be ready. It will be okay. She will make it right. She's already taken the first step.

Tomorrow morning she'll take the next step. He will see the note, and he will have to meet her. He will have to help her, not just by giving her money to leave after graduation. She'll make him admit he duped her as surely as if he'd been a bee orchid, *Ophrys apifera*, which contorts its flowers into the shape of a bee to attract a mate. His smile, his interest in her, telling her she's smart, she's beautiful, a *beaut*. When she came to him, buzzing with interest, he'd laughed at her and pollinated her anyway. She doesn't want to ruin his life. She'll make that clear. But she needs to make him understand. She touches the scar on her ribs, tracing its outline and the smooth but tough patch of scar tissue.

She holds his secret.

The next morning, before first light, she slips out of bed and dresses quietly in the dark. The only sound she makes is when she drops the flashlight on the linoleum floor in the hallway outside her parents' bedroom door. She freezes, listening, straining to hear. No sound comes from their bedroom, but Dean's bed creaks as he tosses and turns. The boy's unable to settle even in sleep. She holds her breath and waits a long moment before bending to pick up the flashlight and backing down the hallway.

Outside, the air is dewy and cool. It's her gem, the loveliness of this time of day. Moving through the empty streets, the overhead lamps illuminate the walkway, so she doesn't need the flashlight until she crosses the highway and enters the park. Still, she decides not to turn it on. Her feet and the sounds of the lapping waves, the scents of the morning glories, Russian sage, and wild lavender guide her to the cliff.

When the sun splits the water and sky, she raises her hand to the dark figure and calls, her voice mingling with the dawn chorus of robins, *Turdus migratorius,* and blackbirds, *Turdus marula*. Then she runs.

Leo

LEO WAKES WHEN a siren stabs the air. He's so tired, he'd have slept through its shriek if the phone's ring hadn't shattered the remaining pane of sleep. He waits for one of his parents to answer it, but after ten rings, no one does, and he forces himself out of bed.

He reaches for the kitchen extension, but only a half-ring chirps before cutting off.

"Damn," he says.

Fuzzy with sleep and exhaustion, he barely discerns the sirens outside his head from the screaming inside it. He pours a glass of milk and drinks it, the liquid sliding cold and sweet down his throat. Before he finishes drinking, the phone rings again.

He picks up the receiver and yells, "What? Who is this?" He glances around to make sure his mother hasn't heard his rudeness. Where are his parents? Still asleep? Or up and out already? His mother is probably grocery shopping or at some neighbors. His father, who knows?

"Leo? Is that you?"

"Yeah," he says, recognizing Kirstin's voice.

"Your voice is all gravelly."

"What is it? Why are you calling so early?"

"It's one in the afternoon," she says.

He looks at the clock above the sink, confirming she's right. The hard glare of the sun should have told him well enough. Man, his eyes hurt. No wonder Joey wears sunglasses all the time. Maybe he'll get himself a pair just like Joey's, with pine-green lenses and wire rims. Wear them all day at school. Make himself look cool and mysterious. He bets Slide wears glasses in the daytime.

He notices a note from his mother telling him she's gone to play piano at the ballet school. No note from Stash of course. He stretches the phone cord to its limit, shuffling to the pantry. The trouble cot is empty, but the covers are thrown back. Dread cuts through his fogginess. Why had Stash slept in there last night? Had there been a fight when they got home, after he fell asleep? It had been late when they arrived back. He assumed his parents went to bed like him. Now he thinks of the conversation he had with his mother outside the silo. Had he given Stash away without really meaning to?

"You have to come," Kirstin says.

"Come where?"

He shoulders the receiver against his ear as he grabs a banana from the bowl on the counter. He peels it and shoves half of the fruit into his mouth before he sees the patches of black on it. It tastes bruised and rotten. Which is how he feels too. Yesterday's music is a vaporous dream. Had it happened? Yes, the two boxes of records stacked next to the stereo console are proof. But something is wrong. He feels it as certainly as the dirty tiles beneath his bare feet. The universe has shifted.

"Don't you hear the sirens?"

"Yeah, of course I hear them. I'm not deaf." But it's only now that he registers the sound is outside of him, not in his head. His whole body spins with confusion. What happened between his parents? Why had Stash slept downstairs? Where is he now? Jeez, his eyes feel like they're on fire. As some emergency vehicle nears, the siren's increasing pitch pinches his glands if he were sucking lemons. Man, his head hurts. The pitch decreases as the vehicle moves away, but his head still pinches.

"What's going on?" he says. "Are those fire trucks?"

"Fire trucks, but not for a fire. From my bedroom window, I can see them at the lake. Police cars too," Kirstin says. "And a county sheriff's car. You know, the lake and park are actually county property."

She says this last bit in the know-it-all tone that annoys him this morning. But it's not her tone that keeps him from saying anything biting back. Where is Stash? His dread rises with the banana bile at the back of his throat. And where is . . . ?

"Emelia?" he manages, remembering her strange mood yesterday.

"What? No, Leo, it's me, Kirstin," she says. "What's wrong with you? Listen, I think maybe—"

"What?"

"I'm afraid."

"Of what?" he asks, not sure he wants to know.

"I'm afraid it's Sonya."

Make it right.

He takes a moment to swallow before saying quietly, "Why do you think that? It could be anything." He allows himself to prize open a sliver of hope. "Yeah. It's probably some stupid kid messing around. Someone we don't know. Or it's nothing. A fox caught in a fishing net." He can see the fox, struggling and snapping against the rope. The wriggling fox is as real as the countertop he drums with his fingertips.

"Just come," says Kirstin. "We'll all meet at the corner and go to the lake together."

"Wait, why do you think it has something to do with her?" He needs her to agree with him that it's nothing. "It's just a fox," he insists.

"Meet me at the corner," she repeats.

"Wait!" he says, angry at her earlier knowing tone and her refusal to defer to him. When did she stop doing that? Has he lost control of everyone, everything? "That's just like you. Why do you always do that?" he snaps.

"What?"

"Say you know things when you don't?"

"Leo, come on."

"Did you talk to the others, to Emelia?" he says. "And Will," he adds as an afterthought. "Do you know it's not a fox? Or it could very easily be—"

"Stop it," she says. She sighs and feigns patience with him. "Leo, I can see from my window. All this fuss, it's no fox."

He glances again at the unmade cot in the pantry, at the boxes of records. Where is his father? He wishes he had one of Joey's cigarettes. He steps into Stash's pantry, again straining the phone cord to its full length. He just barely manages to reach beneath the cot and grab the pint bottle of whiskey he knows his father stashes there. He shoulders the phone, uncaps the bottle, and drinks. The liquid burns differently from the joint, but enough that he barely hears Kirstin say that Will and Emelia will meet them at the corner too.

"So you talked to Emelia?"

"Yes!" she says, exasperated with him now. "She'll be there. Just hurry up."

After they hang up, he dresses quickly, managing to push down his rising fear with another gulp of whiskey. He dribbles water into the bottle, filling it to its former level and crouches down to place the bottle back behind the cot. Thinking again, he says, "Screw you, Stash." He shoves it into his jacket pocket. Just let his father try to hassle him about it.

Outside, the dull glare of the sun behind gathering clouds might as well be glass shards piercing his head. He squints as he ducks behind the Lehmens' hedges and takes the whiskey bottle from his pocket. Placing his lips on the bottle, he remembers the kiss his parents exchanged on the bus yesterday. They'd come so close. So very close to being happy.

Emelia

WHEN EMELIA FIRST hears the sirens, she's lying on her mother's bed, studying a road atlas, identifying places she recognizes from television and magazines. Chicago, St. Louis, Taos, Cheyenne, Tucumcari. No one would have heard of her mother or her aunts in those places. Probably there wouldn't even be a Demski listed in the phone book.

As Ben said, she has choices.

Away from here, she could tell anybody anything about her mother, about herself. Escaping to a place with a name like Santa Rosa, Twin Arrows, or Seligman, she wouldn't have to be *Emelia*. If she can be what Ben said, someone else somewhere else, maybe she can escape being her mother. She can call herself *Lia*. Lia Demon. Even better, Lia Diamond. She just wishes she didn't have to go alone.

Kirstin's call to meet sends her running. She uses the back steps, closing the screen door quietly behind her and jogging down the alley, so as not to pass by the bakery window and be stopped by her aunts, still angry at her for coming home after dark last night. She lied and said she'd been with Kirstin, and that Kirstin had been so excited talking about the college tour, they forgot the time. Aunt Lou and Aunt Genny exchanged doubtful looks, but they stopped short of saying what Emelia could see in their eyes: *Just like your mother.*

She and Leo arrive at the corner at the same time.

"What do you know?" he asks. He smells of bananas, stale sweat, and the holiday fruitcakes her aunts swaddle in brandy-soaked cloths to marinate. Plum circles shadow his eyes. He must have gotten home really late. His father's bus hadn't been in the driveway last night when Emelia passed it on her way home.

After Kirstin and Will arrive, they head toward the sound of the sirens. Kirstin again describes having seen fire trucks from her bedroom window. "It's her," she says. "I just know it is."

"Could be anyone. Lots of people mess around there. How do you know it's her?" says Leo. "A fox maybe. Caught in a fishing net."

"They wouldn't make such a big deal over a fox," Emelia says.

"That's what I told him on the phone," says Kirstin.

"It's her," says Will firmly. "My mother heard it from Mrs. Van Dahl, the fire chief's wife. The body of a teenage girl. Who else could it be?"

"It could be anyone," Leo says, but his face shows what they all fear. *Make it right.* What had Sonya done?

Approaching Lakeshore Drive, the four of them resolve to blend in with the crowd that is gathering. Not a word, they agree. Not a gesture, nothing that will call attention to them or give them away to the neighbors, who form a loose band of neck-stretchers near the fire trucks and ambulance.

They soberly pick up their pace until they're jogging. Passing the marsh, each of them glances toward Water Boy's grave, its pull an undertow. But no one says a word about him, and Emelia thinks, poor Water Boy. Then to her surprise, she also thinks, poor Sonya.

"We should never have sent those notes," Will insists as they cross the field. "If anyone finds out it was us who wrote them, Kirstin and I are going to lose our chance at college."

"No one's going to find out," Emelia says quickly, not nearly as certain as she's forced herself to sound.

"Why don't we just shut up about it?" Leo says when they get in hearing range of the crowd.

Charcoal clouds screen the sun, making the spiraling red and blue lights from police cars, fire trucks, and a single ambulance brighter than they should be at midday. Wind lashes Emelia's hair against her cheeks, but she doesn't brush it back. She tries to stand perfectly still, despite the burning abrasion on her thigh beneath her navy pedal pushers. The cloth irritates the injury, which she mercurochromed and bandaged with gauze last night. She's hidden the bruise on her upper arm, where Ben grabbed her when he was falling, with a washed-out blouse of Aunt Lou's that hangs loose, the ends tied at her waist.

Carrying a stretcher and bundles of rope, firemen hustle from their trucks to the cliff's edge. The vehicles are parked safely back from the cliff's overhang, the tires gashing the lawns of this well-groomed area of the park.

Strange that they cut the grass here, Emelia thinks. Don't they know it's an invitation to toe right up to the edge? Or heel back to it until your foot blindly gropes behind you for earth. Or if you're not careful, the earth crumbles like dried-out cake beneath you.

Police string another red rope tree to tree, presumably to keep gawkers safe from the cliff's edge. Too late, the horse has escaped the barn, as Aunt Lou would say. A few uniformed officers shuffle about just inside the roped area, probably to catch anyone who would think to make a dash for it.

"Bet the body's caught on a boulder beneath the pier. They always get stuck under there." The officer's voice is thick, as if his tongue is slightly too big for his mouth. Or maybe it sounds like this because his body is all thickness, a square head, arms like footballs busting the casings, and a chest of muscles like melons.

"Keep your voice down," says the cop next to him, gesturing to the crowd with his head. He's a beanpole in comparison. Emelia notices the brick red skin at the back of his neck, which looks twice as long as the neck of the square-headed one. The burnt skin is the telltale sign of a farmer, which maybe he is when he's not policing.

Theo's neck was that same brick color, and Danny's. She flushes, recalling their heat against her fingertips. They must have been in the fields earlier that day. She hadn't thought to notice if their hands were clean when they touched her. At the memory of their touch, a small sound escapes her.

The beanpole turns to her and says, "Keep back."

The thick one adds, "Yeah, in fact, why not go home? This is no sight for kids."

Are they still kids? Is she? With her fingertip, she circles the wound on her thigh. A grunt of pain rises, but this time she swallows it. Are they kids, after all that's happened, what they've done, giving Sonya those notes, and what Emelia's done, not just with Theo and Danny, but with Ben too? She lifts a foot and strains to balance on the other foot. The ankle she rolled yesterday shoots pain up her calf. She may not be grown up, but she's not a kid either.

She lowers her foot onto solid earth. Her toes peek through her mud-stained sneakers. She wipes a palm over the sweat on her forehead and glances at the faces of her three friends. She wishes she could tell them about Ben. But yesterday won't make sense unless she first tells them about her mother. And Theo and Danny? How had she accumulated so many secrets in such a short time? How had everything changed so fast? Does nothing stay the same? She slides her hand into her pocket and fingers the twenty-dollar bill Ben gave her. He was supposed to go to agri college and run his family's farm. Now he hobbles through life on a leg named after a car named after a bird.

Both police officers place their hands on their hips, broadening their shoulders as if they think Emelia's about make a run for the path, down the cliff, to the shore. How silly. If she wanted to get to the beach, she wouldn't have to use this path. There is always another way. The four of them know plenty of other ways down. Every kid in town probably does too. The lake had only appeared to be just theirs. But she looks away from the officers and steps back to signal she has no intention of challenging them.

She recognizes many of the people watching with them as regulars from the bakery. They stand in small groups, arms crossed over their chests, fists covering their mouths. Some parents clamp arms around their small children to subdue wriggling bodies. They look to the sky as if searching for funnel clouds, then to the other people who stand with them, tallying up who is here, who is missing.

Will's mother is here. She gave him a relieved wave when they approached. Will nodded to her but has otherwise avoided her gaze. Neither Kirstin's nor Leo's parents are here though. Of course, Lou and Genny aren't here. Even if they didn't have to mind the bakery, they wouldn't come to see such a sight. To them, all unsavory things should be hidden inside dark, cobwebbed closets where no one need look at them. Emelia's forced to admit that she understands her aunts' strategy a little better now that she's got her own secrets to hide.

"Look at all the teachers here," says Kirstin quietly. "Trippsman and Nardinski. There's the principal too."

"Shhh," Will whispers. "Just shut the hell up!"

When another rope is thrown over the cliff's edge, crushing a patch of Queen Anne's lace, waves of whispers undulate through the crowd—*falling, drowning, accident, suicide.* Emelia's teeth begin working the corner of her mouth. Please let it not be Sonya, she begs the clouds. Don't let it be my fault.

Will's right. She should never have pushed the others to send those notes. This wasn't what she wanted. Blood pools over her tongue, and she loosens her jaw, releasing her lip, hoping no one has noticed.

Her friends don't seem to be doing much better than her at keeping still. Leo scowls and drums his thigh. Kirstin gnaws the nails she's been trying to grow out Will's face is crimped with I-told-you-so fear. Physically strong, the best at any sport that requires a ball, he's only recently given up playing with plastic soldiers in his room. In a few years he might really be a soldier like Ben was, fighting in that faraway war, a leg or an arm blown away and left to rot in a rice paddy. Before reading the map this morning, she'd read the newspaper. Until now, she'd mostly searched for articles about the Beatles tour, but today she didn't make it past the headline "Draft Board Sends 37 More for Induction." The group of inductees looked so similar to Will and Leo, the image came to her of Will's face, mud-caked with blood streaming down his forehead and catching in the bow of his lips to create a bloodred mustache.

"ROB-BIEEE!! Has anyone seen my Robin?"

All heads turn toward a fiery-haired deer of a woman who Emelia recognizes as Robbie Stack's mom. Her voice trumpets again, "ROB-BIEEE! Robert!" She canters across the weed-and-wildflower field between the park and the highway, using the shortcut that splits the field in two. Her lemon-colored housecoat slaps her thighs, and her feet are clad in the same slipper-thongs Aunt Lou and Aunt Genny buy for themselves at Woolworth's. The path is awfully rocky for slippers, and Emelia presses her toes inside her sneakers, flexing her calves in sympathy. Pain again sears her ankle, and she has to swallow a gasp.

"Rob-bie!" Mrs. Stack huffs. "ROB-BIEEEEE!" She stumbles, landing hard on one knee and an outstretched hand. But she's immediately up and running again, her agility fueled by fear.

Concerned neighbors scan the crowd for Robbie. A woman Emelia recognizes from the bakery fists the collar of a small boy with white hair. Dean. Her stomach drops. The woman holding him back must be Sonya's mother.

"He's here. Robbie's here!" calls Mrs. Bischell. She raises her hand high and even jumps a little, which Emelia would never have imagined Mrs. Bischell could still do at her age, thirty or forty years old. "He's with Steven!"

Mrs. Stack's relief is written all over her face.

"You know, it could still be anyone," Leo says quietly His gaze darts to the policemen, who shuffle like benched ballplayers wanting to get into the game. Beanpole steps dangerously close to the cliff's edge and peers over.

"Really, anyone, " Leo says.

"You're right," murmurs Kirstin, her teeth working her thumb. "Everyone messes around at the lake. It could be someone else."

A mermaid, Emelia thinks, wishing the stories Kirstin told could be true. She wishes she were a mermaid slinking and slithering through the waves beyond the breakwater. She wishes she were at the campsite, swimming with Ben. She looks to the sky and pleads to the clouds, please don't let it be Sonya.

"Let's go," she says. She has the surreal sensation that it will be her own body they haul up. "We don't have to stay."

"I'm sure it's nothing to do with us," Will says. His voice cracks, and Emelia sees he's holding back tears.

He could come home from the war blind. Or worse.

"I bet it's some drunk college kid showing off to his friends. I heard there was going to be a beer party this weekend," Emelia says, her voice shaky. At the mention of drunkenness though, she actually smells alcohol. Her first thought is of Theo and Danny, but then she notices a bottle peeking out from Leo's jacket breast pocket.

She jostles his shoulder and points with her pinky so the others won't see. He pretends to shiver before zipping up his jacket to hide the bottle.

So this is why he's wearing his jacket in this heat and why he smells of Christmas cakes. Later, she'll tell him not to worry; she'll keep his secrets too. She'll do anything for any of them as long as they don't leave her alone. It's one thing to leave to start a new life. It's another to be left by the people you love most. When Leo climbed onto that bus yesterday, leaving her behind, she'd been bereft. Yet in only a few years, they'll all really go off and leave her. Like her mother. And Johnny Angel. Whoever he was. What will she do when they're gone for good, for college and for music?

Her gaze is pulled to Sonya's mother. What will she do if Sonya is gone? Dean wriggles less now that there is more bustle among the firefighters, but Emelia can see he's poised to run if his mother lets up. When he spots Emelia looking at him, he sticks his tongue out.

"Send down the basket!" a firefighter on the beach calls up through a bullhorn.

In a sudden surge of energy, the firemen rush a rescue litter down the cliff's face. Emelia draws closer to Leo, and Leo to Kirstin, and Kirstin to Will. The small movement brushes Emelia's pedal pushers against the wound on her thigh. She winces, catches herself, and turns the expression into a squint, as if trying to get a better look at the rescue team.

In a surprisingly short time, the litter is lifted back up, the body inside the metal cage covered with an ash-colored blanket. But at the lip of the cliff, one of the men stumbles on a loose rock. He jiggles his end of the metal cage, and the blanket slides off.

The whole neighborhood sucks in its breath.

Sonya's hair, the same dark color as Emelia's, droops through the bars of the metal basket, a clump of seaweed clinging to the ends. Her red pedal pushers, so similar to Emelia's navy ones, are smeared with sand and dirt. The jacket covering a blouse is torn at the sleeve, and her feet are bare and fish white, no polish on the toes. A deep gash along her cheek exposes pulpy flesh.

Bad girls, Emelia thinks, staring at those white toes, at the bloodless gash, one hand instinctively going to the ice pick in her back pocket, hidden by Lou's shirt, the other hand to the wound on her thigh. Wild girls.

We don't deserve this.

A hawk's cry stabs the air, but the sound isn't from a bird. Mrs. Morrow rushes to the red rope. A police officer braces to catch her, but before she makes it into his arms, she drops to her knees, screaming, beating the earth. A moment later, Dean is beside his mother, watching the firemen shove his sister into an ambulance. When the doors close, he looks at his weeping mother curiously. He backs away from the policeman, who moves fast to scoop Dean up and lift him to his shoulder as if burping an infant. Over the navy shirt of the officer, Dean spots them. He stretches his pudgy forefinger and thumb into a gun. Pointing straight at them, he crooks his thumb four times, shooting each one of them dead.

Consequences, Emelia thinks as Kirstin pulls her away. They deserve whatever they get.

Moments later, after the ambulance has driven away, its siren silent because there is no hurry now, the four turn south at the marsh and into the densest part of the woods. They hike in a line along the dirt trail, Will in the lead, bushwhacking with his arms until they get to the clearing where the older kids move their beer parties after being chased off the shore by sheriff's deputies.

Their talk explodes together, so Emelia catches only snippets of who says what.

"Did she . . . to herself . . . accident . . . or someone . . . but how . . . what was she doing there . . . make it right . . . hit her head . . . drowned . . . "

Kirstin's voice breaks through. "I bet Water Boy's father did it."

"Don't be stupid," says Leo.

"Why is that stupid?" Emelia asks, the idea blossoming. If he did it, whoever *he* is, Emelia couldn't be blamed for pushing them to send the notes.

"We don't even know if anyone did anything to her. She was crazy," says Leo. "She did this to herself. She jumped off the cliff. Or she tried to swim to the breakwater."

"Who said she was crazy?" Emelia insists. "What do you know about crazy? What do you know about her?"

Leo says nothing. She watches him rub his chest, at first thinking he's got his hand on his heart and is about to take an oath, but then she sees he's grasping the whiskey bottle as if it holds some answer.

"Listen, it doesn't matter what happened," insists Will.

"Of course it does. If Water Boy's father—" Leo starts.

"No! Will's right," interrupts Kirstin. "She killed herself. Or someone killed her. Or God did it, you know, like act of God, like a tornado. An accident! It could absolutely be an accident. But whatever happened, as long as no one says our names, it has nothing to do with us. *We* didn't kill her, right?"

No one says a word as Kirsten looks from one to the other.

"Right," says Will, rolling index finger circles alongside his head. "The girl was crazy."

It occurs to Emelia that not one of them has used Sonya's name. Suddenly the thought of Emelia Demski being swallowed up by Lia Diamond terrifies her. It's too easy for a girl to vanish. Elisa had vanished, first into the mental house, then on the point of an ice pick. Sonya's barely gone, and she's already disappearing.

"Sonya," she says quietly. It's the least she can do. The very least. "She was a person. Say her name."

"Since when do you care about her so much?" says Leo.

"I'm just saying, she has a name. She's not nothing. No matter what happened to her or what she did. She's Sonya."

They look at her curiously. She can't stand their gaze, and she hollers, "SONYA!"

"Shut up!" Kirstin cries, reflexively backhanding Emelia on her upper arm. Emelia winces at the soft blow, which has hit her fresh bruise. The pain is delicious. If she can feel this much pain, she hasn't disappeared yet.

"What's wrong with you?" says Will.

"Really?" she says, thrusting her arms wide. "You want to know what's wrong with me?"

Tell them, she thinks. Now. She wants them to know. About her mother, about meeting Theo and Danny, about Ben. They are her family as much as Lou and Genny. They're the closest she has to brothers and sisters. They'd have to forgive her for making them send the notes to punish Sonya. They'd have to forgive her for doing anything to keep herself from feeling she's as bad as Sonya and her mother.

With confession on her lips, a blue jay suddenly squawks, but the bird is real this time, swooping at them, angry at the human invasion of its home and hunting grounds. They all flinch. Emelia looks up into the cloudy sky to shoo the bird away. The sun breaks through the clouds and stabs her vision. Oh, God, she thinks, biting her lips and swallowing the words she was about to speak. How can she know they won't turn from her with disgust? Her own mother left her behind. Her aunts betrayed her; even her grandparents had lied to her. With Danny and Theo, and Ben too, she'd been no better than Sonya. Worse. *Almost, nearly. Make it right.* Isn't she worse for having been unkind?

"This isn't getting us anywhere," Leo says finally. "Until we know something for sure, we keep our mouths shut. Just as we always said we would."

"Leo's right," Emelia says contritely. She can't risk telling them. She can't let them see who she really is. She needs her friends. She doesn't trust herself anymore. She purses her lips into a kiss but instead spits hard into her palm and holds it out to them. "Swear it."

"We already did that," Will says, looking at her hand with disgust.

"No, this time it's for real," says Leo, spitting into his own hand, which Emelia notices is trembling as much as her whole body is. But she's not cold, and she would bet neither is he. The surrounding trees have blocked the wind, but the humidity hangs like cobwebs. Her whole body drips knife-edged sweat. Probably there are blotchy sweat stains on Lou's blouse. At the thought that she will be in trouble for borrowing it without asking, a giggle bubbles up in her. It's the sweetest type of trouble she can imagine. Ruining her aunt's shirt. Silly, stupid trouble. Still, she swallows her laugh as if swallowing bad milk.

"I'm serious. Everything's changed now," continues Leo, looking pointedly at Will. "No kid stuff this time. Don't swear if you don't mean it, if you can't keep your mouth shut. We need to know who we can count on and who we can't."

Kirstin spits without hesitation and with admirable force, but Will pauses. He looks at each one of them as if pleading for some other option. His forehead crimps as it does when he's figuring out a math equation in his head. Finally, resigned that he has only one choice, he spits.

They pile hands one on top of the other. Emelia's hand at the bottom of the pile takes everyone's weight. When they shake as one, Emelia wants to cry with joy. How could she have thought they would leave her? All she has to do is keep her mouth shut tight.

After they release their hands, Leo brings out the bottle from his jacket, takes a sip, and passes it to Emelia. She sips, enjoying the burn at her throat. Physical sensation is so much better than everything else. She presses her palm over the bandage on her thigh. She winces as she passes the bottle to Will, who sips and holds it out to Kirstin, who hesitates.

"My mom," she says. "What if . . . ?"

"You're nothing like her," Leo says firmly. "We aren't our parents."

Emelia nods but is not so sure. *E. Demski. Almost. Nearly. Elisa, Emelia.* With this one drink, will Kirstin be sealing her fate as a drunk? Emelia could stop her, could say it doesn't matter, could tell her to spit the liquor out the moment it hits her tongue. But she lets Kirstin put the bottle to her lips and drink. Because maybe, just maybe, Leo is right. Everything's changed. Yesterday Sonya was alive, and Emelia was someone else. Today Sonya is dead, her spirit swept into open waters and buried deep beneath the lake's sandy bed. But Emelia is still here. *Taos, Ensenada, Tijuana.* And so is Lia Diamond, tucked deep inside of her, just in case.

Part Three

Dean

DEAN WOULD HAVE preferred a ride home from the lake atop one of the fire trucks, but the back of a police car is pretty good too. He looks out the window, hoping to be seen by those big-kid creeps from the playground who handed him notes to give to Sonya. He tried to shoot them at the lake. Not fair for them to see her all icky and awful like that, not really his Sonya at all. He's pretty sure they have something to do with her being icky and awful, although when he tries to draw the line in his mind from them to her in the ambulance, his mind goes fuzzy. So what if he can't think what they did? He *pshew, pshew, pshew, pshew* finger-shot each one anyway, the way Crypto would do. But nothing happened, and he hates them even more now because they are untouchable and she is gone.

His tears wet the shirt of the policeman who carried him to the police car. Maybe if those big kids saw he has policeman friends, they'll be afraid and leave him alone. Sonya's left him alone, first disappearing over the cliff, then playing dead doll in that body cage, and then getting locked away in the white ambulance that drove silently away.

If only he were bigger and could have saved her. She can't protect him anymore, and he can't protect her. The whole reason she wanted him to follow her to the lake was to keep her safe. They keep each other safe. And they never tell each other's secrets. Brother-sister secrets, she said, are only for brothers and sisters.

He knew she wanted him to come along this morning because before she snuck out of the house, she dropped something outside his bedroom door to wake him and signal him to come along. He wasn't asleep anyway. He hardly ever sleeps. She knows that. His body doesn't like to be still and quiet. When he does fall asleep, his dreams spin colorful and fast like his comics come to life, and he's the villain and superhero all at once. The dreams wake him up, which is what happened just before Sonya signaled to him. After the noise, he waited for her to open his door and call his name. When she didn't, he realized they were playing not just sneaky but super-sneaky. Only she knows how super-sneaky he can be.

Not knows. Knew.

Oh.

He sniffs as a fresh batch of tears crumple his face.

Now no one knows the best of him.

At her signal, he dropped from his bed to the carpet and felt for his clothes. He could only find one old sneaker and one new sneaker but they were the right feet. He put them on and followed her out of the house.

Super-sneaky, he stayed in the shadows, cloaked in darkness like Batman and Hawkman and Crypto sometimes do.

They would never tell secrets.

Sonya didn't tell when he broke his mother's dumb vase with his spatula sword, and she didn't tell when he dropped one of his father's golf balls into the paint can to watch it disappear into the chocolate-colored liquid, which does not taste like chocolate. She washed his face when he tasted it, and she didn't tell their parents about that either. She didn't tell, and he won't tell, not about the notes from the stinky big kids, or her sneaking out of the house early this morning, or what happened at the cliff. Brothers and sisters don't tell, no matter how bad.

Now in the back of the police car, his mother sits beside him, icky and awful too but in a different way from Sonya. His mother's eyelids are black bruises, smeared with her eyelash goop. She cups her face with her hands, and snot dribbles over her fingers. Why doesn't she wipe her snot away the way she makes him do?

"Aaaaaaaaaawwwww," his mother moans.

He wonders if the policeman man driving the car has turned on the siren to drown out his mother's crying, which sounds like a bird cawing but louder than any birdcall Dean has ever heard, even a hawk's. Sonya taught him about birdcalls. She bought him

Hawkman comics. In his closet, she set up his special drawing place she calls his studio.

"Aaaaaaaaaawwwww," his mother yells.

"Ow," he says. "Too loud."

Birdcalls don't hurt his ears or tie his brain into knots as his mother's sounds are doing right now. He has to stop her noise. Stop, stop, stop her cawing.

He pinches her thigh. He needs to tell her she's hurting his ears. Pinch, pinch. She doesn't notice him, not even to slap his hand away. He tries another place, her upper arm, pulling her skin from the muscle so he can get a good grip and squeezing squeezing, hard hard.

"Aaaaaaaaaawwwww."

Pinch, twist, pinch, harder. Stop cawing!

"Cut that out, little boy!" says the policeman lady in the passenger's seat up front.

Dean scowls at her. Doesn't she know policemen are supposed to be men like his dad, not ladies like his mom? She's probably not a real policeman. She can scold little boys like him, but she can't catch real bad guys in that stupid policeman-lady skirt.

"What's your name?" she says, her voice nicer than before. When he doesn't answer, she shakes her head and says, "Leave your mother alone, son. She's had a shock."

"Shut up, stupid!"

The words are out before Dean realizes what he's said to the policeman lady. He's been trying so hard lately to be good. But sometimes bad erupts from him before he knows it's coming. He braces himself for whatever trouble his bad language will send his way now. If his father were here, he would cuff the back of his head or tug on his ears or swat his bottom, which at least is protected right now because he's sitting down. He looks to his mother to protect him as she sometimes does, but she doesn't see him. Her hands cover her face. She's bird cawing and shoulder heaving. Quieter now, at least, but she isn't paying one jot of attention to him.

"Mom, Mom," he says.

She caws and heaves.

"Mom, Mom, Mom, Mom, Mom, Mom, Mom, Mom, Mom."

He needs her to look at him. If she looks at him, everything will be okay. Sonya may be gone, but his mother will still be here. He pinches her side hard, hard, harder.

"Look at me, look, look, look!"

When he still gets no response, he tugs her hands from her face. She's wrinkled and soaked with tears and snot, which is scary. And interesting. And scary.

He looks to the policeman lady, his fear of being cuffed gone, replaced with fear of his mother.

"It's okay," coos Policeman Lady. "You're not in trouble."

But he wants trouble. Trouble is familiar. He understands trouble. Trouble is bad, but it goes away. Hugs sometimes follow it—and a sweet if he's very good after trouble. But if his mother's bird cawing and nose dripping and not seeing him aren't trouble, and if Sonya's dripping like a wet doll in that cage isn't trouble, what are they?

Strange, that's what they are.

Strange is bad. Strange might stay.

His brain knots, and his belly knots too. He doesn't like strange one little bit. Strange is creepy and black, and he wants to squash it like a spider.

He kicks the front seat with his sneakered foot, which makes him feel better. He kicks again, then drills the seat with his rubber-toed shoes. That feels good. More, more. He punches his mother's thigh. He screams his baddest bad words he's only shouted in his head before now. Big-kid words he's not supposed to know. His mother will hear him and stop her stupid sounds and punish him.

"SHITFUCKDAMNGODDAMNSHITFUCKSHIT!"

He will be in trouble now. Trouble is okay. Trouble he knows. Trouble ends.

He keeps on just to be sure.

"SHITSHITPOOPSHITFUCKDAMNSHIT!"

Still his mother doesn't notice him.

"Ma-ma! Mom-my!" he demands.

He hears the baby talk in his voice. Usually she loves when he plays baby, cuddling him, calling him her bear cub. Now she only

235

cries harder. Doesn't she know that with Sonya gone, he needs her more?

"MAAAAAAAMAAAAAAAAAA!" he wails, drowning out the sirens and sobs in his head.

When she still doesn't look at him, he balls his fists as tightly as he can. He pulls back his arms and punches her thigh, her arm, her rib, rib, rib. When he thinks he feels one crack, he punches again and harder.

"Look at me," he says. Punch, punch. Punch. "Look at me!"

He falls back on the seat when the policeman driver jerks the steering wheel and pulls the cruiser over. Policeman Lady is out of the car like a shot, whipping open the door and yanking him from the car.

Policeman Man swoops in and clasps his torso from behind, holding him there as he kicks and claws the air. He's an upside-down beetle, a turtle on its back. He arches and strains and manages to land an elbow in the man's ribs.

"Ooof," escapes Policeman Man's lips.

Good. He'll be in trouble now. They'll punish him now. Then it will be over. Hugs. Sweets.

"Okay, okay, let it out, kid," Policeman Man says, his clutch firm. "Let it out."

"Shut up!" Dean becomes aware of the man's hot belly against his back. He wriggles harder, his whole body one muscle. He's a snake, a worm.

"Aaaaaaaaaahhhhh! Sonyaaaaa!" he calls.

How could she leave him? She was his favorite. He was her Deanie-Beanie. The weight of her hand felt nice on his head. She had a special smile just for him.

Stupid Sonya. Icky, icky. She's in trouble now. Big trouble. The biggest trouble of all.

Exhausted, his body melts. The car's siren has been turned off. His mother sobs softly. Still huffing, Policeman Man sets him down on the grass by Policeman Lady.

Now he'll be punished. They'll take him to jail, and everything will be okay. He holds out his arms so she can put handcuffs on his wrists.

"Am I in trouble?" he whispers.

"No," Policeman Lady says kindly. Stupid, stupid. She hugs him and coos, "It's okay, hon. It's okay." She rubs his back in circles for a while. When she releases him, she smooths his dripping wet cheeks and pushes his hair from his eyes. She smiles.

He hates her. He wants to shoot her, *pshew, pshew,* but she's still a policeman lady, and he isn't brave enough.

Her brown eyes. The dimple in her chin. She's not his mother. She's not Sonya. He tries to poke her dimple like an eye, but she turns her head to look at Policeman Man, and all he pokes is nothing.

"He'll be all right now," she says. She gives him a warning look. "Won't you, son? Be brave for your mom?"

He grinds his teeth in response. Policeman Lady is not going to punish him. She's worse than stupid Sonya, who promised she'd always be there when he really needed her, but who isn't here now, and won't be ever again, and who's left him alone in something so much worse than trouble.

Leo

"THE CAUSE OF Sonya Morrow's death remains undetermined as investigators await the final report from the Office of the Chief Medical Examiner," Kirstin reads aloud from the morning paper. "They still don't know anything for sure?" she says, giving the newspaper a frustrated shake.

A plume of water slaps the concrete at her feet. Still early in summer, each icy droplet stings Leo's sun warmed skin. Kirstin flinches too, raising the newspaper out of the water's reach. She scowls at the little boy whose gleeful flip into the pool caused the splash. The boy pays her no mind, whooping with pride and scrabbling up the ladder to do it again.

"Little cretin," Kirstin says, looking from Will to Leo to Emelia for confirmation, which only Will gives in the form of a nod. Emelia stares distractedly in the direction of the lake as if she hasn't heard. Leo couldn't care less about the splashing kid. He's desperate to read in black-and-white that his family is in the clear.

In the three weeks since Sonya's death, the four of them have been gathering at the Zailer County pool rather than at the lake. They no longer feel comfortable tramping the beaches and woods, which used to feel like their private wilderness. Before Sonya, it was easy to pretend the tree branches bowed to hear only their conversations and the well-trodden paths rolled themselves out for their feet alone. Of course, Leo always knew this wasn't true. Schlitz cans and empty Ripple bottles were evidence enough that they weren't alone. But they never seemed to see anyone else there until they saw Sonya and Water Boy. Even then, it felt like they had been pulled inside a tent of secrecy. Now the lake holds its own secrets. Whatever it knows about what happened to Sonya, it's not saying.

On the day Sonya died, when Leo finally returned home, he believed he'd be able to read the truth in his parents' faces. Were they involved in Sonya's death, as Leo feared, or not, as he hoped? All the way home from the lake, he nursed his hope. His parents weren't bad, or not that bad. The knife, the whole-note pin, even Nora—they weren't proof that one or both of his parents hurt Sonya. They weren't proof of anything, not really.

Quietly closing the kitchen door behind him, Leo stood listening. Above him, his father's footsteps scratched across the attic floor. The sewing machine whirred in his mother's sewing room.

Relieved at not having to face his parents, he slipped into his bedroom, shut the door, and collapsed onto his bed. Better to think things through before seeing them. Figure out what's.

Feeling sick and smelling the whiskey and nervous sweat that clung to his body, he pictured the wound running from Sonya's cheekbone to her chin, the flesh blooming from the split skin.

A paring knife could have split Sonya's face that way. So could a box cutter like the one Stash keeps handy to cut speaker wire. Leo shook with fear and horror. He crawled under his covers as if his blankets would protect him from what he'd seen.

He squeezed his eyes shut and told himself he had to calm down and think. If his parents were involved, he would have to tell what he knew about Nora and Sonya, and about Water Boy too. He would have to betray his friends and tell about the notes they sent. Weren't these mitigating circumstances? That's what they called it on detective and lawyer shows when one person pushed another person into doing something. *Make it right.*

Or, maybe, Nora, Sonya, and Water Boy were motive. Maybe Leo would have to continue to keep his mouth shut. Could he do that without going crazy?

Maybe he was crazy now.

Wasn't it just as likely his parents weren't involved? What did he really know?

He knew that he and his parents had gotten home from the Silo about two o'clock in the morning. He knew that when Kirstin called and woke him that afternoon, his mother was gone. Her note said she was playing piano for the ballet school, but anyone can write anything in a note. She could have gone to the lake to meet Sonya and then to the ballet studio, or vice versa, or not gone to the lake at all. Of course, his father was gone too. No note. No nothing. So he could have been anywhere. But this wasn't unusual.

Leo also knew the trouble cot was mussed, but his father's bottle of whiskey was plenty full, at least until Leo swiped it. The full bottle wasn't definitive proof Stash was still on the wagon, but his mother's sewing suggested they hadn't fought. His mother never sewed when she was angry, saying she couldn't sew a straight line if she couldn't see straight. Unless she was pretending now. At the Silo, Leo told her his father may have gone too far. Did she understand what he meant? Or had she dismissed Leo's words as frustration at not getting to play the way he wanted?

Finally, he knew Sonya had tacked a whole-note pin to Water Boy's sweater before burying him. The four of them had goaded her by sending notes, the last one urging her to do more than feel guilty. Did making it right mean getting his father to meet at the cliffs? Maybe she planned to take him to the marsh to show him where Water Boy was buried. Maybe his mother followed. Or maybe she intercepted Sonya's message, and she went instead.

A lot of it was speculation. Leo could speculate all day long. In the end, he didn't know anything at all. Not really. Not even how Sonya died. Jumped or pushed? Or slipped?

He pulled the covers tight to his chin and hoped so hard that the cliff gave way or that Sonya slipped that it felt like a prayer. It would be awful, it would be sad, but it would be no one's fault, and he wouldn't have to do anything.

Weary from thinking and drowsy from the whiskey he'd drunk, Leo fell into a hard sleep. When he woke, he found his parents gone and another note from his mother on the kitchen table.

Damn, he hated notes. He'd be happy if he never saw another scrap of paper with writing on it in his life. This one seemed innocent enough though, only saying she and his father had gone

240

to Dora's Dance Palace to hear the Slovenian Swingers play. The information cheered him. Wasn't it a good sign that they were going to hear music together? If his father had fallen off the wagon, she would have refused to go with him. He would have left her home to seethe. And if either one of them were involved in Sonya's death, surely they wouldn't go out to hear music that very night.

His mother also wrote that she'd left Leo a plate of pork chops for his dinner. Realizing he was hungry (that was a good sign too, wasn't it?), he opened the refrigerator and pulled out the plate. Peeling back the wax paper, in the congealed fat on the chops, he saw Sonya's cheek wound, and in the meat's pooling juices, he saw his father's gravy-coated mustache. Repulsed, he tossed the meal into the trash.

"How come it's taking so long to figure out what happened to her?" he says now, knowing he's tempting fate by wanting a definitive answer.

After three weeks, uncertainty has been almost the same as being in the clear. Everyday life has gone on, not quite as if nothing has happened, but normal enough that Leo has wondered if never knowing the truth might be better than knowing. The school year has ended. There was a short memorial for Sonya at the final assembly. At the assembly memorial, Stella had sung "Amazing Grace," and Leo had been stunned at the beautiful clarity of her voice, which broke only at the very end of the song when emotion overtook her.

On the last day of classes, Leo had seen Stella trying on her graduation robe with a group of her theater friends. It was a warm day, and when she took off the robe, the sleeveless shirt she wore showed her muscular arms and elegant neck, and he thought again how pretty she was, fuzzy hair and all. She talked with friends, smiling sometimes as if Sonya never existed. But then Stella broke down crying, peals of emotion shaking her body. Mrs. Nardinski rushed to hug her, patting her on the back. No one had to tell Leo those tears were for Sonya, who should have been trying on her graduation robe with her best friend.

The next day, Leo had seen her working the checkout at Free-Zee Creams. She smiled at the kids as she handed out cones, the traces of her earlier emotion gone. He approached the counter hesitantly and bought a cone from her. She smiled at him as she had the kids. He noticed she had a pretty bowed upper lip. He wished that he'd stayed at the smoker to hear her sing with his father's band so he could have seen up close how her pretty bowed lips opened to hold a note.

As she gave him his change, she said, "Tell your dad I say hi."

Shy and confused, he barely managed to say, "Okay."

Later, Leo turned Stella's comment over in his mind. Had there been a tinge of sarcasm in her tone? Had she meant to imply something more than she'd said, something like, tell your father I know what he did? In the end, Leo could be no more certain of this than anything else. Maybe *hi* just meant *hi*.

As he ate his ice cream, he thought it tasted as good as ever. So maybe with enough time, everything would go back to being as good as ever. Why not be thankful that no one seems to know the truth about Sonya and let it go?

Because uncertainty also feels like treading water, he thinks now, looking at the deep end of the pool. The whole time you're kicking, you know you can only keep your head above water for so long. Eventually, you'll get so tired, you have to stop, and then you'll sink like a stone. As Sonya did.

He looks back to his friends. The four of them have staked a claim on "their corner" of the pool's concrete deck, staying as far from any other group as they can get. They frown away anyone who gets too close while they're reading from the newspaper, as Kirstin has just done. The splashing boy remains unphased though, having moved from flipping into the pool to cannonballing.

"I agree. It shouldn't take so long to figure out that she slipped," says Will, who has decided to take as fact what he wants to be true. In his mind, Sonya slipped until someone proves otherwise.

"If she slipped off the cliff, how come?" says Kirstin, who sticks firmly to the facts. Leo envies her this because for him, a thousand and one plausible scenarios exist in uncertainty. "You'd have to have a reason to be so close to the edge. And if you were that close to the edge, you'd have to have a reason to misstep because who isn't careful on that overhang? I mean, even when we used to play cliff chicken, we were careful."

"Were we really stupid enough to play that game?" Leo says. Had they really thrown dice to see how many backward steps to take? Had there really been a time when they didn't know one misstep could ruin your life or take it from you altogether? More than once, his foot had blindly swished air, and the feeling had thrilled him. They clasped each other's wrists just in case of shaky balance or crumbling clay; the trust you needed had been almost as thrilling as the possibility of falling.

Had Sonya reached out to someone to save her from falling? Had the person also reached out for her outstretched hand, or had the person taken a step back, so Sonya's last sensation was her fingers brushing air?

Uncertainty. Every scenario is possible.

He lies back onto the old quilt Kirstin has spread out, shifting the sun's heat from his shoulders to his chest. He slides a cheap Woolworth's version of Joey Katz's sunglasses up his nose.

What about Joey Katz?

He'd been at the smoker and caught an eyeful of Sonya's peek-a-boo dance number with the letter sweater. Everyone talks about what a cad Joey is. He'll put his sax in any case, right? What if Joey was the real father of Water Boy? Maybe Stash gave Joey a whole-note pin, and Joey gave it to Sonya? Is there any way to find out if Joey left the Silo in time to meet Sonya at the lake?

Kirstin's voice interrupts his thoughts. "The body was found caught in the rocks near Fitzgerald Pier."

"We know all that. We were there. The whole neighborhood was there," says Will. He stomps back and forth from Emelia's towel to Kirstin and Leo, flapping his arms in exasperation like an angry seagull. "What's new? It's not news if there isn't something new. For weeks, all they've reported is that she's—" He drops his voice to a hard whisper. "Dead. Yeah, yeah, yeah, okay, so she went to our high school, she liked science, and she's dead. When are they going to say what's really what?"

"Mmmmm," Kirstin says, scanning the article. "You're right, not much new. Oh, here. Three tennis ball–sized stones were found in her pockets. I wonder why they didn't say that before. They must have seen them when they found her."

"So she put rocks in her pocket, slipped, and accidentally drown," Will says. "She was probably knocked out from the fall. Why don't they just say that?"

"Because nothing is certain. Not until they figure out how she hit her head," says Kirstin. "Or how her head was hit, and how she got that cut on her face."

In addition to the gash on her cheek that they'd seen during the rescue, earlier reports told of another wound near her temple that they hadn't seen in the quick glimpse they'd gotten of her before she was put into the ambulance.

"How else would the rocks get in her pocket unless she put them there?" says Will.

"Someone else put them there?" ventures Kirstin.

For a moment, no one says anything.

"No," Will finally says. "She put them there. They're probably what made her lose her balance."

"Or maybe she put them there so they would weigh her down after she jumped," says Kirstin. "People mistakenly think the lungs act as floats. But it's really the gasses that build up in the body that—"

"Let's shut up about it already," says Emelia.

In a mad switch that Leo still hasn't figured out, Emelia is now the least interested in Sonya. She tightens the waist knot of the giant shirt she wears like a bathrobe over her swim team suit. She hasn't gone in the water once since they've started coming here. The most she does is sit at the pool's edge, dangling her feet. Today, at least, she's unsnapped the button on the waistband of her denim shorts that go down to her knees. Why doesn't she wear a bikini like some of the other girls? She's got a good shape. She never used to be embarrassed about it.

She's gone all weird, and Leo can't tell if it's because of Sonya's death or, horribly, if Sonya's death is because of what's been bugging Emelia. After all, the morning they left for the Silo, Emelia had turned toward the lake. She'd been strange that day too. And why was she carrying around an ice pick? An ice pick could have made the gash on Sonya's cheek.

She's also the one who pushed them to send the notes. She's the one who most wanted to hold Sonya responsible for Water Boy. Could Emelia have met Sonya at the cliffs and challenged her to a game of cliff chicken? Could she have threatened Sonya with the ice pick so Sonya stepped back and lost her footing? Or worse, could Emelia have pushed her?

"Why don't you all just give it a rest," Emelia says.

Leo sits up, piqued by her tone and sick of the endless scenarios turning over in his mind. He wants something definite. Anything. He wraps his arms around his knees and says, "But that's what you wanted, right, Em? For her to feel so bad, she'd kill herself?"

"I never said that."

"What else did you mean by that last note? *Make it right?* What exactly did you want her to do?" he says.

"Keep it down, you two," says Kirstin.

When Emelia says nothing, Leo relents, regretting having jumped on her. He doesn't really think she could have hurt Sonya, does he? Goddamn uncertainty.

He wishes another bottle of booze was hidden beneath Stash's cot; he could swipe it. He wishes for one of Joey Katz's cigarettes. Surely someone from school must sell them, but who? That oily Eddie Skaars looks like he might know where to get his hands on marijuana. How much does one joint cost?

Suddenly, cold water swats him over the head and on the chest. The same kid from earlier laughs as Leo wipes his face with his hand.

"Watch it, squirt!" Kirstin calls to the kid, who flipper splashes his hand in response.

She throws Leo a tattered towel from the stack she's brought.

"It's only water," he says, using the towel as a pillow when he lies back down.

For his part, Leo much prefers the pool to the lake. No matter how anxious he is, he still likes looking at the girls in their little suits. He likes the popcorn smell coming from the snack bar. He likes that the whole place is fenced in with chain link. Sometimes he can almost relax among the astringent scent of chlorine, the solid concrete surfaces to lie on, and the strangely clear water contained in a deep L that's been painted a crayon blue color that the lake could never be. Someone has planned this space to be exactly what it is: safe and sterile and wart free because every foot that crosses the threshold is checked for blemishes. Leo happily spreads his toes as ordered by the stringy-haired girl who sits outside the lockers, examining toe webs. He even flashes her his smile, so now she pretty much just passes him through.

"That's it in the paper today," says Kirstin, folding the newspaper and wiping her hands on another threadbare towel. Does she get these as hand-me-downs from her cousin too? "Agh, the print is all over my fingers. Anyway, the article is on page five, so maybe people are forgetting about it."

"Read it again," says Will.

"I thought we were supposed to *not* talk about this. Isn't that what we swore?" says Emelia.

"I'm beginning to think she's right," says Will, turning in his pacing as if to punctuate his turn of mind. "We should stop talking about it. We should stop thinking about it. It doesn't have anything to do with us, right?" He doesn't wait for their nods of approval. "So let's go swimming already."

"Yeah, okay. Let's go. Last one in is a you-know-what!" Kirstin says, jumping up and pushing past Will to cannonball into the pool over the head of the kid who'd splashed them. Will follows, and the two join a few other kids in a game of beanbag keep-away.

"You going in?" says Leo.

Emelia shakes her head. She picks up the newspaper Kirstin discarded and starts reading. Or pretends to—Leo can't tell for sure.

"Last ones in. I guess we're you-know-whats," he says.

"Like I didn't already know that."

He waits for her smile, but she's hidden her face from him. She turns to the page with the article on Sonya and pulls the paper close, as if to read more carefully.

"I thought you said we should stop looking at the news about Sonya," he says.

"Yeah, we probably should. I can't help it though. I want to know what happened to her. And I don't want to know."

"I've been thinking the exact same thing."

She tosses the paper aside. "Will's right. There's nothing new."

"I know. I read it before I got here."

He reads the morning and evening editions of the paper every day now. What he's found is that in addition to Sonya's tragedy, as the journalists call what happened to her, the whole world is a murky swamp, as muddy as Water Boy's marsh. Until now, the war half a world away and the race riots, erupting all around the country, had played in the back of his mind like the constant whoosh of highway traffic.

Reading the news every day now, even just the headlines, the chaos booms. He's sickened by the photos of boys only a few years older than him shot up and drooping off of stretchers just as Sonya had. He's already resolved he's not going anywhere near Vietnam. Of course, if he ditches the draft, his father will probably call him a coward. Isn't that just perfect, he thinks.

The papers also tell of race riots only miles away from his house, not in faraway places in the South or in big cities like Chicago. He looks around and notes the only brown skin at this pool is from tans. He recalls Slide's black skin under the Silo's spotlight and wishes again he'd had a chance to stay longer, to watch Slide's technique and hear him play more.

With just a little direction from Slide, Leo's own sliding has gotten much better, and he's incorporated it into a few of his songs. The one thing that has helped keep Leo afloat since Sonya's death is that he's followed through on his resolve to start a band, although he hasn't yet been brave enough to tell his friends or his parents. He wants to make sure they'll be good enough before telling anyone. But he's found someone to play piano and, soon, keyboard. Leo's written a few more songs, a couple of them inspired by articles in the newspapers.

Leo couldn't believe it when he read in the paper about kids his own age, many who were once fans, burning Beatles records just because John Lennon said they're more popular than Jesus. He, for one, would much rather go to a Beatles concert than church. Imagine if word ever got out about his father and Sonya? Would they burn the Meitka house to sticks?

"Leo, what do you think happened to Sonya?" Emelia says softly.

"I don't know," he says, exhaling a deep sigh. "Maybe it *was* an accident. I hope so anyway. And I'm sorry about what I said earlier."

He wants to summon back the old Emelia. He misses her. She used to be the one he was closest to in the group. Will and Kirstin have their school smarts connection, but he and Emelia connect in some less definable way. She's the one strangers have mistaken as his sister. He's always liked that, and he thought she did too. And it isn't just that they finish each other's sentences. They just click. Or they used to. These days, she's so far away, he can't fathom what she's thinking.

"An accident? Do you really think so? We saw her swim, Leo," Emelia says. "She had the strongest stroke on her relay team. If she slipped off that cliff and into the water, or off the breakers, why didn't she just swim to shore?"

"The undertow?" he ventures. "Or maybe she was knocked unconscious as Will said."

"Maybe the stones in her pockets were meant to drag her down," she says.

"So what are you saying?" he says. "Do you know something, Emelia?"

"Too much," she snorts. "And nothing. Not anything about anything at all. That's the problem."

"Emelia," he ventures. "That day when I was with my parents, and Will and Kirstin were on the college tour?"

"What about it?"

"You never said what you did all day."

She doesn't respond, but he sees her swallow hard. She looks up at the sky and squints into the sun.

"You were wrong before, Leo. I never wanted her to die. I didn't. And now, well, I wish we'd never sent those notes."

"You do?"

"Yeah. I mean, what was she supposed to do, stuck like that?"

"I don't know," Leo says.

"Trapped like a March hare," she murmurs. "My aunts say that."

"Emelia, what did you do all day?"

She lifts her hand to shade her eyes, but she still doesn't meet his gaze.

"I'm thinking of going by *Lia* now," she says. "I think it sounds sophisticated. Don't you?"

Why won't she answer? What has she got to hide? Why hide it from him?

"The Beatles are playing in San Francisco at the end of the month," she goes on. "I bet it's going to be outta sight."

Leo studies her face, but can read nothing there. Man, he misses the old Emelia, who shared everything.

"Remember, that morning, we talked in my back yard? You wanted to come with me and my parents on the bus," he says. "You said you didn't want to be alone. But you never said what you did that day."

"I think we should go see the Beatles in San Francisco. Maybe we could take your dad's bus. When are you getting your license?"

"Emelia? What—"

"All the kids are going to California," she interrupts. "Why don't we go too? When you get your license, we won't even have to hitch. We could stop in Colorado on the way. See the Rocky Mountains."

He sighs. She won't give an inch.

Finally he says, "The Beatles will be in Chicago a lot sooner than their San Francisco gig. Maybe we could go there. I'd like to see other music in Chicago too."

Slide, for instance.

"Chicago's not that far," he says. "We could go down and be back before anyone misses us. We can find the money somehow."

"I have some money. But just to Chicago? Why bother?" she shrugs and perches soda bottle sunglasses on her nose, covering not just her eyes but half of her face, so Leo can't discern her expression. "Chicago's like going down the block."

"I guess," he says, then decides to try again to spark the old Emelia. "C'mon, let's go for a swim. It's so hot."

"Nah, you go."

Exasperated, he says, "Why are you such a pill these days? At least take off that shirt. Looking at you is making me sweat bullets."

"I'm not hot," she says.

"Jeez, Emelia, we're at a swimming pool. You look stupid all dressed up. At least take your shirt off. You've got a swimming suit on."

"Why do you care so much?"

"Because you're being weird. What's going on with you? Why won't you talk to me anymore? You know you can tell me anything," he says, but before she can answer, a boy with ginger hair and a chest full of freckles approaches them.

"Hey, Meitka!" His legs are as white and thin as birch trunks. "My mom is going out tomorrow afternoon. We can have the house to ourselves."

"You having a party, Charlie?" Emelia asks when he gets close. She seems glad to have Leo's attention taken from her.

"It's Charles. No party," the boy says, giving her a look that says he can't be bothered with something as silly as a party. "Band practice."

"You guys are starting a band?" she says, propping her sunglasses on her head.

"Yeah, so?" Leo says.

"So nothing. So why didn't you say something?"

"Like you're one to talk," he snaps. "Or I should say, *not* talk."

"I think it's great," Emelia says. "I'll come tomorrow too. I could play tambourine. What time's practice, Charles?"

Charles ignores her and turns to Leo. "So? Three o'clock?"

"Great," Emelia says, "I'll be there."

Charles shifts his gaze to her and studies her for a moment. "Can you sing? We could use a singer."

"Her?" Leo laughs outright. "If we want a moose."

"Shut up!" she says. "But he's right. I can't sing."

Charles turns from her as if she has ceased to exist. "Three. Don't be late. And don't bring her."

"Yeah, okay," Leo says, avoiding Emelia's gaze.

"Your dad have an amp you can use?" Charles says.

"My father?" Leo says. "No way he'll let me use it."

"Well, ask him anyway. And bring the sheet music to that song you wrote." Charles gives a one-finger salute before he walks back to his group of friends on the opposite side of the pool.

"You have a band," says Emelia. "That's so cool."

"You really think so?" He can't believe how pleased he is she's excited for him.

"Yeah, of course. It's cool. And it's what you've always wanted, isn't it?"

"Yeah," he says, her excitement fueling his own. "I can't wait for you to hear us play, Em. Charles is really a fantastic musician."

"So you like that guy?" says Emelia, pulling a face. "He seems like such a drip."

"He's okay."

In fact, Leo doesn't especially like Charles, but he likes that he's serious about his music. His mother has a Steinway and a separate music room, and Charles's fingers are fast. He can play any style—classical, jazz, any rock song Leo names. He's better than any of the musicians in his father's band, including Joey Katz, although he's not better than Leo's mother at piano. And he has nothing of Joey's cool style.

Charles has assured Leo he'll have enough money from cutting lawns by the end of the summer to buy keyboards. Then they can play out. Until then, they rehearse at Charles's house when his parents are gone because his mother doesn't like rock and roll, only jazz and classical music. He can only imagine what she thinks of polkas.

Leo likes practicing at Charles's. His house is huge and airy with high ceilings and plush carpeting that compresses sound in a way

Leo likes. It's good they're taking the time to really get good before they play their first gig, as Charles calls playing out. Leo has no intention of embarrassing himself by playing badly or freezing as he'd done at the Silo. For now, they mostly play covers, but Charles has written a few songs, and he likes the ones Leo has written too.

The thought of playing so jazzes Leo, he forgets about everything else for the moment.

"I'm going in!" he says, leaping up, not bothering to wait for Emelia's response. Let her stew if she wants to be a baby. He cannonballs into the numbing water, his splash cascading to the sky.

Later, when he arrives home, his house smells of raspberries. His mother stands at the stove, stirring a pot of simmering fruit. Ball jars have been lined up on the counter, waiting for the jam. His father sits at the kitchen table pasting pictures onto poster board.

He has remained on the wagon since the Silo, and at least on the surface, the harmony between his parents has continued. Yet Leo senses things are off. He can't point to anything definite, but isn't his mother a degree cooler toward his father? Isn't his father a degree less fawning toward his mother? Are they *acting* normal so Leo doesn't suspect something is wrong? Or has the uncertainty surrounding Sonya's death merely created one more scenario in his mind?

"What do you think?" says his father, holding up the poster board. Flamingo pink letters swirl, *The Stash Meitka Band Debut Record Release!* He's pasted a large photo of himself in the top corner and a small one of the band kitty-corner. "Of course, it will be on high-gloss paper. This is just to give the idea to the printer."

His father has spent the last three weeks driving his record to all of the local radio stations, hoping they'd promote it, but only a few polka DJs have played it, and not as much as his father would like.

"Those big radio pooh-bahs won't play me without payola? Who needs them? I'll sell the records myself."

"How come your picture's so big?" Leo says.

"I'm the leader. I'm the reason people will come and buy the record."

Leo leans close and studies the smaller picture of the rest of the band.

"How come I'm not in the picture?"

"You're not in the band, are you? You just played a bit of rhythm."

"Stash," Anne says, "give the boy his due."

"His due? Anyone could have played his part, and he flubbed it besides," his father insists. "He wasted good recording time."

His father sets the mockup on the table and joins his mother at the stove. He dips a teaspoon into the bubbling fruit and blows on it. "I tell you what, kiddo. You decide you're not too good to join the band, you learn to play *with* us instead of showboating your rock-and-roll nonsense, and I'll pay to reshoot the photo so that next time, maybe when we do a full album, your mug will be on the cover. At least the back cover. What do you say?"

As if wielding a wand, he pops the spoon in his mouth and says, "More sugar." He kisses Anne loudly on the cheek.

To Leo's annoyance, his mother sprinkles more sugar into the pot.

"Hmmmm?" continues his father. "You want to join the band? Two Meitkas are better than one. But you've got to follow the leader. A band's like the army. What do you say, kiddo?"

Is this all his father believes he's good for? Goose-stepping after him? He knows the comparison is exaggerated, but why doesn't his father think more of him? Joey Katz and Slide take him more seriously as a musician than his own father. Why doesn't his father want more for him than working at the factory and playing music for the same hundred people every weekend? More than getting drunk and cheating on his wife in cars? Or worse. Sonya, Water Boy, they're so much worse.

Leo makes a show of considering his father's offer, then says in an affected hippie voice, "No way, man. I've got my own band now."

"Hah!" says his father, laughing. "I never heard anything so crazy! As if you would know how to lead a band."

A smile plays on his mother's lips.

The spoon still in his hand, his father grabs his belly and bends over heaving so hard Leo can't tell if he's fake laughing, really laughing, or choking.

"Hey," his mother says, placing her hand on his father's back. A worried look passes over her face until he stands upright. She goes back to her jam, her arm circling and circling the wooden spoon through the bubbling syrup, the worried look still creasing her forehead. "Stash, leave the boy alone. And Leo, don't tease your father. Go wash up for dinner."

Leo's stuck to the spot. He can barely breathe for the anger pulsing through him. Stash's dismissal of him isn't such a surprise. But his mother's dismissal is a slap. She's not laughing at him because she doesn't think he's serious. She thinks he's kidding or lying. Well, he has all kinds of truths to tell that would burn hotter than that jam.

Leo takes a breath before directing his next words to his father, who is no longer laughing but allowing a huge smile to continue to play on his lips as he admires his work on the poster.

"You knew that girl who died at the lake, didn't you?" Leo says. "I saw you with her at the church smoker a while back. You gave her a beer."

The smile drops from his father's face, and his mother slows her stirring. Leo's got their attention.

"I don't—" his father starts.

"Shut up," his mother spits. Leo's not sure if she's talking to him or his father. Probably both of them. "That poor girl has nothing to do with us." The jam burps with heat, and she returns to stirring, her gaze fixed on the red liquid, but a beat later she adds, "Pathetic. Just pathetic."

Leo's not sure what she means. He watches her biceps flex as she lifts the cast-iron pot from the hot burner to a cold one with what seems to him no more effort than she'd take to lift a flute. Arms strong enough to push someone over a cliff?

"Go wash for dinner," she says.

"I'm not hungry," he says.

"Then get out of my kitchen," she snaps.

In his bedroom, he slams the door behind him.

He drops the needle carelessly onto *Revolver*, so it scratches and skips ahead. He cringes, but lets the record play where the needle settles. Grasping his guitar, he shows them just what he can do, the strings bowing deeply as he picks, hammering, tapping out "I Want to Tell You," belting the lyrics.

Old man can't stand for anyone to take the spotlight from him for a second, he rages. Old woman can't see beyond her spoon. They're as bad as each other.

When the record ends, Leo's hands pick random chords on his guitar. He listens and plays them again. He likes them. The energy of composing overtaking his vitriol, he tries a variation, throwing in a B minor. The chord creates a richer melody, but darker. Yes, he thinks, strumming his new tune again. The minor chord adds a black cloud in an otherwise lilting melody.

When he stops playing, the black cloud lingers.

His parents could have gone together to the lake to meet Sonya. When they work together, they're a formidable team.

As angry as he is at them, he doesn't want this to be true. He pulls the whole-note pin from his pool ditty bag.

He rubs the pin's *o*.

Uncertainty is breaking him.

Frustrated, he lifts the needle and starts the George Harrison song again, singing along more melodically.

"I want to speak my mind and tell you. Maybe you'd understand."

With his fingers running the strings, he chases questions over paths and down alleyways. Everywhere they run, they lead back to the same place. He's got to stop treading water. He's got to learn more about Sonya's whole situation and put this whole thing to rest.

Who would Sonya have confided in? Her mother? No, if Sonya told her mother, she wouldn't have taken Water Boy to the lake. She'd have gone to her mother and been taken to a hospital like a normal person. Her brother? Maybe, but Leo doubts he'd get any information from that odd little brat.

Who else knew Sonya well? Of course. He should have thought of her before.

Emelia

EARLY SUMMER HAS been unusually stifling, and it's another still and cloudless day. Walking to the pool, the temperature has already spiked into the eighties. Emelia's got to swim or she'll die, so she's going there before her friends. All this time shrouding her body has made her shy of exposing it, but mostly she wants to go in without having to explain why she wouldn't swim before. If she's already in the water when they arrive, maybe they'll just let it go.

She hadn't meant to make a big deal of not swimming. She just didn't want to explain the injuries on her leg and arm were from Ben catching himself on her as he fell. She can't see a way to tell only part of the story. One detail leads to another and that detail to questions she isn't ready to answer yet, not only because she's promised her aunts she won't tell anyone about her mother, but also because her mother, Water Boy, the notes, and Sonya's death are mixed up with Theo and Danny and Ben in a way she's still sorting out.

But she didn't want to lie to her friends either, which she came pretty close to doing when Leo asked her what's wrong and she said nothing. Is saying nothing as bad a lie as making something up?

She stops herself before she gets too far into calculating degrees of lying. When she woke up this morning, she decided she's sick of sitting on her towel all day, baking in the sun like some slow-proofing bread. Her injuries are gone. She wants to swim.

She shows her summer pass to the boy outside the brick building and pushes through the turnstile into the girls changing room. Inside, a clammy feeling clings to her, and she quickly walks past the lockers and showers, stripping off her blouse along the way. Outside again in the pool area, the sun against her bare skin enlivens her. She can't wait to get into the water.

She removes her sandals and places one foot, then the other on a wooden block, spreading her toes wide. The bored wart-guard girl barely glances at Emelia's feet before waving her through. The pool has just opened, so there aren't that many people here yet. She's able to claim their usual corner easily. She spreads a red-and-white striped towel on the concrete, shimmies out of her shorts, and steps into the pool's gutter. When she slides into the cool water, it stings the scar on her leg, but on her back and shoulders, the water is icing drizzling over her. Delicious.

She floats on her back. Lacy clouds filter the sun, but they won't amount to much, certainly not to rain. Now that she's finally in the water, she wants to stay here all day, like a happy river otter. Actually, her hair billowing around her head brings to mind Kirstin's mermaid stories, and she dunks under. She flutter kicks beneath the surface, pretending she's half fish. *Little girl can swim.* Ben. She wonders what Ben's doing today. Is he driving around in his Falcon? She hopes he found his Falcon leg.

After a few strokes of butterfly, she returns to floating. She wishes Ben were here to float with her. She'd like to thank him. He may have grabbed onto her to keep from falling, but he also tossed her a line. She understands now what he'd been trying to tell her about Sonya, and although he didn't know it, about Elisa too. They were trapped by their own bodies, and no one was there to help them.

To her consternation, she's found out that they didn't have to be trapped. If Sonya could have gotten the new birth control pill, she would never have gotten pregnant at all. Ironically, Emelia only knows about the Pill, and another new way to prevent pregnancy called the Loop, because of her punishment for coming home late the day she'd been with Ben. Aunt Lou made her clean out the rarely used back porch where she stores old magazines and newspapers to be bundled and wrapped in twine for the paper drives at the church. Normally, Aunt Lou keeps the papers and magazines tidily piled, but she must have gotten lazy of late because the periodicals were all helter-skelter. In the process of straightening them so she could tie them up, Emelia found an issue of *The Saturday Evening Post*, which made her gasp and drop the other magazines in her bundle. Right there on the front cover were the words, "The Birth Control Revolution."

Without even glancing at the article, Emelia hid the magazine under the cushion of the wicker sofa. She checked the house to be sure her aunts were in the bakery. When she was sure the coast was clear, she went back to the porch, transferred the magazine from beneath the cushion to beneath her shirt, and dashed to her room where she pushed it between her mattress and box spring. She hurried back to finish bundling the other newspapers and magazines. In doing so, she found that plenty of her aunts' other magazines also had articles about birth control, even *Good Housekeeping* and *Ladies Home Journal*. She stole these away to her bedroom as well.

Hurriedly, she bundled and twined the rest of the newspapers and spent the afternoon reading in her bedroom, her ear trained on the steps in case one of her aunts came up to nap as they sometimes do. The ladies magazines had more warnings about women's promiscuity and the end of the family than real information, but *The Saturday Evening Post* provided her with an eyeful of history and statistics that suggest it isn't just wild miscreants like her mother and Sonya who get pregnant when they don't want to be. Plenty of married women do too, and they have for centuries. These two new birth control methods will let them choose when to have babies and how many. And it's not just women who care. Even President Johnson cares because the population is growing so fast.

As she read, Emelia thought of all her classmates who came from families of six, nine, even eleven children. It had never occurred to her before how hard it must be on their mothers, maybe their fathers too. Plenty of those mothers, she bets, would have taken the Pill or used the Loop if they could have.

But what really burns Emelia is that Sonya *couldn't* use either the Pill or the Loop, and neither could she because only married women are allowed to have them, and then only if a doctor says it's okay, which isn't right. At the memorial during the final assembly at school, Sonya's best friend, Stella, said Sonya wanted to be a scientist and that she was the first girl to win a scholarship to study botany at the university. Hearing this, Emelia thought, no wonder Sonya didn't tell anyone about being pregnant. She'd have had to give up her scholarship. She must have felt, just as Ben had said, trapped by her body. *But she didn't have to be.* Sonya might still be alive if she'd been able to get the Pill or the Loop. And if she wasn't allowed to have them or if they didn't work, which sometimes they don't, she found out, Sonya should have had someplace to go, someone to help her.

Of course, both of these methods were invented too late for Elisa, which saddens her. Sure, Emelia wouldn't be here if Elisa could have used them, but probably her mother also wouldn't have gotten an ice pick to the brain. Who knows what Elisa might have done with her life? Would Emelia trade her own life for Elisa's? It's a hard question, but Emelia keeps thinking that someone else won't exist because that cop stopped Theo and Danny and Emelia just in time, and she sure wouldn't want to trade her life for that someone. And if they hadn't been stopped, she might not know for sure who that someone's Johnny Angel was either. To Emelia, the Pill and the Loop are cops in a cruiser, catching you just in time.

No cop cruised by to stop Elisa and Sonya. They weren't as lucky as Emelia. Maybe one day Kirstin won't be so lucky. Maybe Will and Leo won't be lucky either, and they'll have to choose whether to leave a girl in the lurch or get married and give up on college and music. Emelia may not know what her own future will be, but she wants the chance to find out and wants her friends to have this chance too.

As she floats, the sun shoots points of light through her closed eyelids. Ben's friend had been shot through the head. Alive but blind. Luck is so much more important than she'd ever thought, more than it should be. Eyes or leg? Ice pick or cliff edge? Maybe they never should have been in that war at all.

She'd been lucky twice, first the cops and then when Ben said no. Because her body wanted him to say yes. Sonya's body must have wanted to say yes too. Or, gosh, what if she said no and someone else said yes for her. That's what Ben meant. *Hell, you don't even know if she had a choice at the moment of conception.*

Disturbed, Emelia opens her eyes and sits up. She forgets to kick, and she gulps water, which she snorts through her nose before remembering to tread. She spits and blinks against glare of the sun, the sky and the trees and the pool's blue paint humming and surreal. What if Sonya had said no? But that's too awful to think about. Oh, and then to be stuck as she was with Water Boy, no one to help.

Emelia scoops water and splashes her face as if she might splash the idea away.

Emelia doesn't know Sonya's whole story. Sonya should have had someone to help her, before or after, yes or no.

And she shouldn't have had stupid Emelia making it worse for her by sending her those notes. Even if Sonya hadn't been forced, even if she was wild, a miscreant—and Emelia's no longer sure that she was, or that Elisa was either—those notes were cruel. Emelia knew it too. She believed Sonya deserved it. Maybe she believed her mother deserved her ice pick too. But she was no better than them.

Ben was right about that too. What she did with Theo and Danny, the way she asked Ben to touch her, she could have been trapped just the same. Would she deserve to be punished too? She presses her temple with her wet finger. Does she deserve an ice pick to her brain?

Despite the cold water, Emelia's shame now heats her body hotter than the sun could ever burn her. How could she have involved her friends in her cruelty too? She may have trapped them in a different way. If anyone finds and connects the notes to the four of them, Will and Kirstin will lose their chances at college, and Leo will never get to have his own band.

There's no getting around it. Whatever happened to Sonya at the lake, Emelia had a hand in it. If her friends lose their futures, that will be her fault. And if Sonya's parents find the notes, Emelia will have made their pain sharper too. She's worse than all of them put together.

She pushed Sonya to make it right, and now it's her turn. She's got to do something.

As if summoned by her thoughts, across the pool, Sonya's brother, Dean, screams.

"Aaaaaaaah, no, no, no!"

Wearing denim jeans soaked to black and a wet T-shirt clinging to his cavernous chest and belly, Dean dodges around the pool deck, eluding the grasp of the two lifeguards, who dodge as well, trying to capture him.

"Leave me alone! I want to swim," he shouts.

"Little boy, you can't swim in pants," says a golden-skinned lifeguard, whose graceful strut around the pool Emelia has previously admired. Emelia can't help smiling now. Dean's antics are making the lifeguard look like an old man trying to dance to rock and roll, jerky and ill timed.

"County pool rules!" calls the other guard through a cone-shaped bullhorn. "No suit, no swim!"

Emelia laughs at the bullhorn. Dean's less than two feet away from the lifeguard and hardly needs a bullhorn to hear him.

"Stupid!" Dean spits back, dashing under Golden Boy's outstretched arms and cannonballing into the pool only feet from Emelia, who flinches reflexively as his splash slaps her. He flails and kicks, obviously unable to swim in water that is over his head.

"Help!" he glubs.

"Quit faking, kid," calls one of the guards.

"Mommy," he calls, his panic sounding genuine to Emelia. "Sonya, help!"

Emelia quickly breaststrokes to him. She hooks her elbow beneath his chin the way she has been taught in junior lifesaving. On his back now, he punches air and kicks up water, but he can't reach her, and she holds on, saying firmly, "I've got you. Don't worry. I'll help you. Just relax." Confused for a moment, she nearly calls him Water Boy, but catches herself and says in her best Sonya voice, "Relax, Deanie-Beanie."

And he does.

She guides his thin frame through the water, eventually propping him against the wall. Beneath her fingers, he's all bone and sinewy muscle. He'd been skinny before, but he feels emaciated now. And with the weight of those jeans, it's no wonder he sinks. She continues to press him against the wall until he realizes he can grasp on himself, which eventually he does, huffing and looking stunned. Only then does a red safety ring plop beside them in the pool's gutter, thrown by one of the guards.

"Just in time," Emelia mutters.

Dean manages to grin a little, perhaps understanding that she is mocking the lifeguards. His small teeth are fuzzy with food particles in the spaces. Before she knows it, he shifts his grip from the wall to her neck, cinching her with his small legs. She has no choice but to hold him, her fingers pressing his thin ribs and the knobby bones of his rear end.

Even doused with chlorine water, he smells fishy and faintly of urine. His neck is grubby and his breath hot. Her distaste for him instinctively makes her want to drop him, but his clutch is so tight, she only rubs his back.

"You okay?" says the lifeguard with the bullhorn, standing above her at the pool's edge.

"Yeah," she says, bouncing so as to dip Dean into the water, but the ugly odors cling to him as he does to her. "He's fine. Aren't you, Dean?"

Dean smears his face into the crook of her neck and says nothing.

"I meant you," says the lifeguard, smiling at her. "Are you okay?"

"I'm fine too."

"He can't swim," says the lifeguard, his voice hollow with adopted authority, and she wonders who he's trying to impress, Dean, her, or himself. "Not without a suit."

"Where's his mother? Isn't he here with anyone?" she asks.

"I don't think so. He used to come with his sister. But she was, you know." He drops his voice to a mock whisper. "The one who . . ." He runs one index finger across his throat and jabs the other in the direction of the lake. "You know?"

"Uh-huh," she says, hugging Dean's slithering body to hers. So he's here alone. Without his sister, he's running wild, a miscreant in the making. He's her fault too. *Make it right.* No time like the present.

"All right, I'll take him home," she says.

"He's not your responsibility. You sure?"

"I'm sure," she says.

She swims him to the shallow end and carries him up the steps. Out of the water, he's heavier, dead weight straining her back and legs. She makes it to her corner and bends to set him down. At first, he doesn't release her. He clasps his hands tighter at the back of her neck, refusing to let go. She sits, and when his feet brush the cement, he drops his arms. He lets her pull off his T-shirt, which was probably light blue once but is grimy gray now. She towels him dry and drapes the towel over his narrow shoulders. Despite the hot weather, his lips are blue, and he shivers.

As she's massaging his limbs to warm them, he says, "You're one of them."

Emelia inhales sharply.

"Creep."

His blue eyes hold her like knifepoints, but she doesn't respond.

"My sister didn't like those notes"

She nods. "I'm sorry about those. I'd like to make it up to her."

"She's gone."

"I know." Emelia feels guilt drape her like the wet towel. "Maybe you'll let me make it up to her by taking you home. Will you come with me? I promise I'll take you right home."

"Will you make me something to eat? I'm hungry."

"Yes. If your mom says it's okay."

He doesn't respond. As she gathers her lotion and magazines, the golden lifeguard approaches.

"You know where he lives?"

He's only a year or so older than her. Up close, his skin is less golden and more walnut. He smells of coconut oil. She finds herself wanting to draw her finger down the film of sweat on his chest. She would like to lick the path her finger makes.

"Yeah, I know where he lives."

She adds to herself, he lives at Sonya's house.

"Maybe you could come back after you dump him. I'm off duty early today. We could go to Pig 'N Whistle. Get an ice cream." He steps closer and touches her upper arm where the bruise had been.

Instinctively, Emelia jerks her arm away.

"I don't know," she says, realizing she's parched. Her skin has already dried. She's breathlessly hot. She's so thirsty, she'd like to drink the pool water. She'd like to drink this lifeguard. "Maybe I—"

All of a sudden her leg stings as if hit with a hot pan. Dean stares angrily at his hand, which looks to be stinging too, but he's also poised to strike her again. A red handprint rises on her thigh.

"Ouch! Stop it! That hurt," she says, grabbing his wrist before he can slap her again. To the lifeguard she says, "I should take him home. See you."

"Yeah, okay. Take the little brat home. Then come back."

"I'll see," she says, losing hold of Dean's wrist. She dodges just in time to avoid a kick from his small foot. *Make it right.* No one said it would be easy.

"Stop it now," she says firmly, and to her surprise, he does. "Where are your shoes?"

He shrugs.

"Did you bring any?"

He cocks his head as if the thought of wearing shoes has only now occurred to him. Then he shakes his head.

"Okay, then, let's go," she says.

Dean lets her lead him though the metal turnstile, out of the pool area, and into the park. Emelia walks the path to the street while he boomerangs ahead and back, leaping to pluck leaves from low-hanging tree branches. He chases and nearly catches a squirrel. He finger shoots passing cars once they reach the street. Each time he barrels back to her, he tries to slap her backside or kick her shin. When she manages to parry his blows, he bullets off again, kicking signposts and slamming his small fists against fence pickets.

How had Sonya stood it? His energy exhausts her. She thinks of the cartoon with the devilish beast that spins devastation wherever it goes. Had Sonya actually been able to love this creature? Had Dean been on her mind when she buried Water Boy?

As they turn the corner onto his street, he finds a fallen tree branch. He whisks it up and inserts it between her striding legs. She stumbles but manages to stay upright.

"Do you want me to leave you alone?" she threatens.

"Aaaaaahhhh!" he roars, holding the branch high, a tiny Viking heading into battle with his sword. Her striped towel wafts behind him like a cape as he charges toward his house.

"I'm Crypto! I'm Crypto! Whah! Whah!"

When they get to his house, Dean swishes his branch sword, using all his strength to stab the lawn again and again.

"Dead!" he yells.

"Shush!" she says, glancing around for neighbors. As much as she wants to help him, it occurs to her she probably shouldn't be seen with him. Leo, Kirstin, and Will would be furious if they knew she was here, taking the risk of being spotted at Sonya's house. Maybe she should just leave the boy. She's brought him safely home. Why take any more risk?

Because she owes him. What had Ben said—you make your choices in the moment and deal with the consequences later. Dean is her consequence for sending Sonya those notes. She should at least hand him off to his mother, although she now dreads looking Sonya's mother in the eye.

She jogs behind Dean, over the bluestone path to his porch, up the wooden steps. She takes a deep breath before entering Sonya's house.

"Mrs. Morrow," Emelia calls from the threshold. "I've brought Dean home."

The house has the echo of emptiness.

"Has your mom gone out?" she says, her dread shifting its focus. If his mother is gone, she'll have to stay with him.

Dean points to a closed door at the end of the hallway.

"She's in there. Moooooommmm! Moooooommmm!" he yells, unbuttoning his jeans. "She never comes out."

He peels off his wet pants. His spindly legs jut from baggy, once white, now dirty-gray briefs. He seems happy to be nearly naked, and he sprints across the room and leaps onto the couch. Bouncing on the cushions, he chants in time, "Cryp-to, Cryp-to! She's ne-ver com-ing ba-ack! She's ne-ver com-ing ou-out!"

"What do you mean?" she says. "She's never coming out?"

He stops bouncing and again points to the door at the end of the hallway. "She's stuck in there. She never comes out."

From the state of the place, Dean looks to be telling the truth about his mother having taken to her bed. A shotgun ranch, Emelia can see all the way to the back of the house from the foyer.

"Come in," Dean says. "She won't care. She never comes out."

Emelia steps inside a squat living room, which bleeds into a smaller dining room and a kitchen that Aunt Lou and Aunt Genny would scoff at for its electric stove and Formica countertop. They would jeer at the dirty dishes piled up. Every cabinet door is open with the majority of shelves bare. Strewn over the countertops are empty jars of peanut butter and jelly, and opened cans of soup that have spilled and drip-dried into crusty stains. They linger among black banana peels, withered apple cores, empty Wonder wrappers, dried-up chicken bones, and Jell-O boxes torn open, the contents sugaring every surface.

Dean must have foraged the kitchen like an abandoned bear cub. Where is his father, she thinks angrily, then guiltily. His pain is her fault too.

"I'm hungry," says Dean, once again bouncing on the cushions. "Make me something to eat."

Every fiber of her wants to run screaming out the door, but it's her turn to make it right.

"Okay," she says. "What do you have?"

She walks into the kitchen, her stomach turning at the sight of a furred glass of what must have once been orange juice. She opens the refrigerator and a putrid smell washes out. It can't be the milk; the bottle is empty. It smells like the compost heap in the garden behind the bakery but more fetid. Is there old tuna salad in there? Anyway, there's not much good in the refrigerator besides ketchup, mustard, and other condiments. She shuts the door on the smell and opens the freezer, which offers better options. She takes a frozen block of hamburger to the sink. She rinses a dish, puts in the frozen block, and runs hot water over it.

While the meat defrosts, she washes and puts away the dishes, gagging throughout the process. By the time she wipes down the countertops for the third time—sugar still stuck in the Formica's joints, inviting ants—the meat is thawed enough to form into frost-chunked patties, which she places in a warm, buttered pan. At the smell of the frying, Dean appears in the kitchen doorway. He's subdued now that food is coming.

He places his hands and feet on either side of the doorframe, climbs up a few feet, and suspends himself there, watching her. His steady gaze disconcerts her. Is he thinking of Sonya?

"Do you like burgers?" she says, pressing the patties with the back of a spatula.

He nods.

"Okay, then, go sit down."

He releases the tension in his arms and legs and lands in a squat on the linoleum floor. He hops frog-like to the table. She clears a spot on the table, which is strewn with junk mail and napkins and other random things, like a can of bait and another of tobacco. When the meat is cooked, she places the plate of food in front of him.

As she sits with him while he eats three fat burgers frosted with ketchup, her gaze is drawn down the hallway. There are four closed doors. One for the parents' bedroom, one for the bathroom, one for Dean's room. And one for Sonya's room.

When Dean finishes his food, he drinks down an entire glass of water as she clears and washes his plate and utensils. He follows her to the sink. He wears a dozy expression, and his formerly taut body is all noodles now. He collapses against her thigh, sleepily rubbing his forehead into her leg.

"Where's your room?" she asks, finger-brushing his hair, which is still slightly damp from the pool, but soft.

"There." He points to one of the closed doors.

"Next to your mom's?"

He nods, rubbing his nose into her leg.

"Are you sure your mom is in there?"

"Uh-huh," he says sleepily. "She's always in there since Sonya left."

"Is that Sonya's room?" She points to the door with the poster of a pink flower on a lime background tacked to it.

"Uh-huh. She's gone. I'm tired," he says, drawing the words out into a yawn.

"Want me to tuck you in for a nap?"

He nods and pulls her by the hand to his bedroom, no longer a whirling devil but a little boy no one's taking care of. Her fault. Her consequence.

If the kitchen was a compost pile, Dean's room is a junkyard. Heaped on every surface are clothes, shoes, toys, many of them broken. She steps over pieces of model battleships, race cars missing wheels, little green soldiers in various attack poses. She notices only one area is free of Dean's dross, the closet.

The door is open, and a small table is tidily ordered with coloring books, paper, crayons and pencils, all neatly lined up. She glances at the pictures, finding surprisingly identifiable drawings of a masked figure with a cape and a dagger. One image has been pinned to the wall with *CRYPTO* printed in clear handwriting, obviously not Dean's. Sonya's? But the drawings are his, that's for sure. Violent explosions of black crayon scribble out the drawings he doesn't like.

Dean tugs her toward a bed that's a nest of sheets and blankets and clothes. He climbs in, pulls his knees up, and tucks his fists under his chin, creating a position so familiar, Emelia says, "Water Boy."

"Moon Boy," says Dean, his eyes already closed as he melts into sleep.

Emelia waits a few moments to make sure he's not faking. It would be just like him, she thinks, smiling. Now it's not so hard to believe Sonya might have loved him. When his breath becomes even and deep, she tiptoes across the hall to the door with the flower poster.

Emelia taps the handle with her index finger, half expecting an electric shock. Is entering her room another violation? Make the best choice you can in the moment.

"Okay, Ben," she whispers, turning the handle. "Time to learn more about her story." And to put things right for her friends.

She slips in and finds a cornflower bedspread, a lavender throw rug, and a worn Raggedy Ann doll propped on a shelf above a pine desk. It could be any teenage girl's room. On the walls hang pressed flowers and plants, cross-sections drawn in colored pencils and labeled the way Emelia has done herself in her natural sciences class, but her own are without the beautiful precision of Sonya's.

"She liked flowers," she says. That's why she'd gotten her scholarship. Having built Sonya into a larger-than-life girl, seeing the regular objects of a regular girl is almost more shocking than having seen Sonya on that stretcher. Any girl could be trapped as she had been.

Emelia glances around. Where would this regular girl hide the notes so her mother wouldn't find them? She tries the most obvious place first, sliding her hand under the mattress. Nothing.

She pulls open the drawers of the desk, but finds only pencils and paper and a few old school notebooks. She tries the dresser drawers, rooting beneath sweaters and shorts, noting that she and Sonya are nearly the same size. She searches the underwear drawer, expecting satin or lacy lingerie, but finds only cotton undergarments similar to her own, the same brands purchased at the same places.

She closes the drawers quietly and looks around. The notes could be anywhere. Posters of the Beatles, Bob Dylan, and Joan Baez are tacked to the walls. She runs her fingers over their glossy surfaces to see if the notes might be taped behind them, but she finds nothing.

The suitcase phonograph that sits on a wire rack by the window is similar to the one Emelia has in her own room, which Leo makes fun of for its poor quality, but it sounds okay to her. Sonya has about twenty records in her collection, and Emelia looks inside each jacket for the notes, nervously glancing at the door, expecting Sonya's mother to appear.

Neither Sonya's mother nor the notes turn up. On the turntable, Peter, Paul, and Mary's *See What Tomorrow Brings* has a coating of dust. Drawing a line in the dust with her finger, she becomes aware of a stillness that reminds her of the presence of her mother in her own bedroom. How long do places cling to their people? Or is it people clinging to places?

"Sonya?" she whispers.

But of course, no reply comes. Sonya's gone. Emelia recognizes the wall of nothing from when her mother was dead. Impenetrable. But she's seen Sonya's body. Sonya's never coming back.

Here, in her bedroom, the finality of her death hits Emelia hard. She'll never hear another song or smell another petal. Emelia feels a new urgency to find the notes. Not to protect her friends though. Sonya's parents should remember their daughter only as a girl who played music and liked flowers.

Emelia circles the room. Where would she hide something from her aunts? Eventually she goes to the one place Emelia has always considered her own in Elisa's room.

She slides open the closet door. Hanging there are the clothes Emelia thought were so cool when she'd seen Sonya wearing them at school. She lifts out a navy mini-dress with green and yellow color blocks. Instinctively, she holds it up to her shoulders. Emelia's never worn anything like it.

She'd love to try it on. Would it be so bad to try it on? Would Sonya care? Would it help her understand Sonya's story a little better?

Standing rabbit-still and listening, she glances at the doorway again, her awareness of Sonya's mother in the other room prickling her skin. When she hears nothing, she kicks off her sandals and strips down to her nearly dry suit. She climbs into the dress and slides up the side zipper.

The fit is perfect. She'd thought Sonya was bigger than her, but no, even the chest encases her like a second skin. The smooth lining clings to her stomach and back, slithering against the nylon of her suit.

She addresses herself in the mirror. Not half bad, but it had looked so much better on Sonya. How come? Oh, yes, those matching platform Mary Janes.

She drops to the carpet, ducks into the closet, and paddles through loafers, low heels with pencil-tip toes, ballet flats, and

Keds in a variety of colors, but no platform Mary Janes. At the lake, Sonya's feet had been bare but for a coating of dirt and sand. Could she have worn those shoes to the lake? Who wears platforms there?

Those feet, she thinks as the image returns to her, white and lifeless. No paint on the toenails. She smooths her hands over the dress and her thighs. Sonya wanted nice shoes and dresses. She liked flowers and music. Emelia crawls deeper into the closet, hungry to know more of Sonya's story. She sniffs the dried mud on Sonya's rain boots, the scent of the lake mingling with the odor of rubber. She crawls deeper.

Brushing the area with her fingertips, she finds space in the wall big enough to hide a cardboard box. When she pulls the box out, she recognizes the picture of a one-eyed dog and an impish child with a pageboy haircut. Emelia had once had her own Buster Browns. Backing out of the closet, box in hand, she sits cross-legged on the carpet.

She glances at the door again.

With the box on her lap, she hesitates, again feeling like an intruder. The box was hidden. So it must be filled with Sonya's secrets. How would she like it if someone came into her room, wore her clothes, and snooped into her private things?

She's not so sure anymore that she's doing the right thing.

She looks up at the flowers and records. Emelia guesses that Sonya's mother hasn't moved an object in her daughter's room since she died. But her mother will have to come in some day. And then she'll find this box. If something happened to her, would she want Aunt Lou and Aunt Genny to come in her room and discover her secrets?

No. Never.

Sonya must have hidden her pregnancy from her mother. Of course she would want someone to take the notes away.

Emelia lifts the lid. Nestled beneath ribbons, badges, and a dog collar are all four notes. The other things in the box seem more like mementos, and Emelia has an impulse to linger over them just to learn a little more about Sonya, but those things are for her mother and father and for Dean. She plucks out the notes, covers the box, and crawls back into the closet to return the box to its hiding place.

As she's backing out of the closet, the bedroom door opens.

"Sonya!" exclaims Lorna Morrow.

Through the curtain of hair, which has drooped over Emelia's face, she sees a tall woman with red eyes and sunken cheeks. *Bertha Rochester*. Sonya's mother.

"I'm sorry," Emelia mutters. "I'm so sorry."

Before Sonya's mother can say another word, Emelia has scooped up her clothes and shoes. She doesn't stop to think about her choices or their consequences. Barefoot, still in Sonya's mini-dress and with the notes tight in her fist, she heads for the bedroom door.

Despite her unhealthy appearance, Sonya's mother is fast. She grabs Emelia's forearm as she tries to slip past her.

"Where have you been?" she says. "I've been so worried. The things they've been saying. I knew they weren't true."

"I have to go," Emelia says.

"No. You stay here."

Her fingers dig into Emelia's muscle like a claw, far stronger than Ben's when he grasped onto her. The feeling makes Emelia panic, and she wrenches her arm free. She rushes down the hallway toward the kitchen. She dashes through the living room and keeps going, out the front door and down the porch steps in a single leap. She runs barefoot up the street, notes in one hand, clothes and sandals in the other. A few houses down the street, she stubs her toe on a raised block of concrete.

"Shit," she yells.

"Language!"

Glancing over her shoulder, she sees Sonya's mother has stopped at the edge of the Morrow's porch. Emelia bites her lip at the pain in her foot and trot-limps a few steps, but Sonya's mother isn't pursuing her.

At the corner she leans against a tree to examine her big toe and finds it smeared syrupy red with a flap of loose flesh.

She's glad for the pain. She deserves it for what she's done. It's the very least of the consequences.

Dean

"NO. COME BACK!" yells his mother. "Sonya!"

Crouching in the doorway behind her, Dean understands his mother is broken like the battleship on his bedroom floor. Once he smashed it, he couldn't put that battleship together again no matter what he tried, and he doesn't know how to put his mother back together either.

Dean's father doesn't know how to fix her, to make her get out of bed and go back to doing all the house things and cooking things she used to do for them. Dean's father has tried, urging her, "Get up, it's time. Dean is still here. I'm still here. I can't take care of everything on my own."

His mother only hunkers deeper under the covers.

"Please," his father said to Dean three, five, oh, he's not sure how many breakfasts and dinners ago. "I have to leave. I'll be gone all week. Stay here. Watch her. The neighbors . . ."

His father hadn't finished his thought, but Dean understood that their house is shameful. Their family is shameful. Sonya was the first shame. All those people staring at her at the lake. Now his mother. The neighbors mustn't know.

Since his father left, Dean's stayed in the house with his mother, watching her door and as much television as he wanted. He kept the windows shut and the curtains closed as he played with all of his toys. He drew all the drawings he had inside him. He ate what he could find. This morning though, when he was lonely and hungry, but most of all so steaming, boiling, burning *hot*, all he could think of was the pool. He longed for the cold water in the pool the way he sometimes longs for Sonya to hug him again.

Before he left his house, he forgot what his father said about the neighbors. But he remembers now, as his mother stands on the porch believing that the big-kid girl is Sonya. His mother won't shut up. He's got to hide her from the neighbors. He's got to protect her from their shame.

"That's not Sonya!" he says with a quiet fierceness.

His mother seems not to hear him.

"That's not her!" he yells, forgetting to be quiet.

Damn, shoot, darn! he thinks when he sees a ruffle in the curtains of the Hardingers' house across the street. He grabs his mother's forearm and tug, tug, tugs her toward the house.

He wishes that big-kid girl would come back. He's not mad at her anymore. He needs her help. But she's turned the corner and disappeared like all the nice people and things seem to do.

After a while, when it's clear the girl is not going to return, his mother allows herself to be tugged. Once they are inside and he has slammed the door behind them, she looks at him with surprise, as if a magnetic force brought her inside and not her little boy.

"Oh, it's you," she says.

Her voice has the ring it always has when she talks to him now, which is almost never. But he understands the tone. She wishes it were Sonya here. She wishes he, not Sonya, had gone over the cliff and into the water.

Blink of an eye. There, gone.

Blink, Sonya there. Blink, Sonya gone.

He hasn't told anyone what he saw, and no one's thought to ask him. Not the policeman man or the policeman lady. Not his parents. Even the girl who stole Sonya's dress didn't think to ask what he saw. He wouldn't have told them one single thing anyway because he and Sonya keep each other's secrets.

He leads his mother into the living room. He pushes her down onto the couch, which is covered in his father's sleep sheets and their dirty clothes. Usually she yells at him to keep his shoes off the couch. He's not allowed to eat anywhere but the kitchen table. Pick up his socks. Clean up his toys. But she seems not to notice the mess she's seated on, and this scares him as much as anything else.

Maybe she is blind. He waves his hand in front of her eyes. She flickers to life. She glances around her as if she's trying to remember if she's ever been to this place before.

"Mom?"

"You've cleaned up the kitchen," she says, taking in the big-kid girl's work. "What a good boy you are."

He opens his mouth to say it was the girl who did it. But his mother shifts her gaze from the kitchen to him. And she actually sees him!

Her lips stretch into a smile. A feeling he names *joy* fills him, and he thinks of good things: cold milk streaming down his throat, pumping his legs on the swing until he's high in the air, running so fast he's flying.

But a moment later, her smile dribbles away. Her eyes are empty again.

Thirsty for more smile, he tries doing things that used to make her laugh. He somersaults across the floor. He tells her one of his knock-knocks, although she won't play along, so he does all the parts himself. He drops to his knees and first plays baby, then doggie.

But her stare remains blind and her lips a straight line.

He clenches his fists so hard his arms tremble. He wants to shake her, shake her, shake her and make her see him.

"Come back," he pleads.

What else can he do? There's one thing. But he promised Sonya to keep her secrets.

"Come back," he pleads again.

There. Gone. Sonya is gone forever. His mother is still here. It's up to him to bring her back.

He pads down the hallway. The door to Sonya's bedroom is open from the girl having been in there. He wavers on the threshold. He doesn't like it in there anymore. When it was really Sonya's room, it smelled of Sonya, of flowers and birds and clouds and wind. Sonya told him to knock before coming in, which he only sometimes remembered, and sometimes when he had a nightmare, he sneaked in. He lay on her floor, and in the morning, when she woke up, she tickled his feet and let him crawl in bed with her and snuggle. Sometimes, when she left her door open a crack, he watched her from the hallway.

That's how he knew about the secrets hidden beneath her mattress.

Now her empty bed reminds him of that hole they put her dead box in. The walls are too close. The air is stuffy. After they put her dead box in that hole, he dreamt he was in this room and it started shrinking and shrinking until the walls squished him like a hot dog in a fist. He woke just before the room popped him, and he found himself tangled in his blanket.

He hasn't wanted to come in here since that dream. He went in only one time. When they returned home from putting her box in the hole. Because as he threw dirt on her box, he promised to keep her secrets.

In the silent house, his mother locked in her bedroom, his father at the tavern down the block, Dean stole into Sonya's room. He leaned his shoulder into her mattress as he'd seen Sonya do when he watched her through the sliver of open door. He slipped his hand in and fished around until his fingers hit the sharp edge of paper. He slid out the special-delivery letter that he'd delivered specially to Sonya the day before she left. He couldn't read the words then or now, but he hated the straightness of them on the page—black soldiers, strict and mean, teacher mean, principal mean.

He knew the letter wasn't the only thing Sonya put there, so he cast his line again, going shoulder deep in the fold between the mattress and box spring. His face pressed to the bed's blankets, a waft of Sonya's smell hit his nose, so strong and so lovely that when he found the picture of the man at the cliff and pulled out his arm, he sniffed his skin.

Flowers and birds and clouds and wind.

Now, he needs to smell her again. He crawls onto her bed. He burrows headfirst under the covers, sniffing for her like a hound. Blankets over his head, his nose pressed against her sheets, he inhales a faint what's-left-of-her scent lingering in the cloth. *Flowers and birds and clouds and wind.* He sniffs and sniffs until he can no longer smell her. She's gone again. His muffled tears and snot leak all over her nice sheets.

She wouldn't like that, but she won't know. She won't ever know anything again.

She won't know if he tells. They keep each other's secrets. Sonya will keep his forever. But she's left him all alone with his broken mother and his pleading father.

"I'm sorry, Sonya," he says, his words muted by her sheets.

The moment the words are out, he feels suffocated. He crawls out of her bed. Before leaving, he spots the red-and-white striped towel the girl left. It doesn't belong in here, and he picks it up and drapes it over his shoulder before leaving the room, shutting Sonya's door tight behind him.

He walks to his closet—his studio, Sonya called it. She said it's the place where he can draw whatever he wants, pretty things but ugly things too that he doesn't have to show anyone if he doesn't want to show. In here, he created Cryptic Crypto, who no one can figure out and no one understands except the girl who he's drawn like a flower. He pulls a tablet from the shelf. He opens it and collects both the special-delivery letter and the picture of the man who was at the cliff with Sonya.

Maybe telling Sonya's secrets won't make his mother smile, but they might be like the cord his father pulls on the lawn mower engine. They might make her roar.

"Mom!" he calls, trotting down the hallway, the photo and letter held high above his head like swords. "I have to show you some stuff."

The couch is empty though. He looks down the hallway. His mother's bedroom door is shut again. She's gone. He'd been too slow.

He drops his arms and looks at the photo in his hand. Sonya's secret. She put it in such an easy hiding place. Even if he hadn't seen her hide it, she must have known he would find it. She must have known he would go looking. Did she want him to tell? Is that why she made it so easy to find her secrets? But who will listen to him now? When will his father be home? He doesn't know what day it is. It seems he's been alone for years longer than a week.

He wishes Sonya would come back just for one single second to tell him what to do. How is a boy like him supposed to know things? If he were big like his dad or like Policeman Man, he would know what to do. Crypto would know what to do. With his fingertip, he draws Crypto's eyes over the eyes of the man in the photo. Then he touches his own face, tracing Crypto's features there. The feeling reminds him of watching Sonya draw on her face with the special pencils and brushes and colored sticks that he isn't allowed to use to draw on paper.

"This is only for faces," she said.

He walks back down the hallway. Glancing at his mother's bedroom door, he listens. Hearing nothing, he enters Sonya's room one last time. He roots in her dresser drawer and takes eyebrow pencils and eye shadows, her blusher and lipsticks.

He goes into the bathroom and draws a circle around his eye.

Cryptic boy, Sonya called him.

He fills in the circle with blue powder.

They created Crypto together to do all the things Dean wants to do but can't.

He stripes his cheeks with red lipstick.

Crypto can fly. And solve reading puzzles. And writing puzzles. Crypto has adventures. *Capers*, Sonya called them. He has a friend. A girl who looks like a flower.

Sonya looked like one kind of flower. But there are lots of flowers in a field. Big-kid girl, she's another kind of flower.

He greases his lips black. Crypto doesn't have to always be nice the way everyone tells Dean he has to be. He snarls at the mirror. His teeth are brilliant white inside his black lips, and he giggles. Crypto knows things. He'll find big-kid girl. He snarls at the man in the photo. Crypto's not afraid of him. And only Dean promised not to tell. Not Crypto.

Leo

SINCE HIS VOICE changed two years ago, Leo's vocal range tops three octaves, but his mother has always taught him that only control will allow him to make his singing unique. He's been working on going note to note from baritone to falsetto, clean as a hot knife through cold butter. Rather than show off his vocal control to Charles though, Leo pretends he's his father, belting "We Can Work It Out" just to the left of flat. He wants Charles to see how badly they need a singer. When Charles suggests it, Leo has the perfect voice in mind.

Although Leo has decided he will ask Stella what she knows about Sonya, he understands he can't just walk up to her at Free-Zee Creams and ask her who got her dead best friend pregnant. Inviting her to be their singer is the perfect excuse to talk to her and bring up Sonya at the right time.

First, he's got to convince Charles to let her join the band.

As if hermetically sealed, the air inside Charles's house is cool and dry despite the closed windows and the sultry heat outside. Leo's never been in a house with central air conditioning before. Moments after entering Charles's house, his sweat evaporated, leaving a sticky residue on his skin that he fears makes him stink of body odor.

Nothing stinks in Charles's house. Not a single dirty dish sits on the kitchen's lemon-colored tile countertops. The porcelain sink gleams. Leo bets the living room's powder blue furniture has never felt the weight of a human's backside. Even the rumpus room has neat rows of bookshelves with sets of encyclopedias, fat dictionaries, and a leather-bound set of Charles Dickens's novels. Pillows perfectly placed on matching brown plaid couches prove the television living rooms aren't the big fake-out that his mother insists they are when she's shoving a vacuum around their messy house.

The most curious room is an add-on at the back of the house that juts into the back yard. As they pass it on their way to the conservatory, Leo sniffs earthy scents that remind him of the cigarette Joey Katz gave him. He wishes again that he had one.

Two matching doors—French doors, Charles calls them—separate this room from the others. With tall windows, the room seems to have no purpose beyond growing thin-leafed plants that shoot from colorful pots. The first time Leo visited, Charles laughed when Leo asked about it and said, "That's my mom's *tea* room."

Leo laughed too, although he didn't really understand why tea was funny. Whatever the joke, Leo's confident there are no ropes of drying sausages hanging from the rafters of this house as there are in his father's attic den when his mother is working through the last of a hog or a side of beef. In fact, there are probably sausages drying in the attic right now, getting ready to be cooked at his father's release party tomorrow, which his mother has ordered Leo to attend.

"On pain of death," she said, swiping the air with her chopping knife, minced garlic bits flying. "And be ready to play. If he asks."

The conservatory where he and Charles are practicing now has the same tall windows, but here thick white drapes are drawn halfway across the panes. Having showered before he came over, Leo's still hesitant to sit down on the snowy white upholstery of the curiously named fainting couch. Certain he'll leave sweat and dirt rings if he sits, he sings standing up, which is how his mother has taught him anyway, allowing his diaphragm to fully expand. Charles says the white wood panels of the other walls are especially made for good acoustics, and they are good, but nothing close to the Silo's sound.

However good they are, the panels do little to improve Leo's singing voice today.

"Something's missing," Charles says when they finish the song. Using the insides of his index fingers as sticks, he drums the shelf of the satin-black Steinway.

It's a beautiful instrument, perfectly tuned, with key action that makes Leo feel like he's got extra bones in his fingers when he plays it. He'd love to have a few hours alone with it. Charles is a good pianist, almost as good as Leo's mother, but if Leo had this piano to play anytime he wanted, he'd be the virtuoso his mother tells him he could be if he practiced more. Today, though, he's only half here for the music.

"I think we need a drummer," Charles says.

Leo spots his opening.

"And a singer. Remember, you said so at the pool? You were right. I'm a lot better when I sing with someone."

"Yeah, I guess if we're going to be a real band, we need a beat and a voice," says Charles. "I know a guy who can bang skins, and—"

"I know a singer," Leo gets in quickly, before Charles thinks of someone else and gets stuck on the idea.

"He's good?" Charles says. "I mean . . ."

He means better than Leo just now, and Leo nods enthusiastically, "Yeah, man, she's tops. She sings with my father's band sometimes."

"She? You mean a chick?" he says as if it's just occurred to him girls can sing. "Not that one from the pool?"

"No, not Emelia. Someone else."

"She can sing?"

"Yeah," Leo says. "She's good. You'll see."

Armed with the offer to join the band, Leo rides his bike up and down Stella Bronski's street, pondering ways to bring up Sonya. Should he simply accuse her, Philip Marlow-style: "You know who knocked up your friend, and you're going to tell me now." Or should he play it cool, Lew Harper-style: "Your gal

Sonya keeps lousy company. Had a way of starting conversations that stopped 'em."

Then again, if he were as cool as Paul Newman's Harper, he wouldn't need to know who Water Boy's father was at all. He'd call his parents Stash and Anne and tell them both to kiss off. *Let 'em take their chances with the cops.* He'd douse his face in ice water and be too cool to care. He'd flash his smile and crimp his blue eyes just like Harper. He sure wouldn't be so nervous to talk to Stella.

He supposes he doesn't have bring up Sonya today, but even giving himself this break, his nerves don't lessen much. Man, he doesn't want to make an idiot of himself. She's so pretty. She's older too. And she can sing. He wasn't lying to Charles about that.

Steering his bike in a wide circle in front of the Bronskis' driveway, he glimpses movement in an upstairs window. He panics, jittering his bike and nearly falling. He manages to right himself, but it's too late to sprint off as he'd like to do. A woman he presumes is Stella's mother has stepped out onto the balcony porch and calls, "Young man, what do you want? So you know, my daughter has nothing to say to journalists about that girl!"

"Is Stella home?" he calls.

"Who wants to know? What do you want with her?"

He hops the curb, dismounts, and leans the bike against a maple tree. All hope of Lew Harper coolness has zipped away, and Leo runs to his mommy. "I'm Anne Meitka's son." And his daddy. "Stella sings with my dad's band. Stash Meitka?" His parents are right. What in God's name made him think he could be a bandleader?

"Leopold?" she says.

He winces at the sound of his full name.

"Yes, ma'am."

She waves as if he's just arrived. "Oh, my, you've shot up," she says, her tone suggesting this is an accomplishment. "I hardly recognized you."

"Is Stella home?" he repeats. He sees movement in the curtains of the neighboring house and wonders how long it will be before news of this visit gets back to his parents, either from Stella's mother, who seems to know them, or by way of a nosy neighbor.

"I'll get her. Come up to the porch, Leopold."

The front door opens before he makes it up the porch stairs. Stella pushes through the screen door and steps out. Her hair is fuzzier than ever, but she's tied it back with a scarf dappled with olive-colored dewdrops that match her eyes. Her eyes are red rimmed, and he wonders if she's been crying for Sonya.

Silver hoops loop each of her ears, and a sleeveless midriff of gauzy yellow brings out the golden hues of her tanned skin. Blue jeans rest low on her hips, exposing sharp bones that Leo would like to touch. Peeking past the flare at the cuffs, the toenails of her bare feet gleam a strange purple color that makes him want to tap them like the keys on Charles's piano.

She's a beatnik, he thinks, grinning, clasping his hands behind his back to keep from reaching for that electric hair.

"You're Stash's kid," she declares.

Taken aback at her use of his father's first name, he manages to say, "Yeah."

"What's your name again? Your dad told me, but I forgot."

He blushes. She doesn't even remember his name. To her, he's Stash's kid. He feels sweat dripping down his legs, and he hopes she doesn't notice. Why had he worn shorts? If only he could be cool. Harper cool. Joey Katz cool. Slide cool. Joey and Slide, they changed their names. Why can't he too? Snaggle? No, he needs something cooler.

"Leo Mack," he says. "I go by Leo Mack when I play music."

A smile playing on her lips, she says, "Okay, so what do you want, Leo Mack?" She crosses the porch to sit on a bench swing. Folding her arms over her chest, she pulls one bare foot up, hooking the heel onto the edge of the seat. Her purpled toes spread wide, and he has an urge to place his pinky into the space between her first and second toe. Behind him, he clasps his hands tighter.

He tries to summon some Harper cool, some Mack cool, but he blurts, "You want to join my band?" The moment the words are out of his mouth, he feels humiliated. Of course, his parents were right to laugh at him for thinking he could start his own band. He's just some ding-a-ling kid. She's out of high school. She's sung with the real musicians in his father's band, at least more real than he is. She played with Joey Katz at the smoker. She calls his father *Stash,* not *Mr. Meitka.*

Leo braces for her derision.

"What kind of music?" she says, her forehead crimping with consideration. "Like your dad's?"

"No way." He grimaces and shakes his head.

"You don't like your dad's music?"

"It's not that. I mean, well, in *my* band, not that it's just me, I mean, *we* play rock and roll. The Beatles, Stones. Yardbirds, stuff like that."

"Uh-huh. I see. Anything original?"

"I've got a few songs," he says. At the moment, every song he's ever written seems simple and babyish. He couldn't bear to play them for her. He'll have to write something better. Can he do it, write something good enough for her? His father's voice drums like waves on the shore: *not real music.* What if he can't? What if all he has in him is more of the crap he's already written? He quickly adds, "Charles writes too."

"Charles who?"

"Charles Grady."

"Oh, yeah, he's good. Anyone else?"

"We're looking for a drummer. Charles knows someone who—" He almost says *bangs the skins* as Charles does, but it sounds silly in his head. "—who plays drums."

"Well, I write songs too," she says. "You willing to give my songs a listen?"

Leo's grin overtakes his face without calculation. "You bet!"

"Okay, then. I'll give you guys a try."

For the first time, she smiles a little too. It changes her face, lightening it so he sees just how sad she'd been a moment before. All he wants is to make her smile again.

"We're practicing tomorrow afternoon," he says. "Can you come? And then, if you want, you could come to my father's band's release party in the evening. My mother's making a lot of food."

After the things his parents said about his band, Leo had dragged his feet about going to the release party, but if Stella comes, he'll be glad to go.

"Release party? What's that?"

"Record release." Even to Leo, this sounds impressive, and Stella looks impressed. "He cut a single. I mean, we did. I played on it too."

"Cool," she says, smiling, her bow lip stretching into a sweet arc. "Really cool. Yeah, okay. Let's jam tomorrow. See if we mesh." She interlocks her fingers. Her nails are short, her fingertips calloused in the same places his own are hardened.

"You play guitar?"

"I do," she says, turning her fingers toward her face as if Leo noticing her calluses has made her see them for the first time. "And bass, if I can get my hands on one."

"I've got an old one," Leo says.

"Bring it."

He tells her where Charles lives, offering to meet her and walk her over. Like a date, he thinks. She points out he'll have two instruments to carry, and he'll have to go twice as far to pick her up.

"Might as well meet there. No point in you going farther just to meet me."

He'd go all the way to Mars, he thinks, but manages not to blurt it out.

Only later, as he's riding his bicycle toward home, pushing all his excitement into the gears—he can't wait to hear her play—he can't wait to hear her songs—can't wait for her to hear *his* songs, the new ones he'll write, the good ones—she's so pretty—that one song of his is okay, but he'll have to do better—he *will* do better, he'll write something outta sight—her voice, his brilliant songs—that hair, her green eyes, like another country, another continent, another planet, Mars—without question, he'd get on a spaceship for her—only when he's steering up the driveway at his house and all but collides with the bus his father is backing out of the driveway—only then does Leo realize he hadn't even thought to mention Sonya.

Emelia

HER FEET BARE and her toe bleeding, Emelia gingerly walks in the direction of the pool, hoping to find Will, Kirstin, and Leo there. At a safe distance from Sonya's house, she stops to put on her sandals. Her toe is no longer gushing blood, but the skin flap on its tip won't stay sealed. Greasy and throbbing, her foot slithers against the foam of her sandal, but at least she can walk. Thank God she remembered to grab her own clothes as she ran out of Sonya's room, although she left her towel behind. She wishes there was somewhere to duck into before the pool to change out of Sonya's dress. Each block of color on the dress seems to glow like a neon sign, announcing all the awful things she's done.

She truly thought she was doing something good when she took Dean home and cooked for him. Only after she was there did it occur to her that taking the notes would free her friends from the trap she created, especially Will and Kirstin. No college wants juvenile delinquents, no matter how good their grades. But she also wanted to protect Sonya's parents from learning their daughter hid her secrets in a marsh.

She hadn't meant to make Sonya's mother's pain worse. If only she hadn't tried on this stupid dress. Haven't her aunts warned her against vanity her whole life? Why wouldn't Sonya's mother think her daughter's death was a bad dream? It makes more sense than a strange girl sneaking into her dead daughter's bedroom and trying on her clothes. Now, because of her, Sonya's mother will have to learn all over again that her bad dream is reality.

The hope in Sonya's mother's voice and in her eyes hurts so much worse than Emelia's foot. *And I deserve every painful twinge.*

Sonya's mother wanted so badly to believe her daughter was alive, she mistook Emelia for her. What about her own mother? Has Elisa ever wanted to see her daughter this badly? Alive or dead?

Emelia halts, suddenly dizzy.

Does Elisa think her daughter is dead? If Emelia's grandparents and aunts lied to her about her mother, isn't it possible they also lied to Elisa about Emelia? Is this why her aunts said Elisa wouldn't know her? Because Emelia is as much a ghost to Elisa as Elisa is to her?

Her foot throbbing, she sits down on the curb. She drops her head between her knees and thinks, *I'm not dead.* But her lightheadedness makes her feel ghostly. She inhales a musky scent that must be Sonya's, lingering in the fibers of her dress.

The expression on Sonya's mother's face was hope. What will Elisa's expression be if Emelia walks through the door? Fear? Disbelief? Anger? Will there be any joy mixed in? Will she even know who Emelia is?

So many questions about her mother prick her, and Emelia no longer trusts her aunts to tell her the truth about Elisa. Somehow she's got to see for herself. Whatever her mother has become, whatever she thinks about Emelia, however bad, however scary, Emelia's got to stick her own finger in the wound and see what's real.

But how? After her last two attempts to go to Red River, she doubts can she do it alone.

Wearily, she stands, the notes clasped in her hand. At least her friends are free. Without the notes, no physical connection to Sonya remains. Dean is the only link left. Maybe all the kid will remember are the small kindnesses Emelia showed him, three fat hamburgers and a tuck-in.

She continues walking toward the pool, hoping Will and Kirstin will be there. They'll be so happy. Will gets to escape the draft; Kirstin gets to escape her family. Sadly, she thinks, now they're free to escape her too.

Lying about her mother dropped one curtain between her and her friends. College is dropping another. On a rainy day last week, she and Kirstin went to Will's instead of the pool, but instead of playing board games or cards as they used to do on rainy days, Will and Kirstin spent the whole time reading college brochures and making pro-con lists.

"Let's do St. Stephen's," said Will, propped on the top of his desk. "Pro for me, they have professional programs. Law school and medical school."

"Con for me," said Kirstin, who sat next to him on the wooden chair that matched his pine desk. "It's too close to home. It has to be over an hour's drive away. My mother will only drive an hour from here, so I need to go farther so she won't show up, uh, you know . . . messed up."

"Right," said Will, his manner curt with embarrassment. "St. Stephen's—con for you, pro for me."

"What's their mascot?" Emelia said. She sat on the floor between the two twin beds, her back pressed against Will's mattress, a game of solitaire dealt out on the braided rug. She placed a black ten on a red jack. "Go someplace with a good mascot."

"Who cares about mascots?" said Kirstin, over her shoulder. To Will, she said, "Trina says St. Stephen's has got some good fraternities for you."

"Who's Trina?" Emelia tossed in the deck, having lost the game.

"A fox," said Will.

"Why? What does she look like?" Bored of cards, Emelia tossed up and caught an old tennis ball Will used to increase his grip strength. "Does she go to our school? Why don't I know her?"

"She goes to Holy Trinity," said Kirstin without turning around.

"How do you know her then?"

"She was on the college tour."

"Well, what's so foxy about her?"

"I liked the campus," Kirstin said. "All those brick buildings with fireplaces."

Annoyed at being ignored, Emelia squeezed the tennis ball then flicked her wrist, whizzing the ball between Kirstin and Will and striking the poster of Bobby Hull's gap-toothed mouth dead center.

"Cut it out!" Kirstin said, turning from the college brochure to glare at Emelia. "You almost hit me."

"What makes Trina so pretty?" Emelia caught the ball and threw it at the poster again but this time with less force.

"Who said she's pretty?" Kirstin said, snatching the tennis ball out of the air as it ricocheted off the puck Bobby Hull showed off.

"Will did. He said she's a fox."

"No," said Will, holding his hand out for the tennis ball. When Kirstin handed it to him, he chucked it into the top drawer of his desk. "St. Stephen's mascot is a fox. Trina's so-so pretty."

Both Emelia and Kirstin looked at him with raised eyebrows, then burst out laughing.

"She has nice legs," he insisted.

"She has a huge overbite," Kirstin said to Emelia. "A total horse face."

"Ride 'em, Will!" Emelia whinnied, enjoying the feeling of being included.

"Yeah, Will." Kirstin giggled. "You going to change your last name to Rogers?"

"Shut up," said Will, his face turning crimson. "Where's Leo when I need reinforcements?"

"Probably practicing guitar. Or at *band* practice, I should say," said Kirstin, giggling again. "Isn't it cool he's got a band?"

"I can't wait to hear them play," said Emelia. "Wouldn't it be great if he got famous? We could all travel around with him, be his groupies."

"You can go, but we'll be too busy with college," Will said. He added with irritation, "C'mon, Kirstin, can we get back to the list?"

"Or Hickok, as in Wild Bill," Emelia said, trying to get the joke going again, but it fell flat. Emelia frowned.

"Don't be like that, Emelia," Kirstin said. "We've got to make plans."

"College is two years away," Emelia said.

"If I don't get a scholarship to a good college, my dad is going to make me go to West Point," Will said. "And after West Point . . ."

Emelia thought of Ben and said, "You're right, you can't go to West Point."

Kirstin nodded too.

Brusquely changing the subject, Will said, "Besides, what's wrong with making plans?"

Kirstin elbowed his arm lightly before saying to Emelia, "Not that you need any. You have your aunts' bakery. That's your plan."

"Sure," said Will, his tone adult and lecturing now. He crossed an arm over his stomach, resting the other arm's elbow on it, a loose fist beneath his chin. She'd seen his father adopt the same pose behind the bar. "A family business is a good option. Stable. Certain. People always need bread."

"And booze. So how come you aren't taking over your dad's tavern when you get out of high school? People are always drinking," she said.

"It's not the same for me. Sons are expected to do better than their fathers."

"And daughters?" she said.

"Daughters don't count," he said.

"Shut up," Kirstin said.

"Yeah," said Emelia, glad to be able to be on Kirstin's side. "We're half the population."

"I didn't mean anything," he said. "It's just, you know. Marriage and kids. Unless you're a brain like Kirstin. What else? Anyway, you only have to work in the bakery until you get married, right?" He snapped his fingers as if he's landed on a great idea. "Maybe you plan to marry a baker. Then your husband takes over, and your aunts can retire. You help out in the store sometimes, like my mom does cleaning the tavern, when you aren't taking care of the kids." He wiped his hands together a few times like Aunt Genny brushing off flour. To him, Emelia was done and dusted.

"What if I'm never having kids?" she said. *Unintended consequences. Nowhere to turn to for help. But the Pill, the Loop.* "Women don't *have to* have them anymore, you know."

"She's right, Will," said Kirstin. Her glance flicked to Emelia, who had given her the *Saturday Evening Post* report to read. "Not if you're married anyway."

"Well, it's going to be harder to find a husband with that attitude," Will said. After a moment though, he shrugged. "But I suppose you'll have the bakery anyway if you want to be a spinster like your aunts."

"I'm not working at the bakery my whole life," Emelia said, picking up the deck of cards again and tapping them hard against the wooden floor planks beyond the rug. It bothered her that Will assumed she had no choices beyond what was right in front of her face. He assumed she didn't even want to have choices. "You think you have me so figured out. Maybe I have other plans."

"What plans?" Will said, looking skeptical.

Kirstin nudged him again. "Leave her alone, Will."

"I'm going to hitchhike to California," she said.

"Don't be stupid," Will scoffed. "Only imbeciles hitchhike. It's dangerous."

Imbeciles. The word felt like a slap.

"And all those hippies out there are just crazies," Will said.

Emelia said nothing.

"California, that's far," said Kirstin gently. "All that way? Will's right, it's dangerous."

"Maybe it is. And maybe it isn't. Maybe I'm just an imbecile," Emelia said, shrugging. "Oh, go back to your lists."

She stood up and tossed the cards onto the bed, wishing Leo were here. She walked over to the stack of orange crates where Will kept his records. She thumbed through them without looking. Leo wouldn't call her an imbecile for wanting to do more than work in the bakery. He wouldn't call her crazy. Heck, he wants more than working in the factory like his dad.

He would have put the right music on for this moment, something that would make her feel better and make her dance. He wouldn't dance with her exactly, but he'd play along on his guitar, or he'd drum his fingers and let it be okay for her to sway around to the beat, imagining herself on the road, maybe in a truck, Theo and Danny beside her, sky and trees and black road slipping past like she's in a movie. Leo would help her make fun of Kirstin's and Will's pro-con lists. He'd think San Francisco and Santa Fe were cool places to go. Maybe he could play music there.

That day she'd already felt Will and Kirstin had moved her into the rearview mirror. But now, with the pool in sight, she thinks again that Leo's different. For one thing, he's not college material any more than she is, as their school guidance counselor has informed them both. More than that, she and Leo have always had a special bond that they rarely acknowledge but both feel.

His band won't come between them the way college will for Kirstin and Will. He invited her to listen. He can't wait for her to hear them. She can listen and dance. It's not *so* crazy to think that if he goes on tour, she could go along, carry his guitar for him. She doesn't have to lose him.

Flashing her season pass to the boy at the pool's entrance, she decides she has to ask Leo.

For the second time that day, she pushes through the turnstile. In the changing room, she finally peels off Sonya's dress. But she's unsure what to do with it. It doesn't seem right to dump in the trash something so connected with Sonya. Instead, Emelia folds it neatly and places the notes safely in the folds. She walks to the showers and rinses the blood from her foot. Pressing the bloody skin flap back into place turns out to be a mistake. The wound bleeds again. Maybe the girl who checks feet won't bother to look at hers a second time.

Entering the pool area, Emelia smiles and waves casually at the girl. She strides past her without stopping to put her foot on the block.

"Hey!" the girl calls. "I have to check your feet."

"Oh, it's okay. I was here earlier. Oh, great, I see my friends are here," Emelia says. She's spotted Will and Kirstin in their corner. She waves to them, and Kirstin waves back.

"Well, you've got blood all over your foot now."

"It's nothing. I just stubbed my toe."

"It doesn't matter how you got it. It's gross. Not sanitary. You can't go in the pool area until it heals."

She smiles at the girl and says, "I don't want to swim. I just want to talk to my friends. See? They're in the corner? We come every day. I never swim."

"You swam this morning."

"I won't swim now. I promise. I won't even stay," Emelia says. "I just need to talk to my friends for a second."

The girl twists her mouth and runs her finger over her jaw as if contemplating something. After a moment, she says, "I'll let you in if you put in a good word with your friend."

"Will?" she says, smiling.

"No, the other one. With the feathery hair? The nice smile. Is he coming later?"

"Maybe he is. Probably. He's probably at band practice now."

"Wow, he's in a band," the girl gushes. Without the mask of boredom, Emelia thinks, she's actually pretty. "So? Will you tell him to ask me out?"

"Um, sure, I suppose," she says. "I can't promise he'll do it, but I'll ask him."

As the girl waves her through, Emelia thinks uneasily that she may not lose Leo to music, but she may lose him to girls. He's turned handsome this summer. His dark tan, his longer hair, they suit him. A pang of jealousy twists inside her. Not because she wants him for herself, not in that way anyway. They could never be boyfriend and girlfriend. They're too like brother and sister. He's family.

Which is exactly the point, she reminds herself. If she tells him everything—about her mother being alive, about Danny and Theo, about hitching, about Ben—he'll understand. He'll help her. She'll figure it all out ahead of time. Will's right, there's nothing wrong with planning. She's got the twenty-dollar bill Ben gave her, so they won't need to hitch. She's got more than enough for two Lamers bus tickets. They can leave in the morning. She'll see Elisa, and they can be back for dinner.

She sets her pile of clothing on the edge of Kirstin's towel, her shorts and shirt on top, hiding Sonya's dress. She waves Kirstin and Will into a huddle and whispers, "Don't ask me how I got them. Just be happy." She retrieves the notes from her dress and shows them.

"Holy shit!" says Will.

"Oh, my God!" says Kirstin, grabbing the notes. "How?"

"I *said*, don't ask." Emelia grabs them back and shoves them into her shorts pocket. "Just be happy."

They're both so happy, they pull her up to hug her. Then Will playfully pushes her into the pool. He and Kirstin jump in after her. The chlorine stings her toe, and she glances at the foot-check girl, who grimaces and rolls her eyes but doesn't tell Emelia to get out.

They spend the rest of the afternoon in the pool. By the time Emelia catches up with Leo, a block from his house, her foot doesn't hurt at all. Her hair is damp, and her skin smells of chlorine.

"Hey," she says, jogging up to him. He gently swings his guitar case and hums a song she's never heard before. He's grown a little more this summer, but so has she, and she matches his pace. His hair bounces with each step. He looks a little like the hippie kids she's seen in *Teenset*, not grimy but a little unkempt, a little wild. But not crazy as Will said. Free. Choosing their own paths. Leo and I, we're alike, she thinks. He'll understand.

"Hey girl," he says. He gives her a little salute with two fingers.

The gesture seems forced like that hat she bought at the Woolworths before her birthday. That had been so long ago. She never did return it. They're all trying on these personalities, she thinks, remembering Will mimicking his father's thoughtful pose. Will they ever figure out who they really are? This as much as anything else is why she's got to see her mother. How else will she know what not to choose?

"Hey, have you been swimming?" he says.

"Yeah, finally."

"That's great, Emelia. Why today?"

"Look," she says. She stops walking and touches his arm to still him too. Then she shows him the notes.

"Oh, man," he whispers. "How?"

If she's going to tell him everything, she might as well start now.

"I sort of snuck into Sonya's bedroom," she says, bracing herself for his anger. In the face of it, she doesn't mention she stole Sonya's dress.

"Man," he says again. Then to her surprise, he says, "I wish I'd thought of that."

"Listen, Leo, I told Kirstin and Will I got the notes back, but I didn't tell them I went into Sonya's bedroom. Don't tell them I told you how I got them, okay?"

He pauses for a beat or two, then nods. "Yeah, okay. They don't need to know." He starts to walk again, but she touches his forearm to hold him there.

"There's another thing," she says. "I need a favor."

"What?" he says warily.

His happy countenance is gone, replaced by apprehension. All of a sudden she's sure he won't understand about her mother. Genny and Lou warned her. Were they right? Will he think she's tainted?

"It's nothing big," she lies. "I just need you to come somewhere with me."

"Yeah? Where?"

"First, I have to tell you something," she says, adding without thinking, "It's kind of crazy." Her hand rushes to cover her mouth when she realizes what she said. "Actually, it's kind of real crazy."

"Okay," he says, drawing the word out. "So tell me, I guess."

What she has to tell him is so crazy, she's unsure what words to use. Nothing seems right. She has a moment of sympathy for her aunts on the morning of her birthday. It couldn't have been easy telling her about Elisa. The words themselves are an absurdity. Her doubts return. Once she utters these words to Leo, it's not a family secret anymore. Leo is family. And he isn't.

"Emelia, what is it? Is it about Sonya? What do you know? Is this why you've been so weird lately?"

Things don't have to change, she thinks. She could tell him about having accidentally stolen Sonya's dress instead. She could leave her mother locked away forever. The thought shames her. She's no better than Sonya abandoning Water Boy. She's no better than her mother. No better than her aunts. Maybe nobody is better than anybody.

"C'mon, Emelia. Tell me what you know," he demands. He puts his guitar down and grabs her arm. His thumb digs into her tricep.

"It's not about Sonya. It's—"

"What?"

"Leo, stop it. Let go."

He relaxes his grip on her arm.

"Listen. It's not about her. It's about my mother."

"Your mother? What about her?"

The words catch in her throat.

"Emelia. What? Say it already."

"She's not dead."

"What?"

He smiles as if it's a joke. She'd reacted the same way when her aunts told her. She tries to smile back, but tears press her eyes.

"Elisa Demski," she says, "my mother. Um, she's alive."

It's out. It's done. Relief nearly collapses her.

"You okay?" Seeing her shakiness, Leo puts his arm around her.

"My aunts lied. All this time. She's not dead."

"Jeez, Emelia. That's—far out. I mean. Are you sure?"

She tells him her mother's story and her own story, or at least the parts about riding her bike and hitchhiking to try to see Elisa. Even now, she omits the things she did with Theo and Danny and what she wanted to do with Ben. The rest is bad enough.

Only when she's finished does she remember they are on the street. Anyone might have heard her. Behind every screen door and open window could be listening ears.

"Please, Leo," she says, lowering her voice. "Will you come with me to see her tomorrow?"

"Are you sure you want to go? You don't have to. You don't have to do anything. You said it yourself. Sometimes it's better not to know."

"I have to," she says. "I just do. And Leo, please, whether you come with me or not, you can't tell a soul. Not Will. Not Kirstin.

Not your parents. No one. I know it's not right to ask you to keep it to yourself, but please."

She doesn't realize she's crying until he brushes her cheek.

"It's okay," he says. "What's one more secret? But tomorrow I can't. I have band practice in the afternoon. Then at night I have my father's record-release party."

"If we take the bus, we can go and be back in time for the party. Couldn't you practice the next day, just this once?" She feels tears welling again. "Please, Leo. If I don't do it now, I may chicken out."

He hesitates, biting his lip. "Never thought I'd hear you admit to chickening out."

She doesn't smile. "Please, Leo."

"Yeah, okay," he says finally. "I'll postpone practice."

It's surprisingly easy for Emelia to find out visiting hours on Sundays at Red River Care Facility. All she had to do was call and say she wanted to visit Elisa Demski.

"My mother," she added.

When the phone bill arrives, Aunt Lou will see the long-distance charge, but Emelia will deal with that when the time comes. Having consulted the Lamers bus schedule, she's reassured Leo he'll be back in time for his father's release party.

They leave early, her excitement and nerves building as they move beyond where she's ridden her bike. She passes the lake she went to with Theo and Danny, and she notes the turnoff to Ben's campsite. She searches for his Falcon but can't see through the foliage. She'd like to thank him, and not just for giving her the means to take the bus to see her mother. He was kind to her. He risked showing her his leg. And as strong as he was, he allowed himself to lean on her, even if it made him feel bashful.

It's midday by the time the bus drops them half a mile from Red River. As they walk the remaining distance, Emelia scans the cornfields. A man with one arm in a sling drives a tractor. Its giant wheels kick up clouds of dust behind him. She's reminded of what

Ben said, that it would be easier for him to farm with a missing leg than a missing arm, and she waves at the farmer, admiring him for continuing on despite his injury. He lets go of the steering wheel to give her a curt wave in return.

When they come to a driveway with a sign reading Red River, she stands there for a long time, thinking, *My mother is in there*, and her nerves outpace her excitement.

But the place isn't anything like the images her mind has conjured. There are no scary bars over windows or broken-down stone towers. Red River is a small farmstead with a large garden and a chicken coop. A few hens peck the front lawn. A pretty russet chicken perches on a small stand with a hand-painted sign, reading "Fresh Eggs, Homemade Breads, Vegetables, for Sale Saturdays 9– 12." If she didn't know better, she would have assumed Red River was a regular farm. Even the sign with the image of a river and the name of the place is discrete.

She must look nervous though because Leo says, "You can still turn back."

"No. It's now or never," she says, stepping up to the porch.

"You want me to come inside with you?"

"No. It's okay," she says. "I should do this part alone."

He looks relieved as he sits in a rocker on the porch. Immediately his fingers begin picking some tune that's in his head.

"Leo?"

He looks up.

"Thanks for postponing practice to come with me."

He shrugs.

"What if she doesn't recognize me? My aunts said she wouldn't know me."

"Either way, she's your mother. For better or worse."

"Yeah," she says, opening the door. "Better to know, right?"

"Who the hell can tell anymore?" he says. "But we're here. Go in. Or you'll have to hang out with them." He points to some chickens chattering and pecking the grass.

Inside, her sneakers move soundlessly over the wide-plank floors that smell faintly of lemon oil.

"Hello?" she calls, watching the doorway behind the desk for someone to emerge.

A girl walks out. Her age is obscured by her blurred features, but her smile is big.

"Hello," she says before pirouetting and disappearing through the doorway again, calling, "Dr. Crispan, Dr. Crispan!"

Alone again in the reception area, Emelia has the urge to bolt. As Leo said, she doesn't have to go through with it. No one's making her. She could slip out the door before anyone else sees her. Only Leo would be the wiser. Knowing must be better than not knowing, right?

Before she can decide, a woman enters. She's nearly six feet tall with short chestnut hair that frames her wide face. She has a brisk but friendly manner.

"You're Emelia? I've been expecting you."

"Aren't there other visitors today?"

"A few," she says. "They're with their people. Come into my office for a bit so we can talk."

"Okay."

She follows Dr. Crispan down a hallway with photographs of sunflower fields, mountains ranges, and the ocean. All open spaces.

Dr. Crispan's office is small but neat. Emelia realizes she's never met a woman doctor before. She likes the doctor's sleeveless knit dress with its black peter-pan collar. She likes the easy way Dr. Crispan sits behind her oak desk confidently, as if she's in exactly the right place in the world.

"Please, sit down. Now, let's start with you telling me what you know about your mother," Dr. Crispan says.

"I'm not sure what I know." Her aunts have told her so little, and her own memories might well be made up, that all she has is scraps: bedroom furniture, yearbook photographs, Johnny Angel, the words *wild* and *miscreant*. So she starts with the one solid thing she has.

"The ice pick. I know about that."

"Well, Emelia, that's the worst thing you could know," Dr. Crispan says. "There are so many better things. But if we must, we'll start there. That procedure, the one performed on your mother—"

"The ice pick," Emelia insists.

Dr. Crispan smiles wryly. "They used a leucotome on your mother. A sort of plunger-looking instrument."

"Not an ice pick?"

"People do call it an ice pick, sure." She shakes her head. "That was the original instrument used, very early on, but your mother's transorbital lobotomy . . ." Her confidence seems to slip a little. "Emelia, I'm sorry that happened to your mother. Truly, I am. It's terrible. One of our profession's darkest hours. Set us back a century. It was performed at another facility. I can assure you that we're the future of mental health care here. We believe in community. The residents contribute what they can to our community. Each to his own ability. Everyone is useful. Your mother's been happy here. And as I say, we are a community. Elisa's a valuable member of our community. She understands that."

Dr. Crispan stands and crosses to the front of her desk, leaning her backside against its edge. When she reaches out, Emelia stiffens, afraid Dr. Crispan wants to catch her wrists. Pictures of the witch pulling Hansel into her house come to her. Bertha Rochester comes to her. It's unfair that this is what she pictures in the face of this nice lady doctor, but the stories of crazy people have been with her longer than Dr. Crispan.

She shoves her hands beneath her thighs where Dr. Crispan can't reach them so easily, but the doctor has only placed her palms on her own thighs.

"Emelia, we may be Elisa's community, but you and your aunts are her family," she continues.

"Family," Emelia says, adopting the tone Dr. Crispan had used to utter the words *ice pick*. "I could spend my whole life trying to understand what that means."

Dr. Crispan smiles. "Of course, you're right. You probably will. But I hope today is not a one-time thing. I hope you'll come see Elisa again," Dr. Crispan says, standing again. "You two don't know each other—"

"That's not my fault."

"I'm not saying it is. All I'm saying is it will take some time. Give it some time. Don't expect too much from today."

Emelia says nothing for a moment. Then she asks, "Does she know I'm coming?"

"No."

"Does she know who I am? Does she know I exist?"

"It isn't always clear what your mother understands. I hope she'll understand who you are. But that's not why I didn't tell her you were coming. We don't like to get our people's hopes too high. A lot of families who say they are coming never show up. Better to avoid the disappointment."

Emelia nods contritely. Hadn't she almost run out of the waiting room?

"Do you have other questions, Emelia?"

"Before the ice pick—"

"The leucotome."

"Before *that*." The word feels too strange to say. "My mother was already . . . Wasn't she already crazy? Isn't that why she was put away? People said she was wild."

"What people?"

"My aunts."

"*Crazy. Wild.* Those aren't useful terms. Sometimes they just mean someone won't do what another person wants them to do. For women, that can be almost anything. But from the records I received on her, your mother was ill. Depressed. Sometimes this happens after a woman has a baby."

"So it's because of me she was ill? You know, because she had to have me?"

Dr. Crispan hesitates as if debating whether to tell the truth. Finally she says in a measured tone, "Maybe, Emelia. But even if this is true, that doesn't make it *your* fault. And to be honest, I don't know for sure why your grandparents decided to hospitalize her. Maybe the pressure of being a young mother contributed. Being an unmarried mother. Maybe she wasn't ready. I didn't know your mother then. And her other doctors, their notes, it's just very hard to tell how to interpret them."

"Oh . . . okay." She wanted the doctor to say no, that her mother's condition had nothing to do with her. But at least she's being truthful.

Dr. Crispan smiles sympathetically. "I'm sorry I can't be more concrete. Maybe you should ask your aunts what she was like before she was hospitalized. They would know better than anyone."

"It's okay," Emelia says, realizing Dr. Crispan assumes her aunts are aware she's here. She'll have to tell her aunts now in case Dr. Crispan mentions it the next time they visit. But she doesn't have to tell them Leo came along too. Is this what life is, deciding which truths to tell? Is Dr. Crispan telling her everything? Emelia decides to press her. "I hoped you'd be able to tell me, I mean, do you know . . .?"

"Know what?"

Emelia hesitates.

"Emelia?"

"If I'm going to go wild," she says. "I mean, will I get *ill* like her? Everyone tells me I'm like her."

"No one can say anything for sure about anything in this world. You are your mother's daughter. But you aren't *her.*"

It's a nothing answer, no more than a glimmer of hope. She looks out the window. A russet chicken is perched on the fence.

"And you aren't in her circumstances," says Dr. Crispan.

"Yet," Emelia whispers.

Alarm crosses Dr. Crispan's face. "You aren't . . .?"

Emelia shakes her head to all of the ways that sentence could be finished. "But . . . what if she had never gotten pregnant with me? Would she have been okay?"

"It's not that simple, Emelia. Questions like that, what if, they're—"

"Land mines."

"Yes. That's right."

"But if she'd had a choice. Wouldn't she have chosen something else for herself?"

"Maybe," concedes Dr. Crispan. "Probably. She was very young."

Dr. Crispan searches Emelia's face for a moment, and then as if having run through a debate in her mind and come to a conclusion, she walks to the other side of her desk and sits down. She writes something on a notepad. Pen poised, she hesitates, glances at Emelia again, and writes something more. She rips the paper from the pad, folds it, and returns to leaning against the desk.

She presses the paper between her palms. "You're right about choices, Emelia. We can't know for sure what would have happened if we made different ones, your mother included, but that doesn't mean we don't want—don't need—the options and the chance to make decisions for ourselves." She hands the paper to Emelia. "The first address is a new place. The women there will help you make the right choices for yourself."

"Planned Parenthood," Emelia reads. So Dr. Crispan has recognized something in her that is like Elisa. "Did you give me this because of my mother? Or because of me?"

"Emelia, you're a young woman. *Every* young woman needs a place to go to ask questions and get answers about her body."

"I read about that new pill," she says shyly, her voice edging into a whisper. "Can I get it there?"

"No," Dr. Crispan admits, her expression showing frustration. "Not unless you're married, which is ridiculous."

"So what good is this place?"

"As I said, you can ask questions and get answers. And there are all manner of health issues they can help you with. But as for the Pill, the Loop, we're working on changing that. When we do, we'll be ready right away."

"Who's *we*?"

"Women. The medical staff is fully qualified, but a lot of nonmedical women volunteer there too. We all believe women should have the right to do what they feel is best for their bodies. But it's a fight."

"Jane?" Emelia says, reading the second item on the paper. "Who's she?"

"I can't tell you anything more about her. I could lose my medical license if I do, but if you find yourself in need, Jane can help. I can see you're mature enough to make decisions for yourself, Emelia. Coming here to see your mother is proof of that. So as I said, until things change, if you find you need someone, Jane can help."

"Help?"

Dr. Crispan bites her bottom lip, but she holds Emelia's gaze tightly. She places her palm against her stomach and pats it once.

"You mean if I'm ever . . .?" Emelia says. "But this is just a first name. How am I supposed to find her?"

"I honestly don't know." She raises her palm as if to push Emelia away. "I *can't* know. But if you need her, ask other women."

It's the first time Emelia's been called a woman by anyone, including herself. There's a gravity associated with the term that's alarming, but it feels right too. She's not a girl anymore, not after Sonya and Water Boy, not after Theo and Danny. And Ben. Not after finding her way here.

"But to get back to why you're here," Dr. Crispan says, obviously ready to change the subject. "Emelia, as I said, you're old enough to make some decisions for yourself, about yourself, who you want to be, and what you want to know. So ultimately the decision of whether or not you get to know your mother is yours too. Do you want to see her today? You don't have to. As I said, we haven't told her that you're coming."

With her fingernail, Emelia traces the scar on her thigh, which has reddened from yesterday's exposure to the sun. In battle, you make the best choice you can, she thinks. Deal with the consequences later.

"Yes," she says. "I want to meet her."

"Good. Okay," Dr. Crispan says, standing up fast as if she doesn't want to give Emelia time to change her mind. Like a man, she holds her hand out for Emelia to shake. Emelia stands too and returns the gesture. Dr. Crispan grips Emelia's hand firmly, and in that force, Emelia understands that Dr. Crispan has handed her a choice. For the rest of her life, it will be Emelia's decision whether or not to abandon her mother.

"Elisa's working now, but I think it's a good time to introduce you two." Dr. Crispan says. She escorts Emelia out of her office. "Your aunts have told me you work in the bakery with them."

305

"Sometimes."

"Well, like mother, like daughter," she says, looking over her shoulder and smiling. "It's not always a bad thing, you know."

Emelia hopes the doctor is right.

Elisa

ELISA COUNTS AS she whacks, one, two. BAM, BAM! She loves this. Loves hitting things. The rolling pin solid in her hand. The butcher block shivering. The thump vibrating her wrist and forearm. BAM! With each blow, she releases yeast and sugar and salt, aromas that blanket her mind and keep it calm. The kitchen is the safest place in the world. Her oasis, Dr. Crispan calls it. In here, Elisa puts things where they belong: ladling things go in drawers, sharp things in the wooden block, cooking things on wall pegs. She keeps her hands occupied with the silkiness of flour, the gooeyness of egg whites, the muddiness of baking chocolate, all reminders that hitting is not the only good sensation.

But still.

BAM!

It's pretty good.

"Elisa."

She looks up at the sound of Dr. Crispan's voice.

"Look who . . ."

Elisa smiles at her sister. Which one? She can't remember their names. Names are hard for her to hold onto. The names of people, of objects, of places. Finding names is like separating eggs in her palm—she can manage to keep the yolk of the thing, but the whites go sliding off. The sisters are easier than most things for her mind to grasp. They come regularly to see her. They like her too. They look like her too. Not mirror reflections. They're more like the rippling image she finds when she sees herself in the bottom of the steel thing she mixes ingredients in and whose name she can't call to mind.

She likes the thought that her sisters are like her but not like her. The neatness of it joins like the corners of a turnover to make a tidy triangle. Absently, she sprinkles flour onto the bread dough as she looks up again.

This time when her gaze hits the figure standing with Dr. Crispan, Elisa feels the jolt of time and space colliding. She'd been in a car once with her father when another car had run a red light and hit them. The impact threw her into the dashboard, and she cut her forehead, leaving a small white moon scar near her scalp. This feeling is the same. Time has warped. The past is now, here, standing in her kitchen. This sister is young again. Is she herself young again? Had the good time only been a dream? Is she still in the bad time?

"No," she says.

She won't go back.

She slams the dough with the rolling pin. The past is when the bad things happened, and the past is over. Dr. Crispan has promised the bad time is over.

In the past, they shocked her, and the man with the frozen eyes chipped at her brain with an ice pick, stealing a piece of her. She rubs her head with the rolling pin. She pulls it back to whack, but before she connects with her skull, Dr. Crispan steps forward and catches the pin midair.

They lock gazes.

Dr. Crispan shakes her head once. She reminds Elisa that if she hits herself, she will have to see the nurse and then have quiet time and maybe no baking for days. "Breathe," she says. "Breathe all the way to your belly."

Elisa nods her understanding and breathes as directed. They have been here before. Dr. Crispan releases her hold on the rolling pin and nods in the direction of the butcher block, allowing Elisa to whack the dough instead, which she does.

"Elisa," says Dr. Crispan. "I want you to meet someone."

"No."

"It's okay. She doesn't have to," says the past sister. "I don't want to upset her."

The sound of the sister's voice makes Elisa look up because the voice is strange. The past is different. This isn't one of the sisters after all. The girl from the photos on her wall has materialized. Ghost Girl.

Her ghost girl.

The sisters and Dr. Crispan have told her it isn't a ghost in the photos. But she can't remember who they say it is. It hurts her head to remember. She tries anyway. Thinking. She can't quite . . . the old house where she and the sisters lived . . . the big kitchen there . . . the square yard with the swing set . . . and . . . and . . . Nothing. It's like wearing an eye patch; she only half sees. Ghost Girl. Reaching for dust motes in a sunbeam.

BAM!

With the impact, the cakes come to her clearly.

The telephone cake, the record player cake. Raggedy Ann with her big ropey smile. A funny spiral dog. She remembers now. The sisters bring her cutouts from magazines.

"Can you make a cake like this?" one sister asks.

"For the girl?" the other adds. "It would mean so much."

Elisa doesn't understand to whom it would mean so much, to Ghost Girl or the sisters or Elisa herself. It doesn't matter. She nods and bakes whatever is in the pictures. Sifting, folding, piping. The cakes scream all she can't say. *I am.*

"For the girl," the sisters repeat when they come to pick up the cakes, always so pleased with what Elisa has done. She likes to please the sisters. They pet her, hug her, tell her they love her always, no matter shards have been stolen.

"I am," she says.

"Of course," they say, admiring the cakes.

Later, they bring photos of the cakes. In the photos, Ghost Girl blows out candles someone has pushed into the frosting and set alight. Every year, the girl looks more and more like the sisters. She looks more and more like Elisa used to look in the past. Elisa understands the girl is herself before the bad time. The soul stolen from Elisa by the man with the ice pick roams the world without her.

Soul surgery. That's what pie-face Dr. Euston called it when he introduced the man with the ice eyes and the ice pick.

"Dr. Freeman is here to perform your soul surgery, Elisa," Dr. Euston said.

It happened at the hospital with the bars on the windows, with the locked doors, where she was wrapped in wet sheets like a fruitcake left to marinate in brandy-soaked rags. She was left to marinate in her own juices. For her own good. To cure her. On the day of the soul surgery, leather bracelets encased her wrists and ankles. The cold metal pressing her tongue tasted of rubbing alcohol. The doctor stood above her, his glacier eyes and the sharp steel of the ice pick hovering. A bead of his sweat dropped onto her upper lip. She couldn't reach it to lick it away.

With a few taps, he cut away part of her soul and gave it to Ghost Girl. But no, wasn't the girl there before the ice pick? Confused, she swipes flour onto her forehead as she tries to squeeze memory from her brain.

That was the bad time that Dr. Crispan calls the past. Her cloudy past. The past is over. Dr. Crispan has promised. The sisters brought her here, and the good time has been ever since. But ever since, Ghost Girl has appeared in pictures on her wall. Elisa baked the cakes, and the sisters brought pictures of the piece of her out there in the world. Ghost Girl didn't just eat cakes. She had photos of Ghost Girl swimming, riding a bike, dressed in fancy clothes, and holding a picture of the big water Elisa used to love to swim in. Ghost Girl draws pictures the sisters pin to the wall in her room along with the photos. Sometimes she falls asleep wondering what Ghost Girl is doing right now.

Right now, this now, the here now, Ghost Girl is here, walking toward her. Why is she here? Does she want to steal more of her soul? Elisa shakes her head, no, no. The girl keeps coming. Elisa steps back until she's pressed against the freezer door. Ghost Girl's eyes, steady on her, are grayer than her own. Elisa shrinks back when Ghost Girl extends her arm. She doesn't want this thing touching her.

"No," she says, her voice small and high. "No."

Ghost Girl stops short of touching her, instead picking up the other rolling pin.

Elisa eyes her skeptically. Is Ghost Girl here to whack her like dough and take her place? No, this is *her* good place, *her* oasis.

Is Ghost Girl going to steal Dr. Crispan and send Elisa back to the bad place, the bad time? She tightens her grasp on the handle of her rolling pin. She will beat this Ghost Girl back if she has to.

Her rolling pin poised above her head for whacking, she watches as Ghost Girl sprinkles flour on the butcher block. The girl selects a ball of dough, sets it in the flour just as Elisa would.

BAM!

Ghost Girl brings the pin down with two hands, as if swinging a hatchet, hitting the dough ball dead center.

"I love the way it feels," Ghost Girl says. She hammers the dough again, this time with one hand. "Bam." She smiles. "I love the sound."

"Yes," Elisa says.

Elisa whacks her dough.

Her girl laughs and whacks too.

BAM, BAM!

They laugh.

How wrong she has been to be afraid. The girl's come to play.

They gather dough and press the heels of their hands into it. Gather and press. Her girl knows the right way to do it. Elisa sprinkles the dough with flour. Her girl sprinkles the dough with her tears.

"No," says Elisa gently. "You'll make it bad."

"Yes, gummy," her girl says, wiping her tears with the back of her hand. "And salty."

Elisa nods.

"Okay," her girl says, sniffing.

"Okay," Elisa says, adding sunflower seeds to the dough before gathering and pressing it again.

"That's a good idea." Her girl adds seeds to her own dough.

***

Later, when six loaves of bread are in the oven and Amanda has promised to take them out when they are honey brown, Elisa leads her girl to her room.

"I remember this." Her girl touches the small blanket draped over the foot of Elisa's bed. Elisa has never been able to remember why she loves this blanket. She likes the jungle pictures of giant trees and happy animals, but there has always been something more she can't pin down. Even at the bad hospital, this blanket made her feel better.

"It used to be on my bed when I was really small," her girl says, running her hand over cartoon hippos and zebras. "I'd forgotten all about it."

"It's on my bed now," says Elisa.

"I see."

"I like the animals," says Elisa.

"The elephant is my favorite. He's so jolly." Her girl giggles.

In her girl's smile, Elisa sees the shadow of another smile. A boy's smile. She can't remember the boy's name.

"I used to chew on the satiny part," says her girl.

"I sometimes rub that part against my cheek. See." She runs the satin over her girl's skin, noticing the girl's cheeks are high like the sisters' cheeks and her own, but her chin is square. The boy had a square chin, and earlobes with down soft as a chick's head.

"Soft," she says.

"I remember."

Elisa claps her hands together when her girl gasps at the wall of photos and drawings. Delighted, she sits down on her bed to watch the girl's delight.

"Oh, I remember that bike," says her girl, "the purple banana seat. And there's the old swing set that used to be in the yard. Look how small that maple tree was. Here's Aunt Lou in her navy blue dress. Aunt Genny in front of the Christmas tree. Man, she was young. She was beautiful. I didn't know how beautiful."

"Look," says Elisa, pointing to a corner of the wall.

Her girl steps in and looks.

"Oh, my God, the birthday cakes," she says, pressing her hand to her mouth. "I knew Lou took pictures. She brought them here."

"I made them all," Elisa says quietly, suddenly shy.

"Oh, man, Casper and the phonograph cake. 'Love Me Do.'"

"Did they taste good?"

The girl turns to her. "You made them?"

Elisa nods, her forehead crimping with concern. "Didn't you like them?" she says because the girl is crying again. "Weren't they good? Too much sugar?"

"They were delicious," the girl says. "I loved them all."

The girl sits down next to her on the bed.

"You made them. Every one?"

She nods.

"How long have you been here?" the girl asks, wiping her cheeks and sniffing.

"I don't know," she says. A thousand loaves of bread? Ten thousand?

"Do you know who I am?"

Elisa hesitates, wondering if the question is a trick. She fists her hand gently. How can she explain that it's hard enough to keep her hold on the yolk without breaking it. "The whites slide away," she says.

"Do you know me?" her girl asks.

After a moment, Elisa points to the photos on the wall.

"Yes, that's me. Do you know . . .?"

Elisa feels her girl's hand touch her leg. It's a strong hand, like Elisa's own, but not so red and rough or wrinkled.

"I'm Emelia," her girl says.

Elisa says nothing, but the name laps over her memory like water.

Her girl picks up Elisa's hand and presses it. "I'm your daughter."

"My *girl*," Elisa corrects her.

"Yes. *Your* girl. Your daughter."

"Not a ghost."

Her girl hesitates, her lips pressed into a wire.

"No," her girl says finally, "not a ghost at all. Neither one of us. There's no such thing as ghosts."

But just as the girl says this, a ghost walks through the doorway.

"You okay, Emelia? You've been gone a long time," the ghost says. "That doctor lady said to come in."

The square chin. The soft earlobes.

"I'm fine," the girl says. "This is my mother."

Ears downy question marks, soft as a chick's head, the tip of an angel's wing.

He shuffles awkwardly as he used to do. His blue eyes.

"Hi," he says, holding up a hand to wave.

His fingertips have grown hard shells, but the hands are the same. Smart hands. He used to play that song for her on the accordion.

The sweetest song I ever heard.

He smiles.

That smile. Yes. Oh, yes. It's him. He hasn't changed. Hasn't aged at all.

And the angels sing.

"I'm Leo."

"No."

The names, egg whites slipping away.

"Yes," her girl says. "This is my friend, Leo."

"No. Something else."

She knows when the names aren't right, even if she can't find the right name. But his mouth tightens in the way mouths do when she has said something wrong.

"Music?" she tries.

"Okay," he says. He puts a black circle on the turning machine. "I know this one. My father plays it."

When we touch, the angels croon. . .

Her girl sways her body. Elisa sways her hands. Ghost Boy's smile beams. She lets her girl lift her to her feet, wrap an arm around her waist, and dance.

Leo

"I'M SORRY, LEO," says Emelia.

"That's the five-hundredth time you've said I'm sorry," says Leo, trying to strain irritation from his voice. Up the road, a flock of ravens harasses a red-tailed hawk, squawking and jittering, but beyond the birds, the highway is deadsville. The bus that was scheduled to take them back home, the last bus of the day on this route, hasn't arrived. They've been waiting an hour and a half on a road whose only passing traffic has been a truck stacked with hay bales, going in the opposite direction. "You can stop saying it."

"I know. I'm sorry. But I just don't understand it." Her hand tents her eyes to block a sun that's lowering in the sky faster than either one of them would like. From her purse, she removes a slip of paper on which she's written the time for the bus. "I don't understand it," she repeats, pinching her wristwatch. "It should have come. We should be halfway home by now. Why make a schedule if you're just going to ignore it? How can you leave people in the lurch like this?"

Leo doesn't answer. While they've been waiting, he's already bitten his thumb to blood with worry. He's sworn and kicked a birch tree's trunk in anger. Now defeat thrums his nerves. He's not going to make it back for the release party. He has no idea how they're going to get back home at all.

His parents—or his mother anyway—will be livid. But he doesn't really care about that. He had other plans for tonight.

Yesterday, when he canceled band practice, Stella's voice flattened with disappointment. Although he was sorry they wouldn't get to practice, her tone pleased him. She must really want to play with him, or them, but he's a part of them, so it's sort of the same thing. She cheered up when he invited her to meet him at the party. "I'll be playing on the two songs we recorded," he said with forced casualness, knowing his father allowing him to sit in at the party was probably his mother's doing. "Maybe more too. And then, after a couple of sets, there's going to be a jam. Anyone can sit in. Maybe you could sing."

To himself he added, maybe I could play on those songs too. He'd invited Charles and their new drummer, Van, to the party, and Leo fantasized that they would all play. It would be an impromptu debut of the Oracles, the name he's come up with for the band. Oracles have answers. And right now, music is the best answer he's got.

Playing with Charles and talking with Stella about their band has shown him music may be able to guide him through the quagmire he's caught in. For a while yesterday, when he was talking with Stella about the band, he'd completely forgotten about his parents. Later, just thinking about her eased the sting of his parents doubting his band was any good. With Stella, Charles, and Van on stage at the party tonight, he'd planned show his father and mother how wrong they were to mock him. He planned to show them his band was good. Show them he can be more than his father imagines for him.

As he lay in bed last night, he sculpted the Oracles' debut in his mind with intricate detail. Somehow, they would all be able to follow him in one of his original songs. He debated which song, but whichever one he chose, their performance would be tight, except for a fluffed riff that would turn a good tune into a brilliant one. That one fluff would define their sound. Joey Katz would be so jazzed, he'd jump on stage and sit in. Maybe Slide would show up and sit in too. They would all meld the way he and Joey did when they first played together at the Silo.

In bed, he let his imagination soar. Someone would have an 8mm camera on hand—Stash would be sure of that—or a reel-to-reel audio at least. Leo would send the recordings to Epic or Capitol, who'd offer them a deal. The album they'd record would be admired for its musical finesse and innovation. Singles would shoot up the charts; an international tour would follow; Stella and he would front, with Charles and Van their bedrock backup. Everyone would want to play with them, Mick and Keith, John and Paul, the Yardbirds, the Kinks, Clapton, whose solo playing blows Leo's mind. Leo's not Clapton level yet, but he's close.

He'd fallen asleep bathed in certainty. Music would flow from him like a rushing spring river. Just dip a cup in and drink it down. He and Stella together, gulping and gulping.

Now he thinks of Stella on her porch, her interlocking fingers, the disappointment in her voice on the phone, and his own defeat thrums again. When he doesn't show up, she'll think he's a flake. Who wants to start a band with a flake? Probably she won't ever speak to him again because he won't be able to explain why he was late. Why had he promised Emelia he would keep her secret? At least if he could explain, Stella might forgive him.

"We should have taken a ride with that lady," he says, referring to the bouncing ball of a woman who offered to take them part of the way. They'd said no to her offer because they weren't sure if they'd be able to catch the bus for the rest of the way home where she offered to drop them off. Besides, she seemed weirdly jolly about her husband being in the loony bin. Not that Red River is the lunatic asylum of movies. It's more of a farm, with a big garden and sheep and a pig that the childlike receptionist called Mona.

According to Dr. Crispan, the residents, as she called them when she convinced Leo to come in and make sure Emelia was okay, produce and sell vegetables and cheeses and the bread baked by Emelia's mom, Elisa. Self-sustaining therapy, Dr. Crispan called it. "Work keeps you human, Leo. Remember that."

Emelia's eyes are still red from the crying she did when they left her mother. And although she's genuinely upset at being stranded, she also looks happier than she's been for a while. So despite all he may lose, he grudgingly admits that coming with her was the right thing to do, which is some comfort. He'd forgotten the steadying effect of a good deed. And landing on the narrow strip of right has been so hard lately that he doesn't want to make her feel too awful about the fact that he's going to miss the party.

"If you're not there at the party," Emelia ventures, "will your father go—?"

"Insane?" he fills in for her.

They take a beat to gauge each other's reactions at Leo having spoken the unspeakable. Then together, they crumple into laughter, hysterical, silent, spasmodic laughter.

"Your mother is crazy," he spits when he's able to catch a breath.

"My crazy mother is *alive*," Emelia spits right back. "She bakes!"

They're off again, rocking and clutching their bellies, collapsing into the grassy culvert, so anyone driving by would think they are out of their minds, escapees from Red River, and speed right on past them.

"It's okay," he says finally, wiping tears from his cheeks. "I mean, it's not okay, but it's not your fault. It's the stupid bus company's fault."

How can he be mad at her? Her mother's supposed to be dead. Her aunts are supposed to be honest.

"Blame it on me," says Emelia, "if your folks get mad."

"You mean tell them about your mom?"

"No, you can't, Leo. Really." Her expression is true panic. "My aunts will kill me if they find out you know about her. They're going to kill me when they find out I was here. We'll make up some other excuse."

"You're really going to tell them you've seen your mother?"

She bites on the ragged flesh around the nail of her index finger. When he tugs her hand from her mouth, she says, "They're going to be furious."

"Why do you care? They lied to you for years. Aren't *you* furious?"

He doesn't say, as furious as he is at his father. Damn it, he thinks, why does his father remain a note he keeps reaching for but can't hit?

Emelia takes a few steps but waits for him to follow. She plucks up a tall blade of grass and puts the sweet end between her teeth, gnawing it the way she had her finger.

When he joins her, she says, "Yeah, I am mad. And not just at my aunts. There's plenty of blame to go around. My grandparents,

318

the doctors who used that ice pick, the guy who left her in the lurch. And, you know, maybe if she'd had some choices . . ."

Her voice trails off, and he doesn't know what to say. After a moment, she lightly whips him with the grass blade. "I think my mom liked you."

"Maybe," he shrugs, not certain being liked by a crazy woman is a good thing. Elisa's blue eyes had narrowed at the sight of him as if she'd recognized something familiar about him. In books, the crazy people always see things sane people are blind to, and he's not sure he wants to know what she's detected in him.

"Don't worry about my dad being angry about me missing the party," he says. He cranes his neck to pantomime searching the highway. Not a flutter on the horizon. He listens. Not a whisper of a car engine. "He won't miss me. He knows a hundred guys who can play that guitar part on his song."

"Tell me about your band. The Oracles. It's a good name," Emelia says as they fall into a pace that acknowledges they could be walking for hours. "That Stella, what's she like?"

"She's great." He opens the valve a turn, and Stella comes pouring out. He gushes as they walk, Emelia's stride matching his until a field mouse dashes into the road and stares them down. Startled, Emelia jumps back, but Leo laughs lightly and chases it off the pavement. He lifts his hand to block the descending sun in his eyes. Emelia follows suit, and their shadows turn into two archers shooting the sky.

"Let's keep going," he says. "Maybe I can get there for the end of the party."

"Your dad must be excited about the record."

"Yeah," he says.

His father will be shining; his mother will be beaming. Despite everything, Leo wants to see their joy almost as much as he wants to play with the Oracles.

Eventually a dusty station wagon rattles toward them and slides to a stop, a scrawny, leather-skinned driver at the wheel. A gray-snouted Labrador rides shotgun. The driver has an open can of Pabst tucked between his thighs, and a Styrofoam cooler rests on the passenger seat's floor.

"You kids lost your breadcrumbs, or you running away?" he chuckles. But he offers them a ride. "Hop in back, Hansel and Gretel. Polly always rides up front."

Exchanging glances, they silently decide to take their chances.

"Which one's older, or are you two twins? Irish twins, maybe?"

He's about to correct the guy, tell him they're friends, not siblings, but Emelia raps Leo's thigh with the back of her hand, signaling him to play along.

"Leo's older," she says, which is true and seems to be enough to satisfy the guy, who nods once before turning the knob on the radio to catch the farm report.

Leo checks the time on the guy's wristwatch. His father is stepping on stage right now. His mother is searching the crowd for him. Stella, Charles, and Van are calling him a flake, or something worse.

"Hey, mister," Leo says, "you have any more of those beers?"

As if it's the most natural thing in the world, the guy leans over, flicks the cover off of the cooler, and hands two cans back without looking. "Pop them open out the window and toss the tabs out. I don't want no mess in my car."

The station wagon driver drops Leo and Emelia at the Black Prairie bus station where Emelia pays for two tickets to get them the rest of the way home. They have to wait another two hours for this bus, but at least it shows up.

It's nearly eleven o'clock by the time Leo makes it to the tavern, still a little woozy from the three or four beers—Leo lost count— that the driver had happily shared with them on the ride to Black Prairie. Outside the tavern, fat clouds of his father's accordion and Joey Katz's sax billow through the open windows, playing the "Let's Have a Party" polka. So he hasn't missed it all.

He pauses at the door. Man, he's going to catch hell. He only hopes his mother and father will wait until tomorrow morning to really lay into him.

He tugs open the tavern door. As he expected, his father and Joey Katz are on stage with musicians from other bands. The place is packed. Not as much as it must have been earlier because a few of the tables at the back have empty seats that haven't yet been cleared. It doesn't take Leo long to discover that his friends have all left. At least they won't be here to witness his parents yelling at him.

He spots a nearly full glass of beer abandoned on a table and drinks it down, warm and bitter. A coward's brew, he thinks. The beer does its job though and picks up where the Pabst he'd drunk earlier left off. He feels himself loosen a little. Not enough. Through this song and the next, Leo hangs back as he'd done at the church smoker. His mother dances with a lady Leo's seen before at his father's jobs, a bronze-haired bull with surprisingly delicate hooves.

When the song ends, the flute player and a button-box player wave and step down. Two other guys step up. His mother stays on the dance floor for the next song.

Leo nips into the bathroom to pee, then searches the tables for more booze. There are plenty of castoffs. He swallows three full beers. He finds two abandoned shots of vodka and throws one back as he's seen his father do. It burns as badly as Joey Katz's lovely cigarette.

Where is ol' Joey? When did he stop playing? Someone else is playing clarinet in Joey's place, but Leo doesn't recognize the musician. He's good though. If Leo can find Joey, maybe he can bum another joint. At the next song, though, Joey's back on stage, where Leo ought to be.

As if his father is reading his mind, when this song ends, he leans into the mic. His face is as red as the flesh of a ripe watermelon, and he's dripping with sweat. He's been playing accordion for five hours if he hasn't left the stage, and knowing Stash Meitka, he hasn't stepped aside once to let someone else in the spotlight.

His father waves in Leo's direction and says with heavy breath, "Well, folks, looks like my prodigal boy has finally decided to grace us with his presence." His tone is cutting. Heads turn, and gazes

321

land on Leo. The audience chuckles when his father says, "Folks, be sure to help me out by buying a record. Looks like I got to get the kid a new watch. Give us a drumroll, Clarence, to get my boy up here to play his father's big hit one more time!"

Clarence complies, and Leo can feel the drum's percussion in his chest, but his legs won't move. Everyone's looking at him. Laughing at him. His whole body breaks into a sweat. His throat has tightened so he can barely breathe. For all his dreaming of fronting a band, he's suddenly unable to take a step.

"He's a shy boy, folks. Give him some encouragement."

The audience claps, their low thundering adding to the drum's earthquake. His hands don't feel like his own. He wishes Stella were here. *So what do you want, Leo Mack?* She didn't laugh at him. He barely perceives his hands reaching for the second shot of vodka. The burning liquid works to ignite him, and Leo Mack smiles good-naturedly, striding to the stage steps.

Leo trips up the three steps onto the stage, but no one seems to notice his fumble. His father is busy readjusting the straps on his accordion. The audience's clapping has crested and waned. Joey Katz looks vacantly at him, his eyes bloodshot, his face coated with greasy sweat. He's not drunk, or not only drunk. He's on something else, a marijuana cigarette or something stronger?

Leo lifts his guitar from the stand where it must have been waiting all night. Had his mother or his father brought it for him? He strums it once. The tuning is perfect. His mother's work.

His father counts down, and they play. Couples spin together, chair dance, and pat the rhythm on the bar and tabletops. Their appreciation is genuine.

Leo Meitka's head is fuzzy, but it doesn't get in the way of Leo Mack's hands. In fact, once his head gets out of the way of his hands, they do what they know how to do. Leo Mack adds a little flourish at the end of the song, but it's drowned out by a sax flourish thrown in by Joey Katz. When the song is over, the applause is enthusiastic.

Leo inhales the audience's energy deeper than any cigarette he's smoked. The rushes from singing with Stella have been stronger, but this one's pretty damn good. Someone passes him a cup of beer, and he drinks it down. He'd like to keep playing, but his father nods once and waves him off the stage.

"Home to bed," he says quietly as Leo passes him on the way to the stairs. "You better have a good excuse, kid."

At the words, Leo pauses, irritated by the tone. Who is he to talk to Leo Mack about excuses? Wanting to irritate his father right back, Leo edges downstage. He kisses his fingers, turns his palm, and sends the kiss out to the audience. To his surprise, applause sprinkles over him, cool and refreshing, and he stands until every last drop hits him.

"Ha ha!" Joey Katz cackles behind him. "Kid's caught now!"

"Go on," his father says, giving Leo a little push. "No one likes a ham."

"You love ham," Leo says, "oink, oink." He giggles as he leaves the stage, smiling and throwing off one more wave.

To Leo's surprise, his father laughs lightly, maybe even a little proudly.

Passing the bar, his mother claps his shoulder and shouts over the band, who is already into the next song, "Better late than never. Good for you, facing the dragon, son."

He cocks his head questioningly.

"The stage fright. No amount of liquor got me past it." She rubs his cheek, ending the caress with a gentle slap. "Go home now. Sleep it off. Drink plenty of water first."

His mother has given him his out. If his father chides him tomorrow, Leo will chalk up his tardiness to stage fright.

He leaves out the alley exit, but he has no intention of going home. All he can think is that he wants more. More drinks. More music. More applause.

He wants to share it all with Stella.

Outside Stella's house, leaning on the trunk of an elm tree to steady himself, Leo feels like a character in a play. Should he find pebbles and pellet the blank panes of her bedroom windows, if he can figure out which ones they are? Should he scream the tortured syllables of her name to the star-kissed heavens, Marlon Brando style? What would Leo Mack do?

What Leo Meitka manages to do is stumble his way to the honeysuckle bushes before throwing up and passing out on her lawn, where later she kicks him awake, the toe of her Keds thumping his head. No, she's punting his thigh, but the pounding in his brain keeps good time.

She stops kicking when he manages to open his eyes and lift his head. The pounding soft-pedals to a throbbing backbeat. The sun nosing the horizon silhouettes her legs, which are bare from ankle socks to tennis shorts. She towers over him with her hands on her hips. Her arms are also bared to the shoulders by a scoop-necked shirt. She's bound her wild hair with a scarf, swirling with purple swatches that blend into the morning's shifting light and remind him of throwing up last night or, more accurately, a few hours ago.

"Angel," he whispers.

"No, stupid, it's me," she says, rolling her eyes. "Get up. If my mother sees you like this, that's it for me playing with the band. She hates liquor."

"What are you talking about?" he says, managing all fours, then knees alone. "What liquor?"

"Just because you're stupid doesn't mean I'm stupid. You stink of it."

"Oh," he says, dropping back to all fours, his wrist stabbing in pain. He shakes it, wondering how he hurt it.

"I mean it, Leo. Get up."

She slaps the patch of his back where his shirt has ridden up, a stinging *thwack* cutting into the morning silence. He's pretty sure her handprint is rising on his flesh. The pain focuses him, and he makes it to his feet. She grabs his arm and tromps him up the street and around the corner. When they're out of sight of her house, she drops his arm. His feet still. Swaying, the world looks too dull and too bright at the same time. The sun glints off the windows of a triple-decker with a memory flag hanging down the side.

"Everyone's mad at you," she says, walking on so he's got to move too, but there's no way can he keep up with her quick strides.

"Slow down," he says. "Why are you up so early?"

"Lucky for you." Without slowing, at least not so Leo can tell, she sucks her tongue as if annoyed at conceding to him by saying, "I run. It's good for the voice. You should try it."

"I will," he says.

She rolls her eyes again.

"Hey," he says, "I'm on the swim team. And I run cross-country. Please don't be mad. I really did have something important to do yesterday, and it lasted longer than I thought. Didn't I tell you?" He thought he called her, but he rubs his wrist, unsure of what's real.

"You canceled band practice, but you didn't say you were standing us up at your father's party. So why did you?"

"I can't say. I really can't. I promised someone. A friend."

He's breathless with the effort of keeping up with her. His whole body feels weak. They pass an alley, and he catches a whiff of rotten garbage. He doesn't make it to the can before vomiting again, great spasms that continue long after his stomach is empty. The mess splashes the concrete, dotting his shoes and jean cuffs. When had he eaten a hot dog?

"Are you okay?" she says.

The vein of sympathy in her voice heartens him. He rubs his shirtsleeve over his tongue before returning to her. They walk on at a pace he can manage, turning onto Bradley Avenue. Nordczyk's Grocers, O'Carroll's Hardware, even Demski's Bakery are closed. Only the tavern signs are brightly lit, Heartwood and Nite Awl, welcoming the third-shift workers in.

"Man, I'm never drinking alcohol again," he says. As the words leave his lips, he feels the desire for another drink. Just one. Or a thousand. "That's a promise."

"You make a lot of promises."

They pass Rexall Drugs' corner store where Leo used to buy penny candy with Emelia and Kirstin and Will after messing around at the lake, a lifetime ago it seems, but really just last summer. Passing Morty's liquor store, the smell of baking ham drifts toward them, and he swallows rising bile. His mother will go there later for supplies for the midday band gathering at their house and bring back cases of beer, pounds of ham, and the free sesame rolls from Demski's bakery that you get with your Sunday liquor-and-ham purchase.

"So who's this friend?" she says.

If he tells Stella about Emelia and her no-longer-dead mother, Stella will have to forgive him. More than that, she'll admire him for being such a good friend. He'd love to see Stella's doubtful expression change to admiration. And what would it matter if he told her, if she promised not to tell anyone else? He's got the words on his lips, but he pulls up. Emelia. His promise to her was real. And one lapse leads to another.

Instead he asks, "You were friends with that girl who died, right?"

"Sonya?" she says, taken aback.

"Yes," he says.

"It's funny. No one ever mentions her. My mother says it's in bad taste to bring up dead people."

"I'm sorry. I just wondered—"

"Don't be. She was my best friend. I miss her. People pretend she didn't exist. Or if they do mention her, they call her the worst names imaginable. Right in front of me. As if dying means she's not my friend anymore."

"Yeah," he says. He feels better walking. After a while he asks, "Stella, what did happen to her? I mean, I read the articles in the paper, but they hardly say anything."

She crosses her arms over her chest and scratches a mosquito bite on her back. "She used to go to camp in the summers. She came back so tan, talking about all these new friends she made. I was jealous. I was jealous of her a lot. Man, she was smart. Sometimes now I can convince myself she's just away at camp. I don't know what I'll pretend come September."

They turn right, Bradley Avenue behind them, the lake up ahead.

"Everyone's so concerned about how she died," Stella says. She's scratched the bite open. Blood streaks her back. "As if that will tell them all they need to know about her. I mean, isn't that the *least* interesting thing about a person? Or if it is the most interesting thing about someone, the person probably didn't have much of a life. And Sonya did. She was, well, she was just terrific. She was my best friend."

At the tremble in her voice, his instinct is to change the subject, but not back to why he didn't show up last night. He wants her to smile, and he wants to be the one to make her smile. But he may not get an opening like this again.

"Tell me some more about her," he says, taking the chance that if she keeps talking, maybe she'll tell him what he needs to know without him having to push her.

"She liked science. A lot. She said people were always saying how weird it was, a girl liking science so much. Except the teachers. They loved her. She said she wanted to be a doctor, not a people one, but a flower one. A botanist, I think she called it?"

She plucks a dandelion from a lawn freckled with them before going on. "She had a scholarship to the university. Did you know that?"

"Uh-uh."

"And she was a really good swimmer. One of the youngest girls to make varsity."

"I know. She had a really nice butterfly," he says, realizing he may have given away too much. Trying to cover, he says, "That's the hardest stroke. You have to be really strong."

"That's what gets me, you know. She was such a strong swimmer. And there she goes, drowning. It doesn't make sense."

"Yeah, but . . . the news reports said she had rocks in her pockets." And the gash, the blow to the head, he adds to himself.

"So what?" she says sharply. "Everyone thinks that means something big. But she *liked science stuff*. She used to bore me crazy talking about plants and rocks. She'd go to the beach all the time to look for fossils and stuff she thought was interesting. So maybe she was collecting rocks that day. Did they even think to check what kind of rocks? Maybe they were special or something."

He says nothing, and neither does she as they cover the rest of the block. Swatches of the lake peek between the houses.

"What's weird though is that she was flunking chemistry this year," Stella says. "Even I managed a C– in it, which is good enough to pass. She used to think a B was flunking, but she was barely passing this year. That's not like her."

They've come to Lakeshore Drive, which they cross. The woods are on one side, wild grassland on the other. Dry now, those grasses are marshy in spring, muddy with rain and melted snow. Had they buried Water Boy deep enough that he remains hidden forever, layers of roots and soil burying him deeper still? Or will he rise up next spring or the next?

They take the path between the woods and grassland to the cliffs where he'd seen Sonya for the last time. He studies Stella's face as she looks out at the hard line between the water and the sky. The sun over the horizon has grown glaringly white, the tips of the water glinting like shards of a broken mirror. The wind whips her hair, which strains its scarf. He lets the air push into his lungs, imagining it's cleansing him. But he still feels lousy. He shades his eyes with both hands, waiting for her to go on, knowing if he pushes her now, he will silence her, maybe forever.

After a while, she turns away from the water and walks back the way they've come, all earlier invigoration gone. Once again, they cross Lakeshore Drive, heading toward home.

"She'd been in some trouble," Stella admits.

"What kind?"

"The worst," she says so softly that at first Leo believes it was just the wind. "The absolute worst. For a girl anyway."

He waits, chewing his lip, afraid to frighten her off.

"Yeah," he says when she doesn't continue on her own. He can't let her stop now. She's so close to giving him what he needs. "You know, people say stuff."

"People are stupid!" she spits, her eyes narrowing, her gaze leveling him. Then, more calmly, "But people aren't wrong."

"Did she . . . say?"

"What?"

"Did she say who? Who got her . . . into trouble?"

She stops suddenly and grabs his arm hard. Away from the lake, the air is still. He feels nausea rising again. But her fingers are cool against his skin. He wants to press his lips to hers almost as much as he wants to throw up.

"How do you know she had a nice butterfly?" she says.

He can't think what to say. His mind is cotton.

"I need to sit down," he manages, stepping to the curb where he folds his body and lowers his head between his knees. He feels her sit next to him, keeping a distance though. Of course, he smells awful. The thought awakens his glands, and he smells his own stink. His roiling stomach, his swollen-feeling head, and the heat, press and pressing, so every inch of his body burns and perspires, convincing him he's going to die. All right, if he's dying, what does he have to lose?

He meets her gaze. "Stella, you're saying Sonya was pregnant, right?" His breath is heavy, his tongue thick, but he keeps going. "So who was the father? Who got her into trouble?"

She picks at the scab of a scratch on her ankle but says nothing. The wave of nausea cresting, he makes one last effort.

"She must have told you. You were her best friend."

"No," she says finally. "Sonya never said anything. Not one damn word. I kept waiting. I mean, it got kinda obvious. She wore that stupid letterman sweater thinking no one would notice. Then she took it off at the smoker, remember?"

The sweater she wrapped Water Boy in, the pin on the lapel, and now in Leo's pocket.

"I would have helped her. God, didn't she know that? Why didn't she trust me?"

"Who was the father?" he presses. "You must have some idea."

"He was older. That much I know," she says. "You're right. I should have asked her straight out. I should have made her let me help her."

"Could he have been a musician?" Leo ventures.

"Why would you ask that?" she says, surprised.

As she sniffs deeply and wipes her cheeks, he digs in his pocket for the pin, which he lays in his palm for her to see.

"My dad gives these out to the musicians in his band. Sonya had it pinned to her sweater." Neither of these is a lie, but he hedges now. "I saw her at school."

She picks up the pin and runs her index finger over the embossed surface. She cocks her head, then shakes it. "Uh-uh, this isn't what your dad gives out. I've seen it on those guys in the band. The red background is the same, but the symbol on the one your dad gives out is a whole note."

"That's what this is," he says.

"No, that's an O. They're kind of alike, I suppose. You're right, though, the one on Sonya's awful sweater was the same as this one. She said it was the symbol for . . . what was it? We learned it in chemistry." She snaps her fingers. "Oxygen. Stuff of life."

"Really? How do you know this is oxygen and not a note?"

"Even if it is a note, it's not the one your dad gives out. His is outlined in gold, really fine. This one isn't. See?" She uses her fingernail to show him on the pin.

Oxygen, not a whole note. His parents are in the clear?

"Are you sure?" he says.

It feels too easy. Whatever happened to Sonya has nothing to do with his father. Leo had been so certain. He'd looked at that pin a hundred times. Why hadn't he seen it wasn't the same?

"Leo," Stella says, placing the pin back in his hand. She has beautiful fingers. He could watch them all day long. She has to reach out and lift his chin to catch his gaze. "Why do you have Sonya's pin? That one isn't like hers. It *is* hers."

At her touch, he can't suppress a smile. "I can't say. Anyway, it doesn't matter."

Her features go hard. He braces himself, ready for her to slap him again.

"I want you to tell me right now, Leo. I mean it. Tell me right now, or that's it. I'm out of the band. You can go play with yourself."

"No, come on. Don't be like that."

"I mean it. You tell me what you know, or I'm splitting. And I'll get Charles and Van to come with me. You'll be out on your ear."

He blows out a long breath. The air he expels smells rancid, and she leans away from him. When she leans back in, she shakes his arm.

"Come on, Leo. Spill it."

With the current of secrets and loyalties and promises swirling around him, he thinks it's time to stop treading water. Stella has confirmed that his father is off the hook. His mother is off the hook. Emelia has retrieved the notes, so he and his friends are off the hook too. He could say nothing, and they would all be in the clear. But Stella would be left on an island of uncertainty, and he knows how lonely that place is. There must be a way to tell without telling too much.

"Okay," he says.

He keeps the important parts of his promise to his friends, which is to erase their names and the notes from the story. He describes Sonya at the lake that first day they saw her. He tells her about digging up Water Boy after Sonya left.

"Looked like something dropped from space. My friend thought Sonya killed him. Water Boy, we call him. But I don't think he was ever alive. She wrapped Water Boy in that letter sweater she'd been wearing." He leaves out the hatbox and the time capsule.

Tears wet her cheek, and he almost stops, but Stella squeezes his arm to make him continue.

"The pin," she says. "Sonya said she got it from a boy from the north shore."

"Yeah, the note pin—I mean, the oxygen pin—was attached to Water Boy's sweater. I'd seen the pin on my father's band shirts. I guess, I thought my father . . . I'm not good at science. It never occurred to me it was some chemistry symbol."

"Oxygen," she says.

"Yeah," he says, inhaling some.

"So you don't know who—"

"I don't," he says, relief melting over him as he realizes that not only is this true, he no longer needs to know. He places the pin in her palm and curls her fingers around it. "I haven't got a clue."

"I do," she says through gritted teeth. "Sonya, she may have messed up. But she didn't deserve—. You know, I think I know just what to do with this. Thanks for telling me, Leo."

Despite his stink, she leans in and kisses him.

It was worth it, he thinks, every tortured second, every doubt and fear about his father and mother and Emelia too, worth the worst of it to feel the brush of her lips. All of it has brought him to this warm pool. He wants to swim forever.

After a moment, she shakes her head. "You really thought it was your dad?"

Leo shrugs. At the moment, the idea is ridiculous.

"You're deluded," she says. "It's true, your father's a flirt. But he wouldn't. Not with Sonya anyway."

That last bit nettles him. Not Sonya, but someone. Nora.

But hasn't Stash changed? Isn't he at least trying to change? As Leo's hangover reminds him, it wasn't Stash who drank too much last night.

"Well, someone must have done it with Sonya," he says.

"Yeah," she says, her voice hard again. She rubs her fingertips over the pin's flat surface.

"Oh." In his surprise, he dares to place his hand on her bare thigh. It's velvet, it's silk, it's every soft thing he's ever touched. "You know who the father is."

She says nothing else, and her expression gives nothing away. And after a while, he doesn't care about Sonya. He hugs Stella close, so the silence has no space to settle between them.

As Leo walks home, the dread of his parents' lingering anger over him having been late to the release party is so overshadowed by relief and joy, it hardly matters. Each footfall lands on the sidewalk with a satisfying certainty that his parents had nothing to do with Sonya.

He shakes his head. How could he have thought so badly of his father? Because of Nora, he reminds himself. But he again acknowledges that all signs suggest that his father has changed, or is at least trying to change. So as long as he remains on the wagon, Leo will call it even.

He's got his own band. He's been a good friend to Emelia. He's kissed Stella. This is his time.

"*Bop-bop, bop-bop* . . . *generation!*" he sings, drumming Keith Moon's part with invisible sticks, his head aching from the effort, but the feeling of singing so good that he doesn't care.

He's still drumming when he turns the corner onto his street and sees the ambulance parked behind his father's bus, its red lights slashing his front door. His hangover and the song forgotten, he takes off in a sprint.

Emelia

EMELIA UNCRIMPS THE end of a cardboard tube and pinches out the poster she'd bought at the Hobby Shop in Black Prairie while she and Leo waited for the bus. She unrolls it and admires the black-and-orange daisy sprouting over the yellow background. Drawn in black crayon, the flower's leaves stretch wide like the arms and legs of a stick figure, making the flower both human and plant. In the same black crayon, childlike script reads, *War is not healthy for children and other living things*.

"No kidding," she says softly, looking down at her own two stick legs sprouting beneath the hem of her nightgown. She bends one leg behind her until it disappears. Her ankle strains to keep her balanced. Imagine, wobbling the rest of your life as Ben will have to do, or being blind like the boy who got the deadeye bullet.

"Well, no way are Leo or Will going," she decides, setting her foot down. Not if she has anything to say about it.

She opens the drawer of her pine desk and finds some tape and four black tacks. She turns the poster over and tapes the piece of paper Dr. Crispan gave her to the white backing. She's already checked how far away the Planned Parenthood place is. She'll have to use the rest of the money Ben gave her for the bus to get there. Maybe they aren't allowed to give her the Pill or the Loop because she's not married, but they can give her information. And Dr. Crispan is right. She wants to know her options. She wants to know who Jane is.

She palms the poster to the wall in two different positions, considering and reconsidering. Finally, deciding on the position that will allow her to see the poster as soon as she wakes up, she pierces the primrose wallpaper. A reminder every morning that she has both options and obligations.

She lifts her nightgown over her head and hangs it on the peg on the back of her bedroom door. She selects shorts and a sleeveless blouse from her dresser. Her dresser, her door, her desk. Her bed, her bookshelves, her wallpaper. She hasn't stolen her mother's life. That woman at Red River, her mother, Elisa, one of the Demski sisters—she has her own things, her own life in a community. She's made her own family.

"Will you come back?" Elisa asked Emelia when Dr. Crispan said it was time for her to leave. Elisa had taken Emelia's hands between hers and rolled them like pretzel dough. "You're cold," she observed, then repeated, "Will you come back?"

Her whole life, Emelia had begged her mother for this very thing. *Come back for me.* And Elisa had come back, in a way. Emelia gave her mother the response she'd longed to hear all those years.

"Yes, I'll come back," she said.

Now, looking through her bedroom window at the same houses her mother looked at when she was a girl, at the same trees and sky, at the same triangle of lake peeking through the rooftops, Emelia wonders if she'll honor her promise now that she's uttered it. If she wants more than the bakery, or something different anyway, won't she have to leave here? For the first time, she thinks, maybe not. She has other options right here. Who knows, maybe she'll even volunteer at the Planned Parenthood place. Maybe she'll help other women. Despite what Dr. Crispan said, she owes her mother. And she owes Sonya something. Options and obligations.

She's already broken one promise. She promised Lou and Genny she wouldn't tell anyone about Elisa. She's told Ben and Leo. She'll probably never see Ben again. And Leo's given his word not to tell anyone else. She'll have to trust him.

"Now you know the secrets, so you're part of the family," she said yesterday as they waited for the bus in Black Prairie. "Closest thing I have to a brother." She's pretty sure she'd seen him wince, and she tried not to look hurt. Whatever beef he's got with his parents, they must seem like dreamboats compared to Elisa.

But he'd taken her hand in a friendly way, and he hadn't contradicted her when she let the driver who picked them up believe they were brother and sister. Yet when Leo had bubbled over as he talked about Stella and his band, Emelia silently released him from the hope that he'd leave with her, hitch to California and keep going, to Mexico, maybe South America. Leo's got his own plans. Will and Kirstin will be delighted. She laughs lightly. Man, they ought to love Planned Parenthood.

She glances at the poster she tacked to the wall, assuring herself that no trace of the paper behind it can be detected. Checking herself in the mirror, she takes a breath.

"Time to face the music," she says.

Aunt Lou is alone in the kitchen when Emelia enters. No place is set for her at the table this morning. She smells no waffles or sausages warming in the oven for her, but spots a batch of muffins baking, presumably to replenish the bakery's supply. Lou should be working downstairs, and Emelia proceeds with caution.

With her back to Emelia, Lou washes dishes at the sink. Emelia has to reach around her to get at the half-full coffee pot on the stove. She pours the black liquid into a cup Lou has just washed and adds milk and sugar. Lou leans back to accommodate her reach, but says nothing, and Emelia understands it has been decided that Lou will be the one to deal with Emelia's late arrival home last night, well beyond her streetlights-on curfew.

They'd all but pounced on her as she came through the door, Genny puffing up with anger, Lou collapsing with relief.

"We were so worried," said Lou.

"Where have you been? You tell us right now," demanded Genny.

But Emelia had refused to talk to her aunts last night, ignoring both Genny's anger and Lou's relief. Exhausted as she was, the sight of her aunts reignited her earlier anger. Serves them right, she'd thought, for keeping her mother from her. She waved them away, heading toward her bedroom, saying, "I'm fine. I'm tired. I don't want to talk about it. Not tonight."

To her surprise, they hadn't pursued her. She could only imagine the looks they must have exchanged when she closed her bedroom door.

Thinking about how hard it had been to tell Leo her mother was alive, her anger is dampened. Not gone though. If her aunts had been honest, Emelia might have known her mother her entire life. True, they had their reasons. Were they good enough?

She cuts a slice of day-old bread from the loaf on the cutting board, fanning the crumbs from the board onto her slice. *Waste not, want not* as Genny so often says. She spreads butter and takes a bite. Stale. They rarely have freshly baked bread, only on holidays. They eat what customers don't, but as she chews, salt and butter melting over her tongue, she acknowledges she has always been able to eat as much as she wanted. Genny and Lou had cared for her in her mother's stead. They hadn't abandoned her.

"Sit down at the table if you're going to eat," says Lou. "You're not a cow. And use a plate. We aren't savages either."

Emelia takes a plate from the drying rack, wipes it on her shorts, and sits at the table.

"Well?" Lou says without turning around. "What do you have to say for yourself, young lady?"

Young lady—a sure indication that Lou is fuming. Lou rarely fumes. Genny is the fumer.

She takes time to finish eating the slice of bread before saying, "I went to see her."

"Wherever you went, you should have been back by dark," Lou says, drying her hands on a dish towel. She fills a pot with water, adds salt, and places it on the stove without lighting the burner. She opens the pantry door and hauls a burlap sack of potatoes to the counter. Her back still to Emelia, she sets to peeling them with a paring knife.

How many fields of potatoes have those hands peeled? How many apples for pies? An orchard? Two? Had Lou ever wanted something else for herself?

"Or at least telephoned. Maybe you aren't old enough to take on the responsibility of keeping your own time. Do Genny and I really need to watch you every minute of the—"

"My mother," Emelia says. She sips coffee, hot and sweet. "Elisa. I went to see Elisa."

Lou's hands still.

"How?" she says.

"I took the bus." Because she's determined to be honest, she adds, "And I hitchhiked."

"Hitchhiked? No!" Lou spins around, knife in one hand, half-naked potato in the other. "Emelia, you didn't. That's dangerous. Don't you know what kind of people are out there, just waiting to prey on a young girl alone?"

"I wasn't—" She stops herself before saying she wasn't alone, that Leo was with her. She owes it to Leo to keep him out of it at least as much as he owes it to her to keep quiet. Honesty isn't as easy as she'd like, she acknowledges. Like it or not, she has her own secrets to keep now. "I was very careful," she assures Lou, taking another sip of her coffee to hide the omission her eyes might betray.

"Hitchhiking, Emelia." Lou sets the knife and the potato on the cutting board. She wipes her hands on a clean towel and sits down at the table. "Maybe Genny is right. Maybe you are going wild."

"Aunt Lou."

"I want you to promise me—*promise me*—you won't ever hitchhike again," she says. Her voice is stern, but her fingers nervously knit the cloth of the centerpiece mat. "Promise!"

"I promise," Emelia lies. How quickly the lies pile up. "I won't."

Lou nods once and says, "So now you've seen her."

"Yes."

"And?"

"She made all the birthday cakes."

"She did. She was the best of all of us with cakes. Such a fine touch. She might have been a sculptor if she was a man. She's even better than your grandfather was. He had high hopes for her."

"Did he? Then why did they do that to her? The ice pick. Why did he let them hurt her?"

She expects Lou to balk, but the sincerity of Emelia's questions must come through because she says in a kind tone, "Oh, honey, no one thought it was going to hurt her. You have to understand, when she went into that hospital, the first one, she was so very unhappy."

"Because of me," Emelia says.

"No," Lou says firmly. "She loved you. *Loves* you. But she found motherhood hard. Alone. She was the kind of girl who needed freedom, and she felt trapped. I remember once she told me all she ever saw around her were walls. And then she ended up in that place. Such a waste."

"Why did you let me believe she was—" The word *dead* catches in her throat. Her anger flares. "You didn't tell me. For all those years."

"But we told you as soon as we thought you were old enough to understand."

"Old enough to keep quiet, you mean."

"Well, okay, yes. But until now, you were too young to see her like that too." Lou lays her hands flat on the table and presses, as if pushing the memory away. "The way she looked, the changes in her, they were shocking right after the procedure."

"You mean the ice pick to her brain? The lobotomy?"

"It was supposed to help her, to get rid of her sadness, help her calm down."

"Because she was wild. But what did she really do that was so bad?"

"You had to know her then to understand," Lou says. "She thought the rules didn't apply to her. Out at all hours, dancing, drinking, and with boys. For God's sake, Emelia, she had a child out of wedlock! She might well have had another the way she was going."

"So it was because of me that you stabbed her in the brain."

"You make it sound so awful."

"Wasn't it?"

"It wasn't supposed to be."

"Awful enough that her own daughter couldn't see her?"

"Yes, Emelia, it *was* awful." Lou squeezes her eyes shut and shakes her head. "It *is* completely and utterly awful. So we wanted to spare you."

Emelia can see she should relent. There has been enough anger, enough cruelty, but she can't stop herself from spitting out, "And silence me."

Lou's face and body stiffen. She pushes back the chair, the legs violently scraping the linoleum.

"What would you have had us do, Emelia?" She strides to the cutting board, picks up the paring knife, and stabs the half-peeled potato. She sends the speared vegetable clattering into the sink before pivoting to face Emelia again. "Did you really want to be known your whole life as the bastard girl with the imbecile mother?" Her voice is hard, her eyes steel.

Stunned, Emelia says nothing. From Genny she may have expected such words, but from Lou, they burn like a brand.

"Running around at all hours, hitchhiking." Lou crosses her arms over her chest, and Emelia wonders if this is to keep from slapping her. "You're nearly as bad. You'd best watch yourself, Emelia. You could end up just like her. For all I know you've already—. Oh, yes, young lady, you should watch your step."

Emelia hardly recognizes the ugly woman jeering at her, threatening her. Would they do it? Would they lock her up too if they knew about Theo and Danny and Ben?

"Close your mouth," says Lou. "You're not a cow. Now give me that plate if you've finished."

Mechanically, Emelia hands over the plate, which Lou washes and places in the drying rack. She turns the burner on below the coffee pot, waiting with arms crossed until it heats up. Then she tosses the dregs at the bottom of Emelia's cup into the sink and fills it with the steaming, reheated coffee. She sets it before Emelia with a surprisingly gentle hand before turning back to wipe the counter.

Emelia stares at the black liquid. Dr. Crispan said Elisa's sisters had been good to her. Good to their imbecile sister. Kind to her bastard daughter. *Almost, nearly.* All those years.

"Drink that. You look like you're going to faint."

Emelia drinks, forgetting about sugar and milk. The bitterness braces her, and eventually she manages to say to her aunt's back, "Lou?"

"*Aunt* Lou, you mean. I'm still the adult, and you're still the child. Don't you forget," she says, a bunched rag in her fist. "It's time you remembered that."

"Aunt Lou," she says quietly, her tone measured. She's never been frightened of Lou before, not really. But now. Could they take the ice pick to her?

Yet she senses she has this one opportunity. Once Lou shuts the lid on this topic, Emelia may never pry it open again. She pauses to see if Lou will turn around, but she only circles the rag over the same spot on the counter, over and over, so Emelia presses on. "Aunt Lou, who is my father?"

She steels herself for Lou's anger, but Lou only stops wiping. Slumping forward, she rests her forearms on the edge of the sink.

"I don't know, Emelia," she says, each word a fist. "I don't."

Emelia hears the catch in her aunt's voice. Is she lying? Their lie about her mother's death casts a long shadow. Have she and Genny decided Emelia isn't ready to learn this? That she'll never be ready? Or does Lou sincerely not know?

"I promise that if I knew, I would tell you. It's time enough. But your mother never said. She wouldn't even put it on your birth certificate. But you know that. You've seen it with your own eyes."

Emelia considers pushing her. She must have guessed. Elisa was her little sister. They lived in the same house, shared a bathroom, worked in the bakery together.

But when Lou lays her head in her hands, her shoulders heaving with sobs, Emelia relents, uncertain exactly why Lou is crying. For what she just called Elisa and Emelia? *Imbecile, bastard.* For the little sister she'd once had, who is gone if not dead? For the loss of Elisa's great love? But had it been a great love? Or had it been something else, sadness, fear? She recalls the feel of the ice pick in her hand when she first got into the car with Ben. And Sonya's look the day she buried Water Boy. Ben was right. Men may have war to fear, but women fear sex.

The buzzer on the stove sounds, startling them both.

Emelia releases the breath she didn't realize she'd been holding. If Lou knows the answers to these questions, she isn't ready to tell her. Maybe Emelia's not ready to hear the answers either. Not yet. Maybe some secrets are a relief.

"Blueberry muffins," Lou chokes out. She shakes off her emotion, picks up a dishcloth, and opens the oven door.

She pulls out the tin and expertly flips the muffins onto a cooling rack. She chooses one, places it on the plate Emelia used earlier, and sets it on the table before her. "I know you like them warm."

A fresh muffin, a special treat.

Emelia breaks the muffin open and inhales the scents of blueberries and sugar and flour. She blows the heat away. Her aunts have cooked thousands of meals for her, teaching her how to cook and bake along the way. And although their daily bread was day old, there had been plenty of treats like this muffin too. At Christmas, they'd taught her to wind fruit-laden bread into wreathes, at Easter to mold butter into lambs. All three of them jittered with excitement when the first electric clothes-washing machine arrived. On Saturday evenings, after the bakery closed, Genny would turn up Rosemary Clooney or Bing Crosby records and sing along as they dusted and cleaned the carpets. It's been a long time since they've done that together, since before her birthday.

She feels the loss keenly. In gaining a mother, she's lost her aunts, not completely, but the easiness among them is gone. Revealing truth is like trading marbles; you give away what you have for something heavier or rounder, but until you feel its weight in your palm, you don't know if the deal is sweet or rotten.

She takes a bite of the warm muffin, brown sugar cutting the sourness of the tart blueberries. It hadn't all been dark secrets growing up, she admits. There had been true joy in this house.

"Thank you," Emelia says after the last bite. "Do you want me to take the rest downstairs?"

"No." Lou pulls a tin from a low cabinet and lines it with wax paper. Her motions are slow, as if she's got to think about each one. In the slowness, Emelia can see the old woman her aunt will be. How many more thousands of muffins will those hands make? Millions. She wants so badly for them to make millions more.

"After these cool," Lou goes on, "I'm taking them to the church. There's a service and reception for the Morrow girl."

"Sonya."

"Yes."

Lou doesn't need to say, see what happens to wild girls.

The heat from the oven feels like a weight between them. Emelia stands up and takes her coffee to the window, hoping for a breeze. Looking out, she finds Dean looking up at her. He's tied the striped towel she left in Sonya's room around his neck. Who is she to be angry with her aunts? She's taken this little boy's sister from him. She and Dean hold each other's gazes for a moment before he lifts his hand and waves her outside.

Before she goes to him, she says to Aunt Lou, "What time is the service? I'd like to go with you."

Dean

ON THE WAY to the bakery, the red-striped towel he'd tucked into the collar of his T-shirt slips and falls into a small heap on the sidewalk. He scoops it up and dodges behind a bush. Toilet paper roll telescope to his eye, he scans right, spying porch steps, a landing, and a screen door. He scans left, another porch steps, a landing, and a screen door. A dog. A cat. But no humans in sight. The coast is clear.

He shakes dirt off his striped cape and tucks it back into his collar. When he stands up, the collar of his dirty shirt is so stretched out, the towel falls again. Frustrated, he punches the bush, branches scraping his fist, stinging and burning. Why is everything so hard and wrong? He wants to scream. He strangles the urge, scrunching his two fists hard, hard, hard as he can. Crypto emerges again, and the urge withers. Crypto doesn't need to scream. Crypto is invincible.

Dean's first transformation of himself into Crypto, after the big-kid girl left their house dressed as Sonya and his mother retreated to her bedroom again, had been a revelation. Then, as now, he slashed Sonya's red lipstick over his cheeks. Eye shadow, smeared on and below his eyelids, made two bull's-eyes. Crypto eyes. The way he draws them in the notebooks. He blackened his lips until the dirty boy who couldn't understand anything disappeared. He wasn't, *isn't*, the boy whose sister is gone, whose father is away for who knows how long, and whose mother won't get out of bed. He's smart. Cryptic Crypto knows the answers to all the puzzles. He checks his pocket for the picture he took from under Sonya's mattress the day she left him. Cryptic Crypto wants to tell.

That first day dressed as Crypto, he jogged back to the pool to find the big-kid girl. From down the block, he spotted her leaving, no longer in Sonya's dress but in the clothes she wore to bring him home. He ran to catch up with her, but she was fast. Her long legs cut the sidewalk like scissors. Where was she going so fast? He was about to call out to tell her to stop when she met up with the dark-haired big-kid boy Dean calls Shadow in his drawings. An archenemy. So he kept his distance.

He waited and followed them, and eventually the big-kid boy left the girl at the good-smelling place, the bakery Sonya used to take him to for snowman cookies. The yummy smells and the memory of her handing him the cookie, ruffling his hair, rubbing his back, would have made Dean cry, but not Crypto. Crypto is stronger than Dean.

He waited until the bakery closed for the big-kid girl to come out. The streetlights came on. The darkness buried him, and still he waited until mosquitoes attacked him. By the time he got home, he was more Dean than Crypto. Darkness followed him to his bedroom where he rubbed his face in one of the sweaters that still smelled of Sonya.

He became Crypto again yesterday, waiting for the big-kid girl outside the bakery, but she didn't come out by mosquito time. Has she disappeared like everyone who is nice to him does?

Today, he decided to wait for her one more time. Third time's the charm, Sonya used to say.

The third time for his cape too, and now, instead of tucking the towel into his collar, Dean ties the corners in a knot around his neck. Forgetting he has lipstick on his cheeks, he swipes one with the back of his hand. The blood from his scrapes mixes with the lipstick. He wipes his hand on his shirt and pats his pocket, checking again for the photo.

The photo is really four pictures in a line, the kind taken in one of the booths in the Woolworth's. In the first frame, the man's face is hidden because he's kissing Sonya. In the second frame, Sonya's kissing him. In the last two photos in the strip, Sonya and the man from the lake look straight at the camera. The man's face is serious. Mr. Grim, Dean calls him, having stolen the word from other comics for his own drawings. But Sonya smiles brightly, as if she can't believe her luck.

The morning Sonya left him forever, Dean had followed her out of the house to the lake. He kept hidden the way he often did when he followed Sonya, crouched in the tall grasses so he could watch without being seen. Did she know he was there? He should have asked her. Now he will never know. He will never ask her anything ever again.

He wasn't surprised the man from the photo joined her on the cliff. He'd seen them there together a few times before. They liked to gather rocks and flowers, and Sonya had a few rocks in her hand as he approached her. But the way she put the rocks into her pockets when the man got close—not because she liked them but because she might need them—made Dean pick up a rock too.

He's thought about that rock a lot, wishing he'd thrown it at the man before he got near Sonya, before Sonya yelled at him about the boy in the moon, and before the man lunged at Sonya, making her step back, into air, into nothing, no sound, no scream, no splash. Only later did Dean realize he must not have heard Sonya's last sounds because in his shock, he had raised his hands to his ears. Pressing tight, he watched the man get onto his stomach and inch to the edge of the cliff. Dean must have dropped his hands then because he heard the man call to Sonya. But by the time Dean had scrabbled up and run to the edge himself, the man had bolted.

Dean fell to his stomach too. He inched to the cliff edge as the man had done. He looked over, screaming, "Sonya!"

All he saw was churning, gulping water.

His cape secured, Crypto tells him to get a move on. He cat-crawls from behind the bush, gets ready, gets set, and explodes, leaping, soaring over the sidewalk, the cape catching air before he lands with soft knees, run, run, running and flapping and flying and finally cawing, "SooooooooooonnYaaaaaaaaaa!"

He lands at the door of Demski's Bakery. Through the window, he can see the bakery is crowded with mom ladies, but he doesn't go inside. He doesn't have to.

As if she'd been waiting for him, the girl is at the upstairs window. He waves his Crypto-powered hand, magnetizing her, and pulls her down the stairs and out the door.

"Oh, my gosh, are you okay?" she says.

Today she looks more like a grown-up girl than a big-kid girl, but he can't say why exactly.

"Is that blood?" She kneels down so their eyes are level. She lays her hand on his shoulder in exactly the place Sonya used to put her hand. "Are you hurt?"

Realizing she has mistaken the lipstick on his shirt for blood, he shakes his head and pats his belly.

"Thank goodness. You scared me," she says. "What are you doing here? Is your mom here, in the bakery?"

"I'm Crypto," he says in what he thinks will be a roar, but it comes out more like a kitten's mew. "Crypto knows."

"Does he?" she says, smiling in the way grown people do when they think you are cute and sweet and dumb. But he's not any of these things. "Crypto knows what happened. He wants to tell."

She looks alarmed. "Tell what?"

"What happened." He has to make her understand. "Sonya said never tell, but my mom . . ."

"You've had a hard time," she says. "Your sister. It's so sad to lose someone. Your mom is just sad."

He says nothing.

"I lost my mom a long time ago," she says. "Are you sad?"

He nods, tears welling. This girl has superpowers too. The tears dripping down his cheeks are melting Crypto. He has to tell her before Crypto is all gone. He slides the photo from his pocket and pushes it into her hand. As she takes it from him, he leans in so close that he can smell her floury scent, not as nice as Sonya's, but good.

He whispers in her ear, "Him."

Part Four

Leo

"STAND BACK," STASH says, waving Leo and Anne away. He raises a green metal can filled with gasoline over charcoal briquettes piled high in a grill pan and lets the liquid flow.

"Wait!" Anne calls. Her thongs flap on the concrete of the patio as she skitters to the spigot. She finds the snakehead of the coiled hose. Poised to strike, she calls, "Ready!"

Leo leans against the post that holds the basketball hoop he hasn't used since last summer while his father fishes in his pocket for a match, lights it, and tosses it onto the saturated charcoal. Blackened flames whoosh up. Dark clouds swell, singeing the leaves of the crabapple tree's overhanging boughs.

Leo enjoys the whoosh until his father leans over, hands on his knees, bracing himself against the deep, wheezy spasms erupting from his chest. Watching his father, his mother inches toward the flames, hose still poised, but the fire settles into the grill pan before she has to douse it. The acrid taste of burning gas stings Leo's nostrils and throat, and he covers his nose with his shirttail and waits for his father to stop coughing.

With his father still hacking, his mother trots to the cooler and fetches three cans of beer, pulling the tab on his father's can before handing it to him. She lets Leo pull his own tab, and for a few moments they all gulp in silence until his father's coughing returns and sends him searching his pockets for a handkerchief, which he presses to his mouth. Leo turns his head to keep from watching his father spit into the bushes and wipe blood from his mouth.

The doctors are right. The cancer is progressing fast. It's bad enough the illness is eating his father's lungs and lymph nodes, but it's also eating away his energy; the powerful tree of a man who'd wielded his accordion on stage at the release party last month is more like a sapling bent from the wind.

His mother pointedly keeps herself busy as his father gathers himself. She wraps potatoes in tinfoil, shucks corn, but again and again, her glance is pulled back to her husband. The look of concern on her face is so very different from the narrowed eyes and hard lips of suspicion that used to cross her face. Each morning her forehead crimps and her teeth catch her lip as his father axes through his first cigarette. Now her expression deepens when his father thuds his body into a lawn chair, lights a Chesterfield, and drags deeply. But she says nothing.

Leo says nothing either. His father has insisted that if he's going to die anyway, he's going to enjoy life as much as possible until then. Before his father's collapse, Leo might have thought of Nora and sneered at what his father's enjoyment entailed, but what's the point now? Leo had been so wrongheaded in thinking his father had anything to do with Sonya that for a while Leo could barely look him in the eye.

Only days after Leo gave Stella the oxygen pin, everything came out about Sonya and Mr. Trippsman. Stella told her police detective father. At nearly the same time, Sonya's little brother confessed he'd seen his sister and Mr. Trippsman at the lake that day. Emelia is the one who took the boy to the police station. She had no choice, she said when she told the rest of them what she'd done. The kid had photos of Sonya and Trippsman. She said she didn't think Dean connected their notes with what happened to Sonya, and she didn't say anything either.

"If we have to tell them about the notes, we will—and face the consequences," she said.

"Do we tell them about Water Boy?" asked Kirstin

"No," Will said quickly. "Emelia's right. How would it help? Bad enough for them that Sonya died. They don't need her reputation smeared too."

When confronted, Mr. Trippsman—John Marshall Trippsman, as the paper reported—admitted he'd met Sonya on the cliffs that day to go rock collecting. She'd found some interesting ones she put in her pocket before she slipped and fell into the water right where the current is strongest. Panicking when he couldn't find her, and presuming her already dead, he kept quiet about his involvement in the incident because he worried people would get the wrong idea when they learned he and Sonya had once had a small dalliance.

"I apologize to her family. I should have come forward right away," Trippsman said. "Sonya was an excellent student. A lovely girl."

Together the four of them looked up the word *dalliance* and seethed for Sonya.

But according to the papers, the physical evidence didn't necessarily contradict Trippsman's story. She could have gotten the injuries to her cheek and head in the fall or in the water. And Dean's witness statement backs up Trippsman's story that no one pushed Sonya, so no charges are being filed against him. He might have lost his job at the high school, but he had already resigned to go to graduate school in California.

"Misadventure, they're calling Sonya's death," Kirstin said.

"Misadventure," said Emelia. "What a strange word."

"I can't believe Trippsman called what they did a dalliance," said Leo. Is that what his father and Nora had been?

"Yeah, leaving her in the lurch and getting away scot-free. That's not right," said Emelia, but to Leo's relief, she didn't go on to say it was up to them to do anything about it, only that Sonya should have had more choices, somewhere to turn.

Since they visited her mother, Emelia's changed in a way Leo can't name. She's calmer but more intense. She talks about the war more, but they all do now. The war's become like the constant background presence of a pot simmering on the stove in his mother's kitchen. And she bangs on about how unfair things are for women, but after seeing her mother like that, Leo forgives her for being so strident.

As for Stella, when Leo asked if she was going to tell someone about Trippsman getting Sonya pregnant, she said, "People are saying enough bad stuff about her. Saying anything more would only make it worse." She drew a small cross over her heart. "She's still my friend. I owe it to her to keep some of her secrets."

***

By the time the charcoal briquettes have grayed, his father has recovered from his coughing jag. A car horn honks from the street, and Leo jogs to the porch, where he pulls his guitar case from beneath an old wooden bench. He opens it to check he has picks and the new slide he cut from the top of a Black Bear soda bottle. He's not great with it yet, but he's better. He's practicing. His mother is right. There's no shortcut to being good. And he plans to be more than good.

As he's closing the case, his father says, "You need a stand? You could take mine."

"I don't need one."

Leo braces himself for some crack from his father, that rock music isn't real music and doesn't have to be written down.

"Yes, you have a good memory," says his father. "Always could play by heart after one run-through. I remember once—"

"Just a minute, Dad. Charles is waiting," Leo says. "I'll be right back."

"Right, sure, you go. Maybe I'll come hear you."

"It's not that kind of gig. It's a party. Private."

"Sure, sure," his father says, looking embarrassed and waving him away. For once, Leo doesn't feel dismissed by the wave.

"Another time," he says apologetically.

"Yeah, sure," his father says. "The Jolly Players are at Stan's Danceland anyway. I should go."

He looks so tired, Leo can tell he'll fall asleep in front of the television, his mother next to him, darning socks.

Leo says, "You think I could use your amp?"

His father brightens. "Sure, sure. Get some use out of it. You know where it is."

Leo jogs out of the back yard, up to Stash's attic studio to grab the amp. The room is dusty and hot. The band should be on tour right now, but his father hasn't played a note since the party. He can barely lift his accordion.

At the car, Charles, who's just passed his driver's test, rests his arm on the hood of his father's station wagon, swinging the keys around one finger. In a month, Leo will turn sixteen and be able to take his test. He had his eye on a station wagon for sale at the CITGO. It's a beater, but it would have held all of their equipment. He doesn't need it though. His father told him he can have the bus if he wants it.

Charles and Leo slap five before Charles opens the car door so Leo can place the guitar case and amp in the back seat.

"You want to eat at my place?" Charles says. "Mom's making chicken a la king. We can go together after."

Leo considers it. He's never tasted something as exotic as chicken a la king, but his father's laughter erupts from the back yard. To Leo's surprise, he wants to return to him and his mother, to hear the joke, which, knowing his father, is probably in bad taste.

"Nah, we're grilling," he says. "I'll meet you there."

Charles gives him a two-fingered salute and is about to get back into the car when Leo calls, "Hey, you bring . . . you know?"

"Oh, yeah, right. I forgot. Get in."

They both get into the front seat where Charles hands him three joints.

"My mom says this crop's really smooth."

"Cool," Leo says, sliding them into his pack of Chesterfields, and the pack itself into his shirt pocket. Leo hands him the money he's made playing piano at the ballet school. His mother claims she needed a break, but really she doesn't want to leave his father's side. Leo likes the dancers. Their bodies are lean and strong, but none hold a candle to Stella.

"I'll see you at the beach," he says as he gets out of the car.

By the time Leo gets back to the patio, his mother has set the picnic table with paper plates and bowls of yellow mustard and ketchup. She brings pickles from the basement crock and a platter of watermelon. After another beer each, his father sets down sizzling sausages, corn, and potatoes.

Before they settle in to eat, his father, in a rare flash of energy, ducks inside to turn up the volume on Johnny Vadnal's *Carefree Polkas*. Leo likes this song. It's not rock, but he can't deny, the Vadnals can blow the roof off a song. His father sings along, loud and off-key. When the song finishes, Leo and his mother clap and call, "Encore!"

Leo wolfs down the meal and helps his mother clean up while his father relaxes on the patio. As she hands him cleaned dishes to dry, Leo asks, "You think he'll go see the Jolly Players tonight?"

"He'll be too tired," she says, shaking her head. "I always dreamed someday he'd want to stay home nights with me. Now that he does, all I want is for him to have the energy to go out."

With her shoulders slumped as they are, she's the one who looks tired, but he doesn't say it. For just a moment, he considers hanging around for a while, but once they're settled, he hurries to get out of the house. They don't need him there tonight, and he wants to walk before the party. Stella's right about running being good for the voice, but he finds walking by the lake is good for writing lyrics.

Dusk is coming on by the time he crosses the highway and enters the lake path. He swats his way through a wild mess of mosquitoes and gnats. He inhales the clean scent of water and steak cooking on a grill somewhere. The scent brings back the image of his father bent over and coughing. It hardly seems fair that his father never got to enjoy his record's small success, never got to tour. What will the world be like without Stash Meitka? It's the one thing Leo can't picture.

He lights one of the joints. The beer, the pot, they make his mind ease up a little. It's hard to take sometimes, this ability his mind has to roam into places it should never go, places as vivid as any Technicolor movie, as vivid as the Queen Anne's lace and milkweed he strolls past right now.

He strides with loose muscles, taking in the lake's frosted whitecaps, the paper birch and elm trees fringed with yellow and red leaves. Autumn's coming, but it's still warm, and he removes his shirt, feeling more comfortable in his T-shirt with a violet peace symbol on the front. Stella gave it to him after he admired hers. The sun feels especially hot, and he pulls the T-shirt off too so he doesn't sweat through it before tonight's gig. Besides, he can tell Stella likes him tan, and the sun feels so damn good.

Later in bed or bored in class at school, he'll be able to recall every sensation he has now. He's learned this recall is the most important feature of song writing. Right now, for example, he calls to mind the way the sun backlights Stella's hair, turning it into a halo, dancing on the wind, and with the image comes the exact right chord change, a rhythm to match, and beads of words strung into a necklace of lyrics.

As he walks, he lets his mind see a nightclub, empty but for the front rows. Light from the stage seeps over seats occupied by Emelia, Will, and Kirstin, clapping away, ready to love every note he plays. On the fringe, his mother nods encouragement. Half in shadow, Joey Katz wipes down his horn. Slide's arms cross his wide chest. Beyond the spill of lights, Sonya and Water Boy linger in the chalky haze. His father is there too, in the wings, tongue tsking, head shaking. Leo takes another hit off the joint, blocks the spotlight with his eyes, and lifts the guitar's strap over his shoulder. He clasps the instrument's neck, steps to the microphone, and opens his mouth.

This is as far as his mind can take him right now. He's come to the edge of the cliffs. He backs away. He looks past the fields to the marsh where their time capsule ticks away like a bomb.

He won't go there, not even in his mind. Not tonight. Not ever if he can help it. And what the hell, he's on his way to a party. Stella and Charles are bringing all of the instruments.

Leo hums softly as he walks, at first unaware he's blended a song of his own with one of his father's. He stops abruptly when he realizes this, but then walks on. It's a good tune, and he's making it new. The lyrics he'll write will be deep and moody, they'll say something real, not like—. He doesn't bother to finish the comparison with his father. Instead, he fishes out a stub of pencil and a small notebook from his back pocket. He scratches a few words, a chorus maybe, a nice hook. He can't wait to whisper the words to Stella, let her find the verses for them.

When he's finished, he repockets the notebook and pencil. He stretches to the open sky, arches his back, and shakes out his limbs—the only warm-up he's ever done in swim practice—and he starts to run, his easy cross-country gait. It's the perfect time for a run. Limber up his voice. The lake breeze feels cool and wet, sweet with the scents of wildflowers.

Emelia

EMELIA PUSHES THROUGH a curtain of dogwood and switchgrass, landing on the sand and in a party in full swing. She turns off her flashlight and drops it at the edge of one of three bonfires, illuminating various groups of kids.

Around one fire, they roast marshmallows on sticks, eating charred goo and talking quietly. A few couples hold hands and press shoulders against one another. Some of the more daring or more serious couples make out with awkwardly stretched necks. They seem to have a curious politeness that suggests their bodies aren't overtaking them the way hers did with Theo and Danny. Not yet, she thinks.

All of a sudden, a whooping couple dashes out of the darkness, past her, and into the darkness again.

"Gonna get you, Patsy!" the boy yells, and the girl whoops again. Emelia smiles. She knows Patsy from home ec. When her soufflé came out perfectly, she whooped just as loudly, and it fell right in on itself. It's good to finally be out. She's been grounded for the past month. Her aunts insisted the punishment isn't for going to see Elisa, but for not telling them and for hitchhiking and for staying out so late they thought she was dead in a ditch.

In the light of the second bonfire, Emelia spots Will showing a couple of older boys how to tap the keg of beer they've brought. Would getting caught drinking beer here hurt his college chances? Probably not, she figures. This kind of wildness is okay, at least for a boy. It's different for girls. She'll have to keep an eye out for Kirstin. She'll help her get away should the sheriffs deputies raid the party.

Emelia's about to head over to Will when, at the edge of the halo of bonfire light, the Oracles start up "Barefootin'," and instead she walks toward the music. They sound good enough to be on *Bandstand*. Stella sings, and Leo plays guitar. Charles blows harmonica for the organ's part, and Van pats bongos. She likes the look of Van, who reminds her of a shaggy puppy. Maybe he'll ask her out on a date sometime. Or maybe she'll ask him out. It pleases her to think about how such boldness would shock people.

In the dance area, she's surprised to find Kirstin swinging her arms and hips to the music, and not looking half-bad either. She never used to join Emelia dancing to records in Will's room. She's in a ring of girls from her smart classes, but when she sees Emelia, she hops over and pulls her into their circle. Emelia shifts her body a bit, half-dancing but mostly watching Leo, who's obviously having the time of his life, jigging through the sand like some weirdo combination of Elvis and Mick. It's so sad about his dad, and she's glad to see him having a good time.

Despite his jigging, he never misses a note. He's more than good, she realizes. She'd always known he could play music, but with his father's band, he never put on a show as he is now. She grins with pride.

She leans over to shout to Kirstin. "Look at him go."

"It's what he's always wanted," Kirstin says. After a moment she adds, "I think he really likes that Stella."

"Yeah," says Emelia.

"It's nice. They fit."

Is it her imagination, or is there a trace of jealousy in Kirstin's expression? Before she can tell, Kirstin and her smart friends are deep into the Watusi. Emelia decides Kirstin's right; Leo and Stella fit, even if she is a couple of years older. Of course, no one would think twice if Leo were older than Stella. It's just one more unfairness of the many Emelia has begun to see. So Leo likes Stella, and Stella likes Leo. What does it matter about their ages?

She bites her lip, feeling her own stab, not of jealousy but of worry. What will it mean if Leo gets really close to Stella? Will he still keep Emelia's family secret? Will he tell her about the notes?

There's no way to know. Leo will have to make his own choices. Deal with his own consequences.

When the song ends, Stella's laugh flutters. Kirstin claps, and so does Will, his beer held high in the air. Emelia claps too and whoops as loud as Patsy had.

Leo waves Emelia over, and to her surprise, he squeezes her on the arm and kisses her cheek as if he's been greeting her this way their whole lives.

"You break out, or released for good?"

"I'm free," she says.

"About time. And about time you met someone." He places a hand on her shoulder and another on Stella's shoulder. "Stella, this is my friend, well, more than a friend. Sister-friend?"

Emelia nods and smiles. "That sounds right."

"My sister-friend, Emelia. Emelia, this is Stella."

"You're the famous Emelia," Stella says. "Leo talks about you all the time."

"Oh?" Emelia says, arching an eyebrow. Her lip finds its way between her teeth again. Would he really blab so easily? "What does he say about me?"

"Only the good stuff," says Leo, nodding meaningfully, and she knows he hasn't betrayed her.

"Of course, all good," Stella says, her smile genuine. "Only good. But what else would there be, right?"

"Right," says Emelia.

"You two talk," Leo says. "I'm going to grab a beer before the next song."

Emelia wants to trail after him, but he's already at the keg with all those boys. So she turns back to Stella, whose smile is still wide.

"You guys sound great," Emelia says. "You could be on *Bandstand*."

"Do you think so?" Stella says.

"Yeah."

"We're having fun anyway. We'll see where it goes. I'm off to college soon."

They stand awkwardly for a moment, both of them looking after Leo, who's got Will pouring him another beer.

"The lake's beautiful tonight, isn't it?" Stella says.

"It is," Emelia agrees.

"My mom always says how lucky we are to live near it. I forget that since——. I just forget sometimes."

Since Sonya? Should she say something about Sonya? Offer condolences? Or would that summon the dead girl's ghost and kill this lively party?

"Leo tells me you're the oldest of five brothers and sisters," Emelia says, deciding to stay on safe ground.

"Yeah, my brother Stevie is a year younger than you guys. You should meet him. He's over there." She points and calls to a tall, painfully thin boy, who grins and waves and keeps on play-surfing with a few other boys. "Maybe you'll come over to our house, and we'll all hang out."

"Sure, maybe," Emelia says. "It must be fun to have such a big family."

"It's loud," says Stella. "And annoying. And crazy."

"It sounds fun. I wish I had brothers and sisters." She means it. After all, it isn't that she doesn't want to be a Demski. She just wishes there were more of them, a whole houseful of siblings to share the worst and the best.

"You have Leo," Stella says. "You know, Leo's right to call you sister-friend. You two look like you could be brother and sister."

"I don't know. Maybe. A little," Emelia says, not adding that every kid here could be her sibling for all she knows about Johnny Angel. Some things she'll just never know.

"Well, you look more alike than Stevie and I do, but that's not saying much."

"I guess if I got to choose a sibling, it would be Leo. No question. And our friends, Will and Kirstin." She points to them.

"That's cool how you're all so tight," says Stella, smiling so Emelia can see she really means it, and Emelia likes her for it. Leo could do a lot worse than Stella.

"Play a song!" someone shouts from beyond the bonfire's cloud of light.

Charles breaks away from the boys he's been talking to and says to Stella, "Hey, man, let's play something."

"Keep your shirt on," Stella says. "I'm talking to Emelia."

"Go ahead and play," Emelia says. "We can talk more later."

"C'mon, Leo, guzzle it down," Charles calls to Leo, who is still talking with Will. "We're ready to play!"

Leo has a cup of beer in each hand. He tips his head back and seems to open his throat like a drain to pour them both down before he trots over.

"C'mon, kitty-cats." He picks up his guitar from the boulder where he'd placed it. Without waiting for the others to get set, assured they'll follow his lead, he calls out, "One, two, three, four . . ." He sounds nothing like himself and more like himself than ever before.

They play "All I Really Want to Do," their voices harmonizing at least as well as the Byrds. As the band plays on, Emelia wanders away from the light of the bonfires, toward the water and the dusky half-moon light. She hears the lapping waves before her eyes adjust to the darkness. She picks up a stone and feels its sandpaper surface. She's about to toss it into the waves, but pushes it into the pocket of her shorts instead, not sure if it's a memento of this night or the marker of an end of something. She looks out at the vast lake, knowing there are whole worlds beneath and beyond the surface. She lifts one foot and balances on the rocky shore.

Again, a couple of people breeze past her, splashing in the water. The same couple as before? She can't tell, but they seem to be having fun. She leaves them to it, resisting the urge to warn them about the current. They don't look to be going into the water. They're already in a rolling embrace.

She returns to the party but keeps to the edge of the scene. Had her mother been to parties like this? Maybe on this very spot?

But for now, she tunes in to three boys arguing about the draft. She has thoughts about the draft too. Will and Leo. Her family.

"War is not healthy for children and other living things," she says, making her voice loud enough for the arguing boys to hear. Surprised at the interruption, they scrutinize her for a moment as if trying to figure out who she is. She raises two fingers in a peace sign.

"Right on!" a boy with shaggy hair says.

"Make love, not war," adds a girl with long, stick-straight hair who Emelia hadn't noticed before. Crouched on a rock, she'd been listening to the boys too. The two girls grin at each other in the firelight.

"Peace, sister," the girl says after a moment.

"Right on," Emelia answers, giving her a small wave before backing away and heading to the dance area, feeling her weight shift from leg to leg. She wonders if Ben has made it to his mountain. Maybe she'll go there too someday. Leaving doesn't mean she can't come home again.

The Oracles have segued from "A Groovy Kind of Love" into one of Leo's songs, a moody rock number with a good beat. She rubs the stone in her pocket. Music and dancing, and fire and friends. The beauty of it all wells up in her. Enough mooning around, she thinks.

She gallops over to Will and grabs his wrist. Standing by the keg, she can smell he's had his share of drink. Maybe this is why he lets her pull him into the circle of dancers. Still holding onto Will, she catches Kirstin's wrist and pulls her to them, so together they create their own circle. She raises their arms high and dances them over to Leo, who shimmies his guitar at them. Together they all move, playing on until it seems to her that, for tonight at least, everybody in the whole world is dancing in the moonlight.

Author's Note

This book is a work of fiction, and any resemblance to real people, living or dead, is purely coincidental. I have taken liberties of place and time when narratively necessary. The Silo, where Stash and Slide record their albums, is based on the real recording studio, Cuca Records, and I gratefully acknowledge the exceptional historical work of Sarah Filzen's "The History of Cuca Records, 1959–1973: A Case Study of an Independent Record Company." https://bit.ly/3JKycdr

Although the novel is fiction, its historical milieu is based on fact, including ice pick lobotomies and the lack of availability of the Loop, the Pill, abortion, the Comstock Law, and general information about reproductive rights. I have drawn on the following resources, which include much more information than was needed for this book:
- A Lobotomy Timeline, NPR
  https://n.pr/3H7uWXE
- 100 Years of Birth Control, Planned Parenthood
  https://bit.ly/3Jzd9tW
- "Women in College in the 1950s"
  https://bit.ly/3JJlT0V

Secret Waltz: Discussion Questions

1. Nearly every character in the novel has a secret to keep, but their reasons for keeping them are different. What motivates the various characters to keep their secrets secret?

2. Emelia's attitudes toward Sonya, her mother, her aunts, and even herself change throughout the book. Why and how?

3. What do the different styles of music that Leo and his father, Stash, are drawn to suggest about the experiences of their generations?

4. Sonya's experiences in the book make clear that in 1966 women had very few choices about their futures. How have things changed for women since then? What kinds of challenges are women (and men) confronted with today?

5. At its heart, Secret Waltz is a story about family and friendship. How do these strong forces both support and challenge the characters as they come of age and find their ways in the world?

Acknowledgements

I want to thank William Burleson for creating a press where authors matter and where writing is action. It is my deep honor that you saw and realized my vision in this book, and it has been a joy to work with you.

Early readers of this book allowed me to find the story. Rebecca Sullivan, Dionne Irving-Bremyer, Maureen Reddy, Tina Egnoski, and Elizabeth Winick-Rubenstein, I thank you all for taking time from your own writing and professional lives to give my fledgling work your generous attention.

Writing time and space are invaluable, and I thank Rhode Island College and the Virginia Center for the Creative Arts for both.

I thank both the organization and the dedicated workers at Planned Parenthood and the many other women's clinics I have used throughout my life. You are more than essential workers; you have shaped the future.

To my siblings, who have taught me about family, and to my dear SC, who have taught me about friendship, thank you for dancing, singing, and most of all, laughing with me through the years of writing this book.

To Paul, who is my best thing, every single day.

About the Author

Karen Lee Boren (karenleeboren.com) is the author of *Mother Tongue* (New Rivers Press) and *Girls in Peril* (Tin House Books, a Barnes and Noble Discover selection). She has been nominated for a Pushcart Prize and is the winner of the 2018 Wundor Editions Fiction Prize. Her writing appears in *Women Arts Journal, The Florida Review, BookForum,* and *Fourth Genre,* among other places, as well as the Lonely Planet's anthology *Rites of Passage: Backpacking 'Round Europe,* and *The Best of Lonely Planet's Travel Writing.* A native of Milwaukee, she now lives with her husband, Paul, in Providence, Rhode Island, and teaches writing at Rhode Island College.

Also from Karen Lee Boren

Mother Tongue

Karen Lee Boren, drawing on her midwestern roots, explores the complex relationship between language and intimacy, between the heritage we're born with and our chosen paths. Each character is adrift in her life, searching for a place to land. She is lost when her mother tongue fails her, struggling to find new connections with her loved ones and her life.

Girls in Peril: A Novella

During a 1970s summer, five adolescent girls learn that peril exists where they never imagined: in their neighborhood and homes; in parents who steal their time and freedom (and, in one case, a thumb); in the pull of the world beyond their friendships; and in their own burgeoning sexuality.